ELEMENTS of MIND

© 2014 Walter H. Hunt

Spencer Hill Press

Contact: Spence City, an imprint of Spencer Hill Press, PO Box
247, Contoocook, NH 03229, USA

Please visit our website at www.spencecity.com

First Edition: June 2014
Walter H. Hunt
Elements of Mind/by Walter H. Hunt—01 ed.
p. cm.

Summary: A dangerous artifact is found in Victorian India,
and the head of the English Order of Mesmerists must track it
across two continents to stop it falling into the wrong hands.

The author acknowledges the copyrighted or trademarked status
and trademark owners of the following wordmarks mentioned in
this work of fiction: Webley

Cover design by Lisa Amowitz
Interior layout by Errick A. Nunnally

978-1-939392-08-4 (paperback)
978-1-939392-70-1 (e-book)

Printed in the United States of America

ELEMENTS of MIND

Walter H. Hunt

SPENCE CITY

*For Lisa, my Magnetic North,
and Aline, my elemental spirit.*

Our revels now are ended

"Facts are stubborn things."
—William Davey

Doctor James Esdaile had known for years that this day would eventually arrive—the one on which someone would come to kill him.

For some, the certainty of that fact, and the inevitability of this day, would have been disconcerting; but Esdaile had long since become accustomed to the idea—it was like an old friend, something reassuring and almost comforting. Most importantly, his death was an unavoidable eventuality for which he could plan.

On a cold, blustery Monday morning he rose at his accustomed hour and took his breakfast with Eliza; then, despite the inclement weather, they put on their overcoats and traveled by cab to the Crystal Palace. It had been in Sydenham since March 1854, where it had opened to great fanfare two years after hosting the Great Exposition at Hyde Park. Esdaile and his wife had come down to Sydenham from Scotland shortly afterward. His reasons were anything but coincidence.

Visitors were few at opening hour. In the Great Nave it was relatively quiet; the sound of the wind was muffled by the glass. Thin, wan strands of sunlight found their way through the clouds and the glass-paneled roof that gave the palace its name. They walked along until they stood at the exact middle of the structure. Esdaile verified this to his satisfaction by removing a half-crown from his pocket and balancing it on end atop one of the floor tiles: it remained in place, not rolling in any direction.

As he stood up, Eliza, who had been watching the experiment with curiosity, tugged on his elbow.

"He's here," she said.

"He came in person?"

"You're surprised?"

"No. Not really."

Esdaile licked his chapped lips. If Eliza took any notice, she showed no sign.

"I could—"

"I would prefer that you did *not*."

Eliza seemed to think carefully about it, then nodded. "Very well. But it would be much easier."

"It would only postpone the inevitable," Esdaile said.

He looked away from his wife, carefully disengaging his sleeve from her grasp. A middle-aged man dressed as a vicar was making his way across the great concourse toward the place where they stood.

He waited until the man was close enough that he did not have to shout and said, "Reverend."

"Doctor."

"Welcome to Sydenham. Thank you for coming."

"I am curious to hear what you have to say. It is not as if you could hide forever, Esdaile. You must know it had to come to this."

"I have lived here for more than four years, Reverend Davey, and before that I resided in Perth at an address where I corresponded regularly. I daresay that I have not been *hiding*."

William Davey's glance went quickly from Esdaile to Eliza and back; he did not respond.

"You're not afraid of *her*, are you?"

"Certainly not."

"But clearly *someone* is, or you would have sent some minor functionary rather than gracing me with your own presence."

"You have made your own damned bed, Esdaile," Davey said, looking pointedly at Eliza. "But so that you know that I am a fair man, I will ask you once more, for form's sake: do you have the statue?"

"You know that I do not. I left it behind in Hooghly."

"And you are still at peace with that—*betrayal.*" Davey's face glowered, anger seemingly held back by force of will.

"The statue conveyed access to power that is simply too great for anyone to possess—not me, not you, not any member of the Committee or anyone else. I judged—"

"*You* judged!"

"Yes," Esdaile answered levelly. "*I* judged that while happenstance had placed it in my hands, a deliberate choice was necessary to keep it out of *yours*. You will never have the statue, Reverend Davey. The Committee will never have it—and someday you may understand why this is a blessing and not a curse."

"You're telling me that I don't want something as powerful as this item. Nonsense."

"I stand by my assertion."

"Very well, then," Davey said. He slowly lifted his left hand, palm up.

It became very quiet. Even the wind outside seemed to die down. Esdaile waited…and after a moment he smiled.

For his part, Davey looked baffled—and even more angry.

"This is an unusual building," Esdaile said. "Its structure nullifies mesmeric power. Whatever pleasantries you had in store, you'll be unable to share them with me in here."

"Then I'll simply wait until you depart."

"Ah," Esdaile said. He took a step away from his wife, turning slightly to face her. "But it will be too late by then, I'm afraid."

"What does that mean?"

Esdaile smiled. "I am going to do you a great favor, Reverend—in accordance with a text of scripture with which you are familiar. Despite years of enmity, I am about to *turn the other cheek*.

"My wife—" he gestured toward Eliza—" is of a particular nature. By choosing her, I allowed myself to reach beyond nightfall, a circumstance that has protected me from you and the Committee

3

for these many years. At my death, of course, she would consume me, as all such beings are wont to do.

"But I will not give her the chance: my morning tea included a sufficiently high dose of a particularly efficient aconite compound so that I shall expire..." he slowly removed his watch from its vest pocket and consulted it, then snapped it shut. "...I am reasonably sure...in a matter of a few minutes."

Both Davey and Eliza were speechless; they glanced quickly at each other, then back at Esdaile.

"You should also realize that if I were to perish too soon for... matters to take their usual course, her hunger would remain. Despite your demonstrated skill, you would likely be consumed instead. But once again, the Crystal Palace intervenes." He stretched his arms toward the great ceiling and let them fall. "*Chthonic* spirits are powerless at the place where we stand."

Eliza did not speak: she looked shocked at Esdaile's revelation. Davey stood with his fists clenched, his arms rigid.

Esdaile seemed unsteady on his feet. Eliza looked at Davey and spoke a series of unintelligible syllables; the sounds seemed to float away and disappear into the vast spaces of the Crystal Palace.

"You have cheated the Committee," Davey whispered. "And you have cheated your nightfall companion. And by committing suicide, you have cheated *yourself.*"

"You will understand this better someday, I hope," Esdaile said softly, his attention beginning to wander...

"If you live that long," he added, then said in a whisper, "*Our revels now are ended*"—the words that had been spoken, elegiac, when the Crystal Palace had been closed at its original location in Hyde Park eight years ago.

It was from *The Tempest.*

And as Esdaile's last breath escaped him, Reverend William Davey and Eliza Weatherhead Esdaile gently lowered his body, with the hint of a smile upon its face, to the floor of the Crystal Palace.

PART ONE

A delicate pattern

Aut potentior te, aut imbecillior læsit:
si imbecillior, parce illi;
si potentior, tibi.

(He who has injured thee was either stronger or weaker.
If weaker, spare him;
if stronger, spare thyself.)

Seneca, *De Ira* (On Anger), III:5

CHAPTER 1

Introductions in the half-light

WILLIAM DAVEY

I should be remiss if I do not state, at the very beginning of this narrative, that the last thing I would have wanted to do was to kill James Esdaile. He was a brilliant man, a colleague, and I daresay a friend. It would be trite, however, to state that *I had no choice* or that *he brought it upon himself* or some other such nonsense, for it was clear to the Committee that those statements were self-evident and utterly, tragically true.

I similarly refuse to offer any apology regarding the act itself. Taking another's life is nothing to undertake in haste or without good reason. Neither condition applied when the Committee embarked upon the decision. I was ready, and willing, to punish Esdaile for his betrayal. My clerical profession might demand that I refuse to commit such an act...*perhaps*: but the time for such petty moral self-flagellation was already long past.

If he had not taken his own life, I might have procured the information that it ultimately took me more than two years to obtain. Other consequences might have been avoided. And if he truly wished death, then he should have had it: not by a cruel poison, but at the hands of one who once called him friend.

It might at least have been gentler.

Readers of this narrative must be prepared to forgive its author for the way in which he relates his tale. In order to understand how we arrived at the fateful January morning, I sought to track James Esdaile's course. This effort took me to Scotland and ultimately to India—and at the far end of my journeys I found myself at the beginning of the story. This is not how tales should properly be told:

any tutor at Oxford or Cambridge would be most displeased with my narrative style—commencing with the end and concluding with the beginning. Nonetheless, I liken my search for the truth to Theseus' travels through the labyrinth of the Minotaur: I had my ball of string in one hand to direct my path, and my ball of pitch in the other to thwart any enemy that opposed me.

As I witnessed little of the story myself, I was compelled to depend upon the accounts of many people in sundry places. The reader may rely upon the fidelity of my own recounting of their observations, as in many cases my own skill with the Art assured me that they told what they knew to be the truth—and in other cases there should be no reason to doubt.

Before I commence with their stories, however, it behooves me to offer my own introduction. I flatter myself to think that everyone in the mesmeric world should be acquainted with me, but no writer can be certain of the identity…or era…of his readers.

My name is William Davey. My father, Edward Davey of Honiton, followed his own father's lace-making trade, in the town where the best of the Devonshire craft can be found. Two hundred years before I was born, Flemish refugees came to Devon and brought their skills and styles with them, and from the time I was old enough to take note of it I remember the older men and women sitting outside their thatched cottages to get the best sunlight, bent over delicate work that would become a wedding gown or a christening robe.

I could not imagine growing old that way. My father and mother, my uncles and aunts, and those of my siblings who entered the trade grew nearsighted and rheumatic before their time. There might have been no escape: university was beyond consideration and the law far too expensive.

I was rescued from Honiton by a wealthy Dissenting patron, the celebrated Reverend Doctor G_____, a friend of the renowned Sir William Hamilton whom I later encountered in mesmeric circles. I later learned why a humble craftsman's son might be plucked from such circumstances and taken on as a protégé;

Reverend G_____ saw the mesmeric spark in me, and determined that I would be a useful—and loyal—ally in years to come.

My patron placed me at Manchester Academy in York, where I was transformed from lace-maker to Presbyterian minister. It suited me: I was more inclined toward the academic than the artistic. As a tutor for his children, I could leave the world of Devonshire lace behind.

In the fall of 1837, I read of the extraordinary feats of the Frenchman who styled himself the Baron Dupotet de Sennevoy, an adept of the mesmeric arts transmitted directly from the great Mesmer. I was skeptical of the claims he made: my patron had not yet spoken to me of the Art—yet when I witnessed his skill in person, I was convinced. Dupotet took me aside and told me that he thought me capable of the same feats.

I remember his words as if they were spoken only yesterday.

"Let me assure you that those who can feel the mesmeric forces are few; and they move in a sort of half-light—yet all about them the world is in darkness. When only half-light is available, we must be guided by it alone."

His words were prophetic, and his assistance changed my life. Within a year came the extraordinary examination of the claims of Dr. Elliotson and the exposure of his prize subjects, the O'Key sisters; and though the Committee empanelled to examine such mesmeric claims dismissed the matter, those with actual skill and perception continued to practice. Ultimately, that created alliances—and, of course, enemies. One of the first victims of this struggle for power was my own patron, Doctor G____, who regrettably had a weak heart during a period of dangerous conflict within the society. It made me realize that if choosing sides was a dangerous business, then seeking to avoid alliance was even more so.

Truly there was but one solution: to stitch that society together, like a fine bit of lace-work. Some stitches needed to be dropped and others pulled tighter. Power beckons and those who wield it compel others if they must. The skills and gifts are too valuable to be left unregulated.

I became a supporter of the famous Dr. Elliotson, whom the non-mesmeric world accounted a fraud. Yet he was the first of our geniuses. Despite all of the imprecations against him from outside our society, and all of the bitter rivalries within, he was powerful enough to survive when many did not. He was sufficiently devoted to the Art itself that he found leadership unattractive—he remained on the sideline, protecting and protected by his powerful friend, the famous author Mr. Dickens, observing the developing leadership struggle.

There can ultimately be only one master weaver. It was Edward Quillinan, the sensitive poet, who emerged as the Chairman. He established our codes of conduct and set the tone and direction of our society's development. Four years after the Committee's inception, Quillinan resigned to care for his invalid wife, and though I was no particular friend, he chose me as his successor.

Esdaile and I began to correspond in the spring of 1845 about the statue that he had found; the power he described would have secured for me the Chairmanship of our society, protecting me from the many who sought to wrest it from me; Esdaile would have assuredly had a place at my side. When he informed me that he had left it behind in India I rightly viewed his action as a betrayal. When he died, he thought that he had secured it and its secrets, taking its location to the grave with him.

We were both incorrect...but I am getting a trifle ahead of myself.

I did not yet know where that betrayal would lead. As Dupotet had told me more than two decades before, I was in the half-light. But the rest of the world was still in darkness.

CHAPTER 2

Aftermath

ELIZA ESDAILE

When I opened my eyes I found myself in my own bed—the bed I shared with James Esdaile. A man I knew by reputation but whom I had just met for the first time sat by me, his face composed and peaceful.

He seemed to notice me at once despite my attempt to feign sleep. I reached my hand out, but there was no weapon ready to hand.

"I do not know why you have spared me," I said quietly.

The man unexpectedly smiled.

"Why do you remain?"

"I seek to comfort you, dear lady," he said, and reached out to pat my hand. It was a wonder! Reverend Davey—for it was none other: the man who had sought to kill my husband—was truly acting the part of a vicar.

He was a dangerous man, a skilled mesmerist and a criminal boss—and a *clergyman*. I did not know him in the latter context; indeed, I only knew what James had said of him.

He sees only one side of power. He does not understand what he might let loose.

"I do not *want* your comfort," I answered.

"Then I would have you answer a question."

"What question?"

"Why are you here?"

That was not the question I would have anticipated. I looked around me at the familiar bedchamber: it was near dark and chilly outside of the bedcovers.

"This is my house. Where should I be?"

"I thought you might vanish entirely." He sat upright again, his hands on his knees. "I know what you are—what you were. You were the thing—"

"I am not a *thing*."

"Clearly *not*," he answered. "But you were—you bore the being with which Esdaile made his devil's bargain. When he died—"

I shuddered. "Then I did not dream it."

"No, madam. You did not. I did not kill him, as I had intended. You did not consume him as *you* intended. And when, instead of vanishing, you simply fainted, my…priorities changed."

My first impulse was to ask him what he could possibly mean by that comment. But I knew, and he knew that I knew, exactly what he meant.

"Watching my husband die was good and sufficient reason to faint, Reverend Davey."

"A point taken. It would be more poignant, except that Esdaile's…arrangement was with a *chthonic* spirit, a demon of earth, who has been his guardian since he—you—returned from India. But when such spirits manifest a physical body, they only remain until they accomplish their day."

"You thought—" I paused to consider what conclusion he had reached. "You thought I was the physical form of…"

"Why should I have thought otherwise? But obviously, I was wrong. And as I said, madam, my priorities have changed."

I took a few deep breaths. I felt some combination of relief and terror.

"Then tell me what you intend."

"I intend to learn from you, Mrs. Esdaile. Eliza."

His assumed familiarity put me off, but I was altogether too shocked to object.

"Learn?"

"About the *chthonic* spirit that inhabited you. I wish to understand how you survived this experience without succumbing to madness."

"How do you know I am not mad?"

11

"Because...*because*, dear lady," he said to me, "I understand madness very well, indeed. And you are *sane*. I need to know why."

He looked deep into my eyes. I knew what he was doing: if I had learned anything over the last several years, it was the methods and means by which mesmerists pursue their Art.

I could have resisted. I do not know if I could have withstood his ministrations, but honestly I was not sure it was worth the trouble. I wanted to go back to sleep: I was exhausted.

But I was *free*.

WILLIAM DAVEY

My enemies among the Committee would have had it believed that I was unfeeling, monomaniacal and ruthless. Let me say that I am not monomaniacal: I feel that I steered a middle course and that I sought to keep the Committee directed in that manner as well. Nor am I unfeeling. To the contrary, that Eliza Esdaile was not a manifestation of a *chthonic* being but merely a vessel—and, clearly, an unwilling vessel—aroused my empathy.

She had been taken that morning from the Crystal Palace by house-servants, along with the body of her husband. The local constabulary provided an escort. I accompanied them as a friend of the family and a clergyman: there was no one who would gainsay me.

As I had told her, my assumption had been that she had been *created*. When she remained after Esdaile's suicide, I realized that could not possibly be the case. It made sense: though *chthonic* beings had more physical matter to work with, possession was far more efficient than manifestation for all *stoicheia*, *chthonic* or otherwise, since it was not necessary to construct a body and animate it to resemble life. It was an error due to lack of experience—at that time I had as yet had little to do with any *stoicheia* from any of the elemental realms.

Yet none of these beings are accustomed to human patterns of feeling and thought; they even seem to perceive the passage of time differently. For Eliza to emerge from the traumatic experience with a shred of sanity was so singular that I could not bypass the opportunity to learn how she had done it.

Thus I confess to the third attribution that my detractors place upon me. I do not think it an exaggeration to consider me ruthless. Therefore, far too soon after the tragic events beneath the crystal vault of the exposition hall, I provided Eliza the means to tell her story.

In this way I began at the end of the story—where Esdaile ended.

CHAPTER 3

Adrift

ELIZA ESDAILE

My name is Eliza Weatherhead Esdaile. For the last seven and a half years, my life has not been my own; it has been directed, and controlled, by a spirit—an evil thing, some might say. That I can speak at all is God's miracle.

I am thirty-six years old and a widow. This would be a tragedy worthy of Mr. Dickens, except that it is real life: and no one would pay a penny every week to read what could be considered the ravings of a madwoman. Dickens it is *not*. And a madwoman I am not.

✦

Let me begin again.

In 1847, when I was twenty-four years old, I was hired as a governess for three young children who accompanied their father and mother, Mr. and Mrs. Robert Davis Heath, to Calcutta in the Bengal. Mr. Heath was a prosperous and educated man of business, careful with his money and devoted to work and family. Mrs. Heath, however, was a woman of delicate disposition. She was dissatisfied with her husband's decision to relocate the family to India: it occupied her mind constantly while we prepared for departure. During the long voyage outward she became progressively more ill.

A seagoing vessel is no place for a lady of Mrs. Heath's constitution. Her husband had the luxury of taking strolls on the deck. Children are resilient by their nature: they were soon accustomed to ship life and were adopted by the junior officers, who permitted them liberties that would have caused their mother to faint. Mrs.

Heath, meanwhile, became more and more frail, rarely leaving her cabin and fretting constantly about what awaited them in India.

She never saw India. As the ship made its way across the Indian Ocean, she passed gently into the next world, unsure of where she was. The threads of her life unraveled, leaving the family incomplete. She was interred in Calcutta's English Burial Ground.

A penny dreadful would contain a tawdry romance which would, of course, speed my elevation to the status of the second Mrs. Heath. Such was not the case, nor could I have wished it to be. I was below Mr. Heath's station; I had no desire to bring humiliation upon him or his children. I remained as governess and was accorded proper respect in that capacity for the entire term of my employment. Young Master Heath—Bertram—left for Eton two years after we arrived in Calcutta; his older sister, Henrietta, was sent to live with an aunt in Cape Town, where she married shortly afterward. Only young Rose remained with her father and myself.

I realize, Reverend, that these small details of private life do not matter to you—and I pray you do not protest to the contrary!—because they speak little to the great matters which followed. But you must understand that they belong to that part of my life that is in sharp definition. It is like a warm parlor with a well-stocked fireplace and comfortable furnishings, when compared to a stone balcony exposed to an icy wind. For the last several years I was made to stand out on that balcony, observing the parlor from without, my voice lost in the stiff breeze.

I should tell you more about Rose. I think that she was the key to this—for me, at least. With Mrs. Heath in eternal repose in Chowringhee, a place the children and I visited every Sunday until they left India, Mr. Heath found himself increasingly alone. Rose was always his favorite: Bertram was a fine young man of course, but only came out to India once during his time at Eton, and Henrietta had always been closer to her mother than her father, as young girls often are. But Rose was a darling little girl, clever and quick with her lessons. She was particularly talented with maths—

had she been a boy I am certain that Mr. Heath would have wanted her placed as a junior clerk at an early age.

Then, in the spring of 1851, five years after we had come to India, the unthinkable happened—poor little Rose, not quite eleven years old, was taken by the cholera.

Women are accustomed to the business of mourning, Reverend Davey. We who have lost our men to wars and our babes in childbed, who are caretakers for the old and sick—we know about Death: he is an old and uncomfortably familiar friend. Men have less understanding or experience. They believe that they and all of their seed will live forever. Women accept this fact but men, faced with meaningless loss, are like rudderless ships and simply have no idea what to do.

Robert Davis Heath, gentleman and man of business, conducted himself with perfect dignity as his youngest child was brought down Burial Ground Road and laid to rest in the English Cemetery beside his wife. He escorted me back to the house, and after seeing that I was safely in the hands of the *khansamah*—

What? Of course. Every household in India has a *khansamah*. He is—well, the master butler, the head servant. The best *khansamah* is a kind, wise Indian gentleman of middle age, who knows his city well: who to hire, where to obtain anything his master might desire, how to arrange the thousand little things that keep a household running. He is usually a bit venal—they all are: but any master who expects his *khansamah* to account for every rupee does not understand India very well. By turning a blind eye to a head servant who slightly blurs the distinction between his and his master's funds, a gentleman can assure himself that this activity has strict bounds and will be carefully watched.

A fox set to watch over the hen-house? No, I think you do not understand. In India, servants think every white man is wealthy— for their condition is so mean that he seems so by comparison. Thus, when an opportunity to steal presents itself, they take it. *Surely*, they think, *the master will not miss it.* If it were just one servant this would be nothing: but a well-turned-out household for one such as Mr. Heath had many—kitchen servants, maids, a team for his palky, a *dirwan* at his door—and a governess for his children.

In the weeks of Rose's illness and during the preparations for her funeral, I had never given serious thought to my station in Mr. Heath's household. Gobinda, his *khansamah*, had ever been kind to me, but after Mr. Heath shut himself up in his library—

Oh. I beg your pardon, Reverend. I was distracted from telling the story. And yes, it was many years ago—but the details remain very clear.

After we returned from sweet little Rose's funeral, Mr. Heath shut himself up in his library without a word. He did not appear for tea, nor did he come to the conservatory as we had done in happier times to hear Rose play the little Pleyel piano he had imported from France at great expense. During her illness we had gathered there without her—but not this night.

So there I sat in the conservatory with a book by my side, alone and listening to the rain: and it began to dawn on me that I was without any role or status in Mr. Heath's household. Bertram and Henrietta were no longer present, and Rose slept with her mother.

As I sat alone, the most singular thing happened. I began to hear voices: not the ones from the street outside—the compound was far from the street in any case—but whispers, like the rustling of leaves in the breeze.

They spoke my name—and they told me that I was adrift and alone because of Rose's death. I assumed it was the fears of my own imagination: what would become of me, thousands of miles from England, a governess with no children to care for? Where would I go and what would I do?

Then Gobinda came to me as I sat there in the dim candlelight. He had rarely entered the room while the family was there, unless some matter of business required Mr. Heath's attention; but this evening he not only crossed the threshold but came to sit nearby.

I could not have been more relieved to see any person.

"Miss Weatherhead," he told me. "I come to you because of my

17

genuine affection for you." He said it just like that: he prided himself on proper speech, like a gentleman's gentleman. "I fear that there may be some changes ahead."

"Changes?" I replied. I knew what he meant—had my own fears not represented it to me already?

"I have served in this house for many years," Gobinda told me. "Before Heath Sahib I was *khansamah* to another gentleman who occupied this house, a Mr. Fergusson Sahib, who was from Scotland. Perhaps you know this worthy person?"

I can only assume that to a man from India, all of Britain must seem small, as if we all lived in the same country village. "No," I answered. "I do not know Mr. Fergusson."

"Miss Weatherhead," Gobinda said. "Miss Weatherhead. It may be the best for you if you seek employment with another family. I know that the loss of the young girl pains you severely… we have a different view of such things here in India: these are merely passages, the comings and goings of immortal spirits. But quitting this household will be the best possible thing for you."

"I daresay that is for Mr. Heath to decide," I tartly replied: though he was being blunt, Gobinda was also being kind…I did not know how kind!

"I do not think…" he began, but was interrupted by some noise somewhere else in the house. He stood and offered me a polite bow, then quit the room. I arose to follow him: we made our way into the great hall and up the stairs toward the source of the disturbance, but halfway up he stopped and turned to me, placing his left hand in front of him, palm up—

Yes, I *know* what that means, but of course I did not know then. It quite frightened me that I was left standing on the stairs, unable to follow him: it was as if my shoes were rooted to the stone step, my hand clutching the railing and unable to let go.

Ten minutes later—the great hall's clock had not yet chimed another quarter hour—he returned to where I was still standing. The expression on his face was grave and troubled. He made another gesture with his hand and I found myself suddenly free to move: I lurched forward in my former course, but Gobinda caught me by the shoulders.

"I will thank you to unhand me, sir," I said, glancing around to see if there was anyone else nearby; if so, they kept themselves carefully out of sight.

"There is nothing for you upstairs," Gobinda answered. "You must not go upstairs."

"But, Mr. Heath—"

"Mr. Heath has died, Miss Weatherhead. By his own hand."

CHAPTER 4

Choices

WILLIAM DAVEY

Eliza Weatherhead Esdaile was an easy subject to mesmerize, and her account was clear and detailed—though it obviously exhausted her to give it. A few days after James Esdaile's interment—performed by a local parson—I called upon her. She received me cautiously but politely. As a clergyman, I had a perfect excuse to remain on hand as a friend of the family during her time of loss; she and James apparently had few close friends in Sydenham, and in any case the household and the neighbors seemed terrified of Eliza.

Small wonder. Those with keen perceptions could sense what she was; those with less innate awareness had only a sense of unease. For nearly five years, James and his wife had lived in a little cottage near the Crystal Palace: the retired doctor and a bright young girl twenty years his junior—who had been inhabited by a *chthonic* spirit.

❈

Her revelations thus far had given me a particularly important insight. Eliza's employer had taken up residence in the house where the architect James Fergusson had lived until 1843. I have not yet explained about Fergusson—the stitches in this tale are complex ones—but suffice it to say that he had found the statue somehow and had given it to Esdaile before leaving India. He had also been a key part of Paxton's staff that had reconstructed the Crystal Palace at Sydenham.

There was a connection between them, but I did not understand it at the time. If I had done…

But I had not. Eliza had more to tell me; I had to wait for her to give her own story, at her own pace.

ELIZA ESDAILE

Mr. Heath's death was a tragedy. To be honest, it was something of a scandal. He left a rambling, disturbing note explaining the reason he took his own life: he blamed himself for the death of his wife and daughter. Apparently he was also engaged in dubious financial dealings—though it was not my place to ask, nor my business to know, what was involved. Indeed, it is possible that these details were invented to help explain the tragedy. A man may take his own life in the face of financial disaster—that is considered honorable but unfortunate. But a man is not permitted despair—he must continue to soldier onward.

And so Robert Heath was placed alongside his wife and youngest daughter. For a week, all was calm. I saw to my own meager possessions, knowing that I might soon have to quit the house in search of a new position. I had some money put by, though not enough for passage home.

I was not afraid. I told myself so then, and I believe it now. The English community was large enough for me to obtain another position; I was clean, orderly, well-spoken, and I knew that I had acquitted myself properly in the Heath household. I lacked a reference since my employer was deceased, but I had been with the family for more than five years. Again I am reminded of Dickens: he might have portrayed me weeping with my head in my hands, wondering what would become of me. I do not flatter myself too much, I think, to state that I did not ever venture upon that path. Without the means to return to England, I assumed that I should have to make my own way until I earned enough to do so.

At last, I was called to the office of Mr. Heath's solicitor just off Tank Square—the heart of English Calcutta. I had never had occasion to present myself there: Mr. Rowland, the solicitor, had come to the house a few times but had never before taken notice of me.

I remember the place clearly. A law office is very much a province of men: dark wood furnishings, odors of tobacco and leather, books and papers and ink. Mr. Rowland's place of business was well lighted but seemed almost devoid of air—as if the place had been sealed in a tight jar, to keep the heat and sounds away, to keep *India* away from English courts of law.

I was ushered into a waiting room scarcely worthy of the name—a hard bench, walls full of musty old books, and the disreputable containers into which men discharge their tobacco—spittoons, I believe they are called. The bright sun could scarcely find its way through the yellowed glass and thick curtains, so that by comparison to the outer offices the entire room was cloaked in a sort of hazy shadow.

After some time, a clerk returned for me and directed me to Mr. Rowland's office.

"Miss Weatherhead," he said, without turning to face me directly nor offering me a seat. "As Mr. Robert Heath's executor I am directed to attend, ahem, to certain matters regarding his household."

"I understand, sir," I answered.

"With the unfortunate death of young Miss Rose, your... position in the household is such, ahem, that your services are no longer needed. I trust that you understand the situation."

"I had considered it, Mr. Rowland."

"You must also understand, madam," he continued, still not daring to meet my eye, "that Mr. Heath neglected to make any provision for you. I do not know if it was his intention to do so, but...in the absence, may I say, of a direct instruction, I am unable to give you anything further than your wage through the end of this calendar month."

"That is most generous of you, sir," I replied, not knowing what else I could say. "I had already determined that I might have to seek employment with another family—"

"Yes, yes," he interrupted me, waving his hand which held an unlit cigar. "I am sure that a person of your talents should have no trouble."

He thus appeared ready to dismiss me, but I said, "I would hope that I might obtain a letter of reference—"

"What?" At last he looked directly at me, as if noticing my presence in the office for the first time. "I'm sorry, what is it you wanted?"

"In order to obtain a suitable place, Mr. Rowland, it would be most helpful if I might have a letter of reference that could be shown to a future employer, attesting to my character and responsibility."

At the time I thought it a reasonable request: I had served the Heaths for five years, in a foreign land, during some rather arduous times.

Mr. Rowland seemed unsettled by the request. "Well," he said. "Ahem. It is regrettable that there is no one that could provide you with such a letter."

"Even yourself?"

"I...I beg your pardon, Miss Weatherhead. Please understand that I would normally be willing to do so—if so *directed*—but as I have no personal knowledge of your character or habits, it would be no less than prevarication on my part. As an officer of the court I cannot engage in any activity that might have any chance to cast aspersions upon myself or my firm. I am sure you understand."

"Mr. Rowland," I began, "Surely you must realize that this reference is of great importance to me—"

"I am really quite sorry, madam," he said, as if it were of no matter. "I cannot help you. I am afraid the matter is closed. If you speak to my clerk as you leave, he will provide you with the remainder of your wages."

I did not answer for several seconds: I was shocked and angry at his cavalier treatment. In retrospect, I should not have been surprised: it is the normal way servants are treated—convenient, disposable, *replaceable*.

All that Mr. Robert Heath possessed now belonged to Mr. Bertram Heath. But Mr. Bertram Heath was a third of the way around the globe at Eton, and equally unlikely to give more than a passing thought to his former governess.

As I turned to leave, Mr. Rowland added, "I would also ask that you vacate your present room within the week, as the house must be closed up as well."

"Of course," I said, and walked out of his office, my head held high but with fear in my heart.

Gobinda was waiting for me when I returned; he had already begun the process of closing up the house, having already paid off and sent away a few of the servants—the *chuprasee*, the *meter* and *metranee*, and some of the bearers. The old *dirwan* watched me silently as I passed through the gate of the compound as I had so often done; both he and the *khansamah* might keep their place if Mr. Rowland was able to find someone to let the house, so that the whole cycle of hiring servants might begin again.

The *khansamah* seemed to know already what had transpired with the solicitor. He brought me tea on the verandah and we sat together for a few minutes. The afternoon heat was no less unbearable than usual, but there was at least a welcome breeze.

"I have been considering your situation, Miss Weatherhead," he began without prefacing his remarks. "I may have a solution for you."

"A solution?"

"Yes. I have a cousin in Benares whose brother-in-law has a close friend employed as a *khitsugar* in the household of a proper English family. It is my understanding that they are in need of a governess. I am certain that you would be most suitable."

"Benares," I said. I knew where it was, roughly: three or four hundred miles inland, far enough from Calcutta that it might as well be located on the moon. "I had expected that I would remain here in Calcutta."

"No, no," Gobinda said right away. "You must not remain here."

"I would think that my best prospects—"

"This is an excellent opportunity, Miss Weatherhead," he interrupted. "I am sure that it would be most suitable," he repeated. "Preparations have already been made."

"You might have wished to consult with me first, Gobinda," I said. He seemed genuinely shocked when I stood. After the interview with the solicitor, it was one more example of a situation that was beyond my control.

"I was only seeking to assist you, Miss Weatherhead," he said, his voice unchanged.

"I shall be in my room," I answered. "I must pack my things, as I shall be leaving."

I have reached the same conclusion, Reverend. Gobinda wanted to get me as far from Calcutta as possible. I believe that he knew of the voices I had heard in the conservatory, the night that Mr. Heath took his own life. He sought to save me from them. I also later learned that Benares is the holy city for the Hindu god Shiva, and that his connections with Benares were significant.

The entire matter had been set in train by Rose's death—and Gobinda surely saw it as the hand of Kali. Thus, I do not know if going to Benares would have been enough to keep me safe. Those who come from beyond the Glass Door do not pay heed to distance or time. I was marked by the *stoicheia* and knew nothing of it.

As I lay in my bed that night listening to the steady rain, I wondered if Gobinda's offer might be for the best—for without a letter of reference, a suitable position might be beyond my reach.

WILLIAM DAVEY

I did not know what to make of Gobinda at the time. That he was a mesmerist there is no doubt. That he knew what confronted Eliza, even at this stage, seemed likely. I agreed with Eliza's assessment, however: whether they were agents of Kali in his eyes, or merely elemental spirits as we consider them, it was unclear whether they could have been prevented from taking action even if she had made the trip to Benares, hundreds of miles from Calcutta.

She was already in terrible danger and knew nothing of it. The *khansamah* wanted her to be far away from Calcutta—in Benares, far in the interior; but she was unwilling, or afraid, or perhaps just stubborn.

Her personal strength made a deep impression upon me as I remained in Sydenham to assist her in the many details that accompany a sudden death. She knew well the impression that her former character—or, shall I say, the character of the *thing* that had inhabited her—had given to her neighbors and other townspeople. My own perceptions, somewhat more acute than those who do not even have the half-light to guide them, readily revealed the hesitancy and the fear in their eyes and in their attitudes when they dealt with Eliza, and their shock and surprise when she now seemed somehow *different*.

They may have assumed that her change was due to her sudden widowhood. But their relief was palpable.

A week after Esdaile's death, Eliza received me in the parlor of her small home. I had obtained the beginnings of her own account by placing her—with her permission—in a mesmeric trance. The recollection of her experiences would be made clearer with my help: but she was not Esdaile, not guilty of a betrayal, and not under threat from the Committee. If anything I felt myself to be her *protector*, as she no longer had the powers of nightfall at her disposal to ward off or consume those in the Committee who might have done her harm—as she had done with those who had threatened her late husband.

The sudden absence of her former protector might have been a relief, but even so it must have been a shock after such a lengthy cohabitation. I hoped that my efforts with the Art might calm and center her; I believed, with some justification, that if I befriended

Eliza she might provide me with information about the statue's whereabouts in India. My plans were not well-formed at the time—but I reasoned that for such a prize I *would* journey all the way to India if necessary. Pride is a besetting sin; I possess it in abundance.

That afternoon I told her that I hoped she might continue her account, and would employ a deeper mesmeric trance if she permitted. The inimical *chthonic* spirit had fled, and there was nothing to make her my enemy, nor did I wish to be, nor should she consider me hers.

"This is exceeding kindness, Reverend," she said to me. It was spoken in a level tone—but I detected a hint of irony in her voice. "Do you always seek such tender reconciliations?"

"I think you mock me, madam."

"I am acquainted with the society of mesmerists only to the extent that they have sought to kill my husband," she answered. "And it is I who must bear the memory of how I—how my indwelling occupant—dealt with them. As you are a man of the cloth, sir, you must hear my confession that I am not completely sorry that they received the treatment that was given to them."

"No man deserves that," I answered right away.

"And no man," she answered in tightly controlled fury, "deserves to be hounded and threatened the way your terrible Committee dealt with James from 1851 onward. He made a choice, and I think he made the right one. I say this with no rancor, sir, though my—husband"—her voice caught as she said it, but she continued—"though my husband subjected me to the experience which I propose to relate to you. The spirit is gone and no longer directs my actions, but the knowledge and understanding it gave me remain.

"You all want that terrible thing that James refused to give you, the object that caused my gaoler to come forth. None of you deserve to possess it."

"Perhaps you are right."

I am enough of a judge of human nature to know that she had not expected agreement.

"Do you know what happened to it?" I said at last.

"I don't know. Perhaps James threw it in the Hooghly River."

"I doubt that."

"So do I. I only know that it remained after I…"

At this point the façade of strength seemed to crumble, like the shell of a building being consumed by fire. Her mind had turned to the defining event, the point at which Esdaile made his terrible bargain that introduced the *chthonic* spirit that had inhabited this young woman. I rose from my seat, hesitating between going to her and quitting the house entirely: but she looked up at me, eyes wide as if seeing the past laid out before her, and gestured for me to resume my place.

"It would be easier," she said after a moment, "if you undertook to bring about the deep trance you offer. I submit that my recollections have greater clarity when evoked under the mesmeric influence—and it will help me to keep my emotions more distant."

"As you wish, dear lady," I said.

"I do not know what I *wish*," she replied. "I only know that I wish to tell this story through to the end. Enough choices have been made that cannot be undone, sir. Now I choose to shine a truthful light upon it, and I am obliged to you for your assistance."

CHAPTER 5

A dream of spring

ELIZA ESDAILE

My decision to remain in Calcutta was rational and reasonable. I do not know if it constituted a turning point—but regardless, it seemed more sensible than the contemplated trip into India's interior: a long ride, since there was no civilized thing like a railway carriage in India in those days.

My salvation—how amusing it is to think of it that way now!—came from the Ladies' Society for Native Female Education. This organization was exactly what it sounds like—a group of expatriate Englishwomen firmly planted in English Calcutta, who sought to perform "good works" among the native women, helping them to learn reading and writing and maths to better themselves.

No, Reverend Davey, that characterization demeans them. We easily dismiss the benevolence of good works societies here in England because we see their members as self-serving and pompous. In India—particularly in Calcutta at that time—the Society was engaged in a *noble* pursuit: they sought to teach native women to read and write and handle sums, against the advice and sometimes explicit wishes of their men.

It is more than that. The culture demeans women from beginning to end: when they lose their husbands, they sometimes choose to give themselves over to the terrible ritual of *sati*—in which a widow joins her husband on the funeral pyre. Sometimes this is done voluntarily by a misguided soul or one who can simply not bear to live without her mate—and sometimes it is a compulsion forced upon her by her or her husband's family. Shamefully, it is still done in India today. The Society opposed *sati* through its education of young girls, giving them some measure of self-worth.

They rescued *me*, as well. Two days after the disgraceful inter-view at Mr. Rowland's office, I met Mrs. Martin Shackleford in Cooley Bazaar near Hastings Bridge. I had just been interviewed by the *khansamah* of a well-to-do Company official and had been found wanting, I must suppose, since the encounter was brief and unsatisfactory.

Mrs. Shackleford—a fine and proper lady of middle age—approached me as I examined a bound volume of Coleridge that had seen better days. I had determined that, despite its modest asking price, I could not afford even that modest luxury. But I lingered over the familiar lines that lay before me on that page—

All Nature seems at work. Slugs leave their lair -
The bees are stirring—birds are on the wing -
And WINTER slumbering in the open air,
Wears on his smiling face a dream of Spring!

—long enough that the grinning Bengali before me was convinced that he would make his sale. I was about to replace it next to its other care-worn brethren when a gloved hand touched mine and said, "I have always liked Coleridge myself."

"Then you should have this volume," I answered, turning slightly to face her. "I do not think I can spare even the modest amount this gentleman asks."

"There should always be enough to indulge in poetry, young lady."

I did not know how to properly answer that. She was so firm in her statement, her eye so clear, her smile such a secret indication of knowledge that she was not sharing, that I could not help but smile in return.

"My situation does not commend the extravagance, madam."

"Then it shall be my gift to you," she said, and turned on the book-seller. He was clearly unprepared for her superior haggling skill; it was over in a moment, and the price she obtained was a third of the amount I had declined to pay. She opened her purse and paid it, then pressed the book into my hands.

"And now, young lady," she said, "let us find a quiet place where we may visit."

Georgiana Bales Shackleford—Mrs. Martin Shackleford—had been in Calcutta several years longer than I. Her husband was a custom-house inspector; he had been posted there in 1842. She knew most everything regarding society in English Calcutta, including the news of my employer's recent death. When told of my visit, she deemed Mr. Heath's solicitor's behavior to be ungentlemanly at best; she knew of me from having seen my regular visits to the cemetery with the children. That I lacked a letter of reference was dismissed with a sigh and a wave.

"The Society has plenty enough work to do for five times our number, my dear Miss Weatherhead," she told me as we drank tea in a crowded little shop on Loudon Street. "We would be glad to put you to work."

"I have never been a teacher," I said.

"As a governess, what else *have* you been? You have given children instruction they might otherwise lack. You will do nicely, if you are willing to work."

"Of course."

"And if you have not made other commitments."

I mentioned the "arrangement" that Gobinda had sought to make for me. This too was dismissed perfunctorily.

"Gobinda is a good man, I might even say an honorable man—an unusual quality for one in his station. But Benares? That is no suitable place for an Englishwoman. Varanasi, they call it in Hindi: they say that a god founded the city five thousand years ago. If so, then Lord Shiva must have had a sense of humor. No, my dear, stick to Calcutta."

"I had thought so myself."

"A good decision. Gobinda seeks to do you a good turn, but by the next full moon he will have forgotten you completely." She patted my hand in a friendly, almost motherly, way. "But I shall *not*."

WILLIAM DAVEY

The Ladies' Society for Native Female Education was already more than three decades old when Eliza encountered them; I learned more about their means and objectives after I quit Sydenham for London, but at the time I thought that the appearance of Mrs. Shackleford was altogether too coincidental.

Still, Eliza's initial account betrayed no hint that anyone among the Society was a mesmerist—or, indeed, a *chthonic* spirit. I knew of their work: they were a benevolent society seeking to do good in a land far from home. They sought to bring literacy, numeracy and Christian education to women in a land where such persons were often denied the former two and remained ignorant of the latter. It seemed a perfect match for Eliza's talents.

In the midst of the tropical heat, it must indeed have seemed a dream of spring.

ELIZA ESDAILE

It was not difficult work at first.

The Calcutta I experienced with Mrs. Shackleford was a very long way from the neat compound where Mr. Heath met his tragic end; I never again found myself in Garden Reach, the more affluent part of the city.

Calcutta is like and unlike any city you might know, Reverend Davey. It is crowded—*teeming*—like the poorest parts of London, and dirty in a way that mere words cannot describe. The Hindoos hold certain animals sacred and permit them to roam through their streets unmolested; every native seems to have something to sell, or else is a beggar of the most wretched sort. I saw Gobinda several times over the next few weeks as I walked along the streets or passed through the markets, but he did not approach me.

In that society, native women's faces are often veiled from casual examination and it takes some considerable effort to obtain the merest glance. Ladies of the Society have an easier time of it: evangelizing clergymen must needs communicate the Gospel to men only—in any case, to those who will listen. They must deal with both Hindoos and Mohammedans: there are adherents of both faiths in Calcutta. But unlike the men—skeptical and superstitious—the women seem to thirst for it, all of it, even the simplest lessons of arithmetic. You cannot imagine the joy of a young doe-eyed girl, clapping her hands at having successfully tallied a small row of figures.

I did not forget my former life in Calcutta. Not every Sunday, but still from time to time, I visited the graves in the English Burial Ground—but it was primarily to lay a small bouquet for little Rose.

Life in Calcutta is marked by two things: the weather and the festivals. The most remarkable weather is a fierce rain—the word they give it is *monsoon*. That term has made its way into English vocabulary, like "bungalow" and "verandah"—but no rain here can possibly compare to the deluge that pours from the sky in early summer. It is at the tail-end of monsoon season that the Hindoos celebrate their great feast of Krishna, who is among other things a sort of love god. Some of them paint themselves bright colors, if you can imagine it, and men accost women and offer themselves for carnal pleasure. It is a time for proper persons to avoid the street.

It was at this time that Mrs. Shackleford—who desired that I address her as 'Georgiana', though I found it difficult to do so—removed a number of us from Calcutta to Hooghly, up the river. This smaller town was the site of a prison with an attached hospital; the Society was primarily on hand to work with the women whose husbands and brothers were incarcerated in the jail or being treated in the hospital. Since there was at that time no railway—Mr. Trumbull had only just begun to plan the route—the removal involved packing up supplies and books and arranging for transport for our luggage and ourselves thirty or forty miles upriver on flat-bottomed dinghy-boats. A few of the older ladies dreaded the prospect—but it was something new for me, so I entered into the project with zeal.

The day before we were to leave, I chanced to again see Gobinda while I was on an errand for Mrs. Shackleford in Cooley Bazaar, near where she and I had first met. Where he had previously avoided me—as if he were watching my movements but sought not to be seen—on this occasion he approached directly, his eyes fixed upon me as I haggled with a merchant. I had become rather good at the skill under Mrs. Shackleford's tutelage. I had also become adept at avoiding the multi-colored revelers who offered to share their Holi festival with me. These two things distracted me enough that I was quite surprised when I suddenly found him standing directly beside me.

The merchant seemed eager to conclude the matter quickly— and on highly favorable terms for me—and I found myself in possession of my parcel, looking directly at the old *khansamah*.

"Good afternoon to you, *Memsahib*," he said with a slight bow. "I trust you are well."

"I am, thank you," I answered. "But I am not *Memsahib*." This was a form of address that natives of Gobinda's class reserved for ladies of the household, not fellow servants. "May I help you today?"

"Let us walk," he said.

We passed slowly through the bazaar. Unlike the jostling, crowded experience that was customary, those around us seemed to keep their distance somewhat, so that we passed unhindered along the dry wooden planks laid over the mud of the plaza. It was as if a path opened up before us.

"I see that you remain in Calcutta, Miss Weatherhead, and that you have found a position with *memsahib* Shackleford."

"You are quite knowledgeable about my affairs, sir."

Gobinda smiled. "*Memsahib* Shackleford and I have known each other many years, Miss. She is a good soul. But—"

"But?"

"I wish to tell you once again that I have located a position for you in Benares. My cousin's brother-in-law has a close friend employed as a *khitsugar*—"

"Gobinda." I stopped walking so abruptly that he almost collided with me; but despite his age, he avoided me dextrously. "I see no reason why I should undertake a dangerous journey of some hundreds of miles inland, to a city where everyone would be a stranger. I have been in Calcutta for five years; I have a respectable position with the Society—"

"Miss Weatherhead," he interrupted me. His expression, normally dignified but tinged with a slight smile that crinkled the edges of his eyes behind his round spectacles, had become quite serious. "Miss Weatherhead," he repeated, "I cannot impress upon you too strongly that if you remain in Calcutta you are in danger. *Grave* danger, of a sort that you cannot readily understand."

"Really? From whom, may I ask?"

"Do you remember the night that Heath *Sahib* died?"

"It is etched on my memory, Gobinda. I can never forget it. Why do you ask?"

"Something happened while you were in the conservatory that night, Miss Weatherhead."

A chill swept over me, as if the sun had suddenly disappeared from the sky. I looked around at the bazaar: it looked oddly distant, like a sepia-tint portrait which someone had indifferently colored.

Gobinda reached his hand out and touched my hand where it emerged from my sleeve—and suddenly I saw something in the air, like little scraps of paper fluttering by; but they were not paper—they seemed to be almost immaterial, with a faint glow like burning camphor.

And then, most frightening of all, I heard the same voices that had come to me that night in Mr. Heath's house.

Eliza, they said. *We are looking for you. We have something for you, Eliza.*

"What—" I said, pulling my hand away. The little scraps disappeared; the voices died, and the bazaar returned to normal. Gobinda let his hand drop to his side.

"Did you see—"

"I do not know what you are about," I said angrily. "Nor do I wish to be subjected to any more of your tricks."

"It was no trick," he answered levelly. "You are in danger, Miss Weatherhead. The house of Heath *Sahib* will soon be occupied by another family—but even if they were in need of a governess I would not recommend your estimable self for the position, for you should not remain in Calcutta while they are looking for you.

"While you are here they can fix upon you—but if you leave, Miss Weatherhead, and go far away, I *might* be able to distract them."

I do not know now whether heeding his advice would have saved me. There is no way of knowing. Benares was far away, but perhaps not for them. I might have reached there and been protected by Lord Shiva—though in the Hindoo myth even he is slain. It was all beyond me at the time. All I knew was that Gobinda and his Hindoo fakery had frightened me—and so I left him, hurrying across the bazaar heedless of the mud on my shoes and my skirts. When I looked back he was still standing there, watching me go, his hands by his sides and his expression one of genuine sadness.

CHAPTER 6
Age of wonders

WILLIAM DAVEY

The role of the *khansamah* seemed more and more suspicious and compelling as Eliza told her story. Three times he had intervened: once by halting her on the stairs, once by trying to arrange her departure from Calcutta, and a third time by showing her the presence of the "beings" whom he said were pursuing her. From her description they did not sound *chthonic*, but more resembled *stoicheia* from some other realm—pneumic or photic, perhaps, or even nereic, following the Indian monsoon.

I was eager for Eliza to describe the terrible pact Esdaile had made with the *chthonic* spirit: but while I could anticipate it, my subject was taking her time in preparing the ground. There was no way to hurry it along.

ELIZA ESDAILE

Mrs. Shackleford found me at the Society's offices, packing a crate. She saw that I was disturbed and took me aside to sit; she placed her hands on my own shaking ones and waited for me to return her glance.

"What is troubling you, my dear?"

I told her of my encounter with Gobinda in the Cooley Bazaar—his warnings of danger and the vision he had given me. I tried to keep my voice level but it was obvious to me—and to her as well—that I was terribly angry. I believe that I was waiting for her to tell me that my imagination had run away with me.

Her response surprised me. She took her time answering, as if she was considering the way in which she wanted to phrase it.

"I am a few years older than you, Eliza," she said at last. "There are so many things that did not exist—that had not even been conceived!—when I was a little girl; there were no railways, no telegraph machines…and the mind was scarcely understood. The world has changed so much that I can scarcely encompass it.

"Setting aside Master Gobinda's motivation—we will speak of that another time—what he showed you is quite possibly real. The science of organic magnetism is more than flummery: it is revelatory, an exposition of something quite true."

"But the voices—"

"My girl, the works of Creation are far greater than we can imagine. What are the words from Shakespeare? 'There are more things in heaven and earth…'"

"'…Than are dreamt of in your philosophy,'" I supplied.

She smiled reassuringly back at me. "Precisely. But that does not mean," she added, raising a finger in admonition, "that our friend Gobinda is telling you the *truth*. He may even be evoking those voices for his own purposes. Nonetheless, the science of mesmerism is real and powerful."

"How…do you know all this?"

"Ah. Now, there is a story. My Martin and I have been here in Calcutta for almost ten years. While we were still in London, I had occasion to witness a remarkable exposition of the mesmeric art at the salon of a French practitioner, a *soi-disant* 'Baron' named Dupotet." She wrinkled her nose at this—I suspect that she had little regard for Gallic titles and airs.

I waited for her to continue, unsure what to say.

"This Dupotet was quite singular; he was what I might term to be *effete*, particular about his clothing and deportment. He was elegantly groomed, with the airs of a gentleman. He had established himself in a set of rooms in Hanover Square, where he gave demonstrations of the mesmeric arts. Martin and I attended such a performance and we were astounded."

I listened raptly as she described the scene. A young woman, a servant girl of some sort, had served as the subject: she was made to doze in the presence of an audience of numerous ladies and gentlemen through the use of mesmeric skill. Mrs. Shackleford's description conveyed distaste; the Frenchman's delicate long-fingered hands passing along the girl's body so close that they seemed to brush her sleeve or a loose lock of her hair—effrontery, but apparently insufficient for impropriety. The girl had not seemed to notice.

"I noticed the glint of something at the back of her neck: it looked very much like a seton, a needle attached to a thread passed through her skin to permit the discharge of bodily fluids. Clearly, she was under treatment somewhere for whatever ailment afflicted her.

"At last, he halted the passes and invited the viewers to closer examination—but he would not permit any to touch her, placing his hand in the way. When asked if the girl was sleeping, he replied that it was sleep—but not the usual sort: it was a 'magnetic sleep'."

I believe that she said that this took place in the fall, Reverend—1837, I should say, or 1838. She said that she had come to India in 1842; this would have been a few years prior to that.

1837, then. Very well: I am sure you know more about it than I. And—

Really. That *is* quite singular—do you remember meeting Mrs. Shackleford?

I see. Of course: I imagine that it would be difficult for you to determine with certainty whether you were at the same performance. But that *would* be a coincidence.

No, Reverend Davey. I suppose that I do not believe in coincidence either.

Mrs. Shackleford's account was detailed and became increasingly strange. This young girl was placed into a deep sleep so profound that some believed her to have died; the Baron actually withdrew a small hand-mirror to show that her breath still fogged it. After a few more mesmeric passes he invited the observers to try and awaken her by shouting and shaking, thumping and pinching.

One of the gentlemen even brought out a snuff-box from his waist-coat and applied some of the stuff beneath the girl's nose—enough, the man had said, to bring about a sneeze in a fair-sized elephant—but to no avail. Mrs. Shackleford told me that she was most taken aback by the rough treatment given the child.

When they had satisfied themselves that they could not awaken her, they retreated; Dupotet stepped forward once again and returned to his hand motions, from head to waist and back. As they watched, one of the girl's hands reached slowly out and touched one of the Baron's, causing him to stop his motions.

"As if emerging from beneath the ocean's depths," Mrs. Shackleford continued, "she looked upward at him, and then at the crowd of observers. With an unflinching, liquid gaze, she seemed to take in the entire scene; then she said—and I shall never forget this: 'Why should blushes dye my cheek?'"

"Whatever does that mean?" I asked her.

"I am certain I do not know," she answered me. "Then," she told me, "Monsieur le Baron answered, *Ah, ma chère, si c'est ici le meilleur des mondes possibles, que sont donc les autres?*"

I repeated the words in French, then offered a translation. "'Is this not the best of all possible worlds?'"

"Just so. You have an admirable accent, my dear Eliza."

"Modesty requires a blush to dye my cheek, Mrs. Shackleford."

"Georgiana," she said firmly, smiling.

"Georgiana. What happened next?"

"Ah. Well. The young girl turned her gaze to the Frenchman and stared at him for several seconds and then said, *Qu'importe, qu'il y ait du mal ou du bien?* Then her head slumped to her chest."

"'What does it matter, whether there is evil or good?'" I translated. "But surely she had been *prepared* for this performance."

"She was a servant girl, Eliza. She spoke not a *word* of French. Indeed, when she was revived after a few minutes, she demonstrated that her command of English was quite inferior. It might have been some sort of trick—but the characters of the girl entranced and the one in wakened state were so markedly different that we were all astounded. She had no memory of speaking at all, much less Parisian French—when told of it, a blush did, indeed, dye her cheek. She seemed somewhat flustered by all of the attention, and after only a few questions asked to be excused and she was escorted away.

"During our stay in London I saw several other demonstrations and each time I came away more and more convinced that the Art was functional and effective—and a *science*: something that must needs be drawn out of the morass of mumbo-jumbo and superstition and subjected to critical inquiry.

"We live in an age of wonders, my dear Eliza. Even here in India—poor, backward India—there is no reason to fear such as Gobinda and his flummery. It has the appearance of being learned, but it is founded in no more than superstition.

"It is like turning over a rock in a garden, and exposing what is underneath to the bright light of day. We are in an age of wonders, and every day we turn over another rock in our garden. You have nothing to fear from Gobinda and his tricks."

WILLIAM DAVEY

I know that Dupotet gave this performance in Hanover Square a number of times during the fall of 1837. Indeed, I had witnessed it personally; it was after such a performance that Dupotet himself had taken me aside and made reference to the half-light. What was stunning was the detail in Georgiana Shackleford's description, for it closely matched my own recollection, including the spoken words in French and the matter of the snuff-box. A more cynical observer would dismiss Dupotet's performance as trickery, but for those sensitive to the Art, it was clear that his abilities were genuine. Georgiana Shackleford must have felt it too.

Hard experience had taught me to mistrust coincidence, as Georgiana had said. It was unthinkable to imagine that Georgiana Bates Shackleford, whom Eliza had met by chance, would have been at the exact place on the exact date by mere coincidence.

I began to suggest that Mrs. Shackleford was somehow

complicit in the introduction of the *chthonic* being, but Eliza strenuously exerted herself in denying that any such thing might be true. It took some minutes before she was ready to proceed. I had to be patient and restrain myself in spurring her onward.

At last, she returned to recounting the trip upriver from Calcutta to Hooghly—quitting the teeming city for the more distant hospital. I could hear the trepidation in her voice and felt my own tension: I knew that Esdaile would soon walk onstage.

The details of his initial relationship with Eliza had never been revealed in our correspondence; I did not know of her nature until later—after they returned to Scotland…though, of course, when I speak of her *nature*, I do not refer to the character of the lady with whom I spoke on those chilly mornings and afternoons in Sydenham, but rather the thing that had inhabited her.

Clearly, she felt great affection for James Esdaile, so I inferred that some malign influence had brought the *chthonic* spirit into Eliza's life—perhaps even against Esdaile's will or desire. The devil's bargain I had assumed and of which I had accused him could not, I supposed, have been of his own making.

Regrettably, I could not have been more wrong.

ELIZA ESDAILE

The very first time I laid eyes on James Esdaile was during one of the Society's earliest visits to the prison hospital. He was touring a ward of recovering surgical patients with a native doctor, a man named Noboo. Doctor Noboo reminded me ever so slightly of Gobinda—he showed great deference to James, but had his own rapport with the patients—a gesture here, a spoken word or two there, all the while staying behind his superior, who sometimes took little notice of him.

Haughty? No, not James. He was often simply *tired*. In that, he resembled Mrs. Heath. India was no fit place for him; it weakened and drained him. He would have been better off on the rainy moors of Scotland, if you can believe it. All of the patients were eager to see the man they called Doctor Sahib, but it was clear to me that the patients' personal relationship was with his assistant, Doctor Noboo.

James Esdaile took little notice of us. We were mostly concerned with those patients who had womenfolk visiting or taking care of them. We were servants—background figures, like furniture; for me it was very familiar. He nodded to us in passing and moved on. My first impression of James Esdaile, I do not mind saying, was rather negative.

The first night I was in Hooghly, the voices returned. Mrs. Shackleford had arranged a sort of temporary dormitory for our group; I shared a small room with a younger woman named Amelia, who had no family in the world other than an older brother, who was a soldier in India. She worshipped Mrs. Shackleford and seemed never to be more than a few feet from her Bible.

The night was unbearably hot, and I left my bed and went to sit at the window…and I heard my name being called.

Eliza. It is so good that you have come, the voice said, a whisper on the wind so soft and reassuring that it did not trouble me at first—then I started; I stood and looked out across the fields toward the river, rimmed with the faint moonlight.

"Who is there?" I said quietly, not wanting to wake Amelia. The girl simply muttered in her sleep.

We only want to give you what you most earnestly wish. We want to help you leave India.

"And go home?"

Home, the voice said. *Yes. Home. We want to help you go home.*

I must confess to you, Reverend Davey, that the idea of returning to England after more than five years was more appealing than I can describe.

I think it may have blinded me to…but I am not sure. I am not even sure how to end that sentence.

"How? How will you help me get home? Who are you?"

Friends.

I remember that so clearly, and even after these many years I can still remember my joy at hearing it. Truly, other than Mrs. Shackleford—who was of recent acquaintance—I do not know if there was anyone in India whom I accounted a friend. But here was something—someone—who was offering me the thing I most desired.

There will come a question, the voice continued. *When it comes, you must say yes. Then you shall go…home.* The last word it said came out almost as if the concept were a novel one.

"What question?" I asked. But the whisper had faded away, leaving nothing but the soft sounds of insects in the still, stifling night.

CHAPTER 7

A single word

ELIZA ESDAILE

Among the womenfolk who took care of the men at the Hooghly hospital there was a pecking-order, and Kajari Kaurá sat at the top of it. She was a woman of middle age who seemed to know everyone (and everything) about the hospital and the jail; she operated a sort of open-air kitchen along with her husband Mádhab, which was busy from sunup to sundown. Native women fetched food to bring to the men recovering in the hospital or incarcerated at the jail, and part of the payment for her services was to offer up any tidbits of information about happenings in either. Kajari was a superb cook and amazingly efficient at news-gathering—and dispensing; in the bargain, she provided information with the dal and chapatis.

She was unfailingly polite to members of the Society, though some of my colleagues were extremely short with her. We are all trained to that, are we not, Reverend? By being disdainful of those below us in station and deferential to those above us, we reassure ourselves of our position in society. It was clear to me that Kajari, whether or not she was a simple Bengali cook, had a particular place that I respected—even if others did not. Mrs. Shackleford understood it, as did I, as did her husband Mádhab, who seemed to defer to his wife more than any Indian man I ever met.

Mrs. Shackleford explained to me how Kajari came to have such an important role. It was because her husband, Mádhab, was the first patient whom Esdaile had treated with the mesmeric method. Mádhab had recently received a parole from Governor-General Lord Dalhousie, I am sure due in part to Kajari's efforts—not that any English Governor-General would account that of importance!—and still bore the evidence of having been in irons for his crime. He walked with a sort of limp, but worked hard for his wife—carrying great sacks of rice and bushels of vegetables, bringing in a brace of chickens or a haunch of meat to be cooked, scarcely ever saying a word to anyone else.

To return to Kajari. She prepared our afternoon meal, which we ate in the shade of coralwood trees on a hill overlooking the river. As you must realize, no English person survives in India without learning to eat the native food. Some of the ladies complained, but I found it flavorful and filling. Kajari always made sure to fill my plate, and tell me that she had saved the best for me.

A week or so into our stay in Hooghly, she lingered as she served me and said in a sort of conspiratorial whisper, "You know, *Memsahib*, the Doctor Sahib seems quite taken with you."

"Really?" She meant James; all of the assistant and sub-assistant doctors from Noboo down all called him Doctor Sahib. I hadn't thought that he had even noticed me. "I'm—surprised. I should be flattered, except that I have hardly spoken ten words to him."

"Sometimes only a single word is enough," she answered, smiling.

I hesitated, considering a reply, but could think of nothing to say.

After I had eaten I took my plates and tableware back to where she stood cleaning. She put her hand on my sleeve and said, "It is very important to take advantage of situations, *Memsahib*."

"How do you mean?"

"The Doctor Sahib's time in India is almost over," she answered. "Soon he will return to his home, his Scotland."

"He is a lucky man, Kajari. India is beautiful—but it is not home."

"Not for you, either," she said.

"No. No, of course not for me. But I cannot—"

"Who is to say?" she interrupted, touching my sleeve again. "Situations present themselves. The Doctor Sahib has lost two wives. One died on the way to India, the other while he was in residence here."

"I hardly think—I mean, I do not think this matter even suitable for discussion. This is quite improper."

"In India, *Memsahib*, a husband and wife sometimes do not even see each other's faces until the day of marriage. Such situations occur—and they happen in your own land as well, do they not?"

"I suppose they do, for people of a particular class. I am not…"

"You are not *what*, *Memsahib*? Old enough? You are certainly of age, perhaps past age. Pretty enough? You are quite attractive. They all say so."

I was not sure just who 'they' might be, but I think that I bristled slightly at the notion that I might be the subject of idle talk among Indian servants.

"I do not like such gossip being spread, Kajari. I am not interested in marriage, and even if I were, I do not think that I am a suitable match for the Doctor Sahib—for Doctor Esdaile."

This was the first I had heard of the idea, Reverend. I dismissed it at once. At the time I thought it no more than what I said to Kajari—idle gossip, of the sort that one might expect in a society of women, or among servants; I made no connection between it and the voices I had heard in Calcutta and then in Hooghly.

But I should have. Oh, how I should have.

A single word, Kajari had said. The single word, of course, was *yes*.

A few days later—it could not have been long afterward—a few of our number were asked to assist in the women's ward at the hospital. I was not terribly surprised when I was asked specifically to help.

Many of the women were suffering from the same sort of afflictions as the men, though they were sometimes located in different parts of the body. The most prominent difficulty was a sort of cyst, what was called a hydrocele—a malady common to that area of

India: they grow hard and painful and are sometimes quite large. With the women, Doctor Esdaile found it convenient to have a female assistant on hand to reassure the patient. He found the members of the Society most helpful in this regard.

On one afteroon I was sitting with a young woman and her older sister, who had some command of English, when James passed through the ward and stopped at the bedside.

"And how is Raji today?" he asked, bending down to take the young girl's hand. She was afflicted by a hydrocele, a hardened sac the breadth of a hand, depending from the right side of her face; it clearly pained her greatly, particularly when she moved her head or spoke. Her sister held her hand, and Raji raptly fixed her attention upon the doctor's face. The Doctor Sahib, who had always seemed unruffled, appeared distracted—perhaps by my own presence.

"She seems to be in great pain, Doctor," I ventured.

"Ah, now *that* we will attend to straight away. I think Raji is due for a procedure early this evening, isn't that right, Lekha?"

The older sister was also focused on him. "Yes, Doctor Sahib," she said. "Raji is afraid, but I have told her that there is nothing to worry about; Doctor Sahib will take care of her."

"Quite, quite so," he said. "Of course we will." He looked from Lekha to Raji and then back to me. "Just a little work and she will be just fine."

Lekha smiled and told Raji in rapidly-spoken Bengali what Doctor Esdaile had said; the young girl brightened, as if someone had told her that her fondest wish had come true—which, indeed, it might have done.

The tableau seemed to last several seconds: the older woman, the younger, myself and the Doctor Sahib, like a lithograph in sepia...

"Miss Weatherhead."

I was not sure whether a few seconds or several minutes had passed. I looked away from the young girl in the hospital bed and at James Esdaile.

"I...beg your pardon, Doctor. How may I help you?"

"May I speak to you privately for a moment?"

"Of course." I rose and followed him along the ward to an area set aside with a small writing desk and two simple armchairs; he gestured me to one and took the other himself.

"I have noticed," he began, "that you enjoy a certain amount of rapport with the patients."

"I do my best, sir," I answered.

"Sir." He smiled at me. "Just *Doctor* is sufficient, Miss Weatherhead. Though I should like you to use my Christian name."

It was actually quite a pleasant smile: recall, Reverend, that James was fifteen years older than I—a mature man of middle age, twice widowed and a *Scotsman*. I was quite prepared to be put off by my first impressions, and this desire for informality should have done even more to distance me—but somehow, it seemed all right.

"Mrs. Shackleford wants me to call her Georgiana, Doctor," I said. "I confess that I have trouble with that, as well."

"I understand. Georgiana Shackleford is a force of Nature. But you do not seem to be afraid of her as some of you ladies are."

"There is nothing to be afraid of."

"From her? I daresay she is quite formidable when she is angry." He said it like someone with an acquaintance with such matters. "I understand," he continued, "that you are stranded, after a fashion, here in India."

The change of subject caught me quite by surprise.

"My term of employment ended. I was working for—"

"Robert Heath. The one who…ended his own life. Poor man, he thought he was all alone in the world. I know how he must have felt."

And at that moment, Reverend Davey, I think I gained a glimpse into his soul. James Esdaile must have felt much the same way—alone: he was already preparing for the trip home, knowing that you were waiting for him, expecting him to deliver the statue into your hands or be punished or killed.

That is why he did what he did, sir. He was driven to it by despair. Does it excuse him? No.

Do I forgive him? Yes. Yes, I do. Even with what followed, I came to love him. My indwelling inhabitant never understood that—but I know *he* did.

Especially at the end, Reverend. On that I have no doubt.

WILLIAM DAVEY

The lady ended the mesmeric trance by our agreed-upon signal, leaving the narrative with Eliza and James Esdaile sitting together in the hospital ward. It was not because she was distraught—quite the opposite: she seemed defiant and resolute, as if daring me to criticize.

She rang for tea. We sat and drank for several minutes during which I remained silent. She was flushed, a stark contrast to the black of her mourning dress. Her eyes flashed with anger.

"I am sorry if I have offended you, madam."

"You have not offended me in this interview, Reverend. Your offenses precede you—from the time James made his decision."

"You are very loyal to his memory," I answered. "And ready to criticize me and excoriate the Committee. But while I respect that loyalty, I cannot help but feel it is misplaced."

"I fail to see why."

"He *betrayed* you, Eliza. Whatever he did to introduce the *chthonic* spirit into your person—whatever promise he made, or it made, took away nearly eight years of your life from you and turned you into—"

"A monster."

"Yes. Turned you into a monster." I know that my revulsion was evident in my voice. "It should repel you to think of it. It should anger you—it should make you hate James Esdaile for doing it to you. I understand Christian charity—"

"Not from personal experience," she interrupted.

"I can comprehend," I said, refusing to rise to her comment, "how you might be willing to forgive. But forget? I cannot imagine how the memory of that imprisonment must haunt your rest and bring fear to you even in bright daylight. I cannot see how you do not hate James Esdaile."

"As you do."

"I did not and I *do* not hate him."

"You delude yourself. Of course you did. He did not bend to your will as all of the other practitioners had done. At the moment of truth, he hesitated and judged that the statue he had been given was simply too dangerous for you to possess. That offended you, didn't it?

"Even now, after all that I have told you, sir, you do not comprehend. He would *never* let the statue fall into your hands, or those of other members of your cursed Committee. Only with hesitation did he use the power it gave him to summon the spirit that possessed me. Imagine if you had that power."

I started so suddenly that I nearly dropped my teacup on the floor.

"What did you say?"

"'Imagine if —"

"I beg your pardon. Before that. About the power of the statue. Did you say that he used it to summon the spirit?"

"Yes. Of course." She answered as if summoning a *stoicheia* were the most natural thing in the world. "Why, how do you think it was done?"

"I...assumed he performed the act himself, or used some discipline he had learned in India."

"Oh, he did. But it was the statue that gave him that capability—just as it had enhanced his ability to practice the mesmeric Art in the first place. But ultimately, he was not tempted strongly enough. By protecting him—from you and your kind—it assumed that sooner or later he would call it back to him. He would either prove strong enough to use it, or pass it to someone who would. Someone like you."

"And did he call it back?"

"Not to my knowledge. Only he knew what was done with it—and he has taken the secret to his grave." She dabbed briefly at her eyes, which showed genuine raw emotion. "He made an awful decision, but now he is dead. Not consumed, but just dead. He did what he did because it was necessary."

"Even imprisoning you."

"I am free now. And I am home. What is more, I am not without responsibility. At the critical moment, I accepted the spirit and made my own bargain—I spoke the one word of acceptance.

"You wish to make James the villain. He has much to answer for, Reverend Davey. But I know who the villain must be. He sits in my parlor drinking tea with me."

CHAPTER 8

Betrayal and acceptance

ELIZA ESDAILE

I have decided to continue this narrative to the end for my benefit as well as yours, Reverend. I know that you are surprised, even shocked, that I might be sympathetic to the man that gave me over to possession. But it offered me a way to go home—and a promise that it would go its way when he died. It fully expected to consume him at the moment of death: there was a time that it would have overjoyed me to see it happen. I rejoice now, however, that he cheated the being.

I don't know where it has gone. Back to the nightfall realm, I expect. They speak of the Glass Door, which separates our realm from theirs. Even when closed, each side can see through and be tempted. Maybe it watches this scene, though I doubt it; I don't know what it means for such a creature to give service and be cheated of payment—though I can tell you that it is a member of a hierarchy of sorts, and is among the least of its kind. I tremble to think what a greater one might be like.

This is the power you would have been able to access had James delivered the statue to you. No, I do not believe that you would have been able to resist the temptation. James could not, though he had only used that power once.

After his initial approach, James made a point of speaking with me and working with me whenever possible. I enjoyed the attention, of course, as any young woman might—and Mrs. Shackleford favored me with frequent smiles because I was in such high esteem with our patron. Amelia, my room-mate, was jealous, but tried her best to conceal it—I think she would have been glad to be so prominent.

But she would have been unlikely to be found "suitable".

At the end of a particularly wearying week, Doctor Esdaile invited me to dine with him at his own residence. It was impossible to do so alone, as I am sure you understand: I was therefore accompanied by Mrs. Shackleford. We completed our work for the day and returned to the dormitories; even Amelia seemed excited, and helped me brush my hair and arrange my frock. All of the others were most encouraging—it was as if I were truly being evaluated in some way, rather than simply being accorded a courtesy by the Doctor Sahib.

We walked most everywhere even in the most fierce heat, but this evening Mrs. Shackleford and I were picked up by a palky and delivered in style through a fierce rainstorm directly to James Esdaile's door. His *dirwan*—a younger man, much younger than the ageless relic who had guarded the door at the Heath compound—was ready with a stout umbrella when we arrived, and escorted us quickly inside.

Away from the hospital, I had expected James to be relaxed and more at ease—but he seemed quite tense, for the reason you can imagine. His house was small but well-appointed, with a spacious rear verandah and wide screened doors at either end—making it airy and somewhat cool.

"Thank you for joining me," he said, offering us seats in the parlor.

A house-servant provided us with glasses of Madeira; I am not knowledgeable about wines, but evidently the vintage was sufficient to impress my companion.

We engaged in small talk: discussion of the weather and the festivals, of the Great Exposition then happening in London, and so forth. James was most knowledgeable about ancient cultures: his house was decorated with artifacts and memorabilia from all over India, and he could speak on each one. I was fascinated in spite of myself, though Mrs. Shackleford found it quite wearying.

The discussion continued through dinner. He had engaged a talented chef; Kajari's cooking was excellent as I have already said—but there was a marked difference. Each dish was more flavorful and savory than the last: I can remember them very clearly even after all of these years. And there were so many of them: a spicy soup, *chapati* and savory *naan* breads, a lovely lamb *biryani* dish, fresh vegetables and fruit, accompanied by more of the wine and that excellent sweet yoghurt drink called *lassi*.

At some point short of the end of the meal, Mrs. Shackleford's head began to nod on her chest. She was accustomed to the heat and acquainted with the cuisine; her manners, if not her dignity, should have kept this from happening. Of course, years later I have my own suspicions on this event, but at the time I concluded that she had been working harder than any of us.

I reached to wake her but James said, "No, let her rest a bit. I have a particularly interesting item to show you."

"Really?"

"Yes. It's in my library." He stood and walked toward a doorway. I hesitated: it was a bit improper for me to be alone with him—but I did not wish to contradict the doctor regarding Mrs. Shackleford's rest. "It will only take a minute."

Yes, of course. I should have said no. I should have known. Should have, should have, should have. I assumed he was merely being kind, and enthusiastic about some object he had found somewhere.

I went into the library. It was dark, with only a single lamp sitting on a circular dark wood table in the middle of the room. Almost as soon as I came into the room I knew what he intended to show me.

On the mantel, to the left of an ornate clock, there was a statue. It was tiny; perhaps no more than five or six inches tall. It was a naked native woman worked in exquisite detail, down to the bangles at ankles and wrists; she held one hand upright, almost defiantly, holding a dagger. It glowed as from within, making a second light source in the room.

"You see it, don't you," he said. I couldn't see him in the dim light; I walked forward carefully to look at the object: it was compelling and beautiful.

Eliza, I heard. *You came.*

"What?" I spun around. "Doctor Esdaile? Where are you?"

He has stepped away, Eliza. But he will return. He will be with you.

I wasn't sure what was happening and did not wait to find out. I walked straight for the doorway, where light streamed out from the dining room. But suddenly someone was standing in front of me—a young Indian woman whom I had never seen before. She was barefoot and dressed casually, in a beautiful *choli* and *sari* that seemed to catch the light. She raised her hand as I approached, making the bangles at her wrist jangle musically. It stopped me in my tracks.

Yes, Reverend Davey. That is where I began to be afraid.

"I must ask you a question, Eliza," she said. Not *memsahib*: not Miss Weatherhead. "What is it you most desire?"

"I—I don't know."

"I can answer for you, Eliza. You want to go home. You want to leave India and return to your home."

I wanted to reply angrily—but I could not, Reverend. I could not find words to answer this Indian woman.

She was right. I wanted more than anything to be quit of India—quit of voices, of monsoons, of all that was around me and see my home again.

"I do not know how I will be able to do it."

"I can help you, Eliza. I shall help you."

"How?"

"You must trust me. The Doctor finds you suitable, and I have what you desire."

"You can help me go home."

"Yes, Eliza. I can."

"What must I do?"

"You must say yes, Eliza. You must only say yes."

I do not know what moved me at that moment. Perhaps the *chthonic* spirit had already taken control of my will, or there had been some substance placed in our dinner, or I was overwhelmed by the desire to do as she said—to leave India forever.

I took a deep breath and said, "Yes."

The young girl's eyes began to glow. I promise you, Reverend: I saw it—her eyes became like a pair of bright streetlamps. I opened my mouth to shout, but no sound emerged.

My sight began to fade and I felt faint: my legs seemed to give out under me.

Somewhere in the distance, I thought I heard Gobinda's voice shouting my name.

WILLIAM DAVEY

Her story went no farther for the moment.

There are times when a mesmerist must press a subject to achieve a desired effect. There are many methods and many consequences: pain, loss of memory, emotional turmoil, implantation of false feelings and false recollections—but Eliza Weatherhead Esdaile was not an adversarial subject. She had accepted the trance state at my hands in order to facilitate the telling of the story, and she felt that it had reached its end with Esdaile's betrayal and her own acceptance of the *chthonic* spirit.

I think that her admission of that terrible decision humiliated her before me. She had already declared her disdain and dislike for me, for the Committee, and for all that we represented. Whether that meant that there was more to tell and she refused to tell it, or that she had confessed to as much weakness as she chose to do at present I did not know at that time.

Whatever the case, she summarized for me—briefly and, I think, rather curtly—how she had awoken in the women's ward at the hospital, having fallen unconscious for a few days; how she had found herself trapped, watching her body and her senses under the control of an alien force; and how she had quickly become engaged and then as quickly married to the man who had so casually and callously betrayed her.

Within a matter of a few weeks, Eliza Weatherhead—now Eliza Weatherhead Esdaile, a prisoner in her own body and mind—was boarding a ship with her new husband, bound for Scotland, leaving India behind forever. The statue remained behind: she knew this for certain, since her senses were now attuned to its presence.

When she had finished, I told Eliza that I intended to travel to Scotland to visit Esdaile's brother. When I thus informed her, I thought that she might bid me good riddance—but she softened, and asked that I take a letter with me to Reverend David Esdaile, which she would write and arrange to be delivered to my hotel-room so that I might carry it with me.

"I shall convey it with pleasure, madam," I told her. "I give you my word that I will not examine it."

"If that were my concern, Reverend Davey, I should not send it with you. It does not matter whether you see it or not—there is nothing I care to keep secret. I merely wanted David—James' brother—to know of his death, and some little of what we have learned together these past few weeks.

"I also wish for him to know how terribly sorry I am at his grief at what he…and we…have lost."

"I understand."

"You do not," she replied. "You only think you do. But I would not dream of gainsaying the chairman of the Committee.

"Suffice it to say, sir, that my keeper was by no means the only such spirit abroad in the land. There are certainly others, as I expect you will learn soon enough."

I had no ready answer to that comment, but simply said, "I shall deliver your letter."

"Then I shall bid you farewell, Reverend Davey. I have told you that I believe you to be the villain of this drama, but for all that, I do not wish evil on you."

"I thank you for that kindness, Mrs. Esdaile."

"It is only because evil needs no more help from me, sir. I suspect that it shall have no trouble finding you without me."

And thus I took my leave of Eliza.

As I walked down the lane away from her cottage I turned back for a moment to see her standing at the door. She followed me with her glance for only a few moments, then turned away and closed her door as if shutting me once and for all out of her life.

CHAPTER 9
Weighty things

WILLIAM DAVEY

I had already been waiting more than twenty minutes at the Weathercock, a mildly shabby coffee-house on Piccadilly Square when John Williams Jackson came in from the cold, limping quickly along on his lame foot, clapping his mittened hands to try and dash away the cold and shrugging his shoulders to rid himself of the gray, sooty snow.

I attempted to affect an air of disinterest, but the news that Jackson carried was really too important to bother with that. We were old enough friends that he surely would have seen through it, in any case. I made room for him on the bench, moving my cup and saucer.

John Jackson and I were almost exactly of an age, but he seemed to look older and more worn down. Some of it was due to his lame foot—he had been badly injured when he was thirteen and had limped ever since. But there was clearly more to his appearance than just that: his clothing, while clean and presentable, always appeared just a tad out of fashion and a half-size too small, as if it had been subjected to laundering once too often. The wrinkles in his face, even the ones derived from laughter, were deep creases; he had creaky bones and a raspy cough.

"Glad to have you back in town," Jackson said, placing his hat on the table in front of him and accepting a cup of coffee from a server who arrived without prompting and vanished quickly at my glance.

"Things took longer than I expected."

"We have more than our usual quota attending today, even

given the weather." Jackson brushed snow off his hat onto the floor. "A few extra worthies who would like to turn you over a spit."

"Friends of Ann Braid, I expect."

"May be, maybe not. Engledue is on hand, sharpening his knives."

"He's not even supposed to be in England! Bad for a dead man to show his face."

Jackson sipped his coffee and scowled, then sipped a little more. "It *does* tend to undermine the illusion, doesn't it."

"Indeed, it does."

"He's well known, Will, but he's a crank. Yesterday's news, even as the former editor of the *Zoist*."

"Is there anyone else who qualifies as irrelevant, lying in wait for me?"

"Joseph Baker will be on hand."

"What in God's name is *he* doing here?"

"He's with the American and his wife. Lorenzo and Lydia. They swept in yesterday—Vernon tells me they're looking for a house."

"I'd heard that Lorenzo Fowler was coming to London, but didn't know he'd be here this soon. That's unfortunate."

"You know what he wants."

"Respectability," I said. "Re-spec-ta-bil-it-y," I repeated, articulating each syllable as Fowler always seemed to do in his public lectures, when railed against 'intellectuals' in the phrenological and mesmeric worlds.

"That's right. Spencer Hall and Dr. Elliotson are too smart to let Ann Braid lead them along, and no one listens to Dr. Forbes anymore; he's practically become a laughingstock like poor old Vernon."

"'Poor old Vernon' may be a broken man, Johnny, but he's more canny than most of these poseurs. One of these days someone will turn his back on him and regret it."

"Pray for that," Jackson answered. "But it doesn't solve the problem. They're out for your head."

"If they want my head," I said, "they'll have to constitute a majority—well, *more* than a majority. They have to decide what they would rather do, and which fox they would rather place in charge of the hen-house. But the best approach for me—for *us*"—I touched the rim of my cup to Jackson's—"is to determine in advance what bone we would care to throw them. There must be some things we don't care about."

"What about D'Orsay? You could give him some freedom in recruiting talent from Cambridge. He's been pushing for that for more than a year."

"That's a *capital* idea. Alex D'Orsay thinks he will take my seat away some day—let's find out if he's a threat, or let him fall on his face. Even Fowler might approve of that. Americans." I snorted. "Lorenzo Fowler *understands* who the Chairman is. But giving D'Orsay something to do is a handsome gesture. You're a genius, Johnny."

"Ah, that I were. This isn't like the old days, Will. Fifteen years ago, it was just the lecture circuit and laboring in the vineyards to find new talent. Now…"

"A lot has happened in fifteen years. Let's leave it at that, shall we?"

"It would make a great book. Maybe Mr. D. would like to take it on."

"He'd have to write himself out of it. Though I'm sure that even if the average *Household Words* subscriber never missed him, *we'd* notice his absence."

A few decades earlier, England, particularly London, had been swept up in the reform ideas contained in the People's Charter. When most of Europe was seized by revolution, Chartism was the movement of choice in England—not just for tradesmen and workers, but for intellectuals and reformers as well.

W. John Vernon had been a part of the inner circle of the Committee for a half-dozen years, offering "mesmeric consulta-tions" to the gentry from his fashionable address on Regent Street.

But he had been caught in the backlash to Chartism, spending eighteen months in Newgate Prison and emerging a broken man, dying soon afterward. So went the story.

The Regent Street address was too useful and too valuable to the Committee. John Vernon had been badly done by prison and was a shell of his former self: his debts had mounted and endangered the house—but at my urging the Committee had done something on both counts. Most people whom Vernon had known considered him long dead, a sad artifact of a difficult time…the Chartist movement had largely dissipated…but he had lived on, keeping his quarters and nicely appointed drawing room on the first floor, a few houses up from Glasshouse Street.

We made our way there, walking anonymously among the bustling crowds, bundled and hunched against soot-tinged snow the bitterly-cold wind drove at us. I would have liked a more brisk pace, but Jackson could only move so fast—and I intended that we arrive together.

Let them understand, I thought to myself, *that I have received my briefing.*

As we approached Vernon's rooms, I took note of the idlers on Regent Street. The bobbies moved them along regularly, keeping them from staying in one place—not that they were extremely likely to linger, given the weather. But the constables were oblivious to the true nature of a few among that crowd; they did not sense, as Jackson and I did, that those few were *stoicheia*: elemental spirits disguised as idle hands, itinerants, beggars—the sort of persons that respectable citizens of London walked past every day and certainly would not care to see on Regent Street. I would have disregarded them as well, but for the presence of the *stoicheia*—they were impossible to ignore, and I could hear their whispering voices in my mind.

Can we help you, sir? What do you want, what do you need?

Where are you going today?

*Surely you can find something for us to do…*the last was plaintive, hungry, as if appealing not to intellect but to emotion. I decided that *hungry* was probably the right word: they must have been *eager*, like Eliza Esdaile's *chthonic* possessor had been eager, to pursue an agenda and consume the victim in the end.

There were almost always one or two, hoping for the chance to get inside the building (and thus within the Committee's defenses); today there were at least six, possibly seven. One was particularly notable: a short, fairly well-dressed Levantine, who looked uncomfortable and completely out of place among the idlers.

Despite my alarm I refused to convey any sense of concern. We went past, giving a polite nod to the doorman as we walked into the lobby.

Almost at once, the voices stopped. We brushed the worst of the snow off our overcoats and hats, and slowly climbed the stairs to the next floor.

A servant admitted us to a narrow, short hallway that led to a large drawing room. For a moment it seemed that the voices from Regent Street had returned: at least a half-dozen conversations gave a background buzz of conversation, rising and falling like ocean waves. We gave up our outer clothing; Jackson waited as I took a moment to stand before a mirror and adjust collar and coat lapels before making my entrance.

Within seconds of my appearance every conversation save one had stopped. Spencer Hall—slight and mildly effete—had just stopped mid-sentence in addressing Dr. Forbes, whose pugnacious face was more ruddy than usual; the scholar D'Orsay was a bit further away listening to Dr. Elliotson, who appeared to be trying to make a point; Joseph Baker and the Fowlers were over by the fireplace, beneath the looming black-draped portraits of Admiral Ross and George Combe; and Ann Braid, daughter of the famous surgeon and "debunker" James Braid, had apparently stopped a discussion with two men: one had his back turned to me, but the other was the railway engineer Richard Beamish. Miss Braid had just turned to look at the doorway—and me—with an almost palpable hostility.

The only remaining conversation—if it truly could be called a "conversation"—was taking place near the sideboard, where a familiar figure was holding forth to an audience as if he were the only speaker in the room.

"- *advantage* of me," he was saying. "I cannot fault the man as a *businessman*, but I do not see any reason why propriety cannot be observed. It may be *his* publication, but I daresay no one picks up an issue of it for any reason other than to read my work. If that is not obvious to him, then he is welcome to make any money he can without me. That"—he rapped his knuckles on the sideboard, making a small army of delicate china cups rattle musically—"*that* is why I have founded my own magazine. It is more work, of course, but—"

At this point he seemed to notice, as if for the first time, that I had arrived. He paused theatrically in mid-gesture and converted his stance to a polite bow in my direction.

"Pray do not let me interrupt," I said with what I hoped was the correct minimum of sardonicism.

The other man held my gaze for just a moment, his eyes narrowing and brow pinching, then said, "I was just telling these ladies and gentlemen why I decided to quit *Household Words* and launch a new publication of my own."

"Capital," I said. "What will it be called?"

"*All The Year Round*," he answered. "I think it has a certain charm, don't you think, Reverend Davey?"

"It is an excellent choice, to be sure, Mr. Dickens."

There was some murmur of approval. Charles Dickens was accustomed to being the most important person in the room—and in this society, at this moment, that cachet had ceased as soon as I had arrived. In the rest of the world, Dickens was respected—even revered: but here he was no more (and no less) than a wealthy patron. My comment was not necessarily backhanded or insulting.

However, in this instance, *I* was the center of attention. I do not know if he found it insulting, and at that moment I certainly did not care.

The great author had no response; he waited, as everyone did, for me to indicate my intentions. At last, I nodded to Dickens and turned aside to greet John Vernon, who had entered during the exchange. Jackson made his way to the other end of the room; he would want to see which way the wind was blowing.

Conversations slowly resumed, though Dickens' little audience had dispersed. Only William Engledue remained nearby, and he and Dickens undertook a brief hushed discussion, with the *Zoist*'s former editor casting furtive glances my way.

"I hope there's no danger of running out of tea and cakes, Mr. Vernon."

"I should not think so, Reverend," Vernon answered. He was a small, hollow-cheeked man, not quite as shabby as Jackson—but still a decade out of fashion. Most took him for a bit of a fool; but I sensed his usual, almost feral, intensity. "Those are not the appetites that concern me."

"Jackson told me already."

"Hmm. But did he tell you about *that*?" He gave a slight nod in the direction of Ann Braid, who was again in deep conversation with Beamish and a younger man—another engineer named Begys—and Alfred Higginson, an impossibly pompous surgeon from Liverpool who was forcefully making some point while making a vigorous chopping motion with his left hand.

"Not a word," I said. "What am I looking at?"

"Well, I don't know what Higginson has to do with it—he just barged into that little discussion. But it seems Miss Braid has suddenly taken an interest in railroad engineering. I don't know what to make of *that*, but she—oh, excuse me, Doctor Elliotson, I certainly did not mean to step on your foot, sir."

Vernon danced nimbly out of the way, winking at me. I found myself face to face with John Elliotson, a diminutive elderly gentleman, perhaps the greatest scholar and practitioner of our Art.

"Davey," Elliotson said. After initially ignoring Vernon, he finally gave him a rather disdainful glance: the doctor, like most of our society, dismissed Vernon as a powerless piece of furniture. For his part, Vernon's demeanor had completely changed to one of subservience and mild confusion. He slipped away, mingling with other guests.

"Elliotson. Good to see you, Doctor."

"Spare me," Elliotson answered. "I should tell you as a *friend*, Davey," he added in a barely friendly tone, "that there is quite some dissatisfaction with the way you handled the Esdaile matter. *Quite* some dissatisfaction." The little man jutted out his chin. "You are prepared to *defend* yourself, I assume."

"I had thought you opposed the action."

"Of course I did," Elliotson said, letting his voice drop. "Killing James Esdaile would have accomplished nothing—but there were other alternatives."

"Even worse ones."

"Even so."

"I intend to offer some additional explanation, if that's what you mean by *defending myself*. That *is* what you mean, isn't it?"

"I choose my words carefully, Davey. As you know."

"I find that actions speak louder. Does this mean that you intend to challenge me?"

Elliotson did not look away.

After a moment he said, "You know I find politics distasteful, Committee politics even more so. And antagonizing Mr. Dickens is hardly necessary, either. His money helps provide for *all* of this. But I thought you might like to know that you are on unsteady ground."

"You think so, do you."

I was not fond of Elliotson, though I respected his genius: but as one of the most senior members of the Committee, his opinions and his insights carried weight. He and Dickens were fast friends, and Elliotson had brought him into our society twenty years ago. The doctor was, in many ways, the father of the English mesmerist movement—he had pioneered many of the methods and techniques in regular use by the Committee—which had, after all, been originally empanelled to investigate Elliotson's claims for the Art.

"I shall throw back at you what you constantly *preach*,"

Elliotson said at last. "Over my objections, I might add, you were assigned a task enjoying the full confidence of your colleagues. You bollicksed the damn thing up."

"Do you really believe that?"

"Most of us do."

"Most," I said. "Isn't Esdaile dead?"

"Well, *yes*. As I say, not that it accomplishes anything. Even so, *you* didn't do it—he apparently committed suicide, from what I hear. And you didn't obtain your little trumpery, did you? Or learn where Esdaile put it?"

"I did not. I learned a great deal else, but not the location of the statue. Which, incidentally, I will thank you not to demean, sir. It may be much more important than any of us realized."

"I doubt it. But we did not expect his—we did not expect *her* to remain, and yet she appears to be his 'surviving widow'. I trust that you have not become...*distracted* in any way."

I considered my response. At sixty-eight, John Elliotson was among the oldest members in the room, and deserved—and expected—respect, no matter how he conducted himself.

Your time has come and gone, I thought, but let it be.

CHAPTER 10

And loyal, every one

WILLIAM DAVEY

By tradition, the guests waited until the clock in the outer hall struck three, at which time servants entered discreetly and began moving occasional tables aside and setting up chairs in ordered rows. At the far end of the room, in front of the sideboard and beneath the black-draped portraits of Ross and Combe, they set a somewhat more ornate chair; a portable secretary was placed on a small table on the right, behind which John Jackson settled himself, preparing pens and ink for the meeting to come.

Only a few arrived later than I had done. If there were no weighty matters to discuss I might have taken note of their tardiness, but that day I did not care. When the servants withdrew, a small group of junior members drew lots and the short straw went reluctantly out into the entrance hallway, the doors closing firmly behind him. No one else would be admitted.

I walked to the cleared space near the sideboard and waited for everyone to take their seats.

"Welcome, my friends," I began. "I am gratified for so many of you to take time to be here this afternoon. We have important matters to discuss and I have information to impart regarding my recent time in Sydenham. Mr. Jackson, if you please."

I turned to Jackson, who stood and began to read minutes of the previous meeting, held a few weeks before last Christmas. It had been ill-attended—the weather had been even more wretched than it was today. In the room, the light from the chandeliers and sconces seemed to be fighting against the gloom as Jackson spoke.

My recollections of that meeting were quite sharp. We had taken the decision to accept Esdaile's invitation to Sydenham, and had determined the course of action to deal with him. At the time, I had felt that my clerical collar might have a better chance against the *chthonios*—the earth-demon—that Esdaile had 'married', which had defeated several of our number in previous encounters; I had therefore volunteered for the task.

None of that had ultimately mattered: neither the Committee's intentions, nor my consecration, nor my skill as a mesmerist. James Esdaile had decided how the scene would play out—Esdaile, the Scottish doctor whom the society had so admired, and so reviled, and on whose face scarcely anyone in the room had ever laid eyes. He was a stranger: and now he was dead.

Jackson finished his report, which garnered neither objection nor amendment. He resumed his seat.

"Most of you have heard," I continued, "that our former colleague has died. We had already concluded that it might be necessary; I had gone to Sydenham to carry out the Committee's will. As some are aware, he took his own life—not to avoid having me do that service for him, but in part to cheat the *chthonic* being with whom he had bargained.

"It came as a surprise to me—and I expect it would have done to most of you—to learn that this being had simply *possessed* the woman to whom he was married. His wife was not merely a mani-festation, but rather an indwelling. When he died the creature fled, leaving its host behind—and alive—and, remarkably, sane."

"How did *you* survive it, then?" Elliotson piped up. He had chosen a seat in the front row, as he always did, so that there would be no one to block his view.

"The same way Esdaile did—and the same way he was able to resist my own abilities. We were within the Crystal Palace. Esdaile had discovered its disruptive effect on magnetic auras—both for practitioners of the Art and for *chthonic* beings. Somehow, he learned this and kept it from his...from his wife's possessor."

"And from *us*."

"Almost all of us," I answered, "but perhaps not all. Someone—" I pointed up above the heads of the audience—"*someone*, perhaps someone in this very room, *equipped* him with that information. This is no sudden epiphany: he moved to Sydenham five years ago, just in time for the re-opening on the Crystal Palace on its present site. He had planned this for a long time and kept it secret."

"Why now?" Dickens stood up in the rear of the room. "He waited *five years* to pull you down there so he could commit suicide in front of you? That beggars the imagination, Reverend."

"I appreciate your acquaintance with matters of *plot*, Mr. Dickens," I answered. It made Dickens' brow lower just a bit, and Elliotson's as well. He had a point, but I wasn't going to let him capitalize on it. I continued, "I can only answer that he planned this *ending* more than five years ago—or that something caused him to move to Sydenham when he did in anticipation of the ending. Why he chose to do it at this time—I have no answer to that question. But"—I held up my hand, forestalling the author's retort—"please recall, sir, that *he* invited *us*."

"That is completely *irrelevant*." Dr. John Forbes—Sir John Forbes, KB—stood, a few rows from the front of the gathering. He was heavy-set, with stout side whiskers and no beard; though elderly, he still possessed a strong voice which gathered the attention of everyone in the room. "It doesn't matter who did the inviting. You have clearly mishandled this entire affair. I assume that you do not have the statue we desire—and I further assume you let this— *demon* escape to cause more mayhem, as well."

"I do not have the statue. As for the demon—I flatter myself that I am skilled in the Art, Dr. Forbes, but do not think I had any choice but to 'let it go'."

"It still calls your competence into question, Davey."

"Sit down, Dr. Forbes."

"And your leadership," Forbes added angrily. "And—"

"Sit *down*," I said. I raised my left hand slightly, fingers held together, thumb extended and pointing downward.

Sir John Forbes remained on his feet for only a second or two, then dropped back down.

There was silence in the room.

"It is our custom," Elliotson said mildly, "to refrain from using the Art during our business meetings."

"Except for challenges."

"True," the little doctor answered. "Do you believe that constituted a challenge?"

I let my hand fall to my side. In the quiet room everyone heard Forbes exhale, gasping. No one came to his assistance.

"No. I suppose I did not. Mr. Jackson," I said without turning. "Please note that I shall pay the customary fine."

In the back of the room Charles Dickens looked at Forbes, who was bent down with his hands on his knees, then back at me. Then he, too, resumed his seat.

I told them in some detail what had happened at the Crystal Palace—down to the Shakespeare quote, which made Elliotson frown but drew a smirk from Dickens. It was clear to me that because the account was not especially complimentary to my abilities, they took it to be true.

Of greater interest was the summary of my interviews with Eliza, in which I told the Committee what I wanted them to hear. Calumny about James Esdaile was even easier to accept, since they were already predisposed against him. It would be an exaggeration for the reader to believe that most of my fellow Committee members were actually *sympathetic* to the poor woman's plight: I think that, of anyone present, I may have had the strongest feeling of compassion toward her.

As for the rest, I expect that some of them intended to intrude personally upon her bereavement to obtain further scraps of knowledge. That would certainly *not* happen. I had already arranged with Jackson to have her protected from any predatory challenges. She was not to be interfered with and to be left *alone*. If there was more information to be obtained, I would obtain it in due time.

The only part of the story I withheld—and I believe that it was for the best, at the time—was the relationship between Eliza's *chthonic* possessor and the statue itself. It complicated the tale and converted the item from simply a mesmeric amplifier into a...sort of channeling device. There was truly no need for anyone else to know.

To my surprise—given Jackson's and then Elliotson's warnings—there were no more challenges, not even from Ann Braid. It was not merely the demonstration on Forbes that dissuaded them, though that was a quite satisfactory bit of theater: Forbes was a crank and a fool and, had he possessed an ounce of sense, would have known better. I think it was more a matter of competing interests among those who did not trust each other in the first instance. To challenge me that February afternoon, they would have had to decide who among them would take my seat. None of them wanted to try and fail. None of them wanted the others to take it, either.

Still, I took the step I had suggested to Jackson: I offered D'Orsay the opportunity to recruit talented individuals at Cambridge and—should he find a suitable adjutant to help him— at Oxford as well. My suggestion caught most in the room by surprise, since (as Jackson had observed) I had been previously hesitant to release this responsibility.

But D'Orsay's response, while positive, should have given me warning. I suspect that I was somewhat distracted and did not notice, but neither did Jackson or anyone else among my allies and rivals.

We all should have known better.

"Mr. Chairman," D'Orsay said, "While it is exactly the sort of thing we *should* be doing, I wonder if this effort is not five or ten years too late."

I leaned back in my seat, hands loosely grasping the arms of the chair. "Please explain."

"There seems to be more and more rejection of the disciplines and principles of the Art at Cambridge, Reverend. At certain colleges, mesmerism and other new sciences are even subjected to ridicule."

"We are acquainted with that, sir. We are even accustomed to it."

"Of course. But it is one thing to have mesmerism dismissed in public debate, so long as those who find it of interest can be identified and cultivated. But rigorous 'debunking' is having a deleterious effect. It is not just a matter of ridicule—the perception is forestalling any opportunity to identify likely candidates."

"This is an old problem," William Engledue said from the far side of the room. "We understand that very well, D'Orsay. Very well."

In the middle of the audience Ann Braid sat stiffly, her face passive but her eyes full of fury. For more than ten years, while she had improved her own skill and built a power base among the Committee, her father had been an ardent and vocal opponent of the Art. James Braid, surgeon and scholar, was well respected in the medical community—he had even coined a word, *hypnotism*, to describe the mundane method for achieving the trance state which (he asserted) would require no knowledge of or power over personal magnetic fields.

To Dr. Braid, his daughter's interest in mesmerism was deplorable: he had stated frequently that he felt it to be a hindrance to her marriage prospects—though there had been rumors of an amorous relationship between Ann and Braid's protégé, Dr. Richard Daniel.

Her father's derision was a sore point for Ann Braid. It was a stick often used to beat her.

"You should take it as a challenge, D'Orsay," I said mildly. "We will find new capable people—it just may require some additional effort."

"I will endeavor to do so," D'Orsay said.

Engledue stood again. "Mr. Chairman, we need to combat this problem at the source."

"We have had this discussion before."

"Then I suggest that we have it *again*. This was once merely an annoyance; now it is a problem. It needs to be stopped. There is someone who needs to be silenced."

"He is not readily accessible to our techniques, Engledue," I said, glancing at Ann Braid, who was looking straight ahead.

"Oh, for God's sake, Davey. There are other ways."

"No." I stood up and took a step forward; as I did so everyone in the first row straightened and leaned slightly backward. "I know *exactly* what you mean, Engledue, and I forbid it. James Braid is our opponent, but he is a public figure, a man of stature in the medical community. That is the wrong approach and will only harm the Committee."

"And we are *not* being harmed?"

"Of course we are. But we have tools at our disposal to balance things in our favor."

"But we can't use them against Braid."

"There are some who are resistant to the Art, Engledue. Dr. Braid is one of them. And even if he was not, we do not need to do this. And we will *not* resort to other means."

"Davey—"

"I *forbid* it, unless you are prepared to challenge me right now, Engledue. You are at something of a disadvantage: everyone outside our circle believes you are already dead."

"Davey," Elliotson said, "there's no need for—"

I looked directly at Engledue, holding my hand up to Elliotson—who, sensibly, fell silent.

"Choose right now, Engledue."

"I'm not challenging you."

"Then sit down."

"There was a time," Engledue said, "that debate was a part of our meetings. I see that time is past."

He sat down. The room was absolutely quiet, except for Forbes' still ragged breathing.

"If there is nothing further," I said into the silence, "then this meeting is adjourned."

CHAPTER 11

The collector

WILLIAM DAVEY

I would have preferred to deal with the situations within the Committee other than how I had done. Circumstances, and stubbornness, and a lack of vision on the part of my colleagues forced my hand; like a good parent, I was obliged to enforce my authority in a way that was visible and repeatable.

Still, Elliotson had been right to raise the objection, though we both understood my willingness to flout the regulation. His early experiments, "debunked" by the original, public Committee, had led to the formation of the Committee as it presently existed, and both of us remembered the early days. Challenges—even ones that led to physical harm and death—had been constant and seemed to happen at every meeting. It was not until Edward Quillinan became Chairman that we had any sort of peace.

I succeeded him in 1842, when he chose to retire to take care of his invalid wife. After some initial turbulence, we functioned smoothly under my stewardship.

When we had assumed responsibility for Vernon's rooms after he was sent to Margate, I directed that they were to be considered neutral ground for the Committee. No mesmeric conflicts were to take place there unless it was a challenge. To use one's power with the Art at a regular meeting was punishable by a fine—or worse.

My restraint in the interaction with Dr. Forbes was no more than a point of amusement after the fact. Though he stormed off immediately afterward, I never had the slightest concern about having made an example of the old crank. Engledue, however, though he was in the shadows due to his recent 'demise', still had allies and friends in our community: had I been compelled to defeat him in a challenge, I would have more enemies than desirable. Of course, these would not include William Engledue. I would not leave him alive to challenge me again, a fact of which we both had been aware. He wanted to save his skin, and his dignity was less important than that.

The Esdaile affair would be a point of contention among the Committee for a little while to come—not just those who came to Vernon's rooms in February to see me 'defend myself', but across Britain and beyond. Still, I provided means to protect—or, I might say, shield—Eliza Esdaile from members of the Committee. Esdaile was dead and I was still Chairman. As for the statue—I did not have it, but no one else did either, which was sufficient to conclude the matter.

With a thousand things to attract my attention, time passed quickly; winter turned to spring before Esdaile came to my attention once again—in a way I had not expected.

On a surprisingly warm March afternoon I was poring through the dismal offerings at a bookseller's not far from Vernon's rooms on Regent Street, and came across an edition of *The Rock-Cut Temples of India*. It was an exceptionally well-produced volume, including a series of excellent lithographs illustrating the temples. At a particular page, I happened upon a depiction of a great wall showing a young naked female figure, holding a dagger upraised in her right hand and her left akimbo at her waist. It so precisely matched descriptions and sketches that James Esdaile had sent me that I nearly dropped the book in surprise. I turned to the title page to find the author: James Fergusson.

Suddenly, my interest in Esdaile was rekindled.

I purchased the book and took it with me to a small coffee-house, where I proceeded to read through it. Fergusson was a bit careless in his grammar and more than a bit plodding in his narrative, but nothing if not thorough. It was clear that he had a love for the subject and was fond of seeing patterns even in areas where there might be none, revealing him as somewhat of an amateur. Fergusson had transformed himself from indigo planter to natural philosopher—he was an amateur archaeologist who had traveled extensively and written exhaustively, and his books had been well received.

Yet no part of the volume struck me as strongly as the picture of that temple. It was in the Indus Valley, and the place—and its appearance—was attributed to an unknown culture unrelated to any in recent or distant history.

I determined that I should visit him and see what I could learn. Upon my inquiry he granted me an interview, and a few days later I travelled up Tottenham Court Road to meet him. His workplace was in a small building on Bedford Avenue in walking distance of the British Museum, on a storey shared with the offices of a law firm; a stationer's and a tobacconist graced the ground floor. I was most interested to note the presence of an idler outside the stationer's who was not what he seemed—he was a *chthonic* manifestation, and hastily made: it was scarcely an effort to wave it aside as I entered the building; and it did not seem even capable of trying to follow me. It gave me pause, making me wonder if Fergusson himself was a practitioner of the Art—an undiscovered talent?— able to keep such a being outside the doors of his building.

Fergusson's door was ajar to the hallway, and I found him sitting in a battered armchair with books open on his desk and worktable, and stacks of others on every surface seemingly awaiting his attention. He was peering at a particular volume when I entered, and he removed his spectacles and looked up at me.

"You are Reverend Davey, I presume?"

"I am, sir. Thank you for taking the time to see me."

"Aye. Well. I wasn't making much progress with this, anyway." He rapped his knuckles on the page, which was filled with small type. He gestured to a seat opposite, where a number of dictionaries were stacked. I lifted them and at a gesture from Fergusson placed them on the crowded table.

"Now. Sir. How may I be of service to you? I understand that you were interested in the Indian temples."

"Very much so. But even more…I wished to discuss a mutual friend. Dr. James Esdaile."

As I spoke, I made a small passing motion with my right hand, turning the fingers slightly downward; it was intended to cause him to think on the subject and be immediately forthcoming with his first impression.

For several seconds he did not answer; the sunlight passing through the partially drawn blinds seemed to dim and the fitful breeze died to nothing—but both then returned to their former state. To my surprise the mesmeric gesture appeared to have had no effect—it was as if he had not felt it at all.

"He died earlier this year. I suppose you are aware of that."

"A great loss," I answered, recovering myself as well as I could. "I have visited his widow."

"He was always one for marriage," Fergusson answered. "I do not know the lady. I last saw James Esdaile in India, Reverend, after the death of his first wife."

"You met there, did you not?"

"Yes. We met in Calcutta. 1840 or 1841, I think. We were countrymen, Scotsmen in a foreign land. Both interested in archaeology." He tapped the book in front of him again.

"I had not known of his interest."

Fergusson seemed to take a long look at me. If he had been using a mesmeric technique I should have sensed it—but as far as I could tell, he did not.

"Our perceptions were very different. While I am fascinated by the cultures of Asia, I think that Esdaile was appalled by them. He thought little of India's inhabitants. I…do not think he derived much enjoyment from his time there."

"Yet he wrote about India—and other places in Asia. About his travels. Surely, something must have fascinated him. Like the rock-cut temples."

"I cannot say. Reverend—Davey, is it? You wished to speak with me on that subject. But I have quite a bit of work to do—"

"Of course," I answered. "I appreciate that your time is valuable, sir, so I shall come to the point. Dr. Esdaile and I corresponded for several years, and he mentioned specifically that you were in Calcutta together. He also indicated that you had given him a gift." I reached into my portfolio and drew out the copy of Fergusson's book, opening it to the marked page. "I believe it was very similar to the statue shown in this lithograph."

I presented the book to him; he took it and placed it on top of the volume he had been studying. He grasped a large magnifying glass without looking aside and peered through it at the illustration. After some number of mmhms and ahs, he looked up at me.

"A statue, you say."

"Yes. I recently learned that he obtained it from you, and it was not among his effects…I wondered if you might know its whereabouts."

Fergusson hesitated, magnifying glass still in his hand, as if he were trying to discern my intention. For my part, I kept my face completely impassive.

Let him think, I told myself, *that I am a peculiar collector of unusual things.*

"Esdaile and I exchanged several things over the course of a few years, Reverend Davey. We were both always on the lookout for items that might please the other. Was there something special about this one?"

I realized three things almost at once as Fergusson looked at me, the magnifying glass still in his hand, the book open between us. First, he was *not* a mesmerist: there were no gestures, no patterns, no *sense* of power that I could feel. Second, he had some sort of resistance to my own powers; it might have been something in the room, or something on his person, or an innate ability.

Third, though I had no basis on which to confirm or deny it—and no power to compel a correct answer—I was certain he was lying, or at the very least prevaricating. He surely knew of this particular item, and might even know its significance.

"If it was merely a trifle," I said, "I do not know why he might have mentioned it in his letters to me. But what I do not understand is, if it was an important object, why a scholar such as yourself would give it away."

"This was all a long time ago, Reverend."

"To be sure. But I can no longer ask Doctor Esdaile about it, sir."

Fergusson considered that for a moment, then leaned back in his chair, as if he were sizing me up. I wondered at the time if he was trying to decide what story he would give me—but in retrospect, I realize that much of what he told me had actually been the truth. It was just that his tale did not make sense to me at the time.

JAMES FERGUSSON

I arrived in India as quite a young man and spent eight years there in the indigo trade. Unlike many, I was unencumbered by dependents or spouse; I could focus my attention on my business and devote my leisure to the subject of Oriental archaeology, something that fascinated me—and continues to do so, as you can see.

My agenda, my hours, my choice of activities and even the décor in my house were based on my own decisions. As I have realized in later life, this a direct path to bachelorhood. But if that is the price of having no meddlesome relatives, then so be it.

My residence in Calcutta was in the southern part, in Garden Reach. Houses closest to Hastings Bridge and Fort William were not much improvement over the crowded city, but my compound was significantly more pleasant; a better class of person went through the streets in his palky, his sedan chair. I had engaged the usual army of household servants, and had the good fortune to obtain an experienced *khansamah* to preside over it all. A *khansamah* is—

You are aware of the term? I had not realized that you had been in India, Reverend…ah. Of course. Esdaile would have used it.

My *khansamah* was an Indian gentleman of middle age, a Hindoo named Gobinda Shah Ahmadi. He was a man of tact and skill who had been employed by the house's previous occupant, an East India merchant who had already made the future I hoped to make for myself. He was a likeable man: he knew his place and knew the city—in a short time I came to rely upon him completely.

Gobinda found it unusual that I would choose to decorate my residence with *objets d'art*, and even more that I was competent to discuss their provenance and cultural significance. I suspect that he had never before met a white man who knew and cared about these things. I was moved to redecorate the house, dispensing with stuffed animal heads and racked hunting rifles and portraits of Arthur Wellesley, replacing them with statues of Lord Shiva and exquisitely carved elephants in jade and alabaster. Gobinda had them kept dust-free and properly arranged.

I remember when I brought the statue home. His reaction was abrupt and severe.

"Fergusson Sahib," he said. "This is most inappropriate."

"What?" I asked. "It's quite a pretty thing."

And indeed it was: bronze, six or eight inches tall and in exquisite condition. I set it on the sideboard, in front of a handsome mirror.

"No, no, sahib," he answered. "It will not do." He even made to reach for it—and I had no idea what he might have done with the object! I interposed myself immediately.

"You will take care with this item, Gobinda," I said to him. "And you will mind your place."

He seemed to contemplate a response but held his tongue. I assumed that he valued his position in my household. But he seemed to take a positive dislike to the item thereafter, and so did the rest of the staff. No, not merely *dislike*; the other servants seemed more frightened than anything else—from the old *dirwan*—the door-keeper—to the meanest scullery-maid. They avoided it as much as possible.

What? I don't know. Some taboo, I suppose, some pagan

matter. It was clearly not a Hindoo artifact, but there was some suggestion that it was a representation of their death-goddess, the dread Kali, though she has several more arms.

Where did it come from? I don't recall exactly, sir. I found it in a bazaar somewhere in the Indus Valley while I was on holiday, and I bargained with some local merchant for it. He told me—I remember now—that he thought it might be a fine addition to my collection.

You give them too much credit, Reverend. This was before the Mutiny, of course: most of twenty years ago. We thought then—with reasonable certainty—that there was no backbone to the average man in India, and that their cunning extended only to petty thefts and little intrigues. I scarcely gave a second thought to buying a pretty art object belonging to a dead culture.

Threatening? No, I did not find it so. It was in fact beautiful: a captured moment of some anonymous young girl who lived in the Indus Valley perhaps a thousand years before Christ. The household staff was disturbed by it, and reacted accordingly—all of them refused to touch it, went out of their way to avoid the room where it was placed, and so on. I refused to countenance such superstition and told Gobinda that he should sack any staff who made an issue of it—they could find service in another house if they did not find mine amenable, and despite his excellent service he could take his leave as well.

I *did* ask. He told me that the presence of the statue would ultimately lead to disharmony and violence. All primitive superstition, of course; I should have employed the services of a man of God to drive it out the door with the rest of the dirt.

I confess that the staff's avoidance of the statue made it easier for me to offer it to Esdaile as a gift: I was preparing to leave India and could only take so much with me.

Yes, of course it had value. But quite simply, the item did not match anything—it did not go with anything else in my collection.

WILLIAM DAVEY

I came away from my conversation with Fergusson reinforced with the feeling that something had been withheld. I was already aware that he had lived in the same house as Eliza's patron, Robert Heath, and that this Gobinda had been *khansamah* to both—but I knew that Gobinda was a mesmerist of some sort. Could he have *caused* Fergusson to give the statue to Esdaile?

If Gobinda had been able to influence Fergusson in India, it made me even more suspicious, My efforts during our interview had been ineffective, suggesting the possibility that someone was assisting Fergusson here in London, protecting him as I was protecting Eliza. Perhaps someone else had made a connection between Fergusson and Esdaile.

As I walked along Tottenham Court Road that pleasant afternoon, I concluded that I should ultimately have to deal with this Gobinda—perhaps in person.

How it came to pass

12 June, 1846
Dr. James Esdaile,
Hooghly, Presidency of Bengal,
India.

Dear Sir:

I eagerly read the account of your success with the practice of the mesmeric Art in the April, 1846 number of the Zoist, and wish to take this opportunity to introduce myself and my association.

The Committee comprises the vast majority of active practitioners of the new science of Mesmerism and its related disciplines in the British Isles, and I presently have the honor to be its Chairman. In that capacity, I hope that you will find it of interest to correspond with me so that we may assist one another in our mutual endeavors.

Our society's library has procured a copy of your published work on the Art and it has generated significant excitement and interest; many of our number are curious regarding the origin of your knowledge of the Art and the techniques you employ. I hope that you will enlighten us and, in turn, we will be happy to assist you in any way possible. . .

...I look forward to your earliest reply and remain

Sincerely yours,
Rev. William Davey
London

Walter H. Hunt

22 February, 1847
John Jackson
Bedford Place
London

My dear Jackson:

A fair copy of Dr. E.'s latest missive is enclosed for your perusal, including a sketch of a curious artifact which he possesses, which he claims is an amplifier for mesmeric powers...

This item seems completely singular. No one I have consulted recognizes anything about it, except to note its antiquity—according to what I have read and learned, it is not a Hindoo likeness. As you will read, Esdaile claims that it was given to him by a wealthy gentleman who took leave of India in 1843—a Scotsman named Fergusson.

The only person I have found who meets the description is an amateur archaeologist who recently published a lengthy article in the Journal of the Asiatic Society. I can assume that this Fergusson did not know of the characteristic of greatest importance to us: but the question still remains—why would he give the item away, and why to Esdaile?

...It is, regardless, a great find and probably useful against those who do not understand the limits of their own power. I think that we may well be able to teach them a few cogent lessons.

William Davey

23 July, 1849

Reverend Davey:

I am enclosing for your examination an article sent me from Doctor Esdaile in Calcutta. It contains a number of disturbing assertions that seem out of character for a man of his stature and erudition, particularly given his high level of scholarship in, and contribution to, the Mesmeric Arts. I do not think that this at all constitutes a proper submission to the Zoist, and would like your opinion on the subject.

…I would call your attention in particular to his discussion of stoicheia, and the concept of the "Glass Door"—clearly a metaphor of some kind. It is entirely out of keeping with the highly interesting report appearing in the recent March number, causing me to wonder whether he has been afflicted with some malady peculiar to the tropical climes that might have affected his mind in some way…

If you could inform me of your opinion by earliest post,

William Engledue, M.D.
Editor, Zoist

Walter H. Hunt

11 January, 1851
Dr. James Esdaile,
Hooghly, Presidency of Bengal,
India.

My dear James:

I have received your most recent letter of the 21st of November instant, and appreciate your best wishes for a joyous holiday season; know that they are returned. I realize that your situation is a difficult one and that you are very far from home, a fact which sometimes makes perspective difficult. I trust that it has not clouded your judgment, as well.

Though we have never personally met, all that I know of you and all that is transmitted in your correspondence lead me to believe that you are a rational and prudent man, who understands the consequences of his actions…I cannot help but believe that you have made some of the statements in your last letter in haste, for these imply a complete reversal of decisions we have taken in previous discussions…

Please understand that I am a reasonable man, and believe that I am conducting myself and the affairs of the Committee in a reasonable fashion. This is not universally the case, as many of our members have a tendency to act rashly and peremptorily. Should you return to Scotland without the item we have discussed, they might feel it necessary to take matters into their own hands. I might not be able to restrain them and this might lead to painful, or even tragic, results…

I urge you to reconsider what you have said, with firm reliance that I will do all that is in my power to assure your safety and well-being. Nonetheless, you must keep my warnings in mind.

I hope that you are, and continue to be, well, and remain

Your friend and colleague,
William Davey

PART TWO

Words from dreams

It is impossible for a man to begin to learn what he has a conceit that he already knows.
—Epictetus, *Golden Sayings*, I: LXXII

CHAPTER 12

Confidence

WILLIAM DAVEY

The Committee, ever volatile when there was an issue to consume them, was nothing if not docile when excitement died down. Surgeons and professors returned to their normal activities; articles were composed in public and letters written in private. Calm returned to the mesmeric world as the Year of Grace 1859 wore on.

Esdaile never quite left my mind, particularly since the object of my greatest interest—the statue—was still beyond my grasp. Jackson and I continued to suspect Fergusson, though that line of inquiry was a dead end. As the months wore on we had other matters to distract us.

❖

When the calendar turned to February again, I received a telegram from the Scottish Mesmeric Association. Leaving the Scots alone, in my experience, was usually the best approach: they had their own governance and their own methods and directions of research. Though they were ultimately answerable to me, we only came in direct contact for matters that concerned all of Britain.

They had been happy to leave the matter of Esdaile in our laps when he decamped from Scotland to Sydenham years before. The leader of the Scots organization, Sir Thomas Makdougall Brisbane (Major General, Retired, GCH, GCB), had been more than willing to tell me exactly how happy they were.

Then the old man had died. He was eighty-six and had lived a long and active life full of adventure and heroism—a soldier, a governor, a scholar and of course a powerful mesmerist to whom every Scot practitioner meekly deferred. Death had come quickly and quietly at his country home in Ayrshire at the end of January; he had outlived all four of his children and had left a few things undone—such as designating a successor.

Thus, despite my mild trepidation at leaving England, I felt I must travel north. Preparations took more than four weeks; I took proper precautions to leave all in good hands, and then departed north to make that disposition before it made itself. It was always better not to leave these things to chance, or to the determinations of lesser men.

I felt rather like Edward Longshanks, going north to choose between Bruce and Balliol. I hoped the Scottish mesmerists would not draw the same parallel.

I took the opportunity to travel by way of Manchester: not the most direct route—it was part of the preparation for leaving my direct domain. Readers who may encounter this narrative years from when I composed it might have the wrong idea about the matter of domains—I was in no way constrained from traveling, as will become apparent as I continue—though I was at greatest strength within England. I wanted to make sure that if any of my esteemed colleagues wished to take advantage, it would not go well for them.

And, indeed, there was someone in Manchester I wished to visit.

I arrived at the Manchester Mechanics' Institute just at the stroke of eight o'clock, and found a place in the back of the lecture hall. The figure on the stage, a well-dressed man of robust middle age with carefully groomed side-whiskers and a few stray wisps of hair atop his head, was just completing the answer to a question from someone in the audience; after he had responded—concisely and courteously, as was his wont—he took his watch out and consulted it, then gave a polite nod to the audience of tradesmen who had assembled to listen. He then turned back to the simple lectern to gather his notes.

As the attendees began to file out of the room, he chanced to look up and our eyes met. I remained standing in my position, meeting the glance. *Annoyance* was the emotion that seemed to grip him at that moment, and it was apparent in his expression. He hesitated only slightly and returned to organizing his papers and putting them into his portfolio.

Eventually, the room was empty save the two of us and an orderly of some sort, whose duty it was to gather up any debris from the floor of the hall and to sweep away dirt carried in by the artisans' boots. The speaker gathered his portfolio and walked to the side, as if he had chosen to ignore me—then stopped and sighed, his shoulders conveying the same annoyance mixed with resignation.

"I suppose," he said, "I should be duly appreciative that you did not choose to arrive during my presentation."

"I am not here to disrupt your work, Dr. Braid. I have the utmost respect for your dignity and for your scholarship. I would not dream of disrupting it."

James Braid allowed himself a slight smile.

"I am not sure just why you *are* here, Reverend," he said, turning to me. "But I thank you for that small courtesy."

I did not answer, but merely nodded.

"I have a late dinner engagement. Whatever has brought you here—will it take longer than an hour?"

I walked down through the rows of chairs to stand before and below him. "Most assuredly not, sir. But it does require a certain modicum of privacy."

"Does it." The smile returned, very slightly broader. "Very well—there should be no one in the Institute library at this time. Will that suit your need for…delicacy?"

"Admirably," I answered. "Please lead on."

Braid and I walked through the halls of the Mechanics' Institute, a building erected some thirty-five years before. The Institute itself was an educational body with the objective of *uplifting* the standards of intellectual pursuits for the laboring classes. After hours in the mills and factories and workshops of

Manchester—the *dark Satanic mills*, as William Blake would have it, or what Mr. Dickens characterized as the first circle of the Infernal—they could come and hear Dr. Braid tell them of the form and function of the brain as he understood it.

The Institute's goals, now in practice for a second generation of workers, were noble: my readers must not think me too cynical in offering faint praise for its, or Braid's, philanthropy. Even the lending library into which we walked, established a decade earlier by contribution and public donation, spoke well of *intentions*. But as with so much in England of that time, intentions were not always harmonious with results.

Truthfully, I did not trouble myself so much with it. Indeed, it was this sort of motivation that had elevated me from Devonshire lace-maker to ordained minister—but I owed my present station to hard work, ambition, and skills whose existence Dr. James Braid vehemently denied. I do not believe that the irony of the setting was lost on either of us.

As he had intimated, the library was nearly empty at this hour. We took seats at a reading-table near a banked fire, some distance from the half-dozing proctor who was minding the room at that time. I should have liked the room to be completely vacant, but satisfied myself by making the young man even more sleepy and inattentive. I am certain that Braid noticed the gesture, but let it lie except for a sigh of exasperation.

"Well, Davey," he said when we had taken our seats. "To what do I owe the pleasure of your visit?"

"I am concerned about some recent remarks by my colleagues. You are not well-liked in the Committee, Doctor, though I suspect that is no surprise."

"It most certainly is not. Dr. Daniel keeps me well informed of what he hears."

"What does he hear?"

"Whatever Annie tells him. Which, these days"—and here Braid actually seemed to smile a bit—"is quite a lot. Despite your annoying distractions, she seems finally to be looking to a young woman's proper pursuits."

"Marriage."

"And a family, I pray," Braid added. "This insufferable nonsense that you practice is a burden, Davey. She is nearly twenty-nine years old. Now that she looks kindly on Richard's—Dr. Daniel's—affections, I suspect that she will soon put it behind her."

When I thought about this conversation years later, I was always rueful—Ann Braid was no more likely to give up mesmerism, then or later, than the sun was likely to remain below the horizon in the morning. She was determined and acquisitive…and more. Even then, even on that cold February night.

"We shall see," I said. "In the meanwhile, I can only suggest to you, Dr. Braid, that some of 'my people' would do violence to you, or cause it to be done, as long as you speak against our practices."

"I stand for *truth*."

"Truth is malleable, sir, and depends often on the person speaking it."

Braid's brows furrowed. He folded his hands on the table in front of him. "Reverend Davey—and I speak your title out of respect for your position, not from any belief that you fulfill its requirements—your last statement is itself a canard. Truth is *absolute* and has nothing to do with the speaker. Or the hearer. Or the time or place or method of delivery.

"I know what you believe; but I know what I know. Hypnotism is a natural phenomenon; it does not pay heed to any"—he unknotted his fingers and waved them in the air: the proctor stirred for a moment, gave us a sidelong glance and then settled back into position—"magnetic fluid. Mesmer was a fraud; Puységur, Lafontaine, Dupotet, Elliotson—they were all actors and impostors. I can do all of their parlor tricks, and all of yours."

"You have made your position on this matter patently clear, sir. I am not here to debate mesmerism's merits with you." *Nor*, I thought, *to disappoint you about your daughter.* "I am here instead to warn you about undesirable consequences to your continued public statements."

"You seek to silence me."

"I seek," I replied carefully, "to assure you in the strongest possible terms that there are those in my community who would do you harm—physical harm—for continuing to speak against the practice. They read your books at Cambridge and Oxford, sir."

"I am extremely gratified."

"You are in danger, sir. I do not know why you fail to understand it."

"Danger, is it. I beg your pardon, Reverend Davey. Your supposed 'powers'"—once again he moved his hands; a small log in the fire cracked, throwing a few sparks out—"your 'powers' have no effect on me."

"Let me repeat, sir. I fear actual physical violence against your person. I have forbidden such actions; for nearly a year no one has defied my orders. But after a certain amount of time, such admonitions lose their potency."

"You cannot control your pawns. That is an unfortunate attribute for a chess master, Davey. I really do not see how you can maintain your standing."

"I have come only as a courtesy, Doctor. I do not care to be mocked, sir: neither by you nor anyone else."

Braid did not reply; instead, he reached into his portfolio and drew out three or four closely-written manuscript sheets and spread them out on the table before him. They were written in French in a crabbed hand; another, more careful writer had made annotations in the margins, along with a few strikethroughs and additions.

"This is a letter from a distinguished colleague, Dr. Étienne Azam. I don't suppose you know him?"

"No, sir. I cannot say that I do."

"He is a surgeon in Bordeaux, with a most unusual patient whom he calls 'Félida X'. This young woman suffers from something he calls *doublement de la vie*: two alternate personalities. One is serious and sad—this is the girl's normal state; the other is merry and generous. What is more, they do not know of each other, or say they do not."

To me, it sounded painfully like the situation of Eliza Weatherhead Esdaile—the persona of the *chthonic* spirit overlaid upon that of the woman herself.

"What is of interest to me, Davey," Braid continued, "is the way in which this addresses the entire idea of Self."

"Fascinating," I said.

He picked up the papers and tapped them against the table to straighten and align them. "The reason this is important," he added, "is that between Dr. Azam and myself, we shall evaluate the evidence, examine the patient, and come to a *scientific* and *rational* conclusion. There will be no magnetic fluids, spiritualist table-turning or elemental demons involved. This is an unusual case but not a supernatural one."

"I defer to your knowledge, Doctor," I said—and was sincere: I really had no opinion on the subject.

"This is *truth*, Davey. In that, I have the utmost confidence." He put the pages back into his portfolio. "And this is *science*. You may make all the magnetic passes you want; but someday, perhaps not this year, perhaps not the next, but someday, it will be my party that shall be victorious. Your 'new science' will go the way of leeching and witchfinding and firewalking and all the rest.

"I will concede to you that I perceive an honest concern on your part; whether that derives from your respect for my title, or because of my daughter, or for some other self-interested reason about which I care little, I accept it and appreciate its spirit. But I am in no more danger now than when I was assaulted in public, here in Manchester twenty years ago, for the same truth that I still hold so precious."

I stood; Braid stood as well. I extended my hand, expecting it to be ignored—but to my surprise he took it and shook it warmly. If he believed me to be an enemy, it was an unusual response; but James Braid, though pedantic and bluff, had ever been an honest gentleman.

"I do not seek to convince you by force of personality," he said. "That is more in your sphere. I will let my words and writings speak for me, as they can do that even in my absence."

"I respect your position, sir," I replied. "And I accept your confidence. I hope that my concerns are exaggerated and that all will be well."

I let go of his hand and turned to go. From the corner of my eye, I thought I saw motion in the fireplace; a faint wavering, a shimmer—but then thought myself mistaken.

I walked out of the library, looking backward for a moment at James Braid, who stood near the fire, his face half in shadow and half-lit by the fire and the oil-lamps.

CHAPTER 13

Object lesson

WILLIAM DAVEY

I stood on the platform at Oxford Road Station, bundled against the chill of a February night, waiting for the train that would take me to Leeds and then north beyond the Scottish border. It seemed a far cry from the congenial warmth of the Manchester Institute's library.

It had taken some restraint to keep from telling Dr. Braid that his daughter, despite her affections for his assistant, was deeply devoted to the mesmeric Art. It would accomplish nothing; he would reject the idea in any case. For Braid, truth was truth, and rationality was the cap-stone of his world view.

I had been looking down the track for my train. I turned around and saw a figure approaching. He was a short man, wearing a greatcoat and a felt derby with a slight decoration on the left side, which caught the indifferent glare of the hissing glass lamps and reflected it as he walked.

I felt a chill that was entirely distinct from that caused by the low temperature; and when I caught a glimpse of the man's face—olive-skinned, a Levantine from his appearance—I knew that I had seen him before: among the idlers outside Vernon's rooms on Regent Street.

It was also now quite obvious to me that he was, indeed, a *stoicheion*, an elemental spirit in human form.

"Good evening, Reverend Davey," the man said. He smiled, showing a perfect set of teeth—unusual, in that day and age.

"May I help you, sir?"

"You seem disturbed at my presence."

"You misapprehend my state of mind," I said. "If there is something you wish of me, please state it; I have no interest in—"

"In? In what?"

I considered how to end the sentence. I had intended to declare in no uncertain terms that I was not interested in any conversation with a *stoicheia*. It was his presence in Manchester—as it had been in London—that was disturbing.

In my limited experience, they only came when called. So—*who* had called it?

"I have nothing to say to you."

"Truly. That disappoints me, but does not surprise me. No matter, Reverend: I have something to say to you."

"Very well. Be about it, sir. I have a train to catch."

"To Leeds. It is still a few minutes away." He removed his watch and opened it; I could see neither hands nor numbers on its face—but I heard, or *thought* I heard, terrible sounds of shrieking wind and cracking wood and shouts of terror. When the watch was snapped shut, all again was silent.

I waited out the Levantine, who presently looked up with the closed watch still held in his hand.

"Time is a flexible thing," the Levantine said. "I do not know what it truly *means* for you to have a mere few minutes to wait. I shall say my piece, and we will see what comes next."

"What comes next is I board my railway carriage and leave you here, or you may please yourself by going back to Hell. I really do not care what happens."

"'Hell.'" He said the word as if tasting it, rolling it over his tongue and teeth as if he had never spoken it before. "Is that where you think I am from?"

"I think—"

Once again I did not know how to continue.

"I shall let you revel in your ignorance, just as Dr. Braid revels in his rationality. Truly, Reverend Davey, I have no animus toward you: quite the opposite—I assume that sooner or later we shall become close. Very close."

He tucked the watch—or whatever it actually was—back into its vest pocket. "At least," the Levantine added, "if you want to continue to practice your Art."

"I don't need your help."

"At present."

"*Ever.*" I looked past the Levantine down the track, searching for the elusive pinpoint of light that might be the headlamp of an oncoming locomotive.

"At *present,*" he said, sounding reasonable. "With all due respect, Reverend, you must understand that what Dr. Braid has told you must ultimately come to pass—that cool and rational Science will drive its competitors out of the world…at least until the explanations no longer suffice. But that is well past your lifespan. Ultimately, there will only be one way for you to access the power you desire—and that is through my kind. Through *me.*"

"I would sooner give it up."

"You would sooner gnaw off your own leg, like a wild animal caught in a trap. That is a fanciful lie, a sop to your conscience, a delusion. You are like an opium addict—you *cannot* give it up."

"My soul is important to me."

"In London, used souls are sold a penny a pound on 'Change," the Levantine said. "In the end, you have nothing with which to bargain." He smiled once again.

"I have heard enough."

"Once again, you are mistaken."

The Levantine raised his left hand, placing the thumb over the palm, and swept it outward—

And suddenly the platform began to come alive. The doors to the waiting room opened and a small crowd of passengers emerged: a group of businessmen; a pair of gentlemen and their ladies, accompanied by a wheeled cart loaded with luggage; several disreputable-looking travelers no doubt bound for third class; a half-dozen soldiers in Her Majesty's forces, kit bags on their shoulders, on leave or returning from same…

Every second or third figure was a *chthonic* spirit. My perception was clear on that account.

"We..." the Levantine began: and all around him, I heard the word whispered, spoken, shouted, plucked from the air in a dozen conversations.

"...are..." he continued, and again voices all around took up the word, as if all were speaking it at once.

"...*everywhere*," they finished, and it seemed like a tawdry music hall performance with each of the many figures on the platform and spilling out of the waiting room looking directly at me and saying the word.

I raised my hands in a warding gesture and stepped backward, moving my bag with my right foot. I was a yard from the edge of the platform, and perhaps five yards from its end—and it was truly becoming crowded now: men and women and children, old and young, a menagerie of facial expressions and accents, colors and sights and sounds like the crude moving images of a zoetrope: they edged around me, crowding closer, scarcely troubled by my mesmeric passes as if the magnetic fluid would not, *could* not, bend to my will—

At this point, I had the strangest experience of all. Like the frames of a zoetrope, I began to perceive the scene slowing down, the moments separating one from another as if they were distinct: the group of businessmen, the soldiers, the approaching locomotive—separate instances of time dealt out like playing cards before my eyes, all stopped—except for the Levantine, who was moving normally, flicking a tiny speck of dust from his lapel, adjusting the fit of his gloves and the position of his hat.

The frames came slower and slower—the people, the locomotive, the flickering gas-lamps. At last I noted them separated by moments of blackness where there was nothing there but the Levantine suspended in nothingness, until finally the scene was unchanged: a fixed tapestry that the Levantine stood before, smiling with his perfect teeth.

"This is an object lesson, Reverend Davey. This is the power we command. Right at this moment—which I control—with the minimum of effort, I could push you forward and you would fall... so regrettably...in the path of that locomotive." He gestured toward it, perhaps thirty feet away: the scene jumped forward, a chuff of smoke rising from the locomotive's smokestack, figures in the tapestry taking a single step, gas-lamps letting out a hiss one second in length.

The Levantine reached his hand forward—but did not seem to be able to move past my warding gesture...or perhaps simply preferred not to. Instead, he formed it into a fist and lowered it to his side, then began to back slowly away, his left hand still extended.

"...But that is not why I am here. I continue to hope, and expect, that we will someday do business. And it would not do to discard a potential client."

He lowered his hand—

And with a shocking suddenness, the Levantine—and everyone else on the platform—was gone: there was nothing but an oncoming train and a blast of cold air.

When the conductor's shrill whistle blew, I had taken my place in the carriage; but as the train began to move slowly out of Oxford Road Station, my heart was beating loudly in my ears and my hands were still shaking.

CHAPTER 14

Quid pro quo

WILLIAM DAVEY

A day later, I was in Edinburgh. It had been my intention to go immediately to George Square and convene a meeting of the principal members of the Mesmeric Society, but I was sure that I had not quite recovered from the assault by the *chthonic* being at the Manchester railway station. *Assault* is a fair characterization: the power of the being, its method of attack and the rapidity with which it had seized control of the moment affected me to an extent that I declined to reveal in any way to the Scottish mesmerists.

What troubled me more—if all of *that* had not been enough— was that this being had manifested at all, self-willed and self-motivated, and had been able to undertake such an attack. I believed that it had to have been summoned; *chthonic* beings were not supposed to be able to manifest without the will of a mortal person to compel them.

Finally, the being's last pronouncements—that he sought to provide me with a lesson, that all of our Art would ultimately depend on interaction with such beings. It reminded me of Quillinan's nonsense about mesmerism and the need to worship at the Delphic shrine of technology. Moreover I had the sense that while he had sought *me* out on the Oxford Road platform he had done so almost incidentally, as if that had not been his primary purpose in Manchester. But *why* had the Levantine come? What was the purpose of the Levantine's 'instruction'?

And finally—was he *correct*?

I chose to spend a day or two in a rather modest hotel near the cluster of railway stations beneath North Bridge, a few hundred yards from the High Street. My tiny guest-room overlooked the fruit and vegetable market. Winter precluded much of its activity, thus sparing me the worst of its customary sounds and smells.

In that tiny room I tried to take stock of the situation, of what Dr. Braid and the Levantine had said, and made an effort to restore my lost equilibrium. I have often been criticized about my earnest in the clerical profession; I must confess, however, that I spent some time in St. Giles' in pursuit of that goal. Whether that was in response to the stinging imputation of James Braid, or from a genuine desire for communion with the Lord whom my profession entitled me to represent, I leave it to my readers to decide.

At last, when I was ready to take up the matter that had brought me to Scotland, I sent a letter care of the Mesmeric Institute office in George Square, informing Colquhoun, the secretary, that I wished to meet with the principals on the following evening. I expected an immediate response; what I received instead was a note inviting me at teatime to the sitting room at the Royal Scotsman, the great hotel on the High Street above, a few hundred yards away from my mean lodgings.

I admit that my curiosity was piqued by the note. John Campbell Colquhoun was as willing to talk—and at length—as any man I ever met; he was a polyglot advocate—a Scots solicitor—who fancied himself a mystical scholar—I had a copy of *Isis Revelata*, of course, but would more readily use it to balance the legs of a table than actually take the time to peruse it. I expected, even dreaded, the onslaught of his words as a part of the meeting I desired to convene.

I am not much impressed with public figures. Dickens, for all of his fame, had always been more of a nuisance than an asset in the Committee's deliberations. He was Elliotson's particular friend, and his wealth had helped underwrite our activities, but his self-importance was grating. None of us sought fame for the Art, though many of us had written books about it—my own *Illustrated Practical Mesmerist* continued to enjoy popularity among amateurs. However, the famous who were party to the Committee's work were occasionally compelled to come to terms with the relative value of that fame in the society over which I presided—to wit, not very much.

But it was something they rarely admitted to themselves. Instead, it was most often forced upon them in private.

My companion for tea was one of those public figures: Thomas Carlyle, the Scottish writer and historian, whom I had not even realized was in Edinburgh. He was alone, absent his invalid wife, with whom his relations had long been strained. Some wag had quipped that their marriage had at least made two people unhappy instead of four; I could well imagine.

He had taken a position in one corner of the room, his back to a pillar, a great window nearby overlooking North Bridge. He was perusing a book; he glanced at me as I crossed the room—and set it aside perhaps a few moments too tardily for punctilious courtesy.

I ignored it: this might be his city and his land, but there was no doubt who should defer to whom. He rose and offered me a perfunctory bow, then extended his hand, which I accepted. He gestured me to a comfortable seat.

"I trust your trip north was comfortable," he began.

"March is a wretched month to travel. I hadn't known you were in Scotland, Carlyle."

"I went up to Largs to pay my respects to the General. I was certain you would appear, and wasn't about to leave it to Colquhoun or Holland or the rest of the pygmies."

"That's rather harsh."

"So be it. The General agreed. —Oh, and he told me about Margaret's Law as well; it confirms what I already suspected."

"The cairn? Was there something to 'suspect'?"

"Davey, do you know your all-consuming fault? Your constant assumption that since the majority of the people you govern are fools, that it must be the case with *everyone*. Margaret's Law is not just a cairn—it's where the Brisbanes keep the records they captured from King Magnus. I've seen them now, and it confirms what I have already inferred—that the Vikings, bless them, knew about the odylic force six hundred years ago."

Carlyle could draw upon a vast supply of arrogance; it was *his* all-consuming fault.

"Have you told John Colquhoun about it? I'm sure it would launch him into mystical rapture."

"I've told no one. Sir Thomas passed the secret to me, and me alone."

"So you're his chosen successor."

"I consider myself to be, yes."

"I shall let you know whether I agree after I deliberate on the matter. I am not sure that it is appropriate for a public figure such as yourself to be head of the organization—and as you are not customarily in residence here—"

"Since when has it been your right to—"

"Since May 1842," I said, interrupting him and spreading the fingers of my left hand.

Carlyle gripped the arms of his chair. I could see his teeth clench as his mouth snapped shut; but to his credit, his gaze never left mine.

Five seconds along, I would have expected to see sweat on his brow despite the chilly temperature of the sitting room, but he appeared cool. His posture was rigid, his back leaning hard against the chair, but he still managed to say, "That situation will not prevail forever."

"No," I answered in as reasonable a tone as I could muster. "But it prevails at this moment."

I kept my fingers extended for another few seconds, then formed them into a fist and rapped it lightly on my left thigh. He reacted as if he had been punched in the gut but recovered quickly and smoothly.

His eyes proclaimed contempt. I wondered to myself then whether I had made an enemy, and a dangerous one—he had resisted me more strongly than I would have expected.

"Do you expect an apology?" he managed after a moment.

"You can acknowledge my authority in these matters. If you do, we can continue this discussion."

It had become quiet in the sitting room. One of the features of mesmeric power is its tendency to disperse outward, especially when strong emotions are in play. Several people in the drawing room had stopped what they were doing, their cups raised and held in mid-motion, their attention drawn to the place where Carlyle and I sat. No doubt some of them knew him; I was fairly well assured that none of them knew me.

"This is not a formal challenge," Carlyle said between his teeth. "Set them loose."

"I don't know what you mean, Carlyle. Surely some of them must be wondering what this is about."

"Set them loose," he repeated without moving and without removing his eyes from me. "I do not know why it is necessary to create a public spectacle."

"I am answering your question, Carlyle. You asked 'since when', and I told you. Since May 1842, when Quillinan resigned to take care of his wife Dora. A half-dozen men wanted the position but it was awarded to me. Not, I should add," I said, "without some... spectacle."

"*Set*," he said.

With a force of will that was palpable from ten feet away he managed to unclench his hand from the armchair.

"Them. *Loose*," he finished, making a cutting gesture—not a very demonstrative one, but more than I should have expected him to make.

Somewhere in the tea-room a china cup, a fancy one I imagine, crashed to the floor and the moment was interrupted. The quiet was replaced with the normal hubbub of such a place, dishes and conversation and so forth.

Carlyle was still relatively immobile, but he had broken my hold on him. I decided upon a tactical retreat: no good would come of a further confrontation, the outcome of which I could not readily control.

I relaxed my hand. He relaxed his grip on the chair arms.

"That was completely unnecessary, Davey," he said after a few moments. "And if it was done in an effort to compel my obedience or coerce my conduct, you can be assured that it may result in the exact opposite effect."

"Is that a formal challenge?"

"You know damned well that it is not. At this time."

I picked up a delicate shortbread biscuit with the logo of the hotel baked into its surface, admired it for a moment, and then bit into it.

"I will, therefore, take that under advisement. So tell me. You saw what was in Margaret's Law; did it make any sense to you?"

The abrupt change of subject seemed to catch Carlyle by surprise: he sat forward, his glower dissolving into a sort of baffled frown, and folded his hands in his lap. "I can assure you that it did, but I will not discuss it here."

"Where would you prefer?"

"In public. But first, Davey: tell me what this information is worth."

"I should like to see the merchandise before I pay for it."

"You have the word of a gentleman that it is worth as much as any information you can presently buy. I ask for a quid pro quo: confirm me as your deputy here in Scotland, and I shall consider the debt paid."

"What assurance do you have that I will keep my end of the bargain?"

"The only assurance that anyone could have in this circumstance. I shall have to rely on the word...of a *gentleman*. Tell me, Davey, is that something I should count upon?"

It was a frigid day to walk the streets of Edinburgh, but walk them we did. From the Scotsman Hotel we crossed the bridge above the railway station and strolled along Princes Street, past the monstrosity of the Scott Monument, past Jenners and the Royal Hotel.

Finally, we settled onto one of the benches facing Edinburgh Castle on the mound. The late afternoon sun was bright but gave scant warmth. Carlyle sought to appear unaffected; but he was already sixty-five years of age at that time, and despite his arch Scots superiority it could not have been easy for him to tolerate it.

But what he told me was more than worth the price.

THOMAS CARLYLE

I realize, Reverend Davey, that it is not the habit of most persons—even educated ones—to take an interest in history; to the average gentleman that simple word compels a shudder, reminding him of school days and agonizing lessons. Yet even one fascinated by the ebb and flow of the tides of man's existence eventually comes to realize that there is another story, guided by a hidden hand, of which even the most articulate scholar may not be aware.

I told you that I have seen what is concealed in Margaret's Law. It is one of the greatest treasures of the Brisbane family—and the General himself gave me the key. He worked it out over the course of five decades; it tells us what we should undoubtedly have discerned all along—that though they did not call it that, the Northmen were intimately aware of the Odic or Odylic force, and that they used it to their advantage. They were able to do so because they made contact with *chthonic* spirits and other *stoicheia* when they voyaged to the far north, near the North Magnetic Pole. The *insula magnetum*—not truly an island, of course—is one of their dwelling-places.

When Prince Magnus—remarkable coincidence in the name, don't you think?—ran aground near Largs in Ayrshire in 1263, all of the Northmen's knowledge, all of their tradition, fell into the hands of King Alexander III of Scotland. The whole account of their northernmost journeys had been inscribed in detail on a series of whale-bone plaques, as intricate and detailed as the full-rigged ships that whaling men carve.

It was certainly not intended that the Northmen lose those plaques. King Haakon Haakonsson, Magnus' father, intended that the fleet winter in Orkney; I should think that he would have wanted to take them with him, as they were valuable artifacts. I wonder if the loss of the plaques helped him along to his final reward.

I have considered that possibility as well, Reverend Davey. Of *course* no official account of such a thing exists—but it would hardly surprise me to learn that someone, perhaps some chieftain who was a distant ancestor of Sir Thomas—employed some version of the Art to cloud the minds of the Northmen. Whatever the case, the thirty-eight plaques were placed in a plain wooden strong-box worked with bronze fittings and concealed beneath Margaret's Law. Their existence remained a closely guarded secret, one that was passed down through generations until it became part of the lore of the Brisbane family.

They would have been no more than quaint artifacts if it had not been for Sir Thomas Makdougall Brisbane. At the commencement of the current century, explorers from many lands began to make approaches to the poles, both north and south. Some of these men are well-known, such as Ross and Franklin. Portions of these accounts have been held closely since they were recorded—and other portions were lost with the expeditions. It is clear, however, that these *stoicheia* found their way back to more temperate climes along with...or perhaps in *place* of ...the individuals who found them.

I am approaching my point, Davey. You are impatient as always; I wish to provide you with fair value for your investment.

Both Franklin and Brisbane resided for a time in the southern hemisphere. During Franklin's time there, he mapped the coast of Van Diemen's Land—Tasmania—while Brisbane served as governor of New South Wales. While Franklin spent most of his time at sea, Brisbane had a more bureaucratic and scholarly occupation. One of his greatest accomplishments was in the field of astronomy: his observations led to the identification of more than seven thousand stars in the southern skies: the *Brisbane Catalogue*.

Why is this important? A fair question. When Sir Thomas took up residence on his estate at Largs in 1826, he took upon himself the task of examining the whale-bone plaques of King Magnus, seeking to decipher the coded meaning. What he realized was stunning: the key to the code was the patterns of stars—*southern* stars.

It was the beginning of Sir Thomas' interest in the Art, I suspect. It would be another twenty years before von Reichenbach began to describe the 'odylic force'—but Brisbane learned of it then and there, sometime in 1826 or 1827. He realized what no one else had guessed: every brush with the polar regions, north and south, was a glance through the Glass Door. It is in those regions that the *stoicheia* reside.

WILLIAM DAVEY

When he had finished his description, Carlyle looked off in the distance toward the great hill upon which Edinburgh Castle perched—the Mound, etched in late afternoon sunlight.

"Do you think Sir John Franklin was looking for the 'magnetic isle' on his last expedition?" I asked.

"It would not surprise me. I think Admiral Ross was looking for the same thing. I am even inclined to believe that the mountains he saw—the 'Crocker Hills'—were *real*, and that only a true practitioner could see them. He spent four years in the Arctic and found the Magnetic North Pole."

"And returned with *chthonic spirits* in his foremast?"

"It is conceivable that Ross himself came back…" Carlyle turned to face me, with a knowing smile. "with a more *intimate* relationship with a *chthonic* spirit. Rather like poor Esdaile's wife."

"We would have known."

"Yes. I suppose we would." Carlyle stood stiffly; I joined him. Even the brief time we had been sitting there had had unpleasant aftereffects. "Do you consider yourself sufficiently well compensated?"

"If I said anything other than 'yes', I expect you would show some of that anger for which the Scots race is justly famous."

"Is that your intention?"

"No. Of course it is not. What the information means," I said, "is presently beyond me. But it places an entire new cast on relations with these creatures."

"There, I think you are mistaken," Carlyle said. "They are and remain alien. They are also our enemies, I think; some members of the Scottish Mesmeric Society were victims of that alienness. None of their families will shed a tear for the death of James Esdaile, nor particularly care that the young woman was merely *possessed.*"

I extended my hand to Carlyle once again, removing my glove. He did the same and we shook hands. I do not think that he was much mollified by this modest show of camaraderie; dislike still burned in his eyes. For my part, I saw little basis on which I could build any sort of trust.

But for the moment, at least, we could view each other as allies.

CHAPTER 15

Through a glass

14 March, 1860
William Davey
c/o the Scottish Mesmeric Society
George Square, Edinburgh

Reverend Davey:

I am sure you are aware, as am I, that any subject of Her Majesty has the right to travel wherever he likes within her realms. As the local constabulary is not presently aware of any misdeeds you might have committed, I am certain that you will not be molested on your arrival. Conversely, I am sure that you should not expect to be received in the style of a conquering hero should you choose to visit.

If you arrive before evening on any week-day, you are welcome to join me in the church-yard, where those who have departed us enjoy their final rest. I am sure you will find the experience enlightening. I pray that it does something to prick your conscience as well.

With respect I remain

Sincerely yours,
Rev. David Esdaile
The Manse
Rescobie, Angus

WILLIAM DAVEY

I should like to think that the motivation that drew me north to Rescobie was in part one of Christian charity, based on my intention to reconcile with the family of James Esdaile. I had told Braid, and certainly had intimated to Thomas Carlyle, that I had no desire to be taunted or humiliated—but for some reason I decided that I was willing to submit to such treatment by David Esdaile, James' younger brother, who served the parish of Rescobie. He had dabbled in mesmerism himself when James had first begun the practice, though his demonstrated skill had never brought him to my—or the Committee's—attention. But he might provide some insights into the object—and the true reason James had left it behind.

Thus, I admit that the other part of my motivation was strictly as the Chairman of the Committee. There was unfinished business, even if James Esdaile was dead.

Rescobie was near Forfar, only a few hours' trip from Edinburgh. Even if all I accomplished was to pay my respects to Esdaile's family, it merited the trip. I had sent a letter to the Reverend Esdaile from Edinburgh, resulting in a curt and cold reply—no less than I should have expected.

Reverend Esdaile was going to provide me with more information about his brother's time in Scotland, even if I had to offer to humble myself to obtain it. What constituted humility for David Esdaile might not be too difficult for me to accept.

❖

I boarded the train in Edinburgh bound for Perth with far less incident than in Manchester. Carlyle and Colquhoun were there to see me off—rather surprising for the author, given what I am sure was perceived to be shabby treatment on my part—but I had confirmed his position as Brisbane's successor. That seemed sufficient for him to assume a mantle of courtesy as I made my way out of his new domain.

I only determined to depart after Reverend Esdaile's reply arrived; I had thus remained longer in Edinburgh than I had intended. I passed the time touring Edinburgh Castle at one end of the High Street and Holyroodhouse at the other. One evening featured a festive board with the Scottish mesmerists, none of whom issued a formal challenge or sought to poison my wine. Still, it was easy to see that my well-wishers were eager to well-wish me away from Edinburgh as speedily as possible.

The train took me by way of Stirling to Perth. In more recent years, travelers have been saved this circuitous path by crossing the Firth of Forth by Fowler and Baker's magnificent bridge; but in 1860 that was three decades in the future, making my own journey longer and more wearying. Perth was where Esdaile and Eliza had dwelt during their two and a half years in Scotland after returning from India; I was not sure if there was anything there to see, so I did not tarry. Instead, I boarded a Caledonian Railway carriage that took me through Dundee to Forfar, where I arrived late in the day.

Rescobie was a tiny place, no more than a church with a few houses clustered around it, set at the edge of a small *loch*, or lake; though only four or five miles from Forfar, Rescobie would afford me no lodging; therefore, I engaged a room in Forfar for overnight and settled myself down for rest. The next day would likely afford none.

Some among my professional colleagues put great stock in dreams. For my part, I am always skeptical of what the sleeping mind dredges from its depths and presents to the fevered imagination, particularly when worries and concerns run through it like trains at a busy railway station.

But recent events had suggested that other forces were at work. It would have been foolish to completely discount words from dreams, particularly when those words were spoken by friends...or enemies.

There is a ruined church adjacent to Holyroodhouse, the remains of an Augustinian abbey where the Order of the Thistle once sat. I had walked around it the day I toured Mary Queen of

Scots' palace, marveling at the views and considering the ruins, a sort of *memento mori* to history long past but—like much in Scotland—in unquiet rest. It was to this place that my dreams took me, and it was in those dreams that I heard someone calling my name.

"Davey."

The voice that called me came from a figure seated on a stone bench under a covered archway, all that remained of the abbey roof, which formed the north wall of the palace itself. Away from the sunlight that streamed through the triforium windows, I could scarcely make out the man who sat there, a scarecrow perched on the very edge of his seat, legs crossed, hands clasped across his knee.

It was Edward Quillinan, my predecessor as Chairman. I had not thought of him much at all since his death nine years earlier—but he had come to mind when I was instructing Thomas Carlyle on our relative relationship. Quillinan looked just as he had when he had quit the Committee in 1842 to care for his wife: frail and pale, the physiognomy and pinched expression of a lesser poet.

"It's good to see you, Quillinan," I said, walking closer. I think in my mind I had realized this was a dream—since seeing someone dead many years and whom I hadn't seen for years before that seemed nothing out of the ordinary.

"Really, Davey, don't strain yourself. I don't care." He straightened his legs and stretched them out before him, the knees cracking in the way that always set my teeth on edge. "I just wondered how you were getting on."

"Personally, or professionally? No, wait," I said, holding up my hand, "let me spare you the need for another witty reply. The Committee is doing well, and I am doing well."

"That Esdaile matter hasn't turned out as you hoped, I see."

"You have been watching?"

"Figure of speech." He patted the pockets of his coat and drew out a small commonplace-book, flipped it open and consulted it, then tucked it back away. "I just thought you might be in need of a bit of advice."

"Don't strain yourself."

"Wit. Excellent, good to see you still are capable of repartee at this late date. I'm sure it has served you well in the pulpit…oh," he said, in a voice that encompassed his typical sneer, "you don't spend much time there, do you? No matter. I just thought I might tell you that the conversation with Braid should tell you something important."

"It already has. Whether James Braid believes in mesmerism or the magnetic fluid or not, it exists and I have skill with it."

"So do others. And they are not afraid of it, either."

"You think I *am*?"

"Oh, yes. Yes, indeed. But please understand that I consider that a virtue. One of the few you possess. There is a future for the mesmeric art—but it's not what you think. And it's not what Braid thinks either, for what that's worth."

"Care to give me some insight from beyond the grave?"

"'For we know in part, and we prophesy in part—for now we see through a glass, darkly; but then face to face: now I know in part; but then shall I know even as also I am known.'"

"And the greatest of these is charity," I answered. "First Corinthians is highly quotable. So I don't see and Braid doesn't see. Is there anyone who does?"

"*I* do. And all I can say is what I told Lord Morpeth a lifetime ago." He grinned, the skin pulled tight on his face as always, a skull straining to get out. "Mesmerism will soon have to pay homage at the Delphic shrine of technology."

"I remember you saying that. I had no idea what you meant then, and I don't know now, either. Care to be more clear?"

"No, not in the least, except to observe that it is technology that is shaping the future into the present day by day. The Art would be better served if it were harnessed to Science. You'd best take charge of it or someone will do it for you."

"'Someone'?"

"Someone you don't trust. Someone you should consider fearing."

"Within my circle?"

"Circles. Appropriate metaphor. The wheels go round and round, Davey. You'd best make sure they don't run you over."

My thoughts flew instantly to the scene at the Manchester railway platform and the Levantine, looking to push me in front of an oncoming train.

"I'm not afraid of anything from beyond the Glass Door."

"Because you're so clean and pure?" he sneered again, and folded his arms across his chest. "Please spare me the platitudes and histrionics. No one's hands are clean."

"You have no idea."

"No, old boy. *You* have no idea." In the dream, the sun faded out and clouds seemed to lower.

"Tell me more," I said, stepping closer and under the stone arch. The skies appeared ready to open up.

"No, I shall not," Quillinan answered. "You'll have to peer through the dark glass and find this one out for yourself."

Behind me, there was a roll of thunder. I turned around; when I returned my gaze to the stone bench, Quillinan was gone...but his commonplace-book remained. It had a curious glyph on the cover—a sort of bust with three heads, one looking to the left, one to the right and one looking directly forward.

I reached for it—

But another peal of thunder shook me awake in my tiny hotel-room in Forfar.

I looked out the window, cursing the weather that had roused me. Beyond the dark glass, it had begun to rain.

CHAPTER 16

In the country

WILLIAM DAVEY

I had rarely thought about Quillinan before the dream in Forfar. He and I had never been close; we had arrived on the great level field of the mesmeric world from different directions—he was an intimate of George Howard, Lord Morpeth—who by the time of my dream had been elevated as the Earl of Carlisle. This preferment was a direct result of Quillinan's marriage to Dora, the favorite daughter of the poet Wordsworth. My esteemed predecessor had been a dashing cavalryman in his youth, but as he grew older and Dora grew more and more infirm he had assumed the character of a sensitive, petulant academic and critic, exhuming one or another Portuguese or Spanish poet and rendering their scratchings in the King's (and later the Queen's) English. I, on the other hand, was always 'that damned lace-maker' or 'the Devon vicar' when he chose to speak of me at all.

Yet for all of that, when he decided to step away from the chairmanship of the Committee and devote himself to Dora and to his writing career, he had advised his supporters—primarily Elliotson, Milnes, Hall and Lord Morpeth himself—to support me as his successor. Though he found me personally detestable, he also saw in me the important qualities he knew I must possess in order to direct the affairs of our society. He removed himself from our midst in 1845 when he and Dora moved to the Continent; he had evidently found me satisfactory, since he had never stirred up trouble against me.

But I cannot properly call him a friend—neither during our association, nor afterward. And certainly not as a friendly shade come to assist me in my dreams. Like Dickens' character Scrooge, I thought he might have appeared in my sleep as a result of some bit of undigested mutton, 'more of gravy than the grave.' Still, I was unaccustomed to such nightly visitors, as I customarily slept soundly and dreamlessly, setting the day's worries and affairs aside to take my rest.

✸

The Arbroath and Forfar Railway line traversed the northern shore of Rescobie Loch, but the little hamlet was not provided with a railway station. I accordingly needed to engage the services of a coach to take me the few miles east to Rescobie.

The night's thunderstorm had resulted in a dreary freezing rain, hardly a cheery backdrop for my visit; but while I could control many things, I had no direct influence on the weather, and no expectation that the morrow would bring any improvement. We therefore set off in the morning, following the road eastward, and soon the loch and the little cluster of buildings that comprised Rescobie came in sight.

The church was set back from the road across from the loch, with its cemetery in front; the yard was vacant but for one figure dressed in black, an umbrella held above his head. The entire scene looked like a Cruikshank woodcut from a Dickens novel.

I alighted from the carriage, extending my own umbrella to shield me from the downpour. The coachman climbed down to attend to his horses; I had instructed him to wait until I had determined the extent of my business. Given my liberality, he was content to do so.

I crossed the short distance and entered the graveyard; the other man noted my approach but did not speak until I reached him.

"That puts paid to one rumor," he said. "You can set foot on holy ground."

"You thought otherwise."

"I am not certain what I might be disposed to think," the man said. He was a middle-aged man, about fifty, with graying hair and no beard, dressed as a Kirk minister.

There was the faintest family resemblance to his brother James, but David Esdaile seemed more robust and less weathered. I do not know whether it was merely the work of an overactive imagination, but I felt as if I could scarcely escape the burning hostility of his eyes. I was determined to meet it, not with the same emotion but with its opposite. The Reverend Esdaile was no more my enemy than Eliza Weatherhead Esdaile had been.

"I am here to—"

"We'll get to that in time," Esdaile interrupted. He gestured toward the gravestone before us. "For the moment you should be thankful that I did not simply set the dogs on you." He nodded toward a stand of trees at the north-western corner of the yard, where a trio of setters sat curled, staying out of the rain.

"Very well."

"Look," Esdaile said, and gestured again. This time my attention was drawn to the marker, which read: JAMES ESDAILE. For just a moment I was taken aback—then I read the dates inscribed beneath: AUGUST 17 1774 and JANUARY 8 1854.

"Your father," I said.

"The Reverend Doctor James Esdaile," David Esdaile said. "Formerly of East Church Perth, later of Rescobie. Our father, Jamie's and mine. One more victim of Jamie's wife."

I had no answer to that statement. It did explain his unconcealed hostility, however: if he blamed Eliza, or her *chthonic* inhabitant about which I presumed he knew nothing, then by extension he blamed the Committee.

And therefore blamed *me*.

"Your father was nearly eighty years of age when he died, Reverend," I said at last. "Is it not possible that the Lord simply called him home?"

"Please do not patronize me, sir. I can still call the dogs."

"I would not want you to mar the Scots reputation for hospitality."

I realized that I had made a similar quip to Carlyle back in Edinburgh, but it seemed appropriate here as well.

Esdaile glowered at me—then shook his head. "I know that Jamie once called you friend. Did you entertain him with your wit as well?"

"We only met once."

"Indeed." Esdaile leaned forward and rubbed a spot of some sort from the grave marker. "I am surprised. You seem the sort of person who would press his attentions more directly."

"That is regrettably not the case. I have journeyed a significant distance to meet you, but if you believe that I am pressing my attentions in a way that offends you, I shall offer my condolences—for James, for your father as well, and take my leave." I inclined my head, speaking a brief prayer: despite what my readers may have come to believe, I did respect the dead.

After a moment Esdaile said, "Aye, that's true. All right, Reverend Davey. You have journeyed so far; I can scarcely fail to give you an opportunity to say your piece. Tell your coachman to go to the stable—there'll be a warm mug of tea for him there. In the meanwhile, we should get out of this rain."

Then, to my surprise, the most remarkable thing happened: I was welcomed as a guest at Reverend James Esdaile's table. At eleven o'clock in the morning, Esdaile, his wife and five children were all gathered together, drinking hot tea and eating thick slabs of farmhouse bread with butter and honey. He had four daughters and one son: Ann, the oldest, was about twelve; her sister Mary was a year younger; and Alice—who would be a great beauty as a young woman, I thought—was nine. They were all very helpful to their mother and polite—if a bit wary—of their visitor. The other two children, little Margaret at five or six and James, the only boy, just about to turn three, were spectators more than participants, but were full of energy.

The remarkable aspect of this domestic scene was not the frenetic activity of the five children jostling for slices of bread or the honey-pot; it was that *I* was permitted a place there. Reverend Esdaile had met me in the church-yard, threatened to set his dogs on me, and all but accused me of complicity in his father's death—a matter I certainly wished to discuss—and then had invited me out of the miserable weather and given me hospitality. His wife Mary was much younger—fifteen years younger, I should say—but might well have been a party to his disposition toward me; yet she, too, evinced no hostility…at least not at the table, before her children.

Twenty years in the company of mesmerists had made me suspicious of kindness: in our society that was often, if not always, taken for weakness.

Reverend Esdaile and his wife were not, however, of the *company of mesmerists*. And insofar as he had things to tell me and I had come far to listen, he was in a position of superior power. Had he been a different sort of Scotsman, I suppose I might have been in mortal danger—yet I felt safer at that table than I had felt for several months, at least.

At last the dishes were taken away and the table was cleared. Esdaile's wife and children withdrew from the kitchen; Reverend Esdaile instructed his daughter Ann to fetch him two items—a journal and a commonplace-book—from his study, and he settled into a chair opposite me, his hands wrapped around his own mug.

"You are a very patient man, Mr. Davey. I daresay a lesser might not have survived the onslaught of my family."

"You have beautiful children, sir."

"And unlike one of your…professional colleagues, you will assure me on your honor as a clergyman that you intend no harm to them."

"I beg your pardon?" At that moment I truly did not know what he meant.

"One of the many tactics employed by your humble foot-soldiers over the course of three years was to intimate that something might befall them should Jamie not cooperate. They threatened me, Mr. Davey—me, my wife, my bairns."

"I am appalled by the idea."

"That innocents might be harmed?"

"That is not how we conduct ourselves. Threatening innocents. We only had a disagreement with your brother."

"You got your way at last, now didn't you."

The anger that had been placed on the pantry-shelf seemed to have returned.

"James Esdaile is dead, Reverend. I did not kill him: he took his own life, in front of me and in front of his wife."

"But you were prepared to kill him."

I looked past Esdaile and through the doorway into the other parts of the house. Neither wife nor children were in sight.

"It would accomplish nothing for me to deny it."

"Well." He tapped his finger on the commonplace-book on the table. "At least you are an honest scoundrel, sir. I suppose I therefore know what brings you here."

"I was here to offer my condolences, at least. But pray tell me what you believe my motive to be."

"That statue. You think I have it."

"*Do* you?"

"What makes you think I would tell you if I did? But I do not have it. Jamie didn't have it, either. He left it in India, just as he said. He felt that it was an evil thing, and determined that you should never possess it. To be honest, sir, I expected you to present a more terrifying appearance—a storyteller with any skill would surely have sketched you in more menacingly."

"Appearances can be deceiving," I said.

"If you came here to poke about in Rescobie Manse for the fell object, I shall save you the trouble. It is not presently here, nor has it ever been."

"I believe you."

I do not know if Reverend David Esdaile had expected me to so readily agree with him—nor to suggest, as I had just done, that I had come all the way into the country and be willing to accept his word.

"You do."

"I do. And what I want from you is not the statue—for I know you do not have it. I want to know more about the time when your brother and his wife were in Scotland—and how they came to leave. And why."

"Why? They found a better situation elsewhere," Esdaile said. "Should they have a better reason to have left?"

"Yes. And I believe you know what it was. I suspect…now that we have spoken…that it has something to do with your father, and a great deal to do with you."

Esdaile folded his hands in front of him on the table and looked directly at me. If he feared my mesmeric abilities, he showed none of it as we sat at that table.

"Reverend Davey," he said at last, using my title as well as my name, "if you truly wish to know the entire story, I suggest that you dismiss your coachman or send him back to Forfar for your effects. For Jamie's sake, I think you should have the whole story.

"And that, sir, will take a few days to tell."

CHAPTER 17

Kindred souls

DAVID ESDAILE

My earliest memories are from Montrose, where Jamie and I were born. It is a town by the sea, and my mother used to say that seawater flowed in our veins.

When we were old enough, we were sent to the new Montrose Academy, and it was there we caught the fever for learning. I turned to my father's profession—the profession of the faith. For Jamie, it was the sciences. Every day we would see men who had fought Boney: the original one, not the current one—the lucky ones were hale, but many were not—they would walk with a limp or have a leg off or suffer the consumptive's cough; he wanted to change all that, to heal the bodies as I wanted to heal their souls.

When I was fourteen, Father was granted a living at East Church in Perth. It was a great change for our family, as we left the town we had known all our lives to go to live in the house on Rose Terrace; but it represented a great gain in Father's income—enough that both Jamie and I could enter University in Edinburgh. I had thought to read the law, but I think my head is too hard for that—but just hard enough for the Kirk. My brother never had trouble with any sort of learning, and by the time he was twenty-two had been awarded his degree in medicine, even though he had periods of ill health—but he was determined and stubborn. Yes, all Scotsmen are like that, but Esdailes most of all.

Yes, that's right: it was not too long afterward that he married Mary Ann. She was beautiful—I think a poet might use the word "lissome"—and Jamie was smitten with her. Our father came down from Perth to perform the ceremony, and I—at nineteen—stood up with my brother and held his wedding band. It makes me smile all these years later to think of how happy they both were. How happy we all were.

The Lord giveth and taketh away, Reverend Davey. Establishing a medical practice was much harder than procuring the education for one—and it quickly became apparent to my brother that he would have to seek a better alternative than giving most of his earnings to a more senior surgeon just to have his name on an older man's consulting-office door. Some time the following year—1831, I think it was—he told us that he had taken a position with the East India Company and that he and Mary Ann would be embarking for Calcutta.

I did not see him again for twenty years, and it was the last time I ever laid eyes upon Mary Ann. She was so beautiful, like a figure from a dream; we went to see them off when they took ship for India—and it seemed to me that she looked a bit forlorn, as if she knew that she would never see her home again.

Jamie and I corresponded extensively. I have saved every letter, with fair copies of my replies. Neither he nor Mary Ann enjoyed good health in India or elsewhere. He had a breakdown and was granted leave to travel—they went to Egypt and the Holy Land. Ah, to be with them—he saw the Pyramids and the great Sphinx, and toured the Holy Land and walked in the steps of the Savior—I have a copy of his book: *Letters From the Red Sea, Egypt and the Continent*—all about his travels there.

Did he like the people he met? No, he did not; I should say that he disliked them very much. In Jamie's world there were Scotsmen, and then other Britons, and then other peoples—it is a wonder to me that he was willing to go to India at all. He particularly disliked Egyptians—the modern ones—which I daresay makes some of what I shall tell you a trifle ironic.

I received a letter from him in the summer of 1839. Here, let me show it to you: very clipped, very clinical, as if he were reporting a statistic at his hospital. *My dear Mary Ann passed without pain this morning after a quiet night; I held her hand to the end.*

That was all he had to say. My words of comfort were my best ones—I wrote and rewrote the letter a half-dozen times, showing it to my Mary each time—and it always sounded like no more than words from a dream, something that could mean nothing to him in the harsh daylight of tropical India. His dear wife, whom we had come to love so much, had departed this life like a whisper. Mary keeps her last letter, just as Jamie always kept Mary's last letter to her, sealed in its envelope unread—as it arrived two weeks after her death.

Changed? Of course. It is hard to conceive otherwise. The very tenor of his letters became different—shorter, less substantial. He wrote about the weather and his work and his little expeditions with his friend Fergusson—

When did they meet, you say? Not long after he arrived. Two kindred souls, sons of Scotland thousands of miles from home. I think they were drawn to each other because they were so different: Mr. Fergusson was a prosperous farmer, of indigo I believe, who had come to India to make his fortune—and make it he did!—and because of his love of the culture and the monuments it had left behind. It was completely unlike my brother's views. James Fergusson was a collector, Jamie told me, with shelves and shelves of these things, trinkets and keepsakes and mementoes. They used to sit up late at night and talk about ancient history, and what could be learned from it.

Now, as to my father and how he comes into this story. He was a tireless worker, Reverend Davey, and it caught up with him while I was still in Perth. I had obtained a position as his clerk, as there was no living available for me—and it was much to my liking: Perth was a pleasant burgh in those days; I worked with my father and tutored Latin and Greek at Perth Academy in the evenings, as I was not distracted by any love interests at the time.

And as was my custom, I always called upon my father before retiring. He usually burned the lamp late into the night, so it was not unusual for me to find him in his study, bent over a sermon or the translation of some passage in Greek or Latin.

I returned late one night and knocked on his study door. When he did not answer, I entered—something, I should say, that he had specifically ordered me never to do. I found him collapsed on the floor—he had suffered a fit of apoplexy, or—as Jamie termed it in a letter—a *stroke*.

I remember at the time that though he could hardly speak, he required of me to gather up all of the sheets of the manuscript on which he had been laboring, along with the little book that lay open on his desk. *Keep these to yourself, Davie*, he said to me. *Let no man see them, and I will take them back when I recover.*

All I had in mind was his recovery—and surely there were more valuable things in that study to be secured—but this was his primary concern. I did as I was bid, placing them under lock and key in my own little office after helping him to the hospital.

Did I examine them? I did not. Not until much later. I shall return to that subject when my story reaches it, Reverend; you must possess yourself in patience.

My father labored in his recovery just as he had done with everything else. He was alone in the world now, except for a few distant cousins and myself; our mother had died not long after Jamie took ship for India. He was nearly seventy, a well-respected minister and scholar, with one son following in his calling and another a successful doctor in India. He was proud—not as a besetting sin, but as a man grown long in years who could happily reflect upon a well-spent life. If the Lord had extended His hand and plucked him away there is no one, not even me, who would have said that his time had been cruelly cut short.

After a month he could walk again, more slowly than he had done but steadily and firmly with the slightest aid of a cane. During his convalescence he had resumed his reading, and as soon as he was able he returned to his study. I placed strict limits on his evening hours, packing him off to rest much earlier than he ever desired.

The manuscript? Why, I returned it to his care, of course. While he recovered, during which time I took up his responsibilities as minister in East Church, it was the object of his closest attention. He was copying it by hand; he refused to let me see it, much less assist him with the laborious task. When the task was complete he spoke no more of it—and I never saw the original book again. His copy was placed in a locked drawer in his desk and he did not speak of it further.

My service in his stead was sufficient for my father to make an attempt to find me a living of my own. I think it is possible that his illness had caused a sort of sympathy for him among his colleagues and friends, but I should like to believe that I distinguished myself well enough to merit consideration.

In any case, it took almost eighteen months for his efforts to bear fruit. In the summer of 1844 this parish lost its minister, and Father made application for it on my behalf. There had been a great deal of turmoil in the Church: Father was a Free Churchman, as were most in this part of Scotland, and I was evidently chosen in preference to some patronage candidate. Whatever the case, I was installed here and soon I felt right at home.

My Mary was born and raised in Forfar, Reverend. And while she is nearly fifteen years my junior, she has been as good a wife and mother as anyone I could have imagined. My father was very fond of her, and she him—after the railway reached Perth he would take the cars and hire a carriage and come to visit; when he finally chose to retire in 1849 she welcomed him into our home. He sat up nights with little Mary when she had the colic—he knew as much about bairns as any man I know.

Father's health had almost completely returned by the time he came here to Rescobie; when I broke an arm trying to fix the roof of the church, he stepped into my pulpit as readily as I had stepped into his. He went for walks in the country and spent time reading and writing.

I think I would have liked things to continue that way until Mary and I were old and gray, and the children all grown and gone on to their own lives. But it was not to be.

WILLIAM DAVEY

David Esdaile had a gift for storytelling, and as he warmed to his subject he became animated—he almost transformed into a different person, far removed from the bitterness and anger he had displayed when we first met.

As he began his tale we had taken seats in the parlor, and Mary had kept the children at a polite distance all afternoon; the narrative had carried us halfway through the century, and was even more detailed than the summary I recount. It struck me as odd that he had chosen to pour it out to me—but upon reflection I realized that David Esdaile had been waiting for years to tell some portion of this story; whatever he wanted to convey, whatever secrets he sought to reveal, he had been awaiting the proper ear. If I had possessed a more villainous appearance, I might not have been offered his account; or perhaps there was more to it than that.

Whatever the case, he chose to share it with me without pause until we could barely discern the outline of Turin Hill in the distance. Only when Mary entered the room to light the lamps did we realize that it had grown dark—not the sort that we know in great cities like London, but the dark of the country, bereft of street-lamps and the intrusions of civilization.

Esdaile excused himself from the room, leaving me sitting in an armchair as Mary moved about.

"Your husband has great skill as a storyteller," I said.

She stopped, facing away from me. "You make it sound as if he is fashioning a tale for the children," she answered, without turning.

"I mean nothing of the kind."

"He has told me something about you," she said, turning to face me. "And James told me too, years ago, when I suppose that I was too young to truly understand. When David received your

131

letter a few weeks ago, I asked him why he should want to have someone like *you* in our house."

"I did not expect to be received so courteously."

"You do not know my husband," she answered. She hesitated, then came and sat in the chair David Esdaile had so recently occupied. She folded her hands in her lap and looked directly at me, with the sort of focus I customarily expected from a practitioner of the Art; but there were no gestures or passes, merely the intensity of her gaze.

"I confess that I do not."

"He quoted Scripture, Reverend Davey. 'Love ye your enemies, and do good, and lend, hoping for nothing again; and your reward shall be great, and ye shall be the children of the Highest: for he is kind unto the unthankful and to the evil. Be ye therefore merciful, as your Father also is merciful.'"

"The Gospel of Luke," I said.

"The doctor," she agreed. "He told me that all of this tragedy was like a disease—all of the hatred, all of the anger. He wondered what you would have to say. And when it seemed that you had come not to say but to hear, he told me that he wanted to tell you his…story."

She clenched her hands, gathering up little handfuls of her apron and the skirt below it. "But it is no *story*, sir. It is something that tore apart two brothers and terrified me. I wanted it to remain as far from this house, from Rescobie, from my children, as possible. When James died, I thought it was gone for good."

"I am not here to frighten you, Mrs. Esdaile," I said. "And that which frightened you is no more. I shall not bring it back."

"You have no idea what frightens me. You—you have no idea."

At that moment David Esdaile returned to the parlor. He looked at me, then a bit more curiously at his wife; some unspoken communication may have occurred between them. She stood and without a word made her way out of the room.

"We can continue this later," he said. "It is time for tea."

CHAPTER 18

Far and near

28 April, 1845
Rev. James Esdaile,
8 Rose Terrace,
Perth Angus,
Scotland.

Dear Father:

I apologize for my neglect in correspondence with you. The press of work and my own health have made it difficult to attend to the pleasures of writing and reading. I hope you continue to enjoy the blessings of good health.

I hope to expand upon the topic at a later time, but I wished to share my excitement at the discovery of a new treatment that I have introduced at the hospital here in India. It is a natural curative power that has greatly alleviated human suffering among the Bengali natives in my care. The singular and beneficial process of mesmerism has allowed these patients to be relieved of distresses in a way that is painless and efficacious.

I hesitate to succumb to false vanity but I venture to say that I feel akin to the great Apostle Saint Luke, whose skill confirmed and extended belief in our Lord in times renowned...

...I know that mankind will greatly benefit from the propagation of this curative power, and I hope that my application and perfection of its use will confirm your pride in the humble efforts of your son...

With great affection,

Your loving son,
James
Hooghly,
Bengal, India

WILLIAM DAVEY

I awoke to the early morning sounds of a house full of children. Rescobie Manse was a great rambling structure, scarcely half-full; an attic room had been given to me, and its window overlooked Rescobie Loch, spread out and dotted with echoes of watery sunlight.

Neither Edward Quillinan nor any other unquiet ghost had accompanied me into the country, nor did any spirits manifest.

The younger children were gathered at the table when I descended. From the parlor I could hear Reverend Esdaile conjugating a Latin verb, followed by the solemn recitation of Ann and young Mary. Alice was making a face: she had clearly heard this sort of lesson before, and knew it awaited her soon.

"Good morning," Mary Esdaile said to me. "Children, say good morning to our guest, Reverend Davey."

The three obliged. Little James hopped down from his seat and waddled over to me, reaching up to take my hand; I bent down and took it. His mother turned from the stove, unable to conceal her alarm, but said nothing.

"You have to sit down at the table," he said. "Mama won't bring you tea until you sit."

"I'd best do so," I said, smiling. The lad climbed up onto a chair and I sat next to him. "It wouldn't do to disobey."

"May I have tea, Mama?" he said.

Mary smiled at the show that her son was putting on for the guest, and took down two stoneware mugs from a shelf—one adult-sized and one small one—and poured from a chipped swan-shaped teapot. She placed one in front of each of us.

"Thank you," we both said almost at once. James and the girls giggled and both Mary and I smiled, though she turned away at once to busy herself with something else.

"You seem a bright young lad," I said to James. "Have you decided what you will be when you grow up? A minister, like your father?"

"No, don't wanna," he said, glancing toward the parlor and screwing his face into a frown. "I wanna doctor."

"Really. Well, you know, you have to study a lot to be a doctor, James."

"But not Lapin."

"That's Latin, you goose," Alice said, giggling again.

"Alice," her mother said sternly. "Don't call your brother names."

"You have to learn Latin to be a doctor, too," I said. "All kinds of things are in Latin."

"Then I don't wanna doctor," he declared solemnly. "I wanna sail a ship."

The Latin lesson had apparently ended. David Esdaile emerged into the kitchen, his two daughters following behind, their faces solemn and chastened.

"It seems we shall have to apply ourselves somewhat more," he declared, and sat at the table. He knew the rule as well. Mary poured tea for her husband. "Did you sleep well?" he asked me.

"Very well, thank you."

"I must take advantage of the weather to do some work around the place this morning. We can continue our discussions at midday, if that suits you."

"If I may help—"

"No, that's all right. You are welcome to read in the parlor or enjoy a constitutional."

Another nonverbal conversation took place between David Esdaile and his wife. Once again, that might have been for my benefit: that whatever my purported powers, he was not in the least afraid of me—either on his own behalf or his family's.

I chose the walk.

City life does not encourage long strolls, particularly in London; this has become worse in recent years, but even in 1860 the sooty air and debris, the sights and sounds and smells tended to dissuade such things. But in the country, these things seemed distant and almost imaginary.

The air was brisk but not cold, and the quiet was only interrupted by the distant sounds of livestock and birds. I walked along the loch alone, trying to assemble what I had learned from David Esdaile the day before.

First: it was clear that he had been close with his brother before James' departure for India, but that had been altered because James himself had changed after his first wife's death.

Second: David knew of the statue—possibly not its significance to the mesmeric power, but he clearly understood it was *important*. He knew, also, that I still sought it and, despite any protests to the contrary, might entertain the possibility that it was here at Rescobie.

Third: though I had surely invited it by making James an enemy of the Committee, some of my colleagues had made some rather unsavory threats to *David* Esdaile. I thought I could pinpoint the man responsible: it had most likely been Dr. Horace Eden, a phreno-mesmerist who had been one of the first to offer to come up to Perth and extract information from James on the statue's whereabouts. Eden was a nasty bit of business—and I would have had to deal with him myself. Eliza (or, more particularly, her *chthonic* cohabitant) had apparently done that for me.

But it was abundantly clear that David Esdaile had told me only a fraction of his story thus far. It also seemed to me that when he had finished, I would be expected to depart and never return.

This was my one opportunity to ask questions and obtain answers.

DAVID ESDAILE

Jamie's letters were always full of complaints about his ill health and his misfortune. He had married again shortly after Mary Ann died—a young woman named Charlotte: she had died within a year. We do not even have a picture of her, and Jamie's letters scarcely mention her. As with Mary Ann, there were no children. My father fretted quite a bit about that.

We first heard of his experiments with mesmerism in the summer of 1845, a few months after he had begun. He did not even do most of the work—did he tell you that he did? That was the responsibility of the sub-assistant doctors, who prepared for the trances. The heat, and his poor health, precluded it. From the very first he found it tiring, almost overwhelming. The initial experiment, on a man named Kaurá, nearly defeated him.

It was clear, though, that he felt he had happened upon something extraordinary. His first letter to Father spoke of it as a blessing: he thought of himself like Saint Luke, but instead of the Gospel of Christ his was the Gospel of Mesmerism. His letters to me were even more effusive.

My attentions had been arrested more than a dozen years earlier by Cloquet, the French doctor. He had written of his operation on a young lady's cancerous breast while under the influence of mesmeric trance. The evidence in that case had been so striking—particularly since the renowned Doctor had not been an avowed believer in the powers of the mesmeric art—that I found little reason to doubt its efficacy; but I had dismissed it as chicanery and mummery when Doctor Elliotson's famous experiments had been exposed as false. When my brother brought it back to my attention so unexpectedly, I was forced to reexamine the matter.

As you are aware—and as I recorded in public in Jamie's book, which I was called upon to edit—I endeavored to perform some experiments of my own in the summer of 1846. Once again, I was compelled by evidence laid before me to reverse my ground. I had accepted the efficacy of the mesmeric trance, and then dismissed it as fraud, and then my faith in the practice was restored.

Do I believe in it now? Of course. With certainty. I would be a fool to discredit evidence and firsthand experience. But I also believe with all my heart that there is no man, regardless of how saintly he might be, who is able to resist the corrupting influence of that practice. Not me, not Jamie—and *certainly* not you, sir.

I once said that if we came to believe that mesmerism itself was a terrible engine in the hands of a villain, we could safely rely upon our legislators to draft laws to punish those who would use it—and that it was a tool that needed to be used with care, lest it be used for mischief by the ignorant and unprincipled. Those statements show how naïve I was, don't you think?

The villainy of which I spoke was that someone might use mesmerism to steal a favorite poodle. Yet the work of your Committee is far more sinister, is it not? And with friends like Sir Robert Peel—

Yes, yes. And in the ten years since his death, I am certain that you have found others to replace him in the councils of power. And as for the dangers from the ignorant and unprincipled...I should say that use of these powers by mere criminals is a minimal threat compared to the skill with which true villains could wield them.

No. I am not mocking you. I am explaining to you where I stand—where *we* stand. I am illuminating my position, the rock on which I rest my feet. No one's hands are clean, sir. Likely not even mine, since I helped convey Jamie's writing to the general public in 1846. But all of it might have been no more than the philanthropic exercise he always intended it to be—but for your Committee.

Yes, of course. And the statue. Would you like to see it?

I see you start. No, I repeat what I said yesterday—it is not here. It was never here. But in the fall of 1849, my brother sent me a calotype of it. I know that by that time he had already begun to sense its malignance, though that does not show in the image.

Or perhaps it does. And here it is, Reverend Davey: the object of your desire—the cause of so much grief.

This is what killed my brother and my father.

CHAPTER 19

The object of interest

WILLIAM DAVEY

For the first time, I beheld the statue that James Esdaile had possessed and that he had promised to me.

The picture was indeed a calotype—a sort of early photograph, made by the exposure of a single chemical, silver iodide, I believe, to produce an image. The paper was thick and mounted on a stiff board that had crumbled a bit at the edges; Esdaile handled it delicately, as if he were holding a fair copy of the Magna Carta (or, given the location, the Declaration of Arbroath).

It was a little thing, I knew, and the picture conveyed no sense of proportion. It had been set upon a table, apparently in sunlight, and it showed evidence of having been polished as one might clean the silver flatware—it seemed to shine and glow, particularly where its extremities picked out and reflected the sun.

It was compelling, all the same. It seemed to be looking out of the frame at me, gazing at me from its past—the frozen moment of time at which it had been preserved.

"It's beautiful, isn't it?" David Esdaile said softly. "The object of interest is a work of art."

"And much more," I said.

"To be sure." He took the print from my hands and laid it gently in his lap. He gazed at it for several moments without speaking, then looked up at me.

"The statue is *alive*," Esdaile said. "In his letters to me, Jamie told me that it spoke to him. It was very old—it came from a sort of burial mound left behind by a culture we do not know, located in the Indus Valley. The Buddhist monks thought it to be a *stupa*—a sort of reliquary beneath a small hill, where sacred objects are placed—but it was far older than the Buddha.

"James Fergusson procured this object from a bazaar during one of his treasure-finding expeditions. Jamie told me that Fergusson was very proud of his ability to identify, and acquire, what he called 'diamonds in the rough' from stupid Hindoos."

"It sounds as if your brother did not believe that."

"Not about this object, Reverend Davey. Fergusson did not find it: it found *him*. It had been placed in this mound in an unimaginably distant past, had broken free somehow, and had latched onto the first person it found."

"Fergusson?"

"No, before him. Fergusson was only the recipient of the statue after it had escaped."

"'Escaped'?"

"Yes."

Esdaile picked up the calotype from the table. He returned it to its slipcase, then stood and placed it back on the top shelf of the bookcase between two large folio volumes.

He stood there for several moments with his back to me before he turned to face me once more.

"That is *exactly* the term that applies, sir. According to my brother, the statue—or, more particularly, the being inside it—had been imprisoned."

He returned to his seat. He looked weary, as if the image itself—and the revelation he was sharing with me—had been a tremendous burden.

Outside, the sunlight had given way to clouds.

"The statue spoke to your brother."

"He said that it spoke in his dreams at first, but then in waking hours, as well. It told him that it had been waiting for him, searching for him…or someone *like* him."

I found that I was breathing very slowly and carefully. I forced my shoulders to relax.

"From the beginning," David Esdaile said at last, "my brother was only truly able to accomplish the mesmeric trance and its analgesic effects with the assistance of the statue. Even his first success, the notable experiment on the fourth of April 1845, was accomplished due to its proximity during the procedure. It *helped* him, sir. It guided him to achieve what he had never before done.

"And it led to his death."

"Your brother was inexperienced with such things, Reverend Esdaile. There are forces, and—intelligences—beyond the ken of most people, that—"

He put his hands up, almost a mesmeric gesture.

"Please do not patronize me," he said.

"I mean to do nothing of the kind. I…fear that we have gotten off the subject."

DAVID ESDAILE

Jamie told me that he feared for his life.

I know that after the publication of *Mesmerism In India* and his accounts of the many procedures he performed in Hooghly and on maneuvers with the army, he became quite well-known in the circles of mesmeric enthusiasts. I am also aware that you corresponded with him—and that he had assured you that he would bring the statue back for examination.

Correct. Something did change, and I am not sure what it was. Something convinced him that the statue had an ulterior motive— some clue, some indication that bringing it back with him was wrong.

Then, a few weeks before he arrived, he sent me a letter telling me that he had married again. The young woman, Eliza, was an English girl who had been acting as a governess to some English family in Calcutta, and had lately been working in the hospital with the women relatives of the inmates and patients.

I daresay it *did* seem sudden, but recall, if you will, that Jamie married a second time and became a widower with scarcely any word coming back to us here in Scotland. Our father had already moved in with us here in Rescobie and was eager to see him again.

So were Mary and I. Alice had just been born, and little Annie and Mary were just beginning to talk—we were so looking forward to their arrival.

We met them as they arrived at Edinburgh on the train from London. I scarcely recognized him—no great surprise, given that he had been absent for twenty years. But I knew what Eliza was from the moment Jamie handed her down from the railway carriage. It was as if a chill ran from the nape of my neck to the small of my back—I had all I could do to keep my wits about me.

I knew at once that she was a walking spirit, what esoteric parlance calls a *chthonios*, a spirit bound to earth. More particularly, she was a spirit bound to my *brother*.

Of *course* I knew. I shall explain presently how—but let me assure you that when Father first met Eliza he was just as convinced, and on the same basis as I had known. My brother James had arrived from India in the company of a *chthonic* spirit. When he died—and from his obvious physical debilitation, that possibility was never remote—she would receive the reward that all such creatures crave: the consumption of his soul.

My wife and I traveled by rail to Perth. There were times during the trip that the *chthonios* seemed alarmed, or at the very least surprised, at the sounds and sights of the locomotive and the passenger carriage; she—I shall call it a *she*, for it had the form of a woman—seemed almost unfamiliar with railways. Recall, if you will, that there were virtually none in India at that time; I suppose that the Caledonian car was even more raucous and noisy than the railway they had taken from London.

My Mary, always the gentle soul, sought to befriend Eliza at once but found it difficult—Jamie's wife was aloof, standoffish, thinking before speaking as if everything she heard had to be translated into some other language and then back again. For his part, my brother seemed on edge and on guard.

They had made arrangements to stay in a guest-house on Tay

Street for a month or so while they settled. Jamie had made an advance application to the General Prison on South Inch, where he might find useful employment due to his experience in India. Eliza seemed to cling to him at every moment, but I was surprised when Mary was able to take her aside to examine the couple's new apartments. She was unaware of what I had realized—but had sensed my unease, and determined that I should have a few minutes alone with my brother.

We stood in the largely empty front room that overlooked the street. I confronted my brother at once, unsure how soon Eliza might return.

"Jamie, what in God's name is happening? Do you know—"

"All too well, Davie. I see that you can tell."

"Yes. I can tell."

James seemed surprised, but accepted it on its face. "And Mary?"

"She can tell something's wrong, but doesn't know what. Tell me this first—is she in danger right now, alone with—with—"

"Eliza. My wife."

"Mary Ann was your wife."

"Don't ever say that name," he snapped back at me. "Don't speak of her. Not to Eliza. She is…"

"She is…" I lowered my voice to almost a whisper. "She is not human, Jamie. She is a *stoicheion*, a *chthonios*. I cannot imagine what possessed you to—"

And at this point he laughed, Reverend Davey. It was like a madman's laugh, like the barking of a dog. "Possessed me? No, no. You have it all wrong, brother."

"Is Mary in danger?"

"No. I…believe that Eliza is constrained in what she will do, what she *can* do. We spent weeks on the voyage out from India. She was terribly sick at first, but when she recovered she did not… imperil anyone. She will not imperil your wife."

"Does she know that I know her nature?"

"Quite frankly, I am surprised that *you* know. It isn't just your mesmeric skill—there's something more to it, isn't there?"

"Yes."

"What is it? How do you know?"

Before I could answer—and I am not certain I would have done—Mary and Eliza rejoined us. Mary was smiling, but the look in her eyes indicated that something troubled her severely.

Jamie wrote me a letter from Perth that night—it arrived two mornings later, a day before he and Eliza were to come out to Rescobie to see Father and the children. I still have it—it explained that he had made his contract with Eliza because he feared reprisals from the Committee, and he needed to protect himself from them. He told me that he would explain it all someday, and that he hoped that I—and God—would forgive him for what he had done.

You may find it difficult to believe, but I *have* forgiven him. I do not speak exclusively for the Lord of Hosts, but I pray that James' reasons for taking his own life are sufficient for Our Lord to forgive him. At the time, I found his explanation an unsatisfactory answer.

Before I could frame a written reply to his letter, he and his wife arrived on my door-step.

Father and I had discussed Jamie long into the night after we returned from Perth. I had thought to send word to him that we could not have him visit—the children were sick, there was a problem at the farm, or some such—but Father told me that telling such lies would only hold them for some time. He was eager to see his oldest son, and thought that confronting the problem at once was the best policy.

We cannot be afraid, Father told me. *If the Lord is with us, who can stand against us?*

How could I *not* be afraid? I had never faced things such as Eliza—I had only read about them. But I had my father beside me. He and I prayed, and then he took up a position in the doorway of the Manse and awaited the arrival of his son and daughter-in-law.

When they came into the yard, I saw him immediately stiffen as if he was in pain. Jamie climbed down from the bench first, and came around to help Eliza to descend, and then led her to the door.

He and Father embraced, for quite a long time. Then Jamie introduced him to Eliza.

"*Welcome to the family,*" Father said, and embraced her as well. I saw Eliza grimace ever so slightly; she opened her mouth for a moment, but no sound came out. She opened it again, and I heard something disturbing—a noise that had no sound, like an echo out of nowhere. Father stiffened again, but it passed.

I did not know it at the time, but that was the first time that the *chthonios* attempted to kill my father.

CHAPTER 20

From one to another

WILLIAM DAVEY

When he had finished this recitation, David Esdaile opened his eyes and looked at me. At first his expression was blank, and then it focused into sensibility.

"You were employing a mesmeric trance."

"It was the easiest way to recall the dialogue between James and myself. I remember it…more accurately."

"I would have offered—"

"I am sure you would." Esdaile stood from his chair and walked around the room, rubbing the back of his neck. We had both been sitting in one place for a few hours.

"Did your brother tell you why he had made an alliance with a creature from beyond nightfall?"

Esdaile stopped walking and looked directly at me. "'Beyond nightfall'? I don't think I have heard that description before. Yes, he did, in the end. But Eliza was here primarily because of your people. Jamie knew that he had made powerful enemies, and before leaving India he made this decision."

"Among members of the Committee, it was held that he brought the statue with him, and that it could be taken by force. Your brother was a powerful mesmerist—but not the equal of others. Including myself."

"So you were going to come up to Perth and snatch it away?"

"Essentially, yes."

"You admit it that easily," Esdaile said, returning to his seat. "You *are* a scoundrel."

"I determined long ago," I carefully replied, "that it does no good to avoid titles others apply to you. I am singular in my pursuit of that which I believe to be important. If that makes me a scoundrel in your eyes, then so be it. Your brother and I had an agreement, and he broke it."

"So you sent ruffians after him."

"I did nothing of the sort," I said. "I am not an army general, Reverend Esdaile. I do not command legions of loyal followers. Indeed, our society is scarcely able to agree on anything...except when coerced. But this object was *promised*, and it was a source of considerable embarrassment when the agreement was broken."

Esdaile looked out the window toward the distant hills. His expression was pained, as if the anger had drained out of it, leaving only remorse.

"By my count, there were eight separate attempts on Jamie's life over the course of two and a half years. In five cases, Eliza...disposed of the attacker. Personally."

After a long silence, I said, "There were more than eight."

"I am certain that you know better than I on that matter."

"There was nothing I could do to prevent them from trying. It was clear after the first few attempts that Esdaile was well protected—I did not try to take matters into my own hands."

"Witness your presence here."

"Quite."

"It does not make me think better of you, Reverend Davey. Nor does your polite demeanor or pleasant character. For several years, I have wondered to myself what I might say to you, and now that you are here I find myself at a loss for words."

"You have told me quite a lot, Reverend Esdaile, but some things remain. I should like to know more."

"For example?"

"Why James left Scotland."

"That question has a simple answer, sir. He left in part because I demanded that he leave—and never return."

DAVID ESDAILE

The *chthonic* spirits speak their own language. It is painful for humans to hear it; I wondered, sometimes, if Eliza tormented Jamie in that way…but I suppose that considering his state of health, I suspect that it would have been enough to cause his death. No doubt their contract precluded that.

Every time they came to Rescobie, Eliza would try to speak in their language to my father. I never heard a single word—he deflected them somehow—but these conflicts always left him pale and shaken. Jamie must have known what was happening, as their visits became infrequent. More often, I would travel to Perth to meet with him, as I was assisting in editing his work for publication.

Eliza would sometimes be present, but often she left us alone. She was not particularly hostile toward me, but she considered our father a dangerous enemy; she seemed to save her ire for him.

Jamie was not practicing medicine: there had not been a position open for him, and he had retired to concentrate on his writing. He was making regular contributions to the *Zoist* which related his experiences in India. He had put by some money, allowing them to keep a very respectable house in Atholl Street, a newer and more fashionable part of the town.

Jamie and I managed a supper alone at the Royal George Hotel on a cold, blustery night just before Christmas of 1853. It was more than two years after their return to Perth. I cannot imagine what was occupying Eliza that night: perhaps she was somewhere nearby, listening to the conversation. Jamie was nervous as ever, at loose ends.

"How is Father?"

"He is complaining of weakness on his left side," I told him. "The side on which he was afflicted."

"By the stroke."

"Yes. It has begun to bother him more and more."

"That is usual, Davie," he answered. "The damage done by the stroke never completely goes away."

"It is being made worse. You know why."

Jamie had a pained expression. "Yes. I know why. She...feels threatened by Father. She says that he wishes to destroy her."

"It would not surprise me if he did. He prays for you nightly, Jamie, that the Lord will deliver you from her."

"I am already beyond help," he answered, and took a sip of his wine. "You know that this is *necessary*, to prevent unscrupulous men from having something that it would be catastrophic for them to possess."

"At the cost of—"

"I realize that it is part of your professional brief to fret about me," he said. "But you and Father must accept that what's done is done."

"You know I can't do that, Jamie. God's grace is infinite. He can deliver you from this."

"Not *this*."

"Yes, *this*," I answered. "Of course He can save you from her. If you want Him to."

"Protecting the knowledge of the object is far more important than my life, even my soul, Davie. You must understand that. Someday you will understand. I hope that Father will understand as well—it's not what he wanted, not what he expected. I've...I've been a terrible disappointment to him."

"I don't think that's true."

"Oh, for God's sake, Davie!" he said, rapping the table with his knuckles—it seemed to attract attention all around the dining room. "For God's sake," he repeated quietly. "You don't realize what I have *done*. You cannot imagine. And it is all because of that thing. I left it behind in India, but it has not left me. No one understands—not you, not Father. Here." He reached into his waistcoat and drew out a letter—it was post-marked at Forfar, and addressed in our father's precise copperplate handwriting. "He sent me this."

I took the envelope and opened it. It was a short note, which I have kept.

Walter H. Hunt

Rescobie Manse
19 December 1853

My dear Son:

I have concluded that I must make an attempt to assist you while my strength still remains. I comprehend the obstacle before me, though you keep your reasons for your actions to yourself; but you are not aware of the resources I have at my command.

We are expecting you to visit Rescobie for Twelfth Night, and I will bring this matter to a conclusion. I will do all that is in my power.

My love for you is not bounded by time or circumstance; you are my beloved son and I remain

Your devoted Father,
James Esdaile

"She will *kill* him, Davie," he said in a pained whisper. "I do not know what resources he thinks he commands—but they cannot withstand her."

"He believes otherwise."

"Can you explain this?"

"Not to your satisfaction, I think. But our father has studied many things, Jamie. There is a body of knowledge he possesses that he has begun to communicate to me, and I suspect that is what he intends to use."

"What sort of knowledge?"

"If I tell you, can she compel you to tell her?"

"I…am not sure."

"Then you will have to wait and see for yourself. Father is determined to do this, I see."

"Apparently. It will be one more thing for which I will be judged."

WILLIAM DAVEY

I sat with the senior Esdaile's letter in my hand, rereading it. Clearly, the man sitting near me understood its meaning far better, but was not ready to reveal its import.

The afternoon had gone by quickly and once again the light outside was fading. The sun had returned and was casting long beams of light through the window, but that would soon be gone.

"Your father died not long after Twelfth Night."

"Jamie was right," David Esdaile answered. "Our father was strong, but not as strong as Eliza. If I had possessed his knowledge, I might have been able to withstand her. Our father might still be alive, Jamie might still be alive…"

"What was this knowledge that your father possessed?"

Esdaile stood once again and went to the highest shelf on the bookcase. He removed a half-dozen books and set them on an occasional table, then reached to the back of the case and moved a wooden panel aside. He drew out two small folios and brought them over to where he sat.

"When my father had his stroke almost twenty years ago, he was in the midst of copying out this book." He tapped one of the folios, which looked older and more weathered than the other. "He told me that it was the most precious thing he possessed, and that I would understand someday."

He placed the book in my hand, and then opened the other in his lap. I recognized his own handwriting on the pages of the folio.

"This is my copy of the same book. I transcribed it from my father's volume, just as he transcribed it from another's copy. It is the way this knowledge is transmitted, one to another. It is an esoteric tradition that comes from missionaries in the Near East."

Very carefully, I opened the book. Like the letter I still held, it was written in the elder James Esdaile's precise hand.

I am the Great Name who maketh his light.

I have come to thee, O Osiris, and I offer praise unto thee.

I am pure from the issues which are carried away from thee.

Thy name hath been made in Re-stau when it hath fallen therein.

Homage to thee, O Osiris, in thy strength and in thy power, thou hast obtained the mastery in Re-stau.

Thou art raised up, O Osiris, in thy might and in thy power, thou art raised up, O Osiris, and thy might is in Re-stau, and thy power is in Abtu.

Thou goest round about through the generations of men, O thou Being who circlest, thou Ra.

Behold, verily, I have said unto thee, O Osiris, 'I am the spiritual body of the God,' and I say, 'Let it come to pass that I shall never be repulsed before thee, O Osiris.'

I looked up from the book, and cannot imagine the astonishment that must have showed in my face.

"Sir," I said. "What am I looking at?"

Esdaile looked over at the page before me. "That is Chapter One Hundred and Nineteen. It deals with knowing the true and powerful name of the great Osiris, the judge of the souls of the dead.

"It is from a remarkable book, the contents of which have been passed from hand to hand for many years in the way I have just described. I expect that the text has drifted through so many manual copies. Within its covers, my father thought he had found the key to destroying Eliza and saving Jamie's soul. That he failed to do so is not a fault of the knowledge—it was his own weakness."

I handed the book back to Esdaile, who placed it beneath his own copy in his lap.

"I don't understand—this is some sort of book from ancient Egypt?"

"Aye, that it is. That culture knew more about death and…after death than any other, Reverend Davey. The sort of creature with which Jamie had contracted was known that long ago: it is an enemy that has no doubt existed since man's earliest days.

"The original title of the book is *The Chapters of Coming Forth By Day*, but you might know it—if you have heard of it at all—as the *Theban Book of the Dead.*"

CHAPTER 21

The soul revealed

WILLIAM DAVEY

I have my own commonplace-book from the time, and when I look back at it I can recall my confusion during my time in Scotland that March. The connection between an ancient culture in India, the death cult of Pharaonic Egypt, and the mysteries of Viking polar explorers were like parts of machines—but parts of *different* machines.

Reverend Esdaile had returned the folios to their concealed place, but not in any way that suggested he was hiding them from me. I could have taken them down, or even purloined them, if that had been my wish—but it would have accomplished nothing. My host told me that it was as much *interpretation* as *comprehension*: I should have to be like a Biblical scholar to understand it. As to its relationship with India...and the Northmen...it defied assimilation.

We set the subject aside for the evening. Almost as a relief to the earnest of our discussions, I commented on a piece of finely made lace that Mary Esdaile was using for a formal table covering. It was an exceptional piece of needlework, the kind that could have been made by any of my family—it might well have been: she told me that it had come from Devonshire in her grandmother's day. She was surprised at my interest, and impressed at my expertise.

It made her no less wary of me, however—and she still seemed fearful. I do not know if it was *me* she feared, or just the business in which I was engaged—brought back into her house after she thought it had gone forever.

Though Esdaile had shown me the hand-copied folios of the Egyptian books, this alone did not adequately explain what they

153

meant to him—and how his father had intended to confront Eliza at Twelfth Night six years ago. Therefore, my questions had not been answered, and I was not ready to go.

As it happened, Esdaile had one more thing to tell me before I left Rescobie Manse, something that put much of the rest in perspective.

DAVID ESDAILE

The question I know you want to ask, Reverend Davey, is why a pair of rustic ministers in rural Scotland would take an interest in an Egyptian funereal book. It truly comes down to the same reason why a Devonshire lace-maker would immerse himself in the study of mesmerism. It is a conduit to power: it pays no heed to nationality, or education, or most of all station. The meanest mechanic can become a powerful man. The greatest landed peer can find himself powerless.

The Chapters of Coming Forth By Day explains the precautions that mortals must take when dealing with beings such as these that are not of their kind. What Jamie had done was to make a binding contract with such a being, to protect himself and protect the secret of the ancient thing he had found. He sacrificed all that he had—he committed a terrible crime—and yet he accomplished his goal.

The crime? It should be obvious. I assumed you already understood that. No—no, it was *not* what was done to our father: Eliza did that, and I suppose he was complicit by bringing her here. But he was resolved to stay away—indeed, he had already made arrangements to leave Scotland even before that. My admonition that he must depart—as I told you earlier—only confirmed that decision.

He had determined to remove himself from Scotland, to a place near to London—Sydenham, where the Crystal Palace had been rebuilt. He would not have come with Eliza that January night if Father had not insisted.

There are two ways in which one can dismiss such a being. First, an adept can seek to simply banish it beyond the Glass Door—or back beyond nightfall, as your parlance has it. The harm to the mortal is often irrevocable; Father assumed that if Jamie tried, it would kill him.

The other is more dangerous: to sever the silver cord between the *chthonic* spirit and the mortal bound to it, and then thwart its hunger. It requires the adept to maintain control of the four cardinal points while he severs the cord and banishes the spirit. A stronger, younger man might have been able to withstand it—but Father could not.

You will forgive me for not relating the particulars of that night. It still pains me to think of it—and to know how helpless I was. I had only partly transcribed the book; I was not ready to take my place as an adept. I recollect that he was unable to complete the first invocation, though I think that he came agonizingly close: all of this was done while we celebrated the holiday, with five little children about. It was as if there was a silent struggle taking place that only a few of us could see.

Father showed no sign of having suffered at first—but after my brother and his wife departed the next morning he complained of pain in his chest. He seemed to recover; and then shortly afterward he suffered a final, catastrophic event. The children did not see their grandfather die, but my Mary and I did.

Jamie was far away when it happened. I sent him a letter—an angry one: I shall not show that to you; I do not need to, I think. I told him that he should leave Scotland and go far away, that if Eliza came near Rescobie I would try the same as Father had done and then my death would be on his hands as well.

But as I told you, he had already determined that he should leave on his own.

The Crystal Palace has mesmeric properties? Yes, of course. It is built to precise measurements. I have a copy of Phillips' guide to the palace and park—Jamie sent it to me, though I never acknowledged it, for…I wanted nothing to do with him. But I perused the book. They built it on the top of a hill, set at a precise angle, with two towers placed on either side: all of the indications suggest that the builders employed a first-rate dowser.

But it explains why he chose Sydenham. It came as something of a surprise to you? Really. He must have known that it would have those properties. My brother was misguided, Reverend Davey. But he was also one of the most brilliant men I ever knew.

Yes. I forgave him long ago. Even for Father, even that. I have even forgiven *you*—because I see your ignorance. No: do not deny it—though you have learned a great deal here, you know less than you did when you arrived. Are you sure that Jamie did the wrong thing by betraying you—if it was truly a betrayal?

I rather expected that would be your response. And as my mother used to say, they shall truly write that upon your headstone.

There is something you need to see—something that will make you understand him better, though I am sure your heart is hard enough that it may not change your opinion. I would never have received it but for Mary—he sent it to her, fearing that I might have refused it or left it unopened. She is a kindly soul, and has taught me much about forgiveness: though I daresay at first she wanted nothing to do with you coming here.

Indeed. She told you that. Well, she knows her Scripture well, the affliction of being a minister's wife. In any case, I fear Jamie took exactly the correct approach: I might well have left it sealed, like Mary's last letter to Mary Ann, like words unspoken.

WILLIAM DAVEY

Esdaile opened his journal to a page he had left marked, where a letter was spread out on the pages. I recognized this hand, as well—I had received letters from India that looked just like it. As he turned the book so that I could read it, he hesitated—as if he was not sure, in the end, whether he should reveal this to me. But he pointed to the right-hand page and said, "Here: this is the section of consequence."

I glanced at the date of the letter: December 1858, a bit before the time he had sent word to me that he wished to meet with me in Sydenham.

You have every right to feel as if I have violated the principles that our father and our mother taught us. But time passes without any way to halt it, and the circumstances of the moment sometimes press difficult choices upon us with no alternatives. Thus it was with me.

The being within the statue taught me a great deal about its past—its ancient culture, the means by which its vessel was crafted and the way in which it came to be trapped within. It can break free if it can find a suitable conduit, by which I mean a person, with sufficient power and desire.

For a time, it thought I was that person. For a time, I confess, I thought I was that person as well.

When I realized its true ambition, I turned away from helping it. For indeed, just as it was helping me as I treated those afflicted in Hooghly, I was helping it by feeding it what it most desired: the thoughts and sentiments of those who wished to do violence. It was, ironically, a perfect setting for its hunger. Each week, each month it grew stronger and I grew weaker.

But all of that is past and you understand it. You understand the devil's bargain that I chose to make, and you saw what I brought back with me to Scotland. But I must tell you that Father's objective was right but his analysis was wrong in a way that we could not have known at the time.

I have never described to you the way in which this chthonic being came to be my wife. I was not present at the actual moment at which it took place; the young woman—for there was an actual Eliza: a beautiful, intelligent, sensitive, innocent woman—was taken by the spirit. For these many years I assumed that the persona of Eliza Weatherhead was pushed into the outer darkness or utterly destroyed: after all, such would be my fate.

But I was wrong. I was completely wrong. On a particular occasion last week as I sat in our parlor here in Sydenham and Eliza sat opposite, she seemed to drowse—and for a short span, ten or fifteen seconds, no more— the true Eliza Weatherhead looked out at me from behind those eyes. They pleaded with me—they spoke to me more poignantly than any words could express. I could feel the change in Eliza's aura at that moment.

I knew that the young woman had been seized by the chthonic being and that she lay trapped within. I had not destroyed her existence as I always assumed that I had done. Instead, I had caused it to be imprisoned.

Thus I have embarked upon a course of action that shall free me from the curse I have brought upon myself; that shall protect the secret place where the statue has been concealed; and, God willing, shall free an innocent from an unbearable imprisonment for which I am sure I will be held to account in the afterlife.

I hesitate to ask such a great boon of you, my dear brother, but I ask that you forgive me for wronging you and that you pray for me. We will not speak to each other again in this life.

When I looked up from my reading, I could see tears in David Esdaile's eyes.

"He knew that she was not a manifestation," I said.

"Only at the last. He hoped that she would survive the—his death—and not be mad."

"She is quite sane."

"You have spoken with her."

"Yes, at some length. I remained with her after James committed suicide, and she told me part of the story. I have even brought you a letter in her hand. Now I understand more clearly why she did not hate him."

"No." Esdaile wiped his eyes. "And I do not hate him, either. Nor do I hate you, sir. But I think that it is time for you to leave my house. When I bid you good-bye, I will wish you Godspeed—but I do not expect to see you ever again."

CHAPTER 22

Recoil

WILLIAM DAVEY

I had sent John Jackson a telegraph message from Edinburgh with the time that my train would arrive at King's Cross Station. Amusingly, it was due to come during the early afternoon of All Fools' Day.

John had been my partner as a mesmeric lecturer and co-author for fifteen years before James Esdaile took his own life. He had been clerk of the Committee's plenum since the mid-1840s, when I had concluded that Horace Eden—who had been Quillinan's amanuensis—was far too much of a crazy old fool for my tastes. Jackson was less old; he was also less crazy. Still, most of our colleagues called him 'the cripple', just as I was called 'the lace-maker' to our more well-born members. They knew he was my trusted friend, but it was clear that they thought his brain limped along with his leg.

As the train slowed to a stop on platform 9, I saw Jackson waiting among the crowd. He was watching for me—he had news to convey, but the newspapers I had read en route had already notified me. I now waited for an explanation.

"Welcome back, Will," he said to me as I found him on the platform. "You heard the news from Manchester."

"About Braid, yes. I assume that we have some report of the event."

"We certainly do. There are all sorts of rumors, but Bray is in the city and has some details. You're not going to like it."

"Oh, I'm not?"

"No." Jackson stopped walking, standing beside a pillar to get out of the press. "You should know, Will, that Dickens is demanding

159

an emergency meeting because of it. He doesn't know you're here—but that can't remain secret for long."

"Since you came here to meet me."

"I come to King's Cross often enough, as all of my friends in the Committee know." He smiled, stretching the muscles in his lamed leg. "I come to commune with Boudicca's ghost." He stomped on the platform, and then led the way onward through the crowd.

Charles Bray was waiting in a private room at the Vienna, a small café near the British Museum. He was a middle-aged man, thin almost to being gaunt. When we entered, he looked up with an expression that mixed fear and hunger; he had some sort of drink in front of him that had a cloying, sweet smell. He began to rise from his seat.

"Davey," he began, "I—"

"Wait," I said. The simplest gesture returned him to a sitting position. Bray was much more a spiritualist than a mesmerist—and more of a crackpot than either. But he evidently had something to say.

I made him wait. Jackson and I took our seats; there was a gin bottle on the table that Bray had evidently placed as far from him as possible—I thought I remembered that he was a temperance man as well.

I took a copy of the *Times* from my portfolio and opened it on the table. I had carefully marked Braid's obituary.

"I spoke with Dr. Braid at the Mechanics Institute a bit over three weeks ago," I said to Bray. "I directed that he be left alone. Who violated my order?"

"Reverend Davey, the circumstances of Dr. Braid's death are somewhat complicated."

"That is not what I want to hear." I slammed my palm on the table, directly over the obituary. Glasses and gin bottle jumped an inch. Bray jumped at least two inches. "He was to be left alone. Nothing is gained by his death. Nothing at all. Who—is—*responsible?*"

Bray summoned up all of his energy and some amount of his courage. I didn't know how much he had of either. "It was not a simple matter of roughing him up with a cosh, Davey. Dr. Braid was killed by his daughter. He was killed by Ann Braid."

"He's opaque to mesmeric attack. What could she possibly—"

"She reached beyond nightfall, Davey," he whispered. His hand shook slightly as he raised his glass and drank from it. "She summoned *chthonic* beings to induce apoplexy. She stopped his heart."

The silence in the room was profound—as if someone had draped a cloth over the proceedings. And in that moment I cursed myself for a fool and cursed my own arrogance and cursed Ann Braid, who truly had no interest in making a good marriage and turning her attention to giving her father a house full of beautiful grandchildren.

I had been shown this outcome and I had not seen it for what it was.

That is not why I am here, the Levantine had said to me on the platform at Oxford Road Station in Manchester.

And he and his fellow *stoicheia* had told me one other thing.

We are everywhere, they had said.

I might have come close to being killed on that train platform—or it might have been just an illusion. But the *chthonic* being had told me the truth. It had not come to Manchester to give me an 'object lesson'; it had come because it had been summoned…by Ann Braid.

While I was on the train to Leeds, thankful to have escaped with my life, it was in the process of stopping James Braid's heart.

"Where is she now?"

"This is clearly something she planned for some time," Bray said. "Braid may have been opaque to mesmeric attack, but the structure of the Mechanics' Institute was—"

"Where. Is. She."

I was letting my anger get the better of me. But Charles Bray—

an effete, middle-aged ribbon factory owner from Coventry—happened to be the bearer of evil tidings.

"Trafford. She is in a small private sanitarium. There was—as I understand it—some backlash."

"Explain."

Bray did not immediately answer, but took another drink from his glass. I looked across at Jackson; he had heard some of this before, I expect, and rather than soften the blow for me or make Bray's life easier, had chosen to make him explain it all.

I was glad to count John Jackson as a friend, because he could be a heartless enemy.

"It is my understanding," Bray said at last, "that Miss Braid summoned, or arranged to summon, more than a dozen *chthonic* and possibly other spirits—perhaps including photic ones, since there was evidence of some amount of fire at Braid's office—and used them together to kill Dr. Braid. When they had finished, a few of them turned on her and were only stopped by the actions of their—colleagues. Miss Braid was affected by the encounter."

"How so?"

"I understand that she has lost the ability to walk."

"You have the name of this sanitarium, I trust."

He reached into his watch-pocket and drew out a small visitation card, pushing it across the table at me. "This is the place."

"I shall go there tomorrow morning. She waited—she waited until I was out of the domain. She may have even been in Manchester when I was there, preparing these pleasantries."

"What are you going to do?"

"Do you really want to know?"

Bray didn't look up at me again, but said, "No. Forget it, Davey. Forget that I asked the question."

There was no way to avoid the trouble that Dickens might cause if I simply decamped for Manchester; it was far better to simply confront him. I would have liked to have that meeting take place on neutral or favorable ground—Vernon's rooms, or one of the law-offices or medical offices of a Committee member, for example—but that was not to be. Instead, I was obliged to accept his invitation to come to Tavistock House—anything but neutral ground.

I arrived there in the evening, in the rain—fitting, actually: Dickens had written rather disparagingly about London rain in *Little Dorrit*: how it did nothing but stir foul smells and clog the gutters. Tavistock House had been the author's family home, and he often got up amateur and semi-professional plays on its stage. He was done with that now, as he was largely done with his family.

A servant met me at the door, which was protected by a brick overhang to keep out the weather, and admitted me to a parlor. I had not been in the house for some time; it seemed to me that many of the furnishings and knick-knacks had been removed, giving it the look of a place scarcely lived in.

I was kept waiting ten minutes or so until the great man swept in. He had the look of someone who had a considerable amount of other business and had no interest in departing from it for very long.

"Reverend Davey," he said. He looked at me, then peered out the window onto Tavistock Place, where the rain was fiercely assaulting the cobble-stones. "Have you been offered tea or something else to drink?"

"I have not. But I am not in need."

"Very well." He led us to two deep armchairs. The fire had been banked, and there was a chill, slightly damp air in the room. "Let me get directly to the point."

"Please do."

"I am very disturbed by the events in Manchester, Davey. Very upset indeed. This is not at all appropriate for our organization."

"Doctor Braid's death came as something of a shock."

"I cannot see how it should be that much of a surprise. It is high time that the brutes be removed from the Committee—indeed, it may suggest that we are conducting ourselves in a completely inappropriate manner."

"I do not take your meaning, sir."

"Oh, you don't. Truly. Well, let me clarify it for you."

He rubbed his chin, below his dense beard. I had known Dickens for twenty years, and when I first met him he was clean-shaven and rather unprepossessing, except for an intense gaze and a deep, powerful voice; now he had more the look of the Swiss mesmeric impresario Lafontaine—more heavy-set and bearded. The voice, however, and to some extent the gaze, still remained.

"I would be obliged."

"Organizations such as ours take their cues from their leader-ship. Your demonstrations—if I may call them that—are taken as indications that force and intimidation are the order of the day, and that the ends will justify the means. This must stop, sir. This is not the way."

"Sometimes," I answered carefully, "'demonstrations' are necessary."

"Carlyle tells me that you even resorted to such behavior in Edinburgh. In *public*. Surely it is not necessary every time."

"I think we are agreed on that point."

"Then why in God's name did you permit this to occur? Braid was not an advocate of the Art, but he was a *public figure*, a man of standing. It wouldn't do to simply *dispense* with him."

"How do you think he died, Mr. Dickens?"

"I assume that it was no sudden fit. Men such as Braid do not jump—they are pushed."

"He was killed by his daughter," I said simply.

Over the next few seconds, Dickens' expression moved from hauteur to disbelief to surprise, and then began to verge into disgust.

"How?"

"She reached beyond nightfall," I said. "She summoned—from what I understand—a number of *stoicheia* and overwhelmed him."

Dickens sat silently for a moment, then said, "I think, there-fore, that this only reinforces my intentions. I shall resign from membership, Davey. Effective immediately. You may consider yourself informed that all of my support, including financial support, will cease."

"I am sorry to hear that," I answered. "What do you intend to do?"

"Do? I don't see as it is any of your business."

"I would not dream of prying into your private—affairs," I said, and saw Dickens scowl; his quite public divorce from Catherine was still a current topic at that time.

"Then I see no need to discuss it with you."

"As you wish," I said. "But I will ask you to keep in mind that the Committee does not look kindly upon attempts to establish rival organizations—and I do not look kindly upon them either."

"I am a public figure. You would not dare dictate to me."

"James Braid was a public figure," I retorted, but both of us knew that it was not the same.

"And it astounds me that you would dare to assault him."

"Ann Braid's actions were not at my direction, Dickens."

"Is she not in your control, Mr. Chairman? Will she then come after *me* with her—nightfall allies?"

"I do not expect her to do anything of the sort, at least at present. From what I understand she barely survived this event."

"You are sure of that."

"I am."

"Then I expect that you will have no more such trouble in the future." He stood, and I followed. "I do not intend to remain in residence here in London much longer. I have very little affection for this house after all—I shall remain at Gad's Hill instead. You may convey my regards to our—colleagues."

"I shall do that, sir," I said, not sure what else to say.

He walked me to the door, not even troubling himself to call a servant, though the butler was already nearby with my coat and hat.

"You know your way out," he said, and without another word turned and walked up the stairs.

I thought about framing a reply, but instead shrugged on the coat and took my hat and umbrella.

I know my way out, I thought to myself as I descended the stairs to my waiting carriage, wondering all the way if it were actually true.

PART THREE

The glass door

"Integrity without knowledge
is weak and useless,
and knowledge without integrity
is dangerous and dreadful."
—Samuel Johnson, *Rasselas*

CHAPTER 23

Preliminaries

3 April, 1860
Sydenham

Dear Reverend Davey:

I am in receipt of your letter of the 1ˢᵗ instant, and wish to inform you that I have no interest in revisiting the subjects of our earlier discussions and consider the matter closed. You of all people should be aware of the acutely painful nature of my memories, and my desire not to speak further of them.

It would therefore be my preference that you refrain from calling upon me on this or any other subject in future.

Your obd't s'vt
Eliza Weatherhead Esdaile

WILLIAM DAVEY

On the day I departed for Manchester, John Jackson accompanied me to the train station and expressed surprise regarding my correspondence with Eliza Esdaile. It was not that she should decline to receive me—that was quite predictable, for the reasons she stated—but rather that I should leave it at that.

"It's rather unlike you, Will," he said to me. "Eliza has information you need. She may be the *only* person who has it. I'm not sure why you don't just go get it."

"She is not a member of the Committee."

"And that matters because…"

"John." I looked at him; he was grinning, as if he was waiting for me to reveal that I was joking, or testing his loyalty. But I was not. "It matters because the lady has suffered greatly, and has earned her respite."

"You're sure that you're not feeling unwell."

"I am in perfect health." I looked down the crowded platform and then back at my old friend and lecture partner. "There is a difference between the lady's status and that of members of our society. For you—or me—or Ann Braid, for that matter—we have entered this realm of our own choice, while she was trapped by circumstance."

"And by James Esdaile."

"Indeed. So let me be clear: she has not joined our world, she was pulled into it. She has suffered enough. I am going to see what Miss Braid has to say for herself, and I believe that I now know enough to understand what she has to tell me. I do not need to bother Eliza Esdaile in order to respond appropriately."

"I will be interested to know what you have to say when you return. Assuming she doesn't set her *chthonic* allies on you."

"I do not fear that, John."

"You should, Will. I think you truly should."

I did not respond, as if I had nothing else to say on the subject. Yet I wasn't sure if he might be pointing out a true danger that I might not be able to withstand.

Trafford was a crowded, somewhat run-down borough sandwiched between Manchester and Salford. It did not trouble me to walk through its streets, though I suspect that it might have daunted some of my professional colleagues—certain practitioners of the Art, such as my new Scottish deputy Thomas Carlyle, had little time for the lower classes except as experimental subjects. It would have made Milnes or Lord Morpeth blanch to find themselves in grimy middle England. For me it was no worse than the East End.

Following a few inquiries, I found the sanitarium in a relatively pastoral section of Trafford, not far from the place where the railway passed through; there was a little park nearby, which afforded its residents a pleasant vantage and provided some distance to separate them from the residences and textile mills and the Bridgewater Canal beyond.

Upon presenting myself at the entrance as a clergyman and friend of the family I was escorted into a pleasant waiting-room, set with a few straight-backed chairs and small tables and decorated with vague paintings of flowers—perhaps executed by residents as part of therapy. Presently I was joined by a middle-aged man, who from his dress and appearance was a physician or surgeon.

"Good morning," I began. "I am—"

"I know very well who you are, Reverend Davey. Won't you sit," he said, gesturing—indeed, making the subtlest of mesmeric passes—in the direction of a pair of chairs. His power was almost amusing, particularly since he had identified me and presumably knew of my own prowess with the Art.

I took a chair and he joined me a few feet away.

"I do not believe I have made your acquaintance, Doctor—"

"Daniel. Richard Daniel."

His knowledge of me was thus explained. Daniel was James Braid's close associate, and—it was said—Ann Braid's paramour.

"I am pleased to meet you, sir."

Daniel made no observation about this comment. "I am curious what brings you to Manchester."

"I thought to call upon Miss Braid and inquire about her health."

"She is…recovering." He caught my eye and held it; once again I sensed that he was attempting to engage me using the Art, but its potency was negligible. I met his gaze and applied my own skill until he looked away.

"The death of Dr. Braid is a great loss for science, Dr. Daniel. I am sure that Miss Braid feels so as well."

"To be sure."

"You worked with Dr. Braid for some time, I believe?"

"Nearly twenty years. He was like a father to me, sir, and an excellent mentor and teacher." He was choosing his words carefully, as if examining each of them as they were spoken. "But we must move on with our lives."

Something attracted my attention suddenly: a slight movement, as if some part of a wall behind me had shifted. The air in the room grew very slightly colder.

I turned and noticed someone in the room who had not been there before—a younger woman, perhaps in her mid-twenties, dressed modestly like a lady's maid. Her arms were crossed over her chest, and she gave me a glance that was full of malice. My perceptions were more than sufficient to indicate to me that she was a *chthonic* spirit—not a very powerful one, to be sure, but a spirit nonetheless.

It explained how she had entered the room without my notice, and without a doorway to provide access.

"I see that we can dispense with a certain amount of pretense."

"I am glad that you appreciate the circumstances, Reverend," Daniel said. If he, too, was a *stoicheia*, it defied my perceptions to confirm it, but his quick glances at the servant convinced me that we both knew that *she* was.

"I should like to see Miss Braid."

"No doubt." He leaned back in his chair; the servant saved me the trouble of turning slightly to keep her in view by walking across the room to stand beside Dr. Daniel. As she passed by, I felt the brush of a frigid breeze. "I commend your bravery in coming here alone and unprotected. Most of the Committee would be quaking in their boots."

"I am neither alone nor unprotected, Doctor. And I do not quake easily."

"So Annie has told me. You must realize, sir, that she has considerable admiration for your skill."

"But no respect for my authority."

"In general, no, but that is in part because you have wielded it as such a blunt instrument."

"It is mine to wield. Does she wish to offer a formal challenge?"

The servant opened her mouth to speak. There was a sound that was not quite a sound—like a great chorus taking in a breath before launching into a hymn.

I raised my left hand in a warding gesture, but Daniel looked up at her and said, "No."

She closed her mouth again, her face changing to an expression of mild disappointment.

I lowered my hand to let it lie relaxed in my lap.

"They are very impulsive," Daniel said. "As I am sure you know."

"You have not answered my question."

"Regarding a 'formal challenge'? How very quaint that you even pose the question. No—Annie is in no condition to offer such a challenge at this time."

"Regrettable."

"You think so. Once again, I can only admire your courage."

"And I yours. I assure you, Dr. Daniel, there are very few ways to escape the dire consequences of these sorts of contracts." He began to reply, but I lifted my hand: he stopped speaking at once. "And as I am sure you have been told, the little trick James Esdaile employed is unlikely to work again."

"You understand very little of them."

"Are you sure? My recent education has been very thorough. I think I understand them very well. What I do *not* understand is why anyone would enter into a bargain with them." This time I focused my attention on the lady's maid.

She appeared ready to speak again but seemed unable to do so, which made her appear even angrier.

Daniel looked from me to the maid and back.

"They have very long memories, Reverend Davey," he said.

"No doubt. So do I."

The sanitarium was scarcely inhabited, which ultimately came as no surprise. We passed several closed doors; on a few occasions I heard noises of one sort or another, low moans or mutterings or a soft hiss, but did my best to ignore them.

At last we came to the end of the hall.

Daniel knocked once on a particular door, and the lady's maid from downstairs opened it slightly. If I had not previously been sure that she was a *stoicheia*, her ability to transport herself confirmed it.

"Margaret," Daniel said to her, as if we had not seen each other already. "Is the lady receiving visitors?"

"I will see," she said, and closed the door. I had tensed, unsure what might emerge, and was relieved when she spoke normally.

After a moment she opened the door again. "Yes, Doctor. She is ready now," she said, and stepped aside so that we could enter the sick-room. Sitting in the bed, propped by pillows but looking pale as death, was Ann Braid.

"Why, Reverend Davey," she said, offering me a remarkably pleasant smile. "So good of you to visit."

CHAPTER 24

Recovery

WILLIAM DAVEY

I had been acquainted with Ann Braid for many years—she had appeared at a meeting of the Committee when Quillinan was still Chairman, usually in the company of Reverend Pyne or Dr. Higginson. She was scarcely a grown woman when she had first joined us; her surname had carried some weight, and there were some among the younger members who had sought to use that fact to gain familiarity with her. It was never successful.

She soon proved herself adept at the Art, despite her father's strident denials of its efficacy. She was also clearly disinterested in respecting authority, though she stopped short of open rebellion—preferring to cause trouble without confronting me.

But in all the time I had known her, she had never met me with a smile.

"I had heard that you were hurt," I said. I stepped into the room; Margaret closed the door. Richard Daniel walked to the bed and stood beside it, lifting Ann Braid's wrist to examine her pulse.

"I am recovering."

"I see that," I answered. "I assumed it was worse."

"I've had some help. Margaret, you have met, I see." The smile returned, which was disturbing in and of itself. "And my fiancée." She directed it to Daniel.

"I wasn't aware that you had agreed to marry. It's a shame that your father isn't here to see it."

The smile vanished. Her attention left Daniel as she pulled her hand free; he turned to look at me as well.

"Your attempt at wit falls on deaf ears, Reverend," she said icily. "Perhaps we should dispense with all of this pretense."

"I thought we had left it in the receiving room."

She glanced at Daniel and then back at me. "I think you should come to the point on why you are here, so we do not waste any more of each other's time. I—"

Her words were cut off by a fit of coughing. Daniel took her hand again, and leaned closer to place his hand on the back of her head. She bent down while holding a cloth over her mouth. Margaret took a step closer but hesitated.

I affected an air of total indifference, looking out the window across the park at the city of Manchester, clouded by haze in the distance.

"Perhaps you should take your leave," Daniel said.

"No," Ann Braid said. She looked up at me again. "No, I'm all right."

"You are not 'all right', my dear. You—"

"Reverend Davey," she said quietly, waving Daniel away. "I... am recovering from the effects of a slight miscalculation. But I assure you that it is only a temporary setback. You have a tendency to underestimate others' powers. I suggest to you that you do not underestimate mine."

"Why is that?"

"Because, sir," she said, "you do so at your peril. My new allies have given me...certain insights into the true capabilities that our Art only barely touches. By your *moralistic* constraints—yours, those of that creature Jackson, and any number of others—you have neglected possibilities that can make us ten or a hundred times more powerful than we are. If only your flimsy *objections* didn't get in the way."

"I suppose you'll be demonstrating your powers on me now. As a challenge."

"Not at this time," she said. "I am—" for a moment she looked again as if she was about to collapse into another paroxysm of coughing, but she fiercely clutched the bedclothes and kept her focus on me. "I am...not looking to challenge your leadership of the Committee, Reverend Davey. I neither need, nor desire, to replace you in your present position."

"I am relieved and gratified."

"You are nothing of the sort," she snapped back, and again began to cough. Margaret reached over and touched her leg through the bed blanket; the coughing immediately subsided, but Ann Braid's face took on an unpleasant grimace.

"Reverend Davey," Daniel said, "I would prefer that you leave."

I thought about a retort, then shrugged and walked toward the door. Again I heard the sound like a half-silent chorus—and I turned quickly on my heel, my left hand lifted with three fingers up and little finger and thumb curled into my palm, as if I were giving a medieval bishop's blessing.

Margaret the *chthonios'* mouth hung open for a split-second, then snapped shut like an iron door.

"I will wait in the receiving room," I said, opening the door behind me without looking, and backing through it, never lowering my hand.

✙

You understand very little of them, Richard Daniel had said to me. What I did know I didn't like, but he was certainly right. He characterized them as impulsive—*as I am sure you know*, he had added. Had I seen evidence of that impulsiveness on the Oxford Road train platform, or had that been a lesson that the Levantine and his associates—who were *everywhere*, as he had told me—had prepared specifically for me?

My thoughts chased each other in circles like a pack of hungry dogs. I did my best to compose myself while I waited in the receiving-room; I assumed that my direct interaction with Ann Braid had concluded, at least for the day.

Richard Daniel reappeared at last and crossed to where I sat. His professional manner remained, but there was more than a hint of malice in his tone when he addressed me.

"She is resting as comfortably as she can," he said. "Your interview has upset her, Reverend, as I am sure you can imagine."

"Murdering her father with the help of—what was it? A dozen nightfall beings?—upsets *me*. I assure you, Doctor, her emotional state is of no particular concern to me."

Daniel sat down. He looked angry, resentful—and perhaps more than a little weary. I wondered to myself what his part had been in the death of Dr. Braid.

"She is right, you know. You underestimate her powers."

"They're not *her* powers, Daniel. They come from the creatures who own her soul and who will consume it when she dies. What she can now undertake she does with their sufferance."

"It's not like that at all."

"I beg to differ. It is *exactly* like that, sir. It is a fundamental mistake to think that it is anything different. I cannot help but ask—what deal have you made with them?"

"I am not the least involved."

"Once again, I am forced to point out your error, Dr. Daniel. You are involved from the lapels of your coat to the soles of your boots. You'd best make sure the water doesn't rise and drown you entire."

"Your metaphors are colorful."

"Clerical training," I said, touching my collar. "Denying your involvement wouldn't even hold up in a court of Queen's Bench. Don't expect it to work among those who know better. The question is, though: what am I to do, and what do you intend?"

"I don't believe that you need to do anything, Reverend Davey. You can simply let things be."

"She may not even survive."

Daniel frowned. "I am doing everything medically possible to make sure she survives," he hissed at me. "I will restore her to health."

"Or else," I said, "they *eat* her."

"I will restore her to health," he repeated, his face stony.

"Fair enough. But she has gone beyond even defying my

177

explicit order to leave James Braid alone. She *killed her father*, man. She called upon a whole battalion of nightfall creatures to do it. This is the woman you want to save? This is the one you want to marry?"

"You are very judgmental, Reverend Davey."

I looked up to see Margaret, the *chthonios* and lady's maid, standing a dozen feet away.

"You don't understand *us* at all, either," I said, then returned my attention to Daniel—though it made me nervous to take my attention from the nightfall creature nearby. "We are judgmental by nature. And unless she is challenging me, Dr. Daniel, *right now*, she has defied my authority and spit in the face of the Committee. I am calling her to account for that.

"You asked why I am here, sir. *That* is why I am here. To demand an explanation—and to determine what, if any, extenuation she might have for the heinous crime that we both know she committed. If she has nothing to offer, then I will ask no more questions on that account."

"You are passing judgment," the nightfall creature said.

"I am only gathering evidence," I said, not taking my eyes off Richard Daniel. "The Committee will pass judgment."

"And then?" she asked.

"I do not know."

"Very well," Daniel said. He looked at Margaret. "Leave us," he said.

"I do not answer to you."

Daniel stood up. "Leave us," he repeated. "The person you *do* answer to will cause you considerable pain if you do not do as I say."

She gave him a look of pure hatred, then softened it to mere petulance. She turned on her heel and walked directly into the far wall and vanished.

"Impulsive," he said. After a moment he sat down again.

"I see."

"I will tell you what will happen," Daniel said. "The Committee can choose any verdict it likes. It may assuage its pride by assessing any punishment. But it will not be *levied*. There is no one, even you, Reverend, who can coerce Annie."

"If she survives."

This time it was Daniel whose expression was full of malice. "If you do anything to her—"

"I do not waste my powers on fools or innocents. She is no innocent, Daniel." I stood up and placed my hat on my head. "I have not yet determined into which category I place you."

With nothing further to say, I stood and walked out of the receiving room, down the front hallway and out the door.

As I walked across the lawn toward Trafford, I felt the icy breeze once more, and turned to see the *chthonios* Margaret walking toward me.

"Reverend Davey," she said, stopping a dozen feet away once more—as if keeping her distance.

"I do not have anything to say to you."

"Then you can simply listen. Soon the Glass Door will be open, and all of your—posturing—will mean nothing. You should make provision for that day."

"I am not convinced that day will ever come," I said.

"It will come," Margaret said. "Of that you can be sure. Only the key is needed. When found and employed, the mild amusements I hoped to share with you will seem like love-taps."

"I am not prepared to surrender to—whims."

"I see," she said, making a little pout. "You should be aware, Reverend: when that day comes—when the Glass Door is opened—we will not waste power on fools or innocents. Regrettably, however, you are neither."

Without waiting for me to reply, she turned and walked back toward the sanitarium; but before she reached the steps she apparently tired of the exercise, and simply vanished from sight.

CHAPTER 25

An honest entreaty

WILLIAM DAVEY

A young woman, no more than twenty years of age, answered the door and inclined her head.

"Good afternoon, Reverend," she said. "May I help you, sir?"

A voice called from within the house. "Who is it, Elizabeth?"

"It's a parson, ma'am," she said. "Do you have a calling-card, Reverend—"

But before she could complete the sentence, she turned to see a woman striding toward the door.

"Thank you, Elizabeth," she said. "Please return to your duties. I will deal with this myself."

The young servant offered a slight curtsy and left quickly. The lady of the house did not turn her head to see the order executed, but focused on the guest at the door.

"I told you I did not have any interest in receiving you," Eliza Esdaile said. "I cannot imagine I could be more clear."

"You were very clear, madam," I answered. "The situation has changed."

"I do not care."

"I feel that you *must* care. Your life is in danger," I said quietly.

Eliza glanced back and forth; there were no neighbors in earshot. She was no longer in full mourning, but rather half-mourning. This was before the death of Prince Albert—so the matter was not as formalized as it became later in the century.

Eliza Esdaile had changed a great deal in a year; she carried an air of self-confidence and self-reliance that I had not seen when last in Sydenham.

She turned her attention back to me. Clearly, she was torn

between admitting me to her house and shutting the door in my face; ultimately, perhaps, the utterance of those five words—*your life is in danger*—tipped the balance in favor of the former choice. She stepped back and let me enter, then closed the door behind me.

"I do not have any interest in Committee politics," she said. "I acknowledge your kind assistance in keeping your—colleagues—from my door, but I refuse to be drawn into your world again."

I removed my hat. "I understand. I would not wish to do so. But there is a new threat, one I cannot easily control. I need your help—and your memories."

"You presume on my good will."

"Yes, I most certainly do. I admit that. I fear it cannot be otherwise."

She looked at me once more; for a moment, it seemed that she would open the door and dismiss me: but instead she turned and walked into the parlor, indicating that I should follow.

As soon as Elizabeth brought tea and departed, Eliza fixed me with a stern gaze.

"Pray tell what has brought you back into my home, sir."

"One of our number has reached beyond nightfall and summoned a large number of *chthonic* and possibly other elemental spirits, She used them to kill a prominent surgeon who was an active critic of our practices."

I let this statement sink in for a moment, then continued: "She seems to have survived the experience, though I perceive that she has—changed."

"Is she possessed?"

"I cannot tell. I do not think so, but she is certainly *attended*."

"I do not know how this affects me."

"First, it is clear to me that while I am largely ignorant of the world of these creatures, the woman of whom I speak is scarcely less so. She is fool enough to have done this, but intelligent enough to realize that she must know more.

"Second, she is aware—as are most in the Committee—that

you are the only person who might have that knowledge, and she might undertake extreme measures to obtain it."

"So you have come to warn me."

"I have come to learn more about the creatures, Mrs. Esdaile."

"Or else…"

I sighed. "There is no 'or else'. I am not your enemy, and I do not have any intention of threatening you. To be honest, I have no coercive power over you at all. If Ann Braid had not summoned these creatures and committed this murder, I would not have troubled you again."

"Braid. That name seems familiar."

"It should be, madam. The man Miss Braid killed was her father: the surgeon James Braid."

Eliza seemed genuinely shocked by this revelation. She had been affecting an air of affront and hauteur during the conversation, but the façade was broken by the disturbing statement.

She took a moment to regain her composure, while I waited patiently.

"She killed her father with the aid of *chthonic* spirits."

"So I understand. I had some…interactions with them."

"Reverend Davey," Eliza said, folding her hands in her lap. "You are either a superb actor, or your demeanor has genuinely changed in the months since we last visited. I think, sir, that you are genuinely frightened."

"I am willing to admit that I am."

"And the rest of your Committee. Are they frightened, as well?"

"I suspect that they have no sense of what confronts us, madam. They do not know what I know, and might not believe it even if I told them."

"And what do you know?"

"I know that the creatures who are bound to Ann Braid have their own agenda. They are not merely interested in satisfying their hunger: they want to open the Glass Door itself. They are imprisoned and they want to be free—and they believe that there is a key to unlock that door—and they *may* assume that you know where that key is.

"And I think they are right."

Eliza leaned forward and carefully poured a cup of tea, then added milk and sugar. She took the saucer in her hand and lifted the cup to her lips and drank, then set it back in place.

"Did they tell you the nature of this key?"

"No."

"I suspect that what they desire is the very thing that has caused so much anguish—to James, to me, and to many others. The key to the Glass Door, Reverend Davey, is almost certainly the statue."

"Of course," I said. "It keeps coming back to that."

"It has never been anything but that, sir."

"Do you think that they have reached the same conclusion?"

"There is no way to know. But I fear that you are right—they will come here for answers. But I do not have the statue, and do not know where it is."

"I need you to help me, Mrs. Esdaile. Eliza."

"Help you find the statue for yourself? I truly have no interest, Reverend. There is nothing that they can do—that *you* can do—to threaten me. The worst they can do is kill me, and I have already had years of my life taken by a sort of waking death. I am not afraid."

"I believe you. But you can help me understand the world of the spirits. This is an honest entreaty: if I am to oppose them, I must know more."

"You want me to return to that terrible time?"

"Yes."

"I cannot imagine why you think I would subject myself to that. You are here in my sitting room at sufferance—why should I permit you to further invade my privacy?"

"To be honest, you have permitted me in your sitting room after you told me I should not come. It is because I genuinely need your help, and refuse to force you to give it to me. It is because—

whatever you think of me, and I am sure that in large part you are justified to think so—what I oppose is far, far worse."

Eliza set her teacup back on the tray and stood; I stood as well. She walked to a rolltop desk and opened it, withdrawing a letter.

There was a framed certificate hanging on the wall reading: Mrs James Esdaile MD—Annuitant, Bengal Military Fund. At least he had provided well for her; the house seemed well-furnished and comfortable.

"I received this in the mail last week." She showed me the envelope, which was return-addressed Rescobie, Forfarshire, Scotland. "My…brother-in-law told me that you visited him. His initial reaction was similar to mine."

"He threatened to set the dogs on me."

"David Esdaile is a Scotsman. But he is also a kind and generous man. He asked me to come and visit—Mary wanted to meet me, and he told me that he had something of James' to show me. I confess that I am not yet ready."

I was fairly certain what it might be.

Eliza tucked the envelope back in the desk. "In any case," she said, pulling the roll-top down again, "he said that he expected you to call upon me again and suggested that I might be moved to help you."

"Yet your letter told me not to come."

"But you came, Reverend Davey. You came despite my letter."

"Because—"

She held up her hand: not a mesmeric gesture, but it made me stop, all the same.

"You have explained yourself. Very well: it contradicts my best judgment to allow you this intimacy, sir, but I shall permit it nonetheless."

CHAPTER 26

Impasse

ELIZA ESDAILE

If the being that took control of me had conducted itself as it had intended, I should not be sitting with you today. When I awoke to find a stranger in control, it was clear that it had almost no knowledge of human society. And in the absence of that knowledge, it would be impossible to carry off the role.

It is easier for them when they completely manifest—when some part of their essence is devoted to the creation of a human body. When they do so, they mimic the characteristics of humans they observe, and learn how to speak and walk and carry themselves as humans. Possession of an actual human reserves more power, but it is harder for the less experienced.

My occupant—and forgive me, Reverend, but I shall insist on referring to this being as 'her', for she seemed to be like a young woman—was new to the task, and had little notion of how humans actually interacted. She quite frightened James at first—he did not know what to do with her, and I had been rendered insensible by the transformation, except for that brief few moments when I awoke in the infirmary to learn that I had lost control of my own body. Thus it was that she came to me to ask my help.

❖

My first impression on coming to my senses was that I was cold. Years in India had made me unaccustomed to the sensation— but this was something different from merely waking with the fire out and the bedclothes disarranged: I was freezing, lying on snow and subject to a bitter wind. As far as I could see in any direction there was nothing but an icy wasteland.

And then I saw *myself*, standing in my usual light dress and everyday bonnet, indifferent to the weather.

"What—" I began, scarcely able to speak above the howl. "Where am I?"

"You must help me," my other self said. "You *will* help me."

"I am…f…freezing. Where am I? What is this place?"

"I do not understand. Are you uncomfortable?"

"Yes! Yes, I am, I…" I tried to rise, the ice cutting through the thin garment and into my skin. "I am not attired for this weather."

She seemed to scrutinize me for several seconds, narrowing her eyes. I wondered at the expression: it was like a mirror, but it seemed that her face was animated in a way that was completely alien to me. Finally she seemed to understand what I had said, and waved her hand. My clothing changed to heavy, thick garments and stout boots, with heavy gloves.

I managed to scramble to my feet. "Thank you," I said. "I do not understand what is happening."

"I need your help."

"In what way?"

"I do not understand how to—how to act. How to be like your kind."

The words *your kind* chilled me even more than the biting wind. I tucked my hands into a muff that she had thoughtfully provided.

"Who are you?"

"I am…my name is unimportant and you could not render it," she said. "You may call me by the first few sounds. 'Fi'."

"Very well. Fi. Why have you brought me to this place? And why must you be *me*?"

"I am to occupy you. I was summoned by—" She broke into a series of syllables that I find impossible to reproduce; but they were curious, musical sounds that echoed weirdly across the trackless plain. "I am to be a protector."

"Protector?"

"Against those who seek to do harm to one of your kind. Doctor Esdaile."

"Doctor Esdaile…'summoned' you? From where?"

"From here," she answered. "From my home. Where you are—where we are—is nothing like this place. Instead of being beautiful it is dirty and hot, full of…" she grimaced; it was an expression that I did not think my face could compass, so it looked completely alien to me. "People," she finally finished, speaking the word as if she were saying *vermin* or *pests*.

"India," I said, "is very crowded, yes. But are you saying that we are somehow still there?"

"Of course, Eliza Weatherhead," Fi said. "This is merely a seeming, a place I have remembered so that we can talk. And we *must* talk, for I require you to teach me."

"How to be…a person?"

She smiled, baring her teeth. "How to be a particular person, Eliza Weatherhead. I need to learn to be you."

I need not tell you, Reverend Davey, the shock with which I received that statement. I nearly sat down upon the ice from which I had recently risen; I suddenly felt myself weak and light-headed. In short, I came close to succumbing to panic.

All during these brief seconds, Fi's expression never changed; she looked neither concerned nor triumphant nor any of a dozen other emotions that she might have betrayed. It was then that I realized an important fact—one which surely helped save my sanity and perhaps my life: I knew that Fi, for all that she had taken my appearance and was presently 'possessing' me—whatever that in fact meant—was separate from me.

My thoughts were my own. Trapped though I was—according to her statements—my thoughts were yet my own!

"You have taken possession of me," I said. "Then please tell me why I should cooperate with you in the smallest measure."

"I do not understand. What choice do you have but to cooperate?"

"With what means could you coerce me? What could you do?"

"I could cause you pain."

"You could—" I could scarcely contain myself: I nearly convulsed in laughter. "Pain is no threat. What could you do that has not already been done? You have taken my freedom, my body, my—" I spun around on my heel. "You have me *here*, in the recesses of my mind, I presume, in an icy wasteland that you consider to be home, and you speak to me of *pain?*"

"I was told…I was told that you would fear pain. That you will do *anything* to avoid it."

"You were misinformed."

The grimace returned.

"You do not care about pain?"

"I do not care *for* pain," I said. "But there is nothing about it that I fear."

"What is more," Fi said, as if she were considering the matter, "if you were to feel pain, it would interfere with my duties."

It was a remarkable admission, and I apprised at once that it was valuable intelligence. I had not yet recovered from the elation that had accompanied my realization that I retained privacy in this singular state of captivity.

"Then," I said carefully, "you must find some other coin to pay me with."

"What do you suggest?"

"I want one thing above all others—to have my freedom."

"You know I cannot grant that. I am in this position to accomplish a specific task. You speak of pain, and your indifference to it, but you cannot imagine what pain would be my punishment if I surrendered my duty."

"Then we are at an impasse, I fear."

"But—" she began, then paused. "But I need your help, Eliza Weatherhead. I require it."

"You shall not have it for nothing, Lady Fi."

The grimace took on a more disturbing form—a rather frightening, feral expression that seemed so completely alien to my face that I scarcely recognized it.

"I cannot obtain your help by threat, and I cannot obtain it by force. Therefore I shall take away the only other thing that I perceive to be of any value to you."

"And what is that?"

There was a moment of complete darkness, following which I found myself in a completely different place: the conservatory at the Heath house. I felt tears come to my eyes: it was so painfully familiar—I was sitting in my usual chair near the Pleyel piano, and I could hear the soft patter of rain outside on the verandah—that I thought that I had actually awoken there. I was even attired in a familiar dress, one that I had worn a great deal during my last few years as governess for Rose.

But it was not quite the same. The memory of sound and sight was there, but there were no odors at all. The jasmine blossoms from the garden, the faint scent of wood and polishing-oil from the furniture and the distant smell of tamarind and coriander from the kitchens, all were missing.

"This is another of your remembrances," I said to the empty room.

"It is one of yours, Eliza Weatherhead," Fi said, walking into the room, again a perfect imitation of my speech and my walk; she was wearing the same dress. "This was a place that seemed precious to you, am I correct?"

"You foul it by bringing it before me."

Fi looked confused. "I had thought to please you, Eliza Weatherhead."

"And do stop using my first and last name. You may address me as Miss Weatherhead, or you may use my Christian name, if you must."

"Eliza."

"Yes. I suppose we are intimates now, and on a first-name basis."

The sarcasm was lost on Fi; she was baffled by my response, but

I expect that she concluded that it was some human matter that she could not yet understand. She walked to a nearby seat and settled into it, much as I might do, though her posture seemed altogether sloppy and unsuitable.

"Eliza," she said, "you must believe me that I only sought to place you at ease by bringing forth the memory of this room. You were uncomfortable in the previous surroundings and I thought this would be more to your liking."

I considered an angry reply, but for some reason I refrained. Fi, my own image, seemed suddenly forlorn and sad—and sincere.

"This is a sort of bribe," I said at last. "Do you think that this will somehow make me more tractable? You choose to be kind to me—I recognize and even appreciate that kindness. But I am still your prisoner. There is still nothing you can do to me, nothing you can take away from me."

"But I have, Eliza. While you slept."

I must have now appeared to be baffled.

"Excuse me, slept?"

"Yes," she said. "Since our conversation at my home, nearly a week has passed. I have been very busy, Eliza," she said, smiling, again a bit ferally. "Let me congratulate you: for today you are to be wed."

CHAPTER 27

Passage

WILLIAM DAVEY

"You felt no passage of time?"

"None," she said. "It was as if I blinked and the scene changed from an icy waste to the conservatory in Mr. Heath's house. I could not imagine that a whole week had passed."

"And had it?" I asked.

"What do you mean? Are you asking if Fi told me the truth? She did. Apparently all of the wedding preparations had been made in considerable haste, despite the alien and frightening image that Fi had presented. Her second appeal to me was more urgent: she had no idea how to conduct herself as a bride."

"And she would not free you so that you could do so."

"That is so. She explained to me that unimaginable torture would await her if she did. Instead, she offered me a choice: to assist her in exchange for some unspecified reward, or to experience complete oblivion."

"Could she let you 'sleep' forever?"

"I…do not know. I am not interested in knowing. To lose a week in an eye-blink was terrifying enough—perhaps even more terrifying than all that followed."

"It would not have been better to simply be absent for—for—"

"No. To be completely honest, Reverend, I do not believe that. Imagine if I were to awaken, suddenly, in the Crystal Palace kneeling next to the corpse of a man I had only recently met, to discover that I was thousands of miles away from my former position and that *seven and a half years* had passed in but a moment. Try to imagine that, and how I would have reacted. I should have gone mad."

"Instead of being a prisoner, instead of witnessing what you saw yourself doing?"

"Reverend," Eliza said. "Please, sir. The meanest criminal in the most onerous prison can still dream of freedom. And what Fi gave me instead of oblivion was...enough to keep that dream alive."

"I do not know how I could have survived it. My admiration for you grows by the moment."

"Your terminology is very accurate, Reverend Davey. I *survived*. And I speak of it now against every desire I have to forget all of what happened." She looked down at her lap, as if she were closely examining her hands.

"You have my gratitude."

"Yes," she said. "And your admiration. And not your enmity. You can reserve that for others, since I am so revered."

"Sarcasm ill becomes you, madam," I said. "I do not revere you, and many others among the Committee do not see any reason to separate Eliza the *chthonios* from Eliza the prisoner. They are wrong, just as I was wrong. I like to think that admission is worth something."

"It is not lost on me. But it is not a currency that affects my feeling about you, or makes me less reluctant to speak of my experiences."

"I see." I was very slightly disappointed, but I cannot say that I was surprised.

"Your honesty, Reverend, is why you remain in my sitting room. If the admission had no value, the interview would have never begun."

ELIZA ESDAILE

And thus I was married.

My matron of honor was Georgiana Shackleford. She could not stop expressing her surprise that I had been suddenly swept off my feet by a man many years my senior—but on the whole she was thrilled for me and wished me every happiness.

I was permitted to watch, though not permitted to speak for

fear that I might reveal what was happening—not that anyone would believe it. But if I were believed to be hysteric or a madwoman, Fi's purpose would be ruined as well.

I had determined to continue resisting, but this was my *wedding*. I spoke aloud the proper things for Fi to do and say, and tempered her worst tendencies, so much so that James appeared almost at ease when he spoke the vows. I do not know if they meant anything to Fi—but they were meaningful to *me*. I have never forgotten that they were spoken, Reverend Davey, and it was always foremost in my mind that Fi observe them just as James always did.

Oh, of course. I know that you must think the worst of him for having made the bargain, and for being insincere—but whatever his failings, a lack of kindness was never among them. He was a true husband.

We began to prepare our departure from Calcutta almost as soon as the wedding was over. There was scarce time for a bridal tour; in this, James would have been more considerate, but I assumed that he knew that Fi would not expect it, and he was most interested in leaving India. Fi's emotions on the subject were clear, as well.

Did I fear what was to happen? No, not really: I was not dispatched to oblivion, but we did not have any conversations of the sort that we had done while we were still in India. I did not have a trousseau, as a bride in England might have, but the members of the Society helped assemble much of what I brought with me when we undertook our sea passage.

For James—and for me, viewing the affair from a distance, helpless to interact—this was a voyage back to Britain, back home, though I would be coming to Scotland for the first time. For Fi, however, it was nothing but an agony.

I am not given to seasickness. Mrs. Heath suffered during our outward passage, as I told you earlier; and even Mr. Heath took time adjusting to his sea-legs. James seemed to accustom himself quickly, and was soon calling upon fellow passengers who did not.

I am not sure if my captor had ever seen the ocean—much less traveled on it. She was severely affected, sick and in an extremely poor mood; it's no wonder that James spent so much time apart from her. It interfered with her abilities but did nothing to weaken her hold on me. Still, it brought about our first true conversation since my wedding day.

James and I were sharing a small cabin that was well-appointed and, by the standards of most of the passengers, reasonably comfortable; he was not officially the ship's surgeon, but as a practicing physician he had been given a certain amount of preference when our berth was allocated. She caused me to appear at her bedside so that we could talk.

Fi—in my image—looked awful. She was pale and drawn, as if she had seen little sunlight and had retained little food. We were scarcely two days out from Calcutta, passing through a chilling night fog as our vessel passed along Saugor Island, a low, jungle-covered waste emitting a stench that can hardly be imagined.

"Eliza," she said. "I do not understand why I suffer so, when others on this ship are well and unaffected."

"Different people react in different ways," I said. "I am surprised as well. I have never been seasick."

"This is not my natural domain," she said. "My kind is of the earth, not of the water."

"What does that mean? Are you in danger?"

"No…" she said, and my heart sank: for a moment I had contemplated the idea that a being such as Fi could not survive out at sea, and that I should be freed by circumstance. "Not danger. I merely cannot protect James if I am prostrate here in this wretched cabin on this wretched ship."

"Is he in danger on this ship?"

"I do not perceive any enemies." I wondered to myself what she might be able to perceive. "But I am not confident of my own abilities in this situation."

"What do you want me to do?"

"I want you to tell me what is afflicting me, and what I must do to recover."

"James has administered sedatives," I said to her, as indeed he had done. "But in my experience, the best thing to do is to accustom yourself to the ship—to get fresh air and get your 'sea legs'."

"Fresh air? You mean—you mean walk out on the *deck*?"

"Yes, of course."

She was incredulous. "But—but the ship pitches back and forth. I could fall off it."

I laughed. "No, of course you shall not. The ship rolls with the waves, and there are railings to prevent anyone from falling overboard. The salt air will do you—do us—good."

"No," she said. "That won't do at all."

But it did: ultimately, she concluded that she could not remain in misery in the cabin, and remaining there she could not protect James from whatever might oppose him. Thus, she managed to dress and ascend to the main deck, where she took a very tentative stroll. I was not alongside—I watched from within as I usually did, like the Man in the Iron Mask, unable to speak on my own.

Fi projected an air of hostility, particularly toward people she had not yet met. During the next few days at sea she forced herself to take constitutionals on deck; I instructed her to nod politely rather than glare and suggest affront—they would take her disinterest as a side-effect of her illness. She seemed to be surprised that this would work, but like so much having to do with humans, she simply did not understand how we interacted.

In any case, forcing herself to take fresh air and walk had a salutary effect, making her stronger and less afflicted by the pitching of our vessel.

One moonlit evening, while she stood on a remote part of the ship's foredeck, Fi spoke to me. I could not answer aloud, but apparently she could hear my reply from within.

"There is someone aboard this vessel, Eliza," she said quietly. "Someone who has some ability with the mesmeric art."

"Does he mean harm to James?"

"I must assume that he does. Good evening," she said, her teeth clenched, to a nicely-dressed couple that ventured near. The gentleman tipped his hat to her, but something in Fi's voice or expression caused him to steer his lady away.

"You frightened them," I said.

"I would prefer to be alone. I *am* alone. I see no problem, Eliza. Now as I said before, I sense a practitioner, and I assume that he means harm to James."

"What do you intend to do?"

"Eliminate the threat," she answered.

I did not like the way she said it, and I am sure she sensed my unease. She smiled in an unpleasant sort of way—I felt it, for I could not see it: a sort of tight grin that pulled my lips back from my teeth, as if I were about to bite something.

"I am not sure what you intend."

"Eliza," she said, "I am to protect James. If there is an enemy on this ship, he will be dealt with."

"You mean…"

I did not know how to end the sentence. As for Fi, she showed no inclination to explain.

I slept at night, much as I would have done had I been in control. Either she did not sleep at all: unlikely, I agree, but I have no way to truly know; or else she was asleep when I was. I really cannot say. In any case, she made herself ready for bed each night and settled in next to James, at which time I usually drifted off to sleep.

This night, however, after James began to snore softly, Fi arose and carefully dressed. She let herself quietly out of the cabin. I had not quite fallen asleep, and dressing had awoken me. I do not know whether she was aware that I was paying attention from the start, but as we made our way up on deck I asked, "Where are we going?"

"I am intending to deal with the problem, Eliza," she said. "If I meet with no difficulty, I shall be able to return to the cabin without even awakening James."

I felt chilled to the bone, though the air was stifling and warm. "Do you know where this individual is to be found?"

"At present, he is in the forward lounge with a group of gentlemen who are playing cards or some other such foolishness."

"They are unlikely to permit you entrance."

"I do not intend to *enter*, Eliza," she said. "I intend to wait until he leaves, and deal with him afterward."

"You may attract unwanted attention, Fi," I said. "Depending on what you have in mind. There are many other people aboard this ship and -"

"Be *quiet*," she hissed. "I do not need your advice or your chatter. You can do nothing to assist my efforts and nothing to hinder them. Would you like me to awaken you when I am done?"

I must tell you, Reverend, that it took a considerable act of will to say no to this question. I had the sense that something unpleasant was about to happen, and realized that if I were to 'sleep through' it, I should be sent to this oblivion like a child to her room whenever Fi deemed me to be superfluous. Ultimately, that might well be always.

"I will be silent," I said.

She did not respond to this comment.

It was dark this night; we were well out to sea now, passing along the Coromandel coast north of Madras. There were many places to hide out of sight, and Fi settled herself on a narrow bench along a corridor—what sailors call a 'gangway'—that led out of the lounge where her quarry was presumably enjoying himself.

I was surprised that she should choose this place, for it seemed to me that any gentleman leaving the evening's entertainments would hardly be inclined to take this route; but I did not wish to say anything in case Fi interpreted my comment as interference and sent me to oblivion. In the meanwhile, we could hear the laughter and chatter from within, along with the clinking of glasses and other incidental sounds. It faintly reminded me of the sort of dinner party that Mr. Heath would hold from time to time, entertaining fellow businessmen in Calcutta.

As it happened, Fi knew *exactly* what she was doing. After a few hours—I saw the moon rise from our vantage, lifting itself from the horizon beyond the rolling sea, and climb steadily into the sky—a nearby door opened, and a man emerged, profiled by the light from the lounge beyond. The sound of tables and chairs being moved grew loud and then soft again as the door closed.

The man took three or four confident strides then stopped, and in the moonlight I saw his hands move quickly in front of him. He was slight of form, and dressed in white—not as a card-playing gentleman in evening dress, but instead as a servant. His face was mostly in shadow, but I could see that he wore a carefully trimmed beard and a turban. The line of his jaw and the shape of his hands seemed terribly familiar.

I began to say *Gobinda*—for I was sure that it was he!—but dared not speak, not even within my own mind to Fi. But after a few moments it was clear that, while the man resembled my old acquaintance, he was younger and somewhat taller.

"I cannot see you, servant of Kali," he said in a soft voice, tinged with some accent that I did not know—it was not Bengali. "But I can feel you."

"You are here to hurt my husband," Fi answered.

"I do not care about him," the man said. "It is you I seek."

"It would have been better if you had never boarded this ship."

"Duty overwhelms my personal choices, demon," he said, stepping forward. For the first time I managed a look at his face—and indeed, he looked very much like Gobinda: the same slightly protruding nose and rounded, firm jaw, the same dark, furrowed brows. "I have journeyed very far to confront you."

"Shiva is nothing to me," Fi said. She inhaled slightly and then began speaking a series of syllables. They were nonsense words, like a sing-song nursery rhyme; yet with each phrase there was a sound like a great intake of breath, a sort of non-sound that seemed to soak up every sound around it.

Shiva? I thought. *The ancient Hindoo god?*

"He is—" The man seemed to be straining, as if he was being

pulled toward us, one halting step at a time. "My Lord Shiva sent me from his holy city to—"

Fi continued to speak, and with each sound it became harder and harder to hear anything else. Indeed, it seemed that the moon shone less brightly, and the very patterns of the things on the walls of the gangway seemed to strain and distort.

"I have—" the man said. "I must—"

But whatever he *had*, whatever he *must*, for whatever purpose Lord Shiva had sent him from his holy city to do, was never revealed. The man leapt forward as if a mighty hand had pushed him: but before he collided with us I was subjected to a horrific sight: his body was pulled apart, first his outer clothing and then his skin and then his bones, which seemed to be on fire.

I know that I cried out in anguish and terror, but evidently matters had progressed too far for my exclamation to interrupt Fi's effort. I could not look away: apparently my choice was between oblivion and complete sensory engagement. The latter was my part for the next several seconds, as the fiery remains of the man seemed to flare brightly and then disappear, leaving no trace behind. All through this process he had not even cried out.

Fi stopped speaking and took several deep breaths, as if it had taken some considerable effort.

"Someone will miss him," I managed to say at last.

"No," she said, turning away and making her way toward the stairway to belowdecks. "No one will miss him but his god."

CHAPTER 28

Rubicon

WILLIAM DAVEY

Eliza finished the description of the attack upon the Indian and then seemed to slump her shoulders, as if she was exhausted. I thought to reach out but hesitated. She looked down at her hands resting in her lap and did not speak for a very long time.

Elizabeth entered the room; she glanced at her mistress and then at me, her eyes narrowing, perhaps wondering if I had upset Eliza. But the lady came to my rescue.

"What is it?" she asked.

"I…wanted to see if you were done with the tea things, ma'am, and Mrs. Yells wanted to know if the gentleman was staying for dinner."

"My cook likes to be prepared," Eliza said, summoning a polite smile. "Reverend Davey, shall you be joining us?"

"I would be honored," I said. "Thank you."

"Tell Mrs. Yells that I shall have Reverend Davey at table," she said to the servant, who gathered up the tea tray and teacups, bobbed her head and departed.

"I am sorry to have made you relive that incident, Eliza," I said softly. I truly did feel that I had put her through an extremely unpleasant recollection—but her narrative had told me many things.

"I have recalled that event many times, Reverend. It comes to me in dreams—not because it is the most horrific, but because it was the first such. There were many others. They are all still with me whenever I close my eyes."

"I am even more motivated to keep the Glass Door closed. I apologize once again that I have caused you discomfort."

"Only the memories do that, Reverend."

"This is surely not your fault, Eliza. The being that had taken control of you committed this act, and all of the other acts about which I know—and others about which I know nothing."

"That is easily said, sir. But you forget that I am *complicit*. When Fi committed that terrible act on the ship taking us back to Britain, I realized something critical about my role—by not tempering her dangerous behavior, by helping her to disguise herself as human, I had let Fi act in a way appropriate to her species. I was at fault then, and it was my failing every time she did what she did."

"No, madam, I will not accept that. You cannot take responsibility for this creature's behavior."

"I *can*, Reverend. When she committed that first murder, we crossed a Rubicon of sorts. From that time forward, I chose to teach her what I could in the hope that I might minimize her crimes."

I looked directly at Eliza, who met my gaze with equanimity. This was a strongly held belief: she had decided that the actions of this *chthonic* spirit that had taken control of her body were her fault. Guilt, an important—I daresay a critical—part of my clerical profession, played a strong role with Eliza, and there was no way I could dissuade her.

I should concede that using that guilt to my advantage was somewhat ungentlemanly. But in view of the exigencies of the situation, I could hardly pass up the opportunity to use it to my advantage.

"You acted as you saw best, madam," I said.

She nodded, looking away toward the roll-top desk. Just beyond, hanging on the wall, was a portrait I had not noticed before: James Esdaile, seated in an upright chair, the wall behind him lined with books. He looked completely at ease, a half-smile on his lips.

"I acted to protect myself," she said. "And to protect James, particularly against the Committee."

Walter H. Hunt

With an understanding that I would return the next day, I took dinner with Eliza largely in silence. I had little to say past the polite courtesies of the table, and did not expect to pursue the inquiry further that evening, taking my leave when the meal had concluded.

Her correspondence with David Esdaile suggested that he had reconciled himself somewhat to the idea of Eliza's possession. From his own account, Eliza—or, rather, 'Fi'—had caused the elder Esdaile's death; this, too, would be part of the guilt that Eliza bore. But what, if anything, I could make of this remained to be seen.

In the morning I presented myself once more at Eliza's house and was received politely but cautiously. I had brought a notebook with me with information pertaining to the period between Esdaile's arrival in Perth in the fall of 1851 and his final communication with the Committee in December 1858; I wanted to see how her account coincided with what we already knew.

"Are you verifying my story, Reverend?"

"I am gathering information, madam. No more, no less."

"What information would you care to gather today?"

"I am curious about the world of the *chthonoi*, Eliza. What did Fi tell you about herself?"

"A great deal," Eliza answered. "What I learned was by asking careful questions."

ELIZA ESDAILE

Fi seemed surprised that I knew so little of her race: they had been dealing with humans for millennia, in every culture across the span of history, and even before the time we record. They were certainly known in Babylon and Egypt, where powerful incantations were developed to summon and dismiss *stoicheia*.

She had been brought to James by the aid of a being that inhabited the statue; it is *that* being that is the source of all of our misery. Its provenance was a society about which we know nothing, which dwelt in the Indus Valley a few thousand years before Christ. This

202

being was not one of her kind, she believed, but rather something else: she did not offer any information on that subject, except to indicate that it was something to be feared.

I learned that there had been some sort of great conflict that had forced her race away from the warm lands where they had enjoyed such ready employment by the priests and sorcerers. They had been exiled to the lands of bitter cold near the north and south magnetic poles, toward which they were drawn: whatever means had been used to compel them made use of the Earth's magnetic power to attract all of her ancestors there.

What caused this banishment? I have no idea, Reverend. I suspect that they may have committed some wicked act, or offended some powerful person. According to Fi, this first happened on the Subcontinent, and was then repeated in Babylon and Egypt and in other cultures in other lands. By placing the *chthonic* beings far beyond human ken, they sought to make them unreachable and thus powerless. They would have remained so, except that traders and explorers began to journey to those far reaches. When humans drew close enough, Fi's people were able to make contact with them again and thus once more enter human society.

Fi conveyed the impression that she was quite young by the standards of her kind. Indeed, her possession of my person was the first such assignment she had ever been given; I fear that had a more experienced being been chosen, my services might not have been needed—or even requested. I should have been condemned to oblivion, perhaps forever. I shudder to consider that possibility, and thank God for having granted at least this mercy.

As she gained resistance to the afflictions associated with ocean travel, we made more and more appearances above-decks, sometimes in James' company. I encouraged her to be courteous and polite; she did not understand at first, considering this to be extraneous to her role, but I gradually convinced her that it would better serve her mission to protect my husband if she attracted no undue attention. Thus, her earlier rudeness was ascribed to illness and all was forgiven. Even James observed the difference in her demeanor, though he declined to remark upon it. Thankfully, she did not consume anyone else on the voyage home; whether it was due to her own forbearance or the absence of any threat, I do not know. I am certain, however, that no amount of refinement I imparted to her would have prevented such acts if she deemed them necessary.

I also convinced Fi that she would better comprehend human culture if she read about it. At my direction, she began to spend idle hours reading—anything that came to hand, from newspapers to travel books to James' scientific journals to novels. I was ever willing to consider books as good and faithful friends; Fi had a great curiosity and an insatiable appetite for knowledge that surprised me and astounded James. When the ship docked at the Cape of Good Hope, we went ashore and explored bookshops, returning with a number of volumes that provided us with new diversion, since she had exhausted the available material on board. This habit continued all through my imprisonment; I daresay I have read more in the last eight years than most people will read in their entire lives—to the point at which I must now employ spectacles to discern small print.

We reached Britain in September of 1851, landing in London. Most of our effects were sent directly to Perth, but James had to conclude his business in the city before we journeyed home. He made some particular financial arrangements to which I was not a party, but they included provision of my annuity as his widow and the disposition of certain items we had conveyed home. The statue was certainly not among those things; Fi would surely have noted its presence.

As we traveled north on the train, James' demeanor—which had been reserved and quiet during the sea journey—became more animated and happy. He had been gone from his home for twenty years; he had left with a young bride, whom he had lost, and been married to a second wife whom he had also lost. Now he was returning with a woman who appeared to be some years his junior...and who was, incidentally, inhabited by a *chthonic* spirit capable of consuming his enemies and who, upon his own death, would consume him.

From my peculiar vantage point, I watched this drama play out with morbid fascination—particularly because I did not know what might happen when Fi's service was done.

I first met David, James's brother, when we settled into our temporary residence in Perth—a small house on Tay Street that we occupied before moving to our Atholl Street address. James had hoped to find employment at the prison on South Inch, a park beside the Tay River. To be honest, there was no true need for it: he had handled his money wisely in India and we were capable of living quite comfortably on his investments and pension.

David was a minister at a small parish, Rescobie, a few miles out of town. I know that you visited him there, so I shan't bore you by offering any corroborative details—I expect that you have written copiously in your note-book.

What I should mention is that Fi took an instant dislike to him. He kept his eyes warily upon me from the moment we met, but never openly threatened. He had some skill with the Art—he had corresponded with James about the subject from the time the Hooghly experiments began—but he also seemed to have some other power in his possession, something that made Fi immediately hostile. Had I not urged her to restraint, she might have tried to consume him in an empty front room at Tay Street.

Instead, she held back, clinging to James and seething. Again at my urging, she allowed herself to be taken on a tour by Mary, David's wife, giving the two brothers time to be alone.

"This brother is an obstacle," Fi said to me. "I shall eventually have to deal with him—he poses a threat to James."

"They are *brothers*. James speaks very fondly of David. You must give them some time together."

"I dislike it."

"Fi," I said as placatingly as I could manage, "no harm will come to James in just a few minutes. You must not bring about a crisis here if we are to live in peace."

Fi did not like the idea, but accompanied Mary out of James' sight.

David Esdaile's wife was plain and not especially well-read—certainly not in comparison to our state by that time!—but was as open and kind as Georgiana Shackleford. She had no mesmeric skill whatsoever; Fi did not perceive any threat, though her innate hostility made Mary a little afraid. I supplied my gaoler with the correct responses, and eventually made reassuring noises about various aspects of the domestic arts—suggestions on colors and wallpaper patterns and furniture arrangements—that caused Mary, the kind-hearted soul, to relax, sensing that we had become more at ease.

The house was not that big, and we were not away too long, but as we returned to the front room we could hear the two brothers speak.

"...It isn't just that you have some mesmeric skill—there's something more to it, isn't there?" James was saying.

"Yes." David's voice sounded flat and devoid of emotion.

"What is it?" James asked. "How do you know?"

"I should deal with this threat at once," Fi said to me, and walked ahead of Mary; I could feel her face contract into that grimace that I so hated.

"No!" I exclaimed, which made her hesitate for just a moment, and before she could turn her anger upon me, I quickly added, "No, please, that will do no good. If David Esdaile is a threat, this is the wrong place and time to address it."

"I am a better judge of it than you," Fi said, as we reached the front room and the two brothers turned to face us. For the first time, I noticed how similar they looked—they had the Esdaile chin and facial shape, and seemed to stand with very similar posture—though they had been apart for two decades, they clearly descended from the same stock.

I was alarmed, wondering if she might attack David Esdaile

then and there. He held his hands loosely, as if expecting it; my James looked somewhat baffled, as if unsure what would happen next. So far as I knew, he never learned of the death of the Shiva-servant aboard ship. He might not have known at that time exactly how dangerous she was.

"There you are, dear," he said, interrupting the mood.

Fi did not speak, but did intertwine her hands around James' elbow. I could see that Mary scarcely concealed her concerned expression behind a smile.

"We were just looking at the house with your charming wife, Reverend Esdaile," I supplied Fi. She uttered the words without the pleasant intonation I had provided.

"Mary is always helpful. And I trust that you will call me David, Eliza. Mary and I are glad to have you in our family."

"His words say that," Fi said to me. "But he believes nothing of the sort. He knows what I am. He is a *threat*, Eliza, whether or not you find him amiable."

"I urge you to be patient."

"And we are glad to be here," Fi said to David with my voice. "I am sure that we will have much to talk about."

David and Mary soon took their leave. James told me that he needed a little time to catch up on some correspondence and asked to be left alone; when Fi was unsure what to do, I indicated to her that it was her task to begin making the house ready for our residence.

Interviewing servant candidates would begin within a few days. In the meanwhile, we would have to see to the unpacking.

CHAPTER 29

Unequal to the task

WILLIAM DAVEY

"Between late September 1851 and the end of 1853, I know of at least twelve separate attempts made by members of the Committee to confront James Esdaile. I neither authorized nor directed any of them, though I take responsibility for their actions. As far as I know, the Major-General—Brisbane, my deputy in Scotland—authorized none of them, either."

"There were more than twelve."

"Indeed."

"I cannot tell you the exact number, Reverend Davey. On at least seven occasions Fi 'dealt with' the problem in the same way she had done aboard ship." Eliza looked away again, as if clearly remembering each incident.

"You were forced to witness this."

"I *chose* to witness it," she shot back angrily. "I suffered through each demonstration of Fi's power, and accepted it as part of my guilt for not tempering her actions. Even those who were not consumed by my jailer did not deserve the fright and mental stress to which she subjected them. With one exception."

"Who would that be?"

"Horace Eden," Eliza said with a bitter anger in her voice. "Of all those who sought to do the Committee's unpleasant work in Scotland, I think that Dr. Eden deserved his fate in full measure."

I considered this for several moments and then said, "What about the senior Reverend Esdaile?"

"No." Eliza's face settled into an expression of sad resignation. "No, not at all. Reverend James did not deserve to be consumed—and he was *not*: he died after confronting Fi. But in this he was foolhardy. He was a learned man, but he was old and weak, having suffered some sort of apoplexy years before. David could have mastered Fi: but not Reverend James."

"I see."

"He did not merely speak the Word of God, Reverend Davey; did you know that? He was an adept who had received certain esoteric teachings, and was in the process of passing them on to his son."

"I do know. David Esdaile told me, and showed me their instruction manual—a book about Osiris and other Egyptian gods. I fail to understand how any of it would be useful."

"I cannot say. I am not an adept myself, and it was not a book that David permitted me to see. I can only assume that Reverend James did find it useful, but not in practice, and not in this case. For all of his learning, and all of his good intentions, he was simply unequal to the task."

"So was Horace Eden."

"Quite so—and just as well: he threatened David and Mary and the children. Whatever James thought of me—of Fi, and her methods—this invasion angered him most of all. Eden was a nasty, unpleasant old man—and was exactly what I imagined you to be."

"I hope I have disappointed you on that score, madam."

"I still consider you villainous, Reverend. You are the enemy of an enemy; I am opposing the being within the statue, not assisting you. I ask you to remember that."

"I am chastened."

"You mock me."

"I do *not*," Davey said. "I have known of you—of the persona that inhabited you, in any case—for nine years. When I came to Sydenham on the day of James Esdaile's death, I was certain that I knew all I needed to know about loyalties, about power and about right and wrong. In the last year I have learned more than I ever would have cared to learn about the flaws in my reasoning. I do *not* mock you, Eliza. I am chastened. You find me villainous: I shall accept it. I am not your friend and am unlikely to become such—

that is the way of things. But I do not consider you an enemy—either personally, or as the chairman of the Committee. I pray that you do not consider me an enemy, either."

"You have said that before."

"I mean it no less now."

"Yet it is your Committee that produced Dr. Eden. What do you have to say to that?"

"I am not sorry that he is gone. As I told you before, I cannot honestly aver that any man deserves the fate that a *chthonios* can inflict, but he belongs to an earlier generation of our organization; he occupied a particular role for my predecessor, who died years ago, as well. I do not miss him, and I do not believe that either of the brothers Esdaile missed him, either."

"I do not believe we have anything more to say about him," Eliza said. "Let us not speak of him again."

"Would it pain you to recall your final visit to Rescobie Manse?"

"Yes." She stared grimly at me. "Of course it would. But for the sake of opposing this enemy, I shall recall it nonetheless."

ELIZA ESDAILE

Fi's relationship with David was never cordial, though I believe that I had convinced her against direct action because he would do nothing to harm his older brother. She was fascinated with David's family; evidently the notion of young children was sufficiently removed from her own personal experience that she was endlessly curious about how they changed as they grew older. My own siblings, and my time as a governess in England and in India, proved to be helpful in explaining these things to her.

But Reverend James was another matter. She believed the elder Esdaile to be an enemy—based on all she heard and all she saw. Though it pains me to admit it, sir, her perception was exactly accurate: he was an enemy—to Fi. He knew what she was, or what sort of nature she possessed in any case, and seemed determined to dismiss her from the first time we met.

When we first visited Rescobie Manse, the old man was waiting on the step of the house. He had placed an unseen barrier behind him to see if Fi could pass through. Doorways of various sorts have a special significance to *chthonic* spirits; her ability to pass into Rescobie Manse would not only establish her relative strength, but would institute a level of formal conflict between Fi and the self-anointed guardian of the doorway, the elder Esdaile. He wanted her not to enter—but if she did so, it would be with the understanding that she came within against his will.

Fi began to work on Reverend James as soon as the Manse came in sight from the carriage. She was singing softly under her breath. I know that James felt it; he shifted uncomfortably in his seat. I do not know if he anticipated the conflict between his wife and his father, but I dared do nothing to distract or interrupt Fi in her efforts for fear that she would dismiss me.

James climbed down from the carriage first and then assisted me to descend. He took my arm and led me to the doorway; son and father embraced for what seemed to be a very long time, and then he stepped back and introduced me.

"Father," he said, "let me introduce my wife Eliza. We worked together in Hooghly and she is now my partner in life."

"Welcome to the family," Reverend James said after a moment, embracing me.

It was then that Fi attempted to interrupt the movement of his heart. I am not a *chthonic* spirit, neither am I a doctor; she explained to me what she was doing—clinically, dispassionately, as if it were the most natural thing in the world—and suggested that Reverend James was simply too powerful at this time, in this place, for her to simply consume.

She stepped back and opened her mouth as if to reply, and her soft singing—which had become almost inaudible—turned into a sort of hollow echo. I watched in silent horror as the old man stiffened; only his eyes showed alarm, but I could see that emotion replicated in the eyes of his younger son, who reached out a hand as if to steady him. But the moment passed: it was immediately clear that he had brushed off the attack, or Fi had abandoned it, or both.

I smiled, and felt my hands extend as if in a welcoming gesture. I attempted to silently convey as much warmth as I could, and whatever effect I might have had seemed to help relax the situation.

Our right hand moved, almost imperceptibly, and I saw the barrier placed on the door fall apart like it was made of nothing but spider webs.

Fi could not defeat Reverend James here and now—but the battle-lines had been clearly drawn.

We visited Rescobie Manse several times over the next two years. It was a few hours' travel from Perth; each time we came to the house, regardless of the time of day or night we arrived, and despite all sorts of weather, Reverend James was always outside the door with the invisible barrier reestablished. Fi always passed through it, though it did seem to become more difficult. After the first time, she did not attempt to injure or kill him on the doorstep of the Manse.

That is not to say that she did not attempt to *damage* him. I remember once walking along the lake and glancing over toward the churchyard where David and his father stood talking; for several moments the older man became faint and had to lean on his son for support. But there were also times when I felt that due to the proximity of Reverend James, Fi's grip had very nearly come loose, when I might have been able to cry out—if only to tell someone that I had been trapped and imprisoned. It was like swimming under water and very nearly breaking the surface: coming agonizingly close to that one gulp of cool, fresh air, and then dropping back into the depths.

I shall tell you presently about the last visit, but first there is another incident I must describe. A few days before that, we had marked Hogmanay—the Scottish New Year celebration. James had instructed me—and thus Fi—about all of the customs and traditions, as they were completely different in Scotland, where such events have a life of their own. We were living on Atholl Street by then. It was a good-sized house and it had to be thoroughly clean: Elizabeth, whom you see is still with me, had just become a maid in our household and worked extremely hard to make sure the New Year was welcomed properly.

As I mentioned to you, doorways have a peculiar importance to *chthonic* beings. At New Year in Scotland, it is customary for the master of the house—James—to open the back door so that the old year can escape, and then open the front door so that the new one can enter. Fi, endlessly curious, was amused when James assembled the staff at the rear door and opened it; a swirl of snow and a little blast of chill air came into the house.

This done, he led all of us to the front door, which he ceremoniously opened. We could hear the first bells of the New Year from St. John's Kirk, and there were revelers in the streets—people going from house to house offering the first dram of 1854.

"Fi," I said, "I think I heard something outside."

"There are many noises," she said. James had gone out on the porch for a moment. I wasn't sure quite why, but I wanted to cross the threshold—and I wanted James to see me do it.

"Let's look outside."

"I thought you found it too cold."

"But you do not. Isn't it like your home?"

She was suspicious: I could hear it in her voice. Still, it was quite cold, and I was not bundled up as she had accustomed herself to doing when we went out in winter. After a moment of indecision, she walked across the front entryway—just as James was turning to come back in.

For a moment our eyes met. After these many years, I am not completely sure: but I thought that at that moment, when he looked at me, he did not see Fi's alien gaze—but he looked deeper, into my eyes, seeing my true soul captured in their depths. His expression changed to surprise—as if he had truly seen something unexpected.

"Is there something wrong, James?" Fi asked. Again, I cannot be sure—but I do not think that she knew what had happened, or she would have punished me by sending me to oblivion.

"Nay, lass," he said, grasping me by the shoulders and stepping us back inside. His expression became neutral again. "A guid New Year to ane," he said to me and all of the household, "an' a' and mony may ye see."

We did not speak of that incident, then or later; I wondered if I had imagined it at the time.

A few days later, we journeyed north to Rescobie to spend Twelfth Night with his brother's family. I dreaded the outcome of that visit. As Fi had become more accustomed to her role, she had become stronger and more capable. She had told me early in our relationship that, after James died and she had consumed him, she would quit my body and leave me in control; it was a ray of hope for me, but also something I feared—I was not sure that I could live with what Fi had done, not sure whether I might descend into madness. At least while she was with me, I was equipped with an excuse that kept me from taking any responsibility. As I have told you, that matter has been remedied.

I know that you think I should be absolved. I disagree and will not discuss it further.

I was speaking of Rescobie. We traveled there, arriving after the sun had set. The house and kirk were full of light—candles filled every sconce, an extravagance that they surely could not afford. But it was for a purpose. We scarcely stepped into shadow from the moment at which we descended from the carriage. David greeted us warmly and made a special point of showing us around the kirk, which had been gaily decorated for the season; Reverend James had woven barriers everywhere through which we needed to pass—none very strong, and Fi broke them with ease at first, but became more and more angry as the tour continued. It was clear that they were intended to weaken or distract her. When we reached the house—again, scarcely touching unlit ground—there were more barriers, one in every doorway, and stretched over every piece of furniture. No one else seemed to see or be affected by any of it.

"He thinks this is a *game*," she told me. "This is a challenge."

"I doubt that he considers it a game at all," I answered. "What are you going to do?"

"If he had not defined this as his domain," she told me, "I would consume him with ease. He is old and weak; the aura on his left side is degraded from some earlier injury. But he cannot be consumed *here*."

"I do not see why you think him a threat." Of course I did see: Reverend James knew what she was, and was powerful enough to get her attention, even if he could not hold her back.

"I do not see the need to explain everything to you."

"But—"

"You will interfere with me, won't you, Eliza? You are beginning to feel affection for the old man."

"Of course I do. He is my father-in-law. James loves him very much."

"Love is a weakness," she said.

"I love James."

"I do *not*," she said. "I am responsible for protecting him from his attackers—and from threats like this old man. Just as you have tried to teach me of human society, I have sought to make clear what my duties must be…clearly, I have been remiss."

"Meaning—"

"Only this," she said.

I felt James jostling me. Morning sun shone on my face through the open window of the carriage as it rolled along the cobbled road.

"Look," he said, gesturing out over Rescobie Loch. "Isn't it beautiful?"

The ice of the lake was reflecting the sunlight at such an angle that we could see faint rainbow patterns. Across the expanse of frozen water, the sun was dappling the treetops.

"Oh, yes," I said. "Very."

Fi conveyed only polite emotion, but within, I felt myself

beginning to cry. We were on our way back from Rescobie Manse; clearly Twelfth Night was behind us, and James was happy, but I had been sent off and had seen nothing.

I consoled myself with the knowledge that nothing terrible had happened, for my James was in cheerful spirits. He did not know—he could not have known—that I had been gone. But a few days later we received a letter from David, telling us that their father had passed away quietly.

CHAPTER 30

Departure

WILLIAM DAVEY

Eliza's narrative was evocative: I was almost able to see the ice on Rescobie Loch. I had been there myself and remembered the beautiful view she had described. When she was finished, we sat quietly for a time while Eliza collected herself. I did not wish to disturb her contemplations, so I consulted my note-book for other questions I might ask.

"What did David tell you about the death of his father?" she asked at last.

"His story differs only slightly from yours, Eliza, and only incidentally. He showed me a letter that his father had sent to your husband concerning his intentions. The elder James Esdaile fully expected to confront your captor that night, and James was aware of it."

"I had not known that. I wonder if Fi would have acted differently, had she known."

"I daresay she would not."

"You are probably correct. They are capricious—and cruel. It would have only angered her further."

"But you should realize, Eliza, that David Esdaile has long since forgiven you. He knows that you were not responsible"—she attempted to interrupt; I hastily continued—"primarily responsible—for the actions of the *chthonic* spirit that inhabited you. He came to realize that you were within."

"Reverend James didn't know. He assumed I was a manifestation."

"But I think your husband did."

Eliza did not respond. She stood and walked to the window

and settled herself onto a bench seat. She invited me to join her. The late-morning sun streamed through the window, clear and bright, highlighting her neat, straight hair and picking out a small piece of polished amber in the clasp that held it in place.

"Recounting this story to you is uncomfortable, Reverend Davey—not only for the recollection, which is painful enough, but also because of what it says about my present situation. I am not like some poor Dickensian waif who has endured penury and privation and now at last is free and well-situated, the novel over and the enemy vanquished and the adventures all complete.

"Look at this house, sir: I have a maid and a cook, a generous inheritance and a comfortable pension from James, a successful doctor and author. I am not wealthy, but I am not in want.

"But then I compare myself to my sister-in-law, Mary. She is far happier than I; she has five beautiful children and is married to her dearest heart, while I am childless and my dearest heart—whom, despite all, I came to love—lies here in the churchyard far from his native soil. He is infinitely further from *me*. I wonder whether anything else matters."

"You are still a young woman."

"Thirty-seven is not young, Reverend."

"Among the lace-makers in Honiton in Devon, Eliza, thirty-seven is quite old: their eyes are weak and their fingers are rheumatic. But you are beautiful and intelligent, strong-willed and of independent means. You cannot be without suitors."

"Suitors?" she laughed, not quite merrily—I think it was more rueful than anything else. "I have rebuffed all such petitions. I do not wish to have any sort of captivity, not after my former experience. And that is what it would be—I should surrender my goods and my status as the head of my own household, and for what? The companionship of a man who—of all the attributes you assign to me—would be most interested in my *independent* means. My beauty—such as it is—will continue to fade. As for intelligence and strong will—men do not prize that.

"Which leaves only what I have, Reverend. I simply do not care to give that away."

"Your argument is compelling," I said, unsure what else I could possibly say. In the mesmeric world there had been only a few women, scattered here and there—Ann Braid, of course, Lydia Fowler and Harriet Martineau; Elizabeth Barrett Browning, Ada Lovelace. None had been truly independent, and even Ann Braid would soon be married—and was not, in any case, a free agent any longer.

"You concede what I already know."

"Your intelligence and strong will leave me no choice, madam. And as for your beauty—while I am not bewitched by it, because fifty-two is much older than thirty-seven, it is undeniable."

"If you say so. I am no judge of that. I do not preen or strut, and what vanity I do possess is an unseemly vice. But I thank you for your compliments. I have made clear my opinion of you, so I know that your compliment is genuine, rather than flattery meant to curry my favor."

Again, I was without a response. If Eliza had been trained as a mesmerist, I knew that she could be the equal of any member of the Committee—save perhaps myself. She would be more than a match for Ann Braid, who might have crippled herself to exercise her vindictive revenge. But it was not a career I expected Eliza to pursue.

Still, it occurred to me that if she were perceived to have skills, it might be sufficient to deter any but the most determined among the Committee. I concluded that I should have to put it about that she had acquired some skill during her captivity, or that I had imparted the same to her. I determined also that it was unnecessary for me to consult with her on this strategy.

"I tire of discussing myself, Reverend Davey," she said. "It would be my preference that we moved on to some other subject."

I nodded. "As you wish."

"Tell me. What else would you like to know?"

"I would like to know about your time in Sydenham."

ELIZA ESDAILE

I do not know what my brother-in-law has told you about our move away from Perth, Reverend Davey. Let me clarify on behalf of my late husband.

His brother's demand that we leave was not our only motivation: a plan was already underway at the time Reverend James died. We had been expecting to move for some time. James had already bought this house and engaged the inestimable Mrs. Yells to serve as cook. He had intended to establish our household here in the spring of 1854. The sudden loss of Reverend James merely brought the plan to fruition.

It was a difficult passage for both brothers. James and I scarcely spoke at all to David and Mary at the funeral; we were all polite to a fault, jointly hosting the small gathering that followed the interment, and when we parted it was without any real exchange. It pained James very much; for a time he scarcely spoke to me, though it was clear to me that he understood that the conflict between the *chthonic* spirit and his father was inevitable on both sides.

On the day that James died, Reverend, the reason for Sydenham was finally revealed. At the time we first established ourselves here, I did not know and Fi did not suspect—but she did ask many questions which I tried my best to answer.

James had obtained a favorable situation through some old friends. I was happy to be back in England and was excited to have an opportunity to tour the great Crystal Palace, a wonder I had not seen when it was situated in Hyde Park. This new location was far more extensive, and covered many more areas and periods than the original one had done.

Did Fi sense the effects of the Palace? Not completely, I assume. I was as shocked as she when James revealed the fact as he died. Since you were coming in person, I assumed that you might be her equal, and that if James died, I would be subjected to the final horror of observing my captor consuming the body and soul of the man I loved. Whatever the case, I concluded that it would be unpleasant.

Still, I *can* tell you that Fi did not like the place. I loved it, as did James; he bought me Phillips' guide to the Palace—it sits on that bookcase over there—and I encouraged Fi to read it, so that I could read it as well. Still, the Crystal Palace bothered Fi; she felt almost seasick there at times, she told me, and she thought it affected her ability to protect James. I pointed out to her that it would likely be the case that any enemy seeking to do harm to James would be discomfited as well. As our time in Sydenham lengthened, she became more complacent about it, and we visited often. After a time, she did not even complain about it anymore; instead, she told me of her race's relations with some of the many cultures depicted there.

She was particularly intrigued by the Egyptian Court. She told me that *stoicheia* of all elements had had dealings with that culture, particularly the photic and *chthonic* types; but that most of the artifacts were from later periods. But I should mention that she had difficulty with the place at first—the main arched doorway and the interior ones seemed to have invisible barriers erected across them, stretching between the winged globes atop the door columns. We broke through each time—but after no more than a few minutes, they reestablished themselves. Fi found it quite tiring, but still was compelled by the scene—I particularly remember that she would stand and look at the hieroglyphics and trace the palm-leaf indents on the wall friezes, almost as if she were trying to recapture something she had lost.

There were other parts of the Palace that compelled her—the medieval church, the Alhambra, the Assyrian Court with its great palace—and James and I visited them so frequently that we were recognized and somewhat well-known to the staff and other regular patrons. The only other puzzlement for Fi was why the culture of the ancient Indus Valley was not presented. I assured her that it was unknown to current archaeology. She found this quite amusing.

Yes, I imagine that the final confrontation within the Crystal Palace was part of James' plan all along—though it is a mark of his skill at circumspection that he kept it a secret from Fi for nearly five years. I am sure he was aware of the peculiar geometric properties of the Palace, but accustoming Fi to visiting certainly made it easier to spring his trap.

I do not know why he waited so long—it would certainly have been less painful for me had he not postponed his death until 1859. I have always assumed that he intended merely to assure himself that Fi could not obtain her satisfaction when his life came to an end; he was never completely healthy, though our time in Scotland seemed to energize him. He clearly did know that mesmeric arts could not be practiced there, but…

No, I *do* remember. It was in the summer of 1857; we had been in Sydenham for more than three years. James had been in ill health during some of the previous winter and spring, and Fi was reassuring me that I should soon be free: it was little consolation, for I knew that she was implying that James would soon die.

We had talked about this subject again and again: Fi was devoid of compassion, but devoted to the idea of protecting James—and then consuming him as her reward. She had grown tired of the former, and eager for the latter, but the terms of her employment forbade any meddling. She was forbidden from causing injury or illness to her charge—but I wonder now if she would have let him die if he had some sort of apoplexy or attack, or intervened to save him.

I digress from my point. In July of that year, we began to hear about the unpleasant events in India. It began in Calcutta—the rebellion of a regiment in the Bengal Army—and spread all over the subcontinent. It was like a great wind that spread everywhere, causing small sparks to erupt into fires. There were many injustices and many troubles: India is not a simple place, Reverend Davey, as most Englishmen seem to believe. But the coming of the Mutiny, and the terrible events that took place, made James angry.

Why? It is very simple. He believed that *he* had caused it—by leaving the statue behind. He felt that it had incited the young Bengali at Barrackpore to rebel—and things simply began to unfold from there. It made him so despondent that for a time I thought he might do what Mr. Heath had done—take his own life in despair: he would not even speak to me—to Fi—for a few days, remaining distant even when we were together. He retreated to his study and read his books and wrote letters.

It lasted…well, the worst of his despondency was over in a week or so. He received a letter. Fi tried to keep informed about the post that came into the house, but throughout our marriage James had gone to considerable pains to keep prying eyes away from that which he considered to be his private business.

No, I do not have the letter: I do not know its contents or its import—but James began preparing for *your* visit not long afterward.

WILLIAM DAVEY

Eliza completed her narrative and again turned her attention to looking out the window. I remained silent out of courtesy.

At last I stood and offered Eliza a slight bow. "Madam, your information has been of great help. I promise that I shall do as I have done, keeping our practitioners away from your home. My need to understand the world beyond the Glass Door will help protect you from them, as well, I trust."

"Though I should like to say that I am indifferent to the knowledge, Reverend," Eliza said, "I am moved to ask what you plan to do."

"I am not certain," I answered, though I had already fixed upon a course of action. "I believe that at some point I shall have to place my feet upon foreign soil. Even if you do not wish for me to possess it, for certain others to have the statue would be even worse. It is not here, it is not in Scotland—and I believe that leaves only one place."

"India," she said, with resignation in her voice.

"Yes," I answered. "India."

CHAPTER 31

A tour of the grounds

WILLIAM DAVEY

Considering a trip to India was one thing and undertaking it another. It was certainly not something to do lightly, even if I had made the decision quickly: there were many things to arrange and dispose before leaving my domain—more so than when I had merely traveled north of the Tweed River to Scotland for a few weeks. I might have put it off indefinitely: I tell that to myself now, but I don't truly believe it.

But my hand was forced.

Early in September, Jackson informed me that one of his observers had reported the departure of Richard Daniel on a steamer bound east, for Cape Town, Madras and—likely—Calcutta. Dr. Daniel, now Ann Braid's devoted husband, was no doubt on his way to look for the statue. He possessed less information than I did and fewer resources, at least of the mundane or even mesmeric sort, but he had allies among the *stoicheia*. I wondered at the time what further debt he might need to incur to call upon them for assistance.

We are everywhere, the Levantine had told me.

Everywhere. In England, and in India as well. *Everywhere*.

All roads led back to the statue, and the road to the statue was a passage to India. While I remained in Sydenham, I decided to pay a visit to the Crystal Palace to determine, if I could, what had prevented both Eliza—Fi, as she called her *chthonic* jailor—and myself from carrying out our respective missions on that cold January day more than a year and a half earlier.

It was a much more pleasant day—warm, almost muggy, but a

satisfying change from the oppressive heat of London. Still, by the time I reached the Railway Colonnade attached to the train platform, I was overheated and sweating. I had only a few minutes to compose myself, however, before a train came into the station, bearing expected passengers.

Jackson disembarked haltingly and carefully with Bray beside him. As usual, Bray looked as if he'd not had a decent meal in weeks; he reached out tentatively to help Jackson descend. Whatever assistance was offered was ignored, as always: my lame friend had little interest in showing any sign of weakness. In fact, he looked furious as he made his way toward me, Bray following behind.

"Do you know who is on that train, Will?" he said as he reached me.

"Carlyle."

"Yes. *Carlyle*. In the first-class cabin, if you please. He didn't so much as try to make eye-contact with me—beneath his notice, I suppose. But I assume there is some reason for having him come out here."

"I invited him to join us."

"He despises you," Jackson said. He looked over his shoulder at Bray. "Carlyle despises him," he said.

Bray shrugged, and took my hand. "Davey," he said.

"Thank you for coming, Charles. And I think that Jackson exaggerates Carlyle's feeling toward me. He would despise me if he thought me worthy of it."

I looked past the two men toward the press of disembarking passengers. Thomas Carlyle emerged from the first-class compartment; he looked around, scowling, until our eyes met. Gathering what dignity was possible on the crowded train platform, he strode toward me.

"There had better be a damn good reason," Jackson said.

"He has some expertise in mathematics," I said, stepping around Jackson and Bray and extending my hand to the famous author, who took it briefly and then let go as soon as minimal courtesy was satisfied.

"Reverend Davey," he said. "Mr. Bray. Mr. Jackson." He did not take their hands. His expression was that of someone who had just swallowed something unpleasant.

"I have obtained entry tickets for us," I said, and began to walk along the Colonnade, a covered walkway that led between two rows of plants to the foot of a broad staircase. Without speaking, the four of us climbed them slowly until we found ourselves in a dining hall—the second-class Refreshment Room—and continued onto a second staircase by which we attained the main floor level. The great nave was before us: a huge fountain and, behind it, an ornamental screen that partially blocked our view of the rest of the hall.

"I am sure there is some *clever* reason we are here," Carlyle said as we stood there, letting other guests stream around us.

"Extend your senses, Carlyle," I said. "See if you can perceive the magnetic auras of anyone around you."

Carlyle cocked his head at me, but obligingly closed his eyes for a moment and then opened them.

"This is where Esdaile did away with himself," Carlyle said. "You were to end his life, but he ended it for you."

"Yes. It wasn't quite *here*—we were in the middle of the nave, that way—" I pointed past the screen toward the great hall beyond. "But it was in this building."

Carlyle craned his neck and looked around him. "This hall is quite different from the original."

"The guidebook is quite explicit on the differences. What interests me most is that *this* design interferes with the use of the Art and with the powers of *chthonic*—and possibly other—spirits. I thought it was high time we found out why."

"Is there a specific reason *I* am involved in this grand enterprise?"

"As it happens, Carlyle, yes. If I might have a brief word with you in private." I stepped away toward the stairs; Jackson and Bray obligingly remained in place, while Carlyle reluctantly accompanied me until we were fifty or sixty feet away.

"We are not close," I said quietly. "But I do respect your capabilities and your talents."

"You showed none of that when we met in Edinburgh."

"You demonstrated a remarkable ability to resist my inclinations. That impressed me quite a bit."

"You were making an unnecessary demonstration."

"I am not here to argue about that, Carlyle."

"Nor to offer an apology, I'd wager."

"Not that either. I am not seeking your friendship, nor looking to make any sort of demonstration. More than ever, I am determined to find the elusive statue—though I am no longer convinced that I should possess it. But I *am* convinced that Ann should not."

Carlyle did not answer aloud; he nodded, either in agreement with the sentiment, or merely that he understood my intention.

"I have therefore determined that I must go to India to find it. Richard Daniel appears to have already begun that journey. Accordingly, I have decided to appoint a deputy during my absence."

"I am therefore being asked to cooperate with Mr. Jackson, I suppose."

"Yes, but not in the way you expect. I have determined that I should appoint *you*."

Carlyle was clearly taken aback. "*Me?*"

"Yes. You're skilled, as I say, and you're well known on both sides of the border. The Scots respect you, the English will defer to you. You move in better circles than I do, and you are not perceived as my friend."

His expression confirmed my statement; but he thought for a moment and said, "And if things go awry you can blame them on me."

"Just so."

"Clever. Didn't Quillinan do the same thing?"

"Yes, but for him it was a *permanent* transfer of power. When I return from India, I intend to reassume my former position, and will not expect to have to challenge you in order to do so."

"What makes you think I would give it up willingly?"

I looked over at Jackson and Bray, and then thought for a moment. But this was no more than stagecraft; I already had an answer.

"Because I am certain that, after a few months, you will realize how little you actually desire it."

"And you invited me here to Sydenham to communicate this offer."

"In part. But your mathematical expertise—and skill in the Art—may help give us insight into the reason the Crystal Palace interferes with our practices…and with those of *stoicheia,* as well. If you've seen Magnus's plaques and the Major-General's key and made any sense of them, they may provide additional insight."

"When do you need my answer to your offer?"

"Now."

"That's rather abrupt, don't you think? I would like to think it over."

"You already have all of the information you require in order to make a decision; but I suppose if you need some time…a fortnight, then. If you accept, send me a telegram with the words 'Crystal Palace'. If you decline, send 'Benjamin Brodie'." Sir Benjamin Brodie was the former President of the Royal College of Surgeons; he had taken on Harriet Martineau, and generally held a very low opinion of mesmerism.

"And in the meanwhile…"

"We will explore the mysteries of the Crystal Palace," I said, lazily twirling my walking-stick.

When the Crystal Palace had closed in October 1851, there was considerable discussion as to what might be done with it. For a time, there was a negotiation with an American entrepreneur; but John Bull proved a bit too proud to let this jewel of Queen Victoria's reign be packed off across the Atlantic. A group of gentlemen formed a joint-stock company; it was immediately oversubscribed, giving it the capital to purchase the land on which the new structure now stood, including the surrounding gardens and other facilities.

Not surprisingly, some of the partners were railway men. It was no idle choice: a separate line was laid down to serve the Palace itself, with passenger service terminating at the platform where I had met Carlyle and the others. Tracks also ran underneath the building itself into a twenty-four-foot-wide passageway that (according to the Phillips guide-book) was affectionately titled "Sir Joseph Paxton's Tunnel", after the overall designer of the building. This tunnel led to the furnaces and boilers that ran the machinery and kept the Palace heated in winter and allowed such items as tropical plants to flourish in England's climate.

It also came as no surprise that the revised structure had been planned and executed on a scale significantly more grand than the original. Sydenham's edition was almost twice as long, and its roof soared more than forty feet higher than its predecessor; including the lower level—available due to the sloping ground upon which it was constructed—the new Palace was altogether half again as spacious.

To his credit, Carlyle took to the problem at once, applying his intelligence and background to the Palace's revised structure.

"They have changed the basic layout of the great transept," he said as we stood at the junction of the nave and center transept, where I had met Esdaile many months ago. He gestured to the columns. "These pillars have been moved forward, so as to break up the sight-lines, I suppose, but they will certainly affect the background magnetic aura."

"The spirits would collide with them," Bray ventured.

"Yes." Carlyle scowled at him. "Quite."

"That cannot be accidental," I suggested. "When Paxton redesigned the Palace, he must have chosen the pattern for a reason."

"It breaks the building up into logical parts," Carlyle said. "It might be some faux-artistic effort on Sir Joseph's part. He is not known to be a practitioner of the Art."

"But as Bray suggests," I said, as we walked slowly toward the court that displayed Greek and Roman sculpture, "it *does* interfere with the free passage of non-physical beings. And the arrangement is regular."

"Architecture. And structural dynamics," Carlyle answered. "When they first built it, half of the architects in England thought the damn thing would fall down. It was assumed that the columns could not properly support the girders—but Sir Joseph was smarter than the lot."

We reached Jackson and Bray just as he finished speaking.

"What about the harmonics?" Bray said.

"By which, you mean?" Carlyle asked, giving me a glance as if to say, *Is this why I would not want this job?*

"Could not the…vibrational effects of the structure interfere both with mesmeric auras and the abilities of *stoicheia*? They *are* quite sensitive to sound patterns."

Carlyle considered this for a time, as if he were attempting to determine whether Bray was more or less of an idiot than he had originally thought.

"There may be some merit to that observation, Mr. Bray," he said at last.

Less, I thought to myself. I had told Jackson to bring him along due to his latent interest in spiritualism. Harriet Martineau would have been better, but she rarely traveled; Spencer Hall would have just been difficult and annoying. Bray's insights might make him worthwhile—even if they merely bothered Carlyle, a prospect I found amusing.

"But surely," I said, as we contemplated a series of Roman busts, "this design is intentional."

"As I noted earlier, Paxton is no mesmerist, but he and Dickens were business partners for a short time," Carlyle said. "Paxton has no truck with the Committee, but I do not know his capabilities."

"I can't imagine he'd find the time," Jackson said. "'Busiest man in England', isn't he?"

"You are fond of jumping to conclusions, aren't you, Jackson?" Carlyle said.

"I don't quite know what you mean by that, Carlyle," Jackson said, glancing from me to Carlyle and back again.

"He means that we should take nothing for granted," I said. "I have assumed that neither Paxton nor James Fergusson—who passed the statue to Esdaile, you may recall—has any skill with the Art: but there is no actual evidence to support or contradict such a belief. There is only this." I extended my arms and turned around, looking at the sun coming through the great glass tiles of the roof, a hundred and sixty feet away. "And James Esdaile knew about its properties—before he moved down here."

"You are sure of that?" Carlyle asked.

"Quite sure," I said. "The tableau I experienced in January 1859 was based on knowledge Esdaile obtained years earlier, Carlyle. He planned to be here when he died, so that Eliza's *chthonic* inhabitant would not consume him."

"And to thwart *you*," Carlyle observed.

"Truly, I think that idea came later. Something changed his mind—something that happened around 1858—that led to his final letter to me."

"Perhaps someone"—Carlyle glanced pointedly at Jackson—"should research the newspapers. See if any two-headed cows were born, if the moon was blood-red, or any other such omens presented themselves."

"Your wit is tiresome," Jackson snapped at him.

"And your impertinence is *wearing*, Mr. Jackson. Reverend Davey, I do not require any further tutelage in the arts and sciences, and do not care to spend any more of my valuable time discussing theoretical matters with you. I shall contemplate your offer"— again, he looked pointedly at Jackson, then back at me—"and will respond to you presently. Good day, sir." He tipped his hat to me, turned his back and walked briskly away toward the south entrance and the train platform.

After a few uncomfortable moments, Bray excused himself and followed. I'd learned what I might from him; he might be going off to curry favor with Carlyle, but I didn't truly care.

"What an ass Carlyle is," Jackson said to no one in particular, once Carlyle was out of earshot.

"Tread lightly, Johnny," I said. "You may be working for that ass soon."

"Eh?"

"I have determined that I am finally going to go to India. I have to find the statue before others find it. And in my absence, I've asked Carlyle to assume control of the Committee."

"You've *what?*"

"As I said."

He looked me up and down, as if trying to evaluate what he'd just heard. "I am impressed with you," he said at last. "You have managed to encompass two insane ideas at the same time."

"I think you exaggerate."

"Yes, Will. It's called 'hyperbole'. All the rage."

"Look, I don't see—"

"No. You *don't.* You've decided to travel to India. This is wrong-headed for two reasons: first, Ann Daniel is a ticking bomb, and despite her current injuries she will certainly stir up trouble."

"I'm aware of that."

"Well, I'm quite happy to hear it. But second—" he stared off into the middle distance, then glanced back at me. "Second, this is not a good time to go to India. They're still hanging the mutineers and burning down their villages. I can't imagine that there is any brown-skinned man with a turban on his head who would have any interest in talking with you."

"I won't scruple to ask their permission."

"They are often armed with wicked knives, Will."

I ignored the last remark. "I am going to India, Johnny. It's decided and that's final. It's where the statue is; I need to find it before Ann Daniel—or one of her 'associates'—finds it."

"Assuming the *best* outcome, you'll be gone eight months. Your solution to the possible mischief is the *second* thing that strikes me as insane: your choice of successor."

"I'm not resigning."

"You're going into terrible danger, and there are a good double handful of our friends and colleagues who would be thrilled with the idea that you might never come back."

"I prefer to consider Carlyle my agent, acting on my behalf here in Britain while I am abroad. When I return, I shall take the reins again. If he does well, I will be pleased and he may go from being a rival to being a friend. If he does poorly, he will be a better scapegoat than any of my actual friends."

"You do not have that many friends."

"He will be a better scapegoat than *you*, Johnny."

"I doubt it. I have great skill in that area. But I am also adept at avoiding the usual fate of such creatures. I don't know why you don't just appoint me and be done with it."

"You are not paying attention. I have chosen whom I have chosen not because he is a friend, but because he is not a friend. Quillinan told me—"

"Not recently, I daresay."

You might be surprised, I thought to myself, recalling my dream of Holyrood Abbey. "Quillinan told me why he'd picked me, despite his low opinion of me. I am under no illusions that my deputed agent will conduct himself as I have done. But that's why I have you."

"He'll bring in his own man."

"I doubt it," I said. "He doesn't have that many friends, either."

The gathering in Vernon's rooms was unusually small. We were assembled at a dining-table; I sat at the head, Carlyle at my right and Jackson at my left. Hall and Higginson, Bray and Elliotson and a few others were there, including Lord Adare, a well-born dilettante, and the American 'levitator', D.D. Home, who was visiting London—but fortunately no Forbes. Dickens was absent, of course, as was Engledue: he had been making himself even more scarce than was customary for someone thought to be dead. They were all curious about Carlyle's presence.

Let them wait, I thought.

I presented, in brief, what I had learned in Scotland and Manchester and through my additional interview with Eliza Esdaile. The attendees, quieter and more pensive then they had been a year ago, followed my reasoning and deductions.

When I informed them that I intended to follow Richard Daniel and depart for India, they were less sanguine.

"I believe you should send someone in your place, Davey," Elliotson told me. There were murmurs of approval: with the most difficult troublemakers absent, Elliotson's opinions carried weight. "It is far too dangerous, and your duties are primarily here."

"Who would you propose that I send?"

"Send Engledue," Alfred Higginson said. "No one *there* thinks he's dead."

"I do not think he would carry out either my or the Committee's mandate."

"You find him untrustworthy?" Elliotson asked.

"*Unreliable*, Dr. Elliotson," I answered. To be honest, it did seem to me that Engledue had gone a bit round the bend in the past several months. "Which amounts to the same thing."

"I suppose that it does."

"It is my feeling that the Committee is best served if I take this matter directly in hand. I am the most skilled practitioner we have—" I waited to see if Adare, or Elliotson, or any of the others cared to suggest otherwise; none did. "And I expect that there are things in train there that we have not anticipated. In the meanwhile, I have chosen someone to act on my behalf. He has my full faith and confidence, and has enough skill and discipline to accomplish what is required."

"You have discussed this with the membership, Reverend

Davey?" Lord Adare asked me. His voice had taken on a paternal, somewhat lecturing tone.

"This is not a parliamentary debate, my Lord. It is my decision to make."

"Surely, on a matter of such import—"

"Excuse me, my Lord," I interrupted him. The nobleman stopped speaking. He was clearly unaccustomed to being contradicted. "It is my decision. If you feel otherwise, the Committee has a long-established procedure for contravening or ratifying such decisions."

The men at the table were quiet; they all looked down at Adare, whom I fixed with a steady gaze.

"I…am not making a formal challenge, Reverend. I assume that you will do as you think best."

And if you fail we'll come and cut your throat, he might have added. That was assuming, of course, that some brown-skinned man with a turban and a wicked knife hadn't done it already.

"Yes. And what I think best at this time is to appoint an interim Chairman of the Committee. Gentlemen, I give you my choice: Mr. Thomas Carlyle."

PART FOUR

Future and past

Stultum est timere quod vitare non potes.
(It is foolish to fear that which you cannot avoid)
—Publilius Syrus, *Sententiae*

CHAPTER 32

Lost in crowds

WILLIAM DAVEY

Even with the best of intentions, it took time to arrange a round trip of more than twenty thousand miles.

Jackson continued to be alternately astonished and furious with me for choosing Carlyle to act on my behalf while I was out of my domain. He understood my reasoning: I think his protests were more *pro forma* than anything else—it would not have done for him to acquiesce, and by complaining he preempted complaint from other members of the Committee with whom I had also not consulted before making my decision. Carlyle never acknowledged my efforts on his behalf. I did not expect it.

Reports from Bray and others provided details of Ann Braid's summer wedding. Not unexpectedly, I had not been invited to the ceremony. From what I was informed, the bride was assisted in standing and thereafter was confined to a wheel chair, requiring her maid Margaret to be constantly in attendance.

I could not conceal my plans to leave the domain, but did not intend to put about where I was to travel—at least not in advance: it was not information I wished to share. By mid-autumn, however, it was an open secret, as was Richard Daniel's rather obvious absence from his wife's side. Carlyle did nothing to dismiss the rumors; by the tail end of October I had completed all of my arrangements and had my tickets for the steamer *Empire Star*, departing on the twentieth of November—more than eight weeks after Daniel had departed.

I was about to learn how wide the rumors had spread.

Brunswick Wharf was only twenty years old at the time. It had not yet acquired the patina of grime or the run-down quality that were so characteristic of its later days. There had been a sort of curious railway line powered by two stationary locomotive engines and a series of wires and pulleys, operating between Fenchurch Street and Blackwell Station, terminating alongside the quay; apparently that contraption had been abandoned some years earlier, replaced by the normal train which conveyed me from downtown to the dock.

My trunk and other luggage had been sent on ahead and placed aboard the steamship—all that remained was for me to board with my carpet-bag and small suitcase. It was a bright late autumn day, brisk but not raw, with the faintest hint of the coming change of season.

No sooner had we passed the Minories than I felt a most untoward chill, as if a blast of cold air had been blown through the railway carriage. I knew at once that this was no atmospheric effect: none of my fellow passengers had appeared to take notice.

My first instinct was to turn and scan about to see who might be nearby: I was certain a *chthonios* was aboard, possibly even in a form I could recognize—but I did not want to reveal my awareness. Better to ride the four and a half miles—half a mile of which had already passed—and see what transpired at the dock. Thus, I continued to peruse the *Times*, playing the part of the absent-minded vicar on his way to a holiday. It was the longest half-hour of my life.

I had not planned to have anyone see me off as I boarded *Empire Star*, but to my surprise, I picked out John Jackson standing near one of the gangways. He saw me and touched the brim of his derby without looking directly at me, though I could see a worried expression on his face. In the midst of the disembarking crowd I could still sense the presence of the *chthonios*.

I noticed an elderly lady attempting to move a heavy parcel down the stairs. In a half-dozen quick strides against the tide of passengers I reached her and without a word I handed her down and moved the impossibly heavy package to the platform level.

"I am much in your debt, Vicar," she said, adjusting the veil on her hat. Something about the voice—and the face I could see, not so elderly after all—struck me as wrong at the time, but I was unable to place it: concern about the nearby nightfall creature clearly distracted me.

"Nothing at all, madam," I said to her. I beckoned to a nearby porter who, sensing the possibility of a tip, rushed over to assist her with her parcel. I took the opportunity to drift back into the crowd.

After a few moments, I stopped with the sudden realization that I had just been mesmerically dismissed. When I turned, porter and elderly passenger had disappeared as well.

It troubled me greatly that I had not been aware of the practitioner, or her dismissal gesture, until after the fact.

The departure time for the packet was still a few hours away. I walked away from the boarding area and into a reputable-looking pub, half-filled with respectable patrons who were waiting out the remaining time.

A combination of clergyman's charm and subtle, but tawdry, use of the Art procured me a place near a window, and I received a pint of bitter without too much more effort. From my vantage, I was able to survey the wharf; I could no longer see Jackson, but I did think I picked out Vernon chatting up a group of baggage-handlers who were assisting late-arriving passengers.

At last I identified the source of my concern. Standing at the head of the gangplank, surveying the wharf and scrutinizing the passengers as they boarded *Empire Star* in twos and threes, was a figure I had seen before.

The Levantine was aboard the steamship, and awaited my arrival.

Pint in hand, suitcase and carpet-bag nearby, I tried to take stock of my situation. First, a nightfall creature was aboard the vessel I planned to take to Calcutta, a trip of no less than seven weeks.

During that period, I would be out of my domain and would presumably be without allies; should I relax my diligence at any point, I would be vulnerable to whatever he might choose to do. They were a cruel and capricious race, making them dangerous—and unpredictable.

Second, my allies and friends were watching for the Levantine—and might have already identified him—but there could be others in the vicinity. I did not feel that I could confront the Levantine on an equal footing, and I was considerably more skilled than either Jackson or Vernon. They were least in danger while the Levantine, and any other nightfall beings, were looking for *me*.

My third concern was that a mesmerist of some skill had dismissed me with a gesture and I had not marked it *as it had happened*. Whatever the case, as long as I was bound for the Calcutta packet, and as long as the nightfall beings could isolate me there, I was in terrible danger—they would either seek to suborn me to their purpose or simply kill me outright. Much as I detested the idea of flight, I could *not* board that vessel. My trunk and other effects would have to travel without me.

Once I had reached that resolution, I felt as if my fate had returned to my own hands rather than being controlled by the whim of inexplicable beings.

I finished my drink and then, using whatever skill I could muster to conceal myself, I slipped out of the building and made my way among the crowd and away from *Empire Star*. I do not know if either Jackson or Vernon saw me go.

Blackwell is a busy place, with trains and ocean-going steam vessels and sailing-ships, as well as smaller steamers that ply routes up and down the Thames. It was not difficult to board one of the regular steamers bound upriver; in a matter of half an hour I was at Westminster, and a quick cab ride took me to Victoria Station.

Express trains from London to Dover ran eight times daily in those days; an "express" was two and a half hours from City to

Channel, covering less than a hundred miles. Just as the twenty minutes bound for Blackwell had been agonizing, so the traversal of that short distance was tense—but I felt no icy chill, and sensed no *chthonic* beings following my movements. They may have assumed—as Jackson and Vernon assumed, I later learned—that I had gotten aboard despite their scrutiny.

By the time I reached Dover it was already dark. I boarded the South Eastern and Continental packet scarcely half an hour after the train's somewhat tardy arrival and soon we were out to sea in the Channel. I fancied that I could see the distant lights of *Empire Star* off in the distance, far down near the Isle of Wight…but I concluded that it must, indeed, have been my imagination.

Sleep overtook me during the two-hundred-plus miles between the port of Calais and Gare Saint-Lazare in Paris. It was an unforgiveable lapse in discipline to sleep, since I was forced into a change of plan when traveling out of domain and had to anticipate more enemies. Still, I knew where I would go when I reached Paris.

Manchester Academy had taught me passable French. I had been a tutor for the children of my original patron, and had been expected to be able to teach the language. I had kept up practice as well as I could, and though it was obvious that I was an Englishman speaking a foreign tongue, I was able to make myself understood and to comprehend conversations around me. That may have lulled me to sleep, but the exclamations of fellow passengers jarred me awake. The train was slowly coming around a great curve, and Paris lay before me in the morning sun.

Despite all, it seemed that I had given my enemies the slip… but it meant that I was on my own and short of resources.

CHAPTER 33

Light in autumn

WILLIAM DAVEY

My decision to forego the trip aboard the steamship bound for Calcutta was based directly on the threat posed by the *chthonic* spirits. I wondered at the time why it was necessary for them to travel aboard ship at all: given their propensity to turn up at the most inconvenient time and place, why could they not simply appear in India and let me lead them to the statue? It might have been that while I was threatened by their presence aboard *Empire Star*, I would be more valuable alive than dead. The Levantine had told me in Manchester that I would eventually come to work with the *stoicheia*—they might be looking for another opportunity to convince me.

My decision to go to Paris, however, was not made merely to throw off those pursuers. I had at least one potential ally there. I had expected to have to find him: instead, after a fashion, he chose to find me.

Paris is a city of contradictions. Its residents—at least the ones who frequent its better parts—revel in their republicanism and their emperors, their saints and their apostates. Englishmen—unlike Scots—must overcome a long heritage of dislike when they come to the city. It is enough to underwrite the cost of restaurants and reading-rooms and entire hotels that cater to the Anglophone traveler. Regrettably, those who patronize such places to the exclusion of the rest of the city fail to appreciate the city's complexity and wonder.

I had not been there in more than twenty years. It was immeasurably changed, mostly through the work of the famous Baron

Haussmann—saint to some, apostate to others—who had been given a mandate by Emperor Louis Napoleon to change the face of the city. Much to the consternation of tens of thousands of residents and businessmen, his plan drew a series of broad lines across the map of the city, delineating wide boulevards that ran straight and true and crossed at major intersections. Much of that work was still in progress in the fall of 1860, though the mass expropriation of land and buildings to accomplish this feat had largely come to an end.

As is often the case with older cities, Paris's mesmeric background aura, the symphony that drowned out a thousand other noises, largely derived from its labyrinthine pattern of streets and alleys, hills and waterways. Haussmann's modernization changed all that, at least for the majority of the city. It was due to this alteration that I was noticed.

Just before tea time—a time of business in the City of Light, since Parisians are fond of long midday pauses, causing consternation to many foreign visitors—I was enjoying a strong cup of coffee and a delicate pastry in a café on one of the metropolis' newest streets, the Rue Saint-Antoine. My good French had obtained me adequate service from the staff, but my English accent earned only disdain from the other patrons. The coffee was a beverage best drunk either very slowly or all at once. The pastry, however, I had brought to ruin in a fraction of the time it had taken to carefully erect its delicate edifice.

As I watched the day's shadows slowly lengthen, a man approached. He was attired somberly but fashionably, and had an overly serious face. He had no hair atop his head: it appeared as if his tonsure had decamped from there and made for the sides, where it curled loosely around his skull. What was more, though he held his hands loosely at his sides, his left was slightly raised, palm turned. In short, he was attempting to cause me to rise from my seat to greet him.

He was a mesmerist. And if he could not perceive my own capabilities, he was a terribly incompetent one.

I relaxed in my seat, placing my hands on the table in front of me, palms down. I caught his glance and then slid my left hand forward, turning it very slightly at the wrist toward an adjacent seat. Without letting him go, I directed him to that chair. He obligingly sat in it. As soon as he had settled, I removed my hands from the table.

The gentleman started, as if I had just jostled him awake.

"Excuse me, Monsieur," he began in French. "I—"

"You are quite right," I interrupted. "Garçon," I added, catching the waiter's eye. "Please attend my companion here, Monsieur..." I looked at the man, who still looked somewhat startled. "I'm sorry, I did not get your name?"

"Leconte de Lisle," he said obligingly. "Charles Marie Leconte de Lisle."

"Yes. Of course. Coffee for you, Monsieur? Or something else?"

"Coffee."

"It is not the best," I said conversationally, "but it is strong and full-bodied. Another coffee." The waiter nodded curtly.

I turned my attention back to Leconte de Lisle. "Good of you to join me, sir," I said, adding quietly, "but you must work on your technique. If I were of a more unforgiving disposition, I *might* find it necessary to teach you a lesson."

"I don't know what you're talking about."

"Do not make me change my mind."

He paused, as if gauging my earnest, then nodded. "Very well. But may I have the honor of knowing with whom I speak?"

"My name is William Davey."

His raised eyebrows pushed his hairless forehead comically upward.

"Monsieur Davey," he said. There was some indication that he at least recognized the name.

"I am looking for the Baron."

"Baron?"

"Baron Dupotet."

"*Le Maître?*"

"Is that how he styles himself these days? Yes, I'm looking for *Le Maître*. I shall be most obliged to you if you can tell me where I can find him."

"He does not receive visitors, Monsieur Davey."

"He will receive *me*. Where does he reside?"

"I do not know, precisely," Leconte de Lisle answered. He seemed nervous and uncomfortable. "But," he added, as I frowned slightly and placed my hands back on the table, "he often takes a constitutional in the Tuileries gardens an hour or so before sunset. He does not go out in the open very much."

"Why is that?"

"He...does not wish to accidentally...lose contact with the earth."

"Indeed."

"So I am informed."

"So you are not an intimate of Baron Dupotet. Of *Le Maître*."

"I must admit I am not. But his direction is that we should be vigilant for...auras we don't recognize. You were a stranger, Monsieur Davey. I did not mean to offend...but I did not recognize you."

"Yet you know who I am."

He swallowed. "Yes. There are few English practitioners whose reputation is greater. I am...surprised that you are here."

"In this café?"

"In Paris."

"It was a spur of the moment decision. I shall await *Le Maître* in the gardens—but if I should fail to meet him today, I ask that you send him a message."

"*Certainement,*" Leconte de Lisle said. He seemed relieved: apparently my reputation was something to be conjured with.

"Tell him that you met me, Monsieur, and that...an old intimate...I need his help."

"He has—" Leconte de Lisle began. "He is...have you been in contact with *Le Maître* recently? You may find him changed."

"Only by letter. But I have not actually seen him in many years. What do you mean when you say he has 'changed'?"

"I am...not the intimate of *Le Maître*. I expect that you will find it out for yourself."

On my way to the gardens I stopped into a small bookshop. There, to my surprise, I came upon several volumes bearing Leconte de Lisle's name on the spine; they were collections of poems with classical themes. The work was ponderous, monotone, abstracted feelings and scornful phrases and declamations. I was no expert on poetry—then or now—but I thought they were complete rubbish. The shopkeeper, however, a diminutive, hyperactive little man with pince-nez and a little waxed turned-up moustache, set aside his natural Parisian disdain for foreigners when he noticed my interest; he gushed uncontrollably about the genius who had penned the works. I allowed myself to be separated from several francs and left the shop with a copy of *Poèmes antiques* in my possession, wondering if there might be a table somewhere in my future with a fourth leg that might need bracing.

It proved useful cover when I reached the Tuileries. In the waning afternoon sunlight I sat on a bench and puzzled through the poems, reinforcing my opinion of the man and his work. Passersby did not disturb me, because there was apparently some unwritten law regarding the interruption of a reader of poetry, even if obviously foreign. Still, I remained alert, and took note when Charles Dupotet de Sennevoy, walking-stick in hand, made his way toward my chosen bench, the breeze stirring fallen leaves around him as he approached.

He looked indeed much different from when I had last seen him, more than twenty years earlier, when I had been his student in London: then he had been most fashionable in his dress, almost flamboyant. Now his attire was somber and conservative, even a bit out of fashion.

He had aged—so had I: but now he walked in a peculiar way, gliding along the ground, his feet rising slowly and then falling rapidly, as if his boots were heavy. He recognized me at once and smiled as if we had not been apart for many years.

"William," he said. "May I join you?"

"Of course." I gestured to a seat beside me—not with a mesmeric gesture: Dupotet was at least my equal in skill with the Art. "I presume you heard of my intention to meet you."

"One hears things."

"Your…student?" I held up the little book, which I closed and set on the bench. "An interesting fellow."

"An interesting choice of phrase."

"He's a buffoon, actually. I chose to exercise restraint because I am in your domain, Charles. But he is ill-prepared. I hope that you do not have him employed in anything serious."

"Buffoon." Dupotet smiled. "We are concerned about visitors. You have stirred a great deal of trouble across *la Manche*, William. I cannot imagine what you think you're doing—but it is more dangerous than you know."

"I'm not doing anything."

"You are still Chairman, *non?*"

"Yes."

"Then you are *responsible*. You must put a stop to these activities before they go any further. There is no good that can come of making bargains with elemental creatures of that sort. Even if you do not care about the next life—and many do not—the *stoicheia* are fickle and capricious and will not fulfill your desires in *this* one."

"I know that."

"Then stop it *now*. Too many of their kind have already made the journey into our realm. The means to *dispose* of them are not readily available—we have all we can do to *control* them."

"I know. That's why I'm here, Charles."

"Ah. I assumed you would get to that eventually. Very well, my old friend: why, exactly, *are* you here? Don't tell me that you need my help."

"I need your help."

"Did I not just expressly request that you *not* tell me that?"

"I assumed that was merely a rhetorical flourish."

He smiled again. My dry English wit always entertained him, for some reason I could not fathom: it seemed impenetrable to most Frenchmen, even in their native language.

"It is not," I said.

Baron Dupotet took a moment to reply, as if my earnest answer took him aback.

"My dear William, my Society has no interest in your quarrels and petty violence. I thought I had made that clear on many occasions."

"This is not a power struggle within the Committee, Charles. Well, I suppose that it *is*, to some extent, but it is far more than that. It involves a more fundamental challenge to the way in which these beings are contained."

"You *know* how they are contained, William?"

"They call it the 'Glass Door'," I answered. "Someone is trying to open it."

"I don't think I have heard that term before."

"This is *their* term, Charles. For centuries many—most—of them have been trapped in the polar regions. Only recently have they found their way back into temperate lands."

"Due to—"

"Polar explorations."

"Eh, *oui*?" Dupotet lifted one foot and settled it, then did the same with the other. The sound of his boots was heavy and solid. "*Recently*. That makes sense. Polar regions, you say?"

"Without doubt. I have it from an unimpeachable source—the testimony of one of the beings."

"I told you that bargains with—"

"It was not testimony I received directly, Charles. It was an account—" I let my sentence drift off. An elderly couple, she in a long dress a little out of fashion, he in a handsome suit, walked by, the woman clinging to the man's elbow. He moved with military precision: he might have been a soldier with the first Napoleon. He offered us a tip of the hat which we returned with a polite nod. When they had passed, I continued. "It was an account given to James Esdaile's wife by her—inhabitant—and relayed to me. It was very revealing."

"And you credit it with being true."

"I am convinced of it. And I concur with your concerns, Charles. These beings pose a *direct* danger to us: all of us—English, French, Hindoo and Moor and Chinaman, too. I must prevent them from their goal."

"To open the 'Glass Door'."

"Precisely. It is my intention to go to India for that reason."

"India? Why India?"

As succinctly as I could manage, I outlined the role of James Esdaile in the events of the past two years. I refrained from mentioning the nature of the object I believed to be the key to the Glass Door. He was distant and detached as he listened. Dupotet had changed from the man I had known when we both were younger and less burdened by responsibility.

I have always been inclined to the belief that information should be in the hands of the minimum possible number of people—for their protection as well as the guardianship of my own interest. I would be beholden to Dupotet should he choose to help me; there was no need to involve him further.

By the time I had finished the sun had vanished beyond the Champ de Mars and lamps were being lit. Dupotet continued to sit quietly for several moments, then turned his attention directly to me.

"You have told me only half the story, my friend. Or—is it the entire story, fashioned from half-truths?"

"I have told no lies, Charles. But I have kept some details to myself."

"Then I ask you. What help do you wish? How do you intend that I assist you?"

"I need to travel to Calcutta. I expect now to make much of the journey by a route I had not planned. I do not think that it is critical that I reach India before the *chthonios* that boarded *Empire Star*. Richard Daniel is already ahead of me in any case. Still, I do not think that my mission brooks further delay. You have contacts across Europe—or once did: I wish to prevail upon you to write to them, so that I may obtain introductions and assistance."

"I should call in favors on your behalf."

"Essentially, yes."

"The Committee is held in...less than high regard in certain quarters, William. I assume you know that. Your methods—*your* methods in particular—have excited some controversy."

"I have done what I felt was necessary, Charles. I am not here to make apologies or amends."

"I had asked that you not request my help." He sighed. "And you took it for a rhetorical flourish. Very well, William: for the sake of our old friendship—and because the need is great—I shall do this. But there will come a time that I will call in this favor—doubled or trebled, I imagine. I trust my meaning is clear."

"Extremely so."

"Good." Dupotet, once resolved, seemed almost relaxed. He stood up and I joined him. "Then I think we should attend to the next pressing concern before us."

"Which is?"

"Dinner."

CHAPTER 34

To the window

WILLIAM DAVEY

I ultimately spent two days in Paris. I lodged at the Hôtel des Étrangers in the guise of a visiting scholar.

Though internally I fretted about the lost time, I tried to make the best of it; Dupotet provided me an introduction to a few of his colleagues, including a formal one to the poet Leconte de Lisle. This encounter confirmed my earlier opinion—the man thought altogether too highly of himself. He had a reputation for deep thinking that was built upon a foundation of shifting sand; but such is the relationship between Frenchmen and their poets. Even Dupotet spoke highly of his literary feats, while admitting that his skill as a mesmerist left something to be desired.

In any case, I did not intend to remain in Paris long enough to ingratiate myself with the resident mesmerists, at least the ones over whom Charles Dupotet de Sennevoy presided as *Le Maître*. The *Société de l'Harmonie Universelle* claimed direct descent from the original body formed by the legendary Mesmer himself; it possessed a more mystical and philosophical bent than our own Committee.

Overall, despite its pedigree, it was not a particularly practical instrument for effecting useful action. With Dupotet—*Le Maître*—at its center, it had been turned into a cult of personality; in comparison to our rather brutal meritocracy, it was neither forceful nor efficient.

While I was personally known and my skill was respected, my Englishness was mildly disdained. As long as I obtained the help I needed, I cared very little for their opinion. Deflecting their questions and dismissing their frivolities were a matter of merely exercising patience and world-weariness. The rest was simply bluff and arch superiority.

My time in Paris was both gratifying and frustrating. Dupotet, once he determined that he would help me, was courteous and insightful; but I was eager to get on my way and had to wait until he was able to make dispositions on my behalf.

I had expected to depart from Gare Saint-Lazare for a destination somewhere to the east—Amsterdam, perhaps, or Berlin; instead, on the second night following my arrival, *Le Maître* directed our steps to the new railroad station, the Gare de Lyon, where he provided me with a first-class ticket for Marseilles and a steamship billet for Alexandria.

"I have sent letters on your behalf, William. Expect help in Alexandria, at least. I have further arranged for someone of approximately your height and build to don a suit that matches this drab and highly unfashionable one you wear. He will be on the express for Munich this evening," he told me as we stood in the smoky concourse. "And before you complain, William, it is someone who is well-skilled in the Art."

"I was actually going to react to the jibe about my clothing."

"Really, I think that was *quite* on target. Minister or not, you really must consider returning here after your business in the East is finished. I shall introduce you to my tailor."

"I appreciate your concern."

"I truly *am* concerned about you," Dupotet said. He paused and glanced up and down the wide concourse; I did as well, wondering if I might catch a glimpse of the Levantine somewhere nearby. There was no such apparition.

"Why?"

"It puts me in mind of a cartoon I saw some years ago," Dupotet answered. "Before the late revolution. It showed our former king, Louis-Philippe, sitting on the cover of a teapot that was boiling over.

He had talked about the 'storm in the teapot' to his ministers—but it erupted on him and gave us a republic."

"For a few years."

Dupotet snorted. "Yes. Well, that is the politics of my country. When I consider your situation, William, I am put in mind of that cartoon. You are sitting atop a major problem that has already begun to erupt."

"I am working to avoid the worst."

"Yes. Yes, of course. But if it were truly under your control you would not be here—and asking for my help." He embraced me after the custom of the French: a bit unseemly, except we were in France, after all. Then he held me out at arms' length. "I shall call upon you in future. But in the meanwhile—" and his face went from merry to serious. "Do not let matters reach the stage at which your people are unwelcome in my domain."

"I shall do my best, Charles."

"I know you will."

At that time the railway from Paris to Marseilles was not an express route: it was a new line, scarcely a dozen years old, and I am sure that if I had been traversing it by day I would have found it remarkably scenic. Instead we passed ghost-like through Dijon, Châlons-sur-Saone, and then—deep in the night—Lyons, before leaving civilization behind and climbing into a remote, tree-covered region. From there we were to descend to the port and see the Mediterranean. In the dark compartment I made my best effort to sleep, but as we were obliged to make a number of stops on sidings, my rest was fitful at best. Once in the night I wondered if we had stopped to allow Hannibal's elephants to cross in front of us…but it was my imagination, or more likely the wind.

Awakening at night when a train halts on a siding or a train-platform is a curious feeling. It is not always quite possible to determine what interrupted one's sleep—and then suddenly the scene comes into focus. It is as if there is no one else awake: then in the quiet a whistle is blown and the train shudders into motion.

I wondered as I traveled southward what might be happening at home; however, I had chosen to put all of that aside by embarking upon this journey. Dupotet had, at my request, sent a two-word telegram to Carlyle just after my departure from Paris: "Chairman safe." He would, I hoped, convey that assurance to the other principals of the Committee—or not: I had not imposed any constraints on my deputy's style except to protect the interests of the organization. He might well choose to keep Vernon, Jackson and others in the dark, either from his own arrogance or to demonstrate his strength of will. Meanwhile, he would use the fine pretext of keeping information from the Committee's enemies. Carlyle was a Germanophile and unimpressed with the French, after all, though that was nominally only in the realm of literature.

When it began to become light I could see Marseilles spread out like a beautiful painting, with the Mediterranean shining beyond from the rays of the sun not yet visible. I had come through the night, traveling from darkness into light. My journey had only lately begun, but in a way, I felt that I had been freed from the perilous corner in which the *chthonios* had sought to trap me. I told myself that whatever lay ahead I would meet with firm decision, with my eyes open and in full possession of the initiative.

In that respect, I was totally and completely wrong.

I will not dwell upon the two days I spent in Marseilles waiting for the Alexandria steamer. The light rain sweeping off the sea dampened my spirits somewhat, but it was the forced patience that irked me the most, as I remained eager—I might even venture to say *anxious*—to be on my way. When the vessel finally arrived, the weather had at least turned pleasant. I boarded along with several other passengers and a large number of huge sealed cartons and sacks labeled with the mark of the French Emperor's postal service—some, I noted, with destinations in India—like myself.

But most cargo and passengers were bound for the Italian coast, despite the unrest there owing to the *risorgimento*.

We traveled for three days, following the southern shore of Provence. If my mission had not been driving me on I should have enjoyed the trip far more: the Provençal coast with its tree-covered hills dappled with sun and rocky promontories jutting into the sea is extraordinarily beautiful for anyone not condemned to the scourge of seasickness. I was not afflicted in the slightest by that malady, but despite my earlier feelings of freedom I could not avoid being troubled by what lay immediately before me. Still, the balmy and sunny pattern that replaced the recent intemperate weather was utterly different from the damp and foggy city of London in the autumn.

However, as I sat on the deck with the smokestacks and a straw hat affording me shade, I encountered some difficulty focusing on the matter at hand—*chthonic* spirits, Ann Daniel, the death of James Esdaile, Eliza—all of it; these things seemed distant, matters that elicited someone else's concern.

Our second day at sea we passed Corsica; the mountains were already covered with snow and their tops disappeared into the clouds. While we steamed along the coast of the island, we were followed by a whale for a time; it was a frequent companion and apparently the sailors considered it a good omen.

The ship halted at Naples for almost a full day and departed by night. From the stern I watched the light from brooding Mount Vesuvius until it disappeared below the horizon.

Those ships that do not pass between Scylla and Charybdis in the Strait of Messina follow the coast to the north-western tip of Sicily. This cape is rocky and decorated with a scattering of small islands. In sailing days, ships had to weather that promontory to begin their travels eastward, but a modern steam vessel need only travel wide enough to avoid any hazard that such rocky islands might present. I had been drowsing in the midafternoon sun and noted the course change, turning our path east and south, placing the sunlight to starboard instead of ahead—and I was suddenly struck with the unusual feeling that we were being pitched *downward*, as if the sea itself were inclined in the direction we were traveling.

I could not account for this sensation, which grew greater as afternoon wore into evening. We passed a sward of green on our right—the island of Pantelleria, a bucolic-looking place that was a possession of the King of the Two Sicilies; it was swiftly left astern and was clearly not the source of my unusual feeling. I did not receive confirmation until early the following morning when, standing on deck in gray pre-dawn, I saw us drawing near the distant land.

By late morning I could at last resolve features on the horizon. What I had taken to be Malta—not being completely versed in the geography of the central Mediterranean—was in fact the rocky island of Gozo, the northwestern of the main islands in the Maltese archipelago. We were to steam along the north side of the islands to Grand Harbour on Malta proper; Gozo was not on our itinerary, merely a place to view just as Pantelleria had been on the previous evening. Still, I obtained the use of a spyglass from a crewman so that I could take a closer look.

As I swept the glass along the horizon, I picked out a singular formation of rock—a sort of arched bridge on the coast of Gozo, extending a number of feet out into the water; the waves of the Mediterranean crashed at its base and washed through the opening between the single pillar out in the ocean and the mainland.

I lowered the spyglass with astonishment. The crewman who had lent me the device squinted at me, then took the glass from my hands and spied in the direction I had been viewing.

"*Bien, oui,* that's a pretty one," he said. "Not sailed this way before, Monsieur?"

"What? Oh, no, never," I said. "What…would you tell me what we are looking at?"

"Oh, that? Quite a natural wonder. It's called the 'Azure Window', Monsieur. At low water you can climb right up into it—it's, I should say, a hundred fifty feet high—less when the tide is up. You can see right through it; that's why they call it a window, I think."

"Quite," I said, and accepted the spyglass back from the man. To the naked eye it was as he had said—a rock arch with the rough headland of Gozo visible through the 'window'…but when I trained my spyglass on the formation, I did not see land beyond, framed by the stone arch.

It looked to me like a firmament dotted with pale stars scattered across a dark night.

CHAPTER 35

Antipodes

WILLIAM DAVEY

I thought it possible that Dupotet might have planned my route so that I could experience something in Malta, but I ultimately discarded the notion as the workings of my own suspicious mind. After all, Leconte de Lisle's warning—as well as my own observations—had shown me that *Le Maître* had indeed changed, but the gravity of the threat and his ready acquiescence to my need for assistance suggested that he did not seek to provide me any particular epiphany. Therefore, as far as I could tell, Charles Dupotet de Sennevoy had not arranged a learning experience for me.

But as we anchored in Grand Harbour, the beautiful port of Malta's principal town, Valetta, I still lacked the answer to what had caused the sensations I still felt—and what I had seen when gazing through the Azure Window.

We made port late in the morning and were not scheduled to depart until the next day after the ship recoaled. Those passengers who chose to do so could disembark and spend the day and night ashore, with the strict admonition that they should be aboard by eight o'clock the following morning. I concluded that I could use a respite from my cramped quarters and the full heat of the day on the ship's deck, and went ashore along with a few others. I engaged a room at a small hotel in Birgu.

Malta was a colony of the British Empire, but that was a relatively recent evolution in its history. For a few centuries it had been the home of the Knights of St. John, a military order that dated from the Crusades; it had taken up residence on these barren rocks after the Ottoman Emperor Suleiman had ejected them from

Rhodes in 1530. Their occupation of the strategic little island chain and their zeal as corsairs annoyed that prince, causing him to invade it thirty-five years later to further dislodge them. While most of the Christian world remained on the sidelines, a handful of Knights and a few thousand inhabitants had prevailed against absurd odds; their resistance to the might of the Turk conjured up images of superhuman—and perhaps supernatural—bravery. Only Napoleon—not his lesser nephew who led France at the time of my journey, but the great one who had conquered most of Europe—had managed to overcome these knights, seizing Malta in 1798. After the tyrant was finally deposed, the islands became property of the British crown.

Other than its history, I knew blessed little about Malta—in the middle of the century, as at present, the British Union Jack flies everywhere in the world: every continent, on the shore of every sea, fluttering in every wind. Malta was just another colony, though one that—like Gibraltar—was close to the home islands and in a particularly strategic location. If it had not captured my attention, I might well have simply passed it by on my way to more momentous things.

A bit after noon, with most of the town dozing through the midday hours, I began my journey away from Fort St. Elmo. I felt the unusual tugging of the strange phenomenon as I walked slowly, stick in hand, across the broad peninsula of Mount Sciberras. I had not chosen to hire a guide to share my journey, despite many offers of the same; I assumed that I should not need one, given the size of the island. In any case, I preferred to be alone for my explorations. As I had departed Birgu to be rowed across Grand Harbour, numerous residents had looked askance at me—certainly I did not look the sort who could survive crossing the water, much less a hike across the vast limestone hills of Malta: but like most natives in most places, they assumed that I would receive my due comeuppance.

A mile or so from the fort, with the Mediterranean still well in

sight, I came upon a narrow footpath that led me to a small defile.
I scrambled down, heedless of the obvious fact of which the average
Maltese was aware—that were I to fall and injure myself even this
close to civilization on this small an island, I would lie uncovered
and subject to the elements for some time at best, and perish igno-
miniously due to exposure at the worst. Nonetheless, I managed the
descent without incident and shortly found myself confronted with
a rock overhang beneath which I could see a concealed
cave-mouth.

I had thoughtfully packed a lantern for just such an eventuality.
A torch might have been better; but though pitch was a readily
available substance on an island full of sailors, wood was still at a
premium. Thus the lantern. I struck a match and lit the wick,
shielding it from the stiff fresh wind that blew even into the defile
where I now stood, and prepared to enter the cave.

Once again, had I considered the possibility that I might
somehow become trapped, alone and at some remove from the
towns of the island, I might have reconsidered my precipitate
action. Of such sturdy foolhardiness are heroes made.

I thus bent down almost to my knees, my lantern held out in
front of me like Diogenes, and moved under the rock overhang and
into the narrow cave entrance. Just beyond, I discovered that I could
stand almost upright; I found myself in a narrow gallery that sloped
slightly downward, agreeably to the incline which my perceptions
indicated. After ten or fifteen feet the passageway bent sharply to
the left, cutting off my view of daylight; I stepped forward carefully
and found myself in a larger chamber, one which afforded me the
ability to stand fully erect.

No sooner did I do so but a strong gust of air from somewhere
put out the light of my lantern, leaving me unexpectedly in
darkness.

With my light suddenly extinguished, I was seized with a panic
that prevented me from drawing breath for several seconds. As I
knelt and fumbled for a match to reignite the lantern, I was able to

discern that the darkness around me was far from absolute: there were faint glowing spots visible on the walls. I also noted that the chamber was much more vast than I had originally thought—I stood on a sort of balcony, and it extended some considerable distance up and down from my current position.

It was also apparent that this place was the source of the feeling that I had experienced from the time we had rounded Sicily. *This* was the location that had drawn me.

And finally, I realized that in that chamber there was a presence—perhaps several presences—that was so strong that I was almost unable to rise from my knees. Were I of weaker character I might not have been able to stand at all: I cannot imagine the consequences of that circumstance.

Instead, I left the lantern where it was and got to my feet.

"Who is it—" I began.

Man, a soundless voice said. **Man.**

I felt rather than heard it, echoing throughout the chamber, not all at once, but slightly out of phase. As the word was spoken, each of the glowing patches seemed to become brighter for a moment, then returned to its former state.

"Yes." I glanced behind me: the corridor was there, daylight was only a few dozen feet away. "And you are not."

It is far from what we are, the voices managed simultaneously.

"I should like to know with whom—with what—I am speaking."

That is not under discussion at this moment, Man, the initial voice said, the one that all the rest had echoed. **We deliberate on quite another matter.**

I strongly considered retreating; once again I felt as if I should be driven to my knees by the voices in the chamber, and suspected that retreat was not an option.

"I should be honored to know what you discuss."

It is your demise, Man.

"I do not take lightly to the idea that others are deciding my fate," I said.

WE DO NOT CARE ABOUT YOUR OPINION.

"Clearly you *do*," I ventured. "Or you would not trouble yourselves to keep me informed of your discussions."

I believe that it goes without saying that I was frightened. I am more than willing to admit that fact. But it occurred to me at that moment that if these beings—whatever they were—wished to simply slay me, they could have done so without the trouble of deliberation or debate. I told myself that I therefore remained safe as long as they kept talking. Their silence, not their speech, was dangerous.

YOU ARE BOLD TO SPEAK THUS, MAN.

"I shall even be sufficiently bold to introduce myself."

WHY DO YOU SUPPOSE THAT WE CARE?

"It is merely rhetorical. For convenience and courtesy. And I would have your names as well, should you possess them."

YOU WOULD BE BETTER SERVED TO EXPLAIN WHY YOU ARE HERE, MAN, THAN TO TROUBLE US WITH MEANINGLESS IDENTIFICATION.

"Nonetheless," I continued, "I have the honor of presenting myself. My name is William Davey, and I have come here because I sensed your presence. I think—I believe I even saw you from far away. Through the Azure Window."

CURIOSITY.

"Just so."

A WEAKNESS OF MEN. WHAT DO YOU WANT FROM US, WILLIAM DAVEY? OR IS YOUR CURIOSITY SATISFIED?

"I should think that it is not. I want, however, only to return to the light. Other duties await me."

SHOULD WE PERMIT YOU TO CARRY THEM OUT.

"I hope that I might have some say in the matter. Again I ask you—how are you called?"

NAMES ARE UNIMPORTANT, the voice replied. IN ANY CASE, OUR RACE IS LONG FORGOTTEN BY YOURS. WE WERE OLD WHEN NATIONS OF

MEN YOU NO LONGER REMEMBER WERE ALREADY DUST. YOUR MOST
ANCIENT ACCOUNTS BEAR ONLY THE SMALLEST HINTS.

"Are you *stoicheia*, then? Elemental spirits?"

I felt a wave of resentment—possibly even anger—that made
me unsteady on my feet.

THEY ARE CHILDREN COMPARED TO US. WILLFUL, ARBITRARY,
CRUEL AND QUICK TO ANGER. THEY PLAY AT THE GAMES OF MEN FOR
THEIR OWN PURPOSES. BUT...WE ARE NOT LIKE THEM.

"I meant no offense."

WE DO NOT CARE ABOUT YOUR COURTESY.

"What do you care about? Is there something...you want?
From me?"

IT IS POSSIBLE.

It was the most interesting response I could have imagined.

"And what should be my reward for this service?"

WE WOULD NOT TERMINATE YOUR EXISTENCE.

I squared my shoulders and took a breath. "While I am most
gratified that you should grant such a favor, I do not believe that is
in the nature of a reward. If you wished to slay me, you would have
done so. If you do not wish to offer me something for my service,
you should perform the act yourself and I can be on my way."

I attempted to step back, but found my feet rooted to the spot,
as surely as if a powerful practitioner of the Art had commanded me
to stay in place.

WE HAVE NOT CHOSEN TO DO SO, the voice said at last. WE
REMAIN HERE AT THE MAGNETIC ANTIPODES. IT IS SURROUNDED BY THE
SEA IN THE MIDDLE OF THE EARTH. THE CHILD SPIRITS DO NOT DARE
TO COME HERE.

"Why?"

THEY ARE AFRAID OF US. THEY ARE CAPRICIOUS AND FLIGHTY.
THEY CREATE WITHOUT HEED OF CONSEQUENCE; THEY DESTROY
WITHOUT A THOUGHT. THEY DO NOT KNOW WHAT THEY DO—AND
THEY DO NOT KNOW AT WHOSE BIDDING THEY ACT.

I felt a chill run along my back.

"And you do."

YES.

"They are more powerful than *I* am," I said carefully. "If you want me to move against them, you must realize that I am a poor instrument."

YOU UNDERESTIMATE YOURSELF, WILLIAM DAVEY, the single voice said. YOU HAVE SURVIVED THIS LONG FOR A REASON.

"I am careful and plan ahead."

WE MEAN, the chorus of voices said, YOU HAVE SURVIVED THIS CONVERSATION FOR THIS LONG FOR A REASON.

I paused for a moment, and then replied, "You have given me no choice."

THERE IS <u>ALWAYS</u> A CHOICE.

"What would you have me do?"

YOU MUST STOP THE POWER THAT CONTROLS THE SPIRITS YOU CALL <u>STOICHEIA</u>. IT IS KNOWN TO US—AND TO YOU.

"By which you mean the statue."

THAT IS NOT QUITE CORRECT.

"I await your explanation," I said. I did not know if I was antagonizing them by my banter, but as long as they were still talking to me it gave me some illusion of control over the conversation.

THE <u>STATUE</u> IS NOT THE POWER THAT CONTROLS THE SPIRITS, WILLIAM DAVEY, the voice said. IT IS A PRISON THAT CONTAINS THAT POWER. THERE IS A BEING TRAPPED WITHIN THE STATUE: AN ADEPT FROM THE CIVILIZATION THAT CREATED THE STATUE CAPTURED THE BEING AND RENDERED IT POWERLESS.

"How did he do that?"

IT WAS A MOMENT OF WEAKNESS. THE BEING WAS NOT THE MOST SKILLED AMONG US, AND THE ADEPT WAS THE MOST SKILLED AMONG THEM.

It took a moment for that to sink in. "You mean—that the inhabitant of the statue is one of *your* kind?"

YES.

"And you want me to rescue it?"

CERTAINLY NOT, the voice said. IT FAR EXCEEDS YOUR CAPACITY. NO: IT WAS TRAPPED—LET IT REMAIN SO. IT IS NOT THE BEING'S

ENTRAPMENT THAT CAUSES OUR ATTENTION; IT IS THE POSSIBILITY THAT IT MIGHT ESCAPE, DESPITE ITS LONG IMPRISONMENT. WHEN IT WAS TRAPPED WE DID NOT CARE. ONLY WHEN IT EVOLVED A SCHEME FOR ESCAPING DID WE TAKE AN INTEREST. FOR YOU—OR ANY MAN—TO THWART IT WOULD BE FAR BETTER THAN IF WE WERE ROUSED TO ACTION.

"And if I choose to decline this singular honor?"

AS YOU OBSERVE, WILLIAM DAVEY: THERE IS <u>ALWAYS</u> A CHOICE. BUT KNOW THIS. IF WE WERE ROUSED TO ACTION, WE WOULD BE INDIFFERENT TO ANY CONSEQUENCES THAT MIGHT AFFECT YOU, OR THE STOICHEIA, OR ANYONE OR ANYTHING ELSE. IT WOULD BE BETTER FOR YOU IF THIS PROBLEM IS SOLVED WITHOUT OUR INTERVENTION.

"Better that you remain here in this cave."

THAT IS NOT QUITE CORRECT.

"That it's *better*?"

THAT WE ARE HERE IN THIS CAVE. THIS IS FOR <u>YOUR</u> BENEFIT. All the voices chimed in at this sentence.

I did not quite know what to make of the statement.

WE WILL NOT WARN AGAIN, WILLIAM DAVEY, they said, and the ground around me began to shake.

I found myself able to move, and without hesitation I turned and ran back along the tunnel's brief dogleg. Dirt and rock were starting to fall even as I ran upward along the passageway, which I seemed to do at an agonizingly slow pace, as if I were running uphill into a strong wind. I ducked barely low enough, diving through the short opening below the overhang, then crawled on hands and knees as quickly as I might manage.

Some bit of falling rock must have struck my head at some point; when I next possessed my senses, day had turned to night. My vision was blurred, my eyes were watery; I reached into a pocket of my coat and drew out a kerchief. There was a nearly full moon partway up in the sky.

Behind me there was no trace of an overhang, a cave or any sort of rock formation. The feeling that I had experienced for the last few days remained, but it was muted and dim—the aura of the anti-magnetic island and its elemental inhabitants had been muddied.

At every turn, the tale seemed to be getting more complex. As I picked myself up and prepared to make my way back, I allowed to myself that I might, indeed, have had a very close brush with death.

CHAPTER 36

Guided through the Orient

WILLIAM DAVEY

It is fair to say that I was shaken by my brief stay in Malta. My understanding of the situation had begun to fall into place; it was now clear why the *chthonoi* were so interested in the recovery of the statue. I wondered how much of this Esdaile had known, and how much he had merely suspected.

A day's sea travel from Malta placed us in a different sort of Mediterranean than I had previously experienced. It was warm and dry—even the sea seemed a different color. As our vessel steamed along toward the Egyptian coast, I watched from the deck and felt as if I was transported into another world.

When the land mass of Africa first came into sight, it was almost indistinguishable on the horizon. It lay scarcely above sea level, featureless, with hardly anything that could be called a hill. Only when we were hard by Ramleh, a resort for wealthy Egyptians, were there any distinguishable features—primarily windmills, catching the fresh breeze from the sea and turning steadily, modern improvements that surely must have been an innovation by His Majesty's government when Egypt came under British influence at the beginning of the current century. There was little evidence otherwise that the land had changed since the time of Exodus and the Pharaohs—at least until we came in sight of Alexandria itself. The great ancient wonder, the Pharos, had long since been destroyed, leaving us to make our own way into the great natural harbor.

The city of Alexandria, its red-tinted stone walls bleached to a pale color by the unrelenting sun, bore little resemblance to the great and famous one about which every school child had read and every scholar lamented—and upon reaching the dock it was even less so. Neither truly Middle Eastern nor truly European, it seemed to bear traces of the worst of both worlds.

I knew that my ultimate destination would be the port of Suez, accessible by Stephenson's new railroad linking the two locations. It had only been open for a few years, but had been revolutionary for communications and commercial interests—something which the Canal, only in its infant stages at that time, would redouble. Dupotet had suggested that I might find some help here; nonetheless, I was somewhat wary when I disembarked at Alexandria—and since I was not directly met by a porter or a servant, I was set upon by all manner of individuals speaking a combination of English, French, Greek and patois culled from half a dozen other languages, offering to assist me with bags, with transport, with hotel accommodation and with every sort of fruit imaginable and available from the local *suq*.

Fortunately, the siege was lifted by the arrival of a singular individual. He was a military man—though his uniform was unusual, not least because the jacket seemed to be of an unusual cut. He was also one of the tallest soldiers I had ever seen, standing well over six feet, though weighing no more than fourteen or fifteen stone.

He knew how to deal with the crowd that beset me. He dispatched them both verbally and physically until he stood alone before me, at last giving me a good look at him. He was young—certainly not quite thirty years old—with quite a military bearing, and wore his hair neatly trimmed and his moustaches long and drooping—but no beard; he shielded his face from the sun by means of a broad straw hat similar to the one I had employed aboard ship, though his was fitted with a fold of cloth that covered his neck and touched his shoulders, protecting him yet further from the fierce glare of the sun.

"Mr. Davey," he said. His accent was not quite English—it sounded almost American, but not quite.

"Whom shall I thank for my rescue, sir?"

"My name is Dunn," he answered. "Alexander Dunn." He touched the brim of his hat. "Major in the 100th Regiment of Foot, sir."

"I thank you very much."

"All part of the service," he said, guiding me by the elbow. "Do you have luggage? A trunk, perhaps, or a portmanteau?"

"I am traveling rather lightly." I gestured to my carpet-bag and suitcase. My heavier luggage was, of course, traveling without me aboard a steamship bound for Calcutta.

"Don't tell me you have no more than that, coming all the way from Paris?" He lowered his voice and added, "I cannot imagine that *Le Maître* let you get away without a visit to his tailor."

"He merely threatened it for my return trip."

"You should certainly accept his offer, Reverend," Dunn said. He clapped his hands and gestured at one of the less disreputable-looking individuals, who bowed and picked up my suitcase. He followed respectfully behind us. Dunn led me to a carriage which looked vaguely like a London hackney a decade or so out of date; instead of a grimy coachman, a dignified-looking Arab in a long blue robe and a scarlet turban sat up in the driver's box. We climbed into the passenger compartment; the porter handed up my case, and Dunn handed the man a few coins, eliciting a number of bows and thank-yous in a few languages I recognized and several I did not. As soon as the door closed, the carriage got underway.

"I assume that I have Monsieur Dupotet to thank for my reception," I said, looking out the window at the crowded street. To my recollection, there was nothing to see that I had not seen in Naples—or, for that matter, in London: it had an Oriental cast, with women carrying jugs on their heads and men lugging goods on their shoulders—and everywhere poverty and all that went with it. The encroaching fog of London was simply replaced by the burning sun.

"He telegraphed several days ago to a mutual friend, who asked me to look after you while you were in Egypt."

"Where you just *happened* to be."

"I am to depart at the end of the month for Abyssinia," Dunn said. "I am here on holiday, but always glad to help out a fellow subject of Her Majesty."

"Where are you *from?*"

"York. Or, as it is now called, Toronto," he said. "Ontario, in Canada. A lovely little town that, I'm afraid, I've seen precious little of since I was a lad."

"Soldiering?"

"Quite. I was in the the Crimea and India with the Eleventh Hussars."

"Eleventh Hussars—you were in the famous Charge, weren't you? The Light Brigade at Balaclava."

"Yes." He placed his hand over his heart, placing his index and middle finger on a bronze medal in the shape of a cross, depending from a red ribbon. Around the center of the cross were the words FOR VALOUR. "I have this from that battle."

"A Victoria Cross," I said. It was an extraordinary honor—and my companion, as I had noted, was scarcely thirty years of age. "I am in the presence of a hero."

"For rescuing you from street Arabs?"

"For—for whatever service you performed in the uniform of the Eleventh Hussars, Major Dunn. How many such medals were awarded for that battle? Not many, I expect."

"Very few, and actually among officers only one." He let his hand fall to his lap. "There were many brave men that day, Reverend. But I am not here to speak about that."

"I do not mean to offend, Major Dunn."

"And I do not mean to brag, Reverend Davey. I mean to fulfill my brief, which is to see you from here to Suez safely, as I have promised. I am confident that I can do so."

"You should be aware," I said the carriage moved along slowly, "that my enemies are not necessarily the sort that valor and determination can easily overcome."

"Valor and determination may count for more than you think," Dunn answered.

"I don't doubt it—and you have the right to speak to that subject. But I stand by my remark."

"We shall see," Dunn answered. "I am not unaware of the nature of your enemies, sir."

"All right," I said. "I am eager to depart as soon as we can."

"You will not stay long in Alexandria?"

"Not that I wish to dismiss its charms," I said, "but what compels me to travel is far more important than what might attract me to stay."

"Evening train, then. Traveling after dark is far more comfortable."

"How long does the trip take?"

"About five hours to Cairo, then another three to Suez." He reached into his vest and withdrew a watch. I felt a momentary chill: the gesture reminded me of the device that the Levantine had displayed last winter on the Oxford Road train platform in Manchester.

Dunn noticed my discomfiture. "Is there a problem?"

"No, Major. Nothing. A memory."

He gave me a curious glance, as if I echoed something that he had been thinking. He held my eyes as he snapped the watch shut and slowly tucked it away.

"We can pass the time at the Hôtel de l'Europe," he said. "The chops are acceptable, and at least we will be out of the sun."

Europeans tend to take their comforts and their customs with them, even when venturing into alien lands. The Hôtel de l'Europe, on the Place du Mehmet Ali—not far from the port, and adjoining a pleasant tree-lined avenue leading down to the main post office and, beyond, the promenade along the harbor—could have been transplanted from any European city. The salon and dining-room were quiet, the servants attentive and almost unctuous, the fare considerably beyond *acceptable*.

Dunn was extremely pleasant company. He was not a mesmerist, but was—as he observed—conversant with the world of the Art. He had been asked by an old friend of Dupotet, an Egyptian named Mehmet Nour, to await my arrival at the harbor, and to keep me safe as far as Suez and a steam packet bound for India.

"He is some form of grey eminence, I presume," I said, as we sat in the dining room finishing the last of an excellent bottle of wine that had accompanied our dinner.

"I suppose you might characterize him thus," Dunn answered. "He is…unusual."

"Everyone in my world is *unusual* to some degree, Major. Even yourself."

"I am no more or less than I seem."

"That does not contradict my statement."

He chuckled, sipped his wine and then carefully wiped his long moustaches with his napkin. "No, I suppose it does not. Well. Nour is a practitioner of the Art, though I daresay he is not of the same school as you. He is nowhere near as circumspect."

"I find that ostentation only attracts enemies."

"From what I was told, sir, you seem to be having no trouble attracting enemies."

"I see no reason to increase their number by flaunting my moderate skill."

"That may be so," Dunn said, dropping his napkin on the table. "But sometimes one must demonstrate that skill to best effect. Modesty is only seen to be a virtue if it is occasionally left behind."

It was my turn to be amused at my companion's phrase. "I would like to know something, if I might."

"Ask away. After battling street Arabs, I have no fear."

"You are not a practitioner, Major Dunn; I suspect you are less an intimate of Baron Dupotet de Sennevoy than I am, even at this point in my life. How do you come to be involved in this?"

"Well. There's a bit of a tale to tell in that."

I glanced outside through the large glass windows, now thankfully covered by blinds and thin drapes; the sun had descended, but was still some distance from the horizon. "I daresay we have time."

"My father, Reverend, was a regular correspondent with a man of deep faith and conviction—Reverend Simeon Calhoun, a missionary in Syria. I do not know if you have ever met this gentleman."

"I confess that I have not, though I have heard the name—he is still alive, I believe."

"Very much so. He has been at Damascus for most of twenty years, bringing the light of the Gospel. When my father died some years ago, I had the duty of writing to him to pass on the sad news. When I first came to Asia I was provided an introduction to this worthy individual, and I spent some short amount of time with him.

"The Reverend Calhoun is in many ways no more than he seems: an upright, modest"—he smiled as he echoed my words—"and extremely learned man; motivated, I might say *driven*, in his life's goal of spreading the divine Word. But in one important respect he is much more than the casual observer might expect."

"I am eager to learn how."

"You are familiar with the work of the Frenchman Jean-François Champollion?"

"Of course. He was one of the translators of the Demotic script of the Rosetta Stone."

"Exactly. Reverend Calhoun took great interest in this work, since it is so germane to the study of the Old Testament—and for an additional reason, having more to do with *your* area of expertise: in particular, your current area of concern. You see, more than anywhere else in the world, this area—the Holy Land, Mesopotamia and the Nile Valley—seems to attract the creatures called *stoicheia*."

"I thought they were restricted to polar regions."

"*Chthonoi* might be so restricted—but not *photoi*: elemental spirits of fire. If anything, these beings are more violent, more anthrophobic, more difficult to tame. From early in his mission in

Damascus, Reverend Calhoun was troubled by their interference. But as a scholar of Champollion and his successors, and with the help of ...scholars and others...he was able to derive and implement certain methods to combat their influence, and in some cases banish them entirely.

"This powerful and esoteric knowledge has been transmitted carefully over the last dozen years, being passed from one man of God to another. Mehmet Nour—who is a Coptic Christian—is skilled with it as well, and I know that it has been passed to others all over Europe."

Such as Reverend James Esdaile, I thought to myself. "You are referring to *The Chapters of Coming Forth By Day*."

"That's right. Are *you* -"

"No. Apparently I was not included on the subscription list. But I have met a few others who have been trained in this manner. And as for you -"

"No." He tugged at his uniform collar. "Regrettably, I am in the wrong line of work."

And I am in the right 'line of work', I thought to myself.

"In any case, Mehmet Nour asked me if he might prevail upon my old friendship with Reverend Calhoun, as a favor to his friend *Le Maître*. I could not say no. And—" He spread his hands. "Here I am, enjoying your company."

"And preparing to employ valor and determination."

"And whatever else comes to hand, Reverend."

The main station—the Gare du Caire—lay just beneath the great fort of Kôm-ed-Dik in the middle of the city. We boarded our train before dark, when the remnants of the sun still painted the bleached stone buildings of Alexandria with orange and crimson; the carriages were crowded and noisy, but we were favored with seats in a relatively clean and quiet portion of second-class, and soon the locomotive was huffing its way across plains as flat and fertile as any land in the world. Plantations of cotton, grains and vegetables alternated with rows of date-palms. Flocks of birds scattered at the train's approach, their wings dappled with the last rays of sunlight before it also vanished, cloaking us in night.

"It does not take long," Dunn told me as we traveled onward, "to see why this race worships the Sun."

"No doubt," I answered.

"And the Moon," he added, gesturing out the right-hand window of our carriage. Our route had taken us southward along the right bank of the Nile; the moon was rising over the desert land beyond the fertile, cultivated places near the river. "The Muslims revere it as well. But I think that the people of this land have never quite let go of the beliefs of their ancestors."

"Your Reverend Calhoun seems to suggest that we still have something to learn from them."

"Did you ever doubt that?"

"Major Dunn, after the last few months, I cannot properly say what I believe, or what I doubt, or what I even *expect.*"

"Then," he said, settling back in his seat, "I should think there is only one course of action."

"That being?"

"Sleep," he said. "A soldier always gets rest while he can. I suggest, sir, that you endeavor to do the same."

With that advice in mind, I settled myself as well; and though I had told myself that I was too troubled for such distraction, the movement of the train and the buzz of conversation gradually lulled me into sleep.

CHAPTER 37

Borrowed moments

WILLIAM DAVEY

The arrival of the train in Cairo jolted me awake, but Dunn was already alert; I could see his eyes even in the dim light from the station platform.

"Cairo?"

"Yes. A message-boy came to the window a few moments ago." He held a slip of paper in his hand. "Mehmet Nour is expecting us."

"How long are we to stay in Cairo?"

"We have to take on water and more coal. But the length of the stopover doesn't matter."

"What do you mean?"

"You'll see, I imagine. Come."

He stood up and slid the door aside; passengers crowded the corridor, along with porters and food-sellers and luggage. I was still fogged with sleep; I began to pull down my suitcase, but Dunn waved his hand. I followed Major Dunn through the passageway until we reached the end of the carriage, where we disembarked onto a platform. I glanced at a large clock at one end: it showed the time to be just short of 2 A.M.

"Not exactly the Great Western Railway," Dunn said, shrugging. "Nearly seven hours since Alexandria, and I expect that we will be laid over here for an hour or more." He led me along the platform toward the station's main concourse.

Another carriage, with another Arab coachman, was waiting outside. Some non-verbal communication passed between the Egyptian and Major Dunn to confirm that this was the vehicle he expected. Unlike our carriage in Alexandria, the present conveyance did not conform specifically to European custom, for it had an unpleasant odor and we found the floorboards to be damp and somewhat slick underfoot.

"We are apparently headed for his villa," Dunn said to me. He reached into his own carpet-bag and lifted his hand just enough to show me that he had a small pistol in his possession. Any hint of sleep that might have plagued me was immediately banished.

"Will this man have hostile intent?"

"No, I do not expect so. But he has used the knowledge of the *Chapters* in a way that might lead to complication. He has his reasons for this, as you will see—but it is best to be armed."

"I wish I had been informed that I might do so myself."

"You possess more formidable weapons than I do, Reverend. In fact…" he let the pistol go and it landed soundlessly inside the bag—"I daresay that my precaution is no more than a palliation of my own fears. I do not know if it would do any good."

"Against—"

"*Stoicheia*."

The term *villa* was a frank exaggeration. In Devon it would have been scarcely allocated the term *farm*. It lay on the outskirts of Cairo, some distance from the road leading back northward along the Nile. Its buildings, limned by the light of the setting moon, consisted of a main house and two other structures: one, from the odor and the night-time animal sounds, had an obvious purpose. The contents of the other were unknown until my senses told me that there were *stoicheia* present, of a different sort than I had hitherto felt.

Dunn may not have had the senses of a practitioner of the Art, but he was on his guard as we approached. The carriage had stopped at the edge of the property; a brisk exchange between my companion and the Arab coachman, which seemed to grow quite warm, concluded with the outcome that the carriage should not go up the lane; thus we disembarked at the ramshackle gate, the horses snuffling and whinnying as if they, too, objected to the idea of entering the property.

"Major Dunn—"

He gestured for quiet—not with a mesmeric pass, but with the authority of a soldier. I complied, and we walked up toward the main house, our boots sinking into the soft soil as we went.

As we passed the second outbuilding, I saw that there was a sort of yard attached to it, like an animal pen. It was bounded by a low wall consisting of old, irregular stone blocks between which some sort of woven reed mats had been placed. They were secured by stout pegs, and each had symbols inscribed upon it, impossible to discern in the fading moonlight. Within the pen, I could see several men, Egyptians I presumed, wearing little other than kilts and turbans; they approached—but did not touch—the wall, and watched us as we trudged by.

Can we help you, effendi? I heard in my mind, so clearly and plaintively that it stopped me in my tracks.

I made eye-contact with one of the men. He offered me a polite bow. I felt Dunn's hand touching the sleeve of my coat.

What do you want? What do you need? I heard. I opened my mouth to reply, but I felt Dunn's firm hand on my shoulder. He spun me firmly to face him, but did not speak: instead he merely shook his head in the negative.

No, I heard the voice say as Dunn and I moved away. *No. Do not go in the house.* The words were echoed by a half-dozen other voices.

The soldier did not let go of my arm as he directed my steps to the main house.

We were met at the door by an elderly gentleman, who looked like an Arab—but who wore a large, heavy pectoral cross of an unusual design. He was otherwise dressed simply in the Egyptian fashion—a shirt and trousers, with slippers on his feet. He had a neatly-trimmed beard and was going bald on the top of his head, but his most striking feature was his steel-blue eyes, illuminated by the candle he held in his hand. I could still hear the voices from the pen outside.

"Come," he said, stepping aside so we could enter the house.

"Good evening, sir," I said. "My name is William Davey."

"You are a friend of the Baron Dupotet," the man said in perfect English, closing the door behind us. The voices stopped abruptly.

"Yes."

"I am Mehmet Nour. And you," he said, looking at Dunn, who had needed to duck his head when entering the house, "must be Major Dunn."

"Your servant, sir."

Nour's right eyebrow elevated just a bit, as if considering this comment.

"This way," he said, leading us from the entryway into the house. It was laid out simply, with a sort of parlor in the middle and rooms off to each side. To the left, the door was nearly closed; I could hear the gentle sound of soft snoring from beyond. Nour led us, candle in hand, through the other door into another room.

I stopped at the threshold, unable to continue for a moment. The windowless chamber was lit by two or three dozen candles, leaving no part of it dark. About halfway in there was a sort of ornate wooden wall that reached to about waist-level, with a small gate in the middle; on the far wall I could see a beautifully-painted mural of the Saviour, surrounded by a Heavenly host, inscribed with symbols and writing in an alphabet I could not read. A table covered with white linen held some object concealed by another cloth made of the same material; to either side a lectern was placed, each bearing an open book. One was beautifully rendered in the same unknown script; the other was more like a copy-book, with careful handwriting.

Nour did not speak, but opened the gate and stepped within, bowing to the covered table and touching the first and second fingers of his right hand to his lips and then to his heart. Dunn did not follow, but removed his hat, which I had already done.

Nour spoke quietly in a language I did not understand, then set the candle down on another table on his side of the barrier, and turned to face us.

"Tell me what you require, sir," Nour said, at last.

"I am here at your request."

"Just so. But you have a mission, I believe? You have not been in Egypt before."

"I have not. And my...*mission* is not here. I am merely passing through."

"We are all 'passing through', Mr. Davey. We all tarry for a season."

"I would normally be happy to engage in wordplay with you, sir," I said. "But Major Dunn and I are expected back in Cairo— our train leaves soon, and we must be on it."

Nour let his eyebrow rise once again. "You need not trouble yourself about that, Mr. Davey," he said. "Your train will not leave without you. There is all the time we need."

"You have some influence with the railroad company?"

"I have some influence with...*time*," he answered.

It was a rather bold statement, and I would have considered it no more than bravado—except for my experience with the Levantine in Manchester some months ago.

"Convenient."

"Tell me of your mission," Nour said, and it was more a command than a request. It was not accompanied by an overt mesmeric gesture, but I felt as if I were being compelled. Suddenly, I perceived that Nour was not alone—that there were others beyond the little barrier.

While Nour was clearly more skilled than someone like Leconte de Lisle, he was by no means my equal—even with the help of whomever, or whatever, aided him. I made a warding gesture with my off hand and stepped forward; whatever was going on here, I was not about to be manipulated. Nour seemed surprised by my sudden action, and took a step back. I reached for the handle on the little gate—

"*No*," Nour said, his hands raised. "Do not touch that. You are not permitted."

My hand stopped short, a few inches from the handle—not because of some compulsion, but by my own choice.

"Then tell me," I said, "what this is about."

"Step back," Nour said.

I glanced over my shoulder at Dunn, who stood completely still.

"He is not a party to this discussion," Nour said, following my glance. "This is between adepts."

"Tell me about the men outside," I said, lowering my hand to my side but remaining ready to deflect anything else that might come from Nour.

"They are not *men*," he said. "There is no need to dignify them with that title. Why? Do they interest you?"

"They spoke to me."

"They will be punished for that. They are to speak to no one. But that is not your concern. What did they say?"

"They asked me what I wanted."

"Did you tell them?"

"I did not. Mr. Nour, once again I ask you what this is about. Please tell me at once."

"This is my sanctuary, sir. My *domain*, as I think you would term it in England. Do not trifle with me."

"Then you should be so good as to refrain from trifling with *me*." I gave in very slightly to my annoyance: it might have appeared as anger to Nour, but I decided that it was necessary for me to take control of the situation, whether I was in his domain or not.

Nour had no answer: the blue eyes merely stared back at me, as if waiting for me to continue.

"Major Dunn and I are here at your request; I am prepared to either step forward"—I lifted my hand slightly, as if I was to reach for the handle to the gate once more—"or back, and return to my carriage and my train. I understand that I am obliged to you for assistance in remaining safe as I pass through this part of Egypt: you have my thanks, and should I return to England safely I will offer you the thanks of the Committee. But my presence in your domain is at *your* request. Get to the point, sir—and I would ask that Major Dunn be permitted to observe, if not actually participate, in this discussion."

There is a point in most conflicts between mesmerists of a certain level of power, when each determines that the other is a worthy opponent—and the effort required to vanquish such an opponent is not worth the price to be paid for it.

Most conflicts of this nature, however, are not between equals. When Forbes challenged me in Vernon's apartments, he was not capable of resisting me; Leconte de Lisle was defeated without even realizing it. Carlyle was another matter—but neither he nor I had had a particularly strong desire to take the matter to its logical conclusion.

Nour might have expected to best me at once, in his domain, with the power of—whatever there was—behind him: but I proved to be possessed of power of my own.

"Very well," he said. He touched his cross, and the sensation that I had hitherto experienced faded away, leaving only the three of us—Nour, Dunn and myself—in the room.

I heard Dunn clear his throat behind me, and wondered what he might have just experienced.

"The beings in the pen outside are photic spirits, Mr. Davey. They are devils of a particular nature. I am given to understand that you have beings of a related type in England, and that they are presenting difficulties for you."

"That is generally true."

"I should like to make you aware of another sort of being," Nour said. "I have asked that you come here so that I could provide you with first-hand knowledge."

"I am obliged to you, Mr. Nour," I said, feeling in no way obliged. If I had been aware at the time what had already transpired, I suspect that I would have been less short with him.

But my knowledge at that time was incomplete.

"Come," he said, taking up the candle. Once again, he made obeisance to the altar and then opened the gate and stepped through; I made room for him, as each of us avoided coming into contact with the other.

We came within several feet of the outside pen. Nour set the candle down on the ground beside him. There were six individuals, gathered together at about the same distance from the wall within as we were without; Nour stood a bit in front of the two of us, his hands raised slightly.

"These creatures were foolish enough to stray close and be captured. I have turned them to useful work."

"At what price?"

"Price?" Nour looked over his shoulder at me. In the moonlight his expression, a mixture of light and shadow, had a distinctly unpleasant appearance. "They are doing the Lord's work now. The price for me is merely vigilance."

"He is very proud of that," one of the photic spirits said, crossing his arms in front of him. Nour's face was suffused with anger and his shoulders tensed.

Before Nour could reply, I said, "Should he not be, sir? You are captive—and he is your gaoler."

"You should not speak with them, Mr. Davey," Nour said, turning to face me. "You have no idea—"

I held up my hand; Nour let the sentence trail.

"He is our jailor," the spirit continued. "For *now*. His prized vigilance cannot last forever. Neither," he added, "can his life."

Nour turned to face them. He raised his hands, and the beings stepped back; the one who had spoken staggered, as if physically struck.

"We shall see who lives longer, devil," Nour said, his hands still raised.

"He does not fear us, but he should," the being said raggedly, his left hand clutching his chest. "But there is something he *does* fear."

"What is that?" I asked.

The being lowered its hand slowly to its side as it stood erect. It pointed past us with its other hand, toward the flat land to the west—the cultivated fields, and beyond, the desert.

"Our father," he said.

With a sensation that I had experienced just a few days earlier on Malta, I was then nearly overwhelmed with the presence of a being: powerful, malign and—unlike the pale points of light in the cave—*immense*. From our remove, it appeared to be a vague sort of storm, a distortion in the air, whipping up sand and dust.

I heard a sound that was like a distant chorus of pain, a moan that chilled me despite the tropical heat. It reminded me once more of the sound I had heard from the Levantine's pocket-watch in Manchester.

The being inside the pen began to speak, but its words seemed to dissipate, despite obvious effort on its part to articulate them. I had before heard, or almost heard, words in that language—at the Crystal Palace on the day James Esdaile died.

But, as in the Crystal Palace, the being seemed to be without the capability to work its will.

"I am not afraid of *that*, either," Nour said, again without turning to see the manifestation. "As long as you are here and my captives, it dares not attempt to do me any harm."

"Every day we gain back a little of our strength," the being said. "And though you use us to borrow moments, every day you grow a little bit older. And our father grows slightly more…impatient."

Nour lowered his hands and turned, stepping between us to face the distortion. He placed one hand on his pectoral and raised the other in a gesture that seemed mesmeric; he spoke a series of words in a language I did not understand, then lowered his ring and little finger and made the sign of the cross.

The distortion slowly faded and the sound died away. Nour

turned to face us, and he looked as if he had expended considerable effort in dismissing the phenomenon.

"There are only so many moments he can borrow," the photic spirit said quietly. "Time can be slowed, but it cannot be stopped. No human lives forever."

Nour did not answer. He took up his candle and led us back to the main house. We followed, while the photic spirits murmured amongst themselves.

Once we were inside, Nour looked at us. He appeared gray and shaken, but his eyes were still deep and animated.

"I am looking for a way to banish the great devil," Nour said. "The one they call their 'father'—it is far more powerful than these photic spirits."

"You play a dangerous game, sir," Dunn said. "If I may say so."

"It is no game," Nour answered.

"Whatever it might be, it is fraught with danger, as my companion intimates," I said. "My mission—I believe—involves another being of this sort, similarly held at bay. I know what the other one wants; what does this being desire?"

"I...am not sure. In my limited intercourse with it I have sensed a sort of childish nature: it has simple, straightforward wants, and a long-standing enmity for the great Nile and for the sea beyond. I believe that it is a remnant of a race that existed before the Flood, and considers all that came after the great inundation to be its enemy. But I *will* defeat it and put it in its place.

"If you know of another such," he concluded, "you must do the same."

It was clear that there was much about this being, and his conflict with it, that remained unspoken. In other circumstances I might have wanted to inquire further; but an understanding was not necessary to accomplish my goal. I let the matter lie and said, "That is my objective, sir."

"Then I wish you well with it. I...cannot borrow too much more time for you, Mr. Davey. You must return to your train. But think well on what you have seen tonight."

"I will do that."

Nour opened the door and gestured us out. Dunn offered Nour a polite bow, and then set off at a brisk pace down the lane. The photic spirits watched us as we went.

"No human lives forever," I heard one of them say as we went past the pen. Neither Dunn nor I turned our heads as we walked away.

CHAPTER 38

A miraculous east wind

WILLIAM DAVEY

The muezzin had not yet called the faithful to prayer when our train reached Suez, a dismal little town overlooking the gulf of the same name. In the fall of 1860 it was a fairly sleepy place, the end of a hastily built rail line; when the Canal was finally complete it became much more impressive—but that lay years in the future of the time I describe.

Unlike the journey from Alexandria to Cairo, Major Dunn and I did not sleep at all between Cairo and Suez. As Nour had promised, we had no difficulty re-boarding our train—according to the clock on the platform, perhaps ten minutes had passed since we had left the station. Our borrowed moments had given me some insights; Dunn provided a few additional explanations.

"Nour," he told me as the train trundled along, "is playing a very dangerous game with the photic spirits he has captive."

"You observed that at the time."

"So I did," Dunn said, running a finger along one of his moustaches. "Still, I am not surprised—all that I learned of him from Reverend Calhoun is reinforced by our interview. Nour assumes that the photic spirits are devils, and that their 'father' is a creature from before the Great Flood." He paused, looking out the train-window at the cultivated fields, lit now only by a clear, star-filled sky. "What do you think?"

"There is more and more scientific evidence that the Biblical Flood is a myth, or perhaps an exaggeration of some lesser event. I do not know quite what the greater photic spirit is, but I doubt its antediluvian origin."

"You know this."

"About the creature—or the Flood?"

"The Flood," Dunn said.

"I do not tell parishioners that the tale of the Flood is metaphorical." I didn't truly have regular parishioners, so I did not quite speak falsely. "But it is clear that there are events that transpired before *recorded* history, whether or not the Flood actually happened in one form or another. This greater being is of a different order than the ones Nour holds captive. It is also not the first such being I have encountered."

"Say on."

I summarized for him my experience on Malta. In the retelling, it seemed more like a dream than an actual experience; I suspect that had I recounted this adventure prior to our visit to Mehmet Nour's villa, he might have dismissed it as a flight of imagination… but both of us had seen and heard the photic manifestation. For my part, I had *felt* the thing looming out in the desert, approaching close enough to be sensed. I do not know what Dunn might have felt—Nour, after all, had stolen a few of *his* personal moments as well.

"Is that the being to which you alluded when we spoke to Nour? The one that is 'held at bay', I believe you put it?"

"No. That is yet *another*, trapped in a sort of artifact. It is a long and complex story, Major, one that is becoming increasingly more of both, but I remain determined to follow it through to the end."

"In India."

"I do not truly think that the tale ends there. What happens next depends on what I find—but I am not the only one seeking this artifact in India. I am certain that this journey is the correct course of action."

"You shall do it—or die trying, I daresay."

"Banish the thought, Major," I said, but without too much earnest—he had, after all, done just that in the Crimea: the *correct* thing. He had certainly been *willing* to die trying and bore a medal honoring his valor and service. For my part, I was undertaking the former and hoped I might be able to avoid the latter.

But even in my waking hours, watching the night fade away as I rode along on the crowded, dark train between Cairo and Suez, I could not be rid of the image of the terrible photic being and the power it represented.

The steamer did not arrive at Suez for four days, leaving me to wait once again for something to happen. Nothing really *did*—trains arrived and departed, depositing passengers for the steamer to take us down the Red Sea. They queued and crowded the hotels that overlooked the Gulf; there was brisk traffic between the main station and the station on the low island across the mud flats, at the basin docks where the Pacific and Oriental steamship office was located.

Suez was structurally little different from Blackhall, though it was hotter and drier. A steady breeze blew off the Gulf; the pace of activity was languid, particularly away from the hotels that catered to Europeans, who demanded alacrity and efficiency in their service in exchange for Swiss francs and English pounds. To an Arab, particularly in sultry Suez between departures and arrivals, the customary answer to what or when was: *Insh'Allah*, or *if Allah wills it*. It was the verbal equivalent of a shrug.

The wait was not vexing for Major Dunn; he was eager to see the beginning work on the Canal. Most of the excavations had already been made at the northern end on the Mediterranean near the new port of Sa'id, but engineers working for the redoubtable Frenchman M. de Lesseps had marked out the entire route from the Port Sa'id settlement, through the city of Ismailia, the Bitter Lakes, and down to the Red Sea.

One afternoon we obtained horses and rode up along the railway line toward Ismailia; the terrain above Suez was hilly and rough, but the work to level and prepare that part of the canal route was years in the future. It was difficult for me to imagine what it would look like—but Dunn had a soldier's eye, and I imagine that he was more aware of the consequence of that great building effort, how it would change the world. It put me in mind of the miraculous east wind—the one that parted the Red Sea and permitted the Israelites to escape the host of Pharaoh. This channel, however, would not close again over those who would follow it.

From where we sat on our horses at the top of a bluff beside the marked-out works, we could look southward and see Suez and, beyond, the Red Sea; eastward, into the Sinai where Moses and his followers wandered for decades—and Asia beyond; and westward, at the cliffs of Genef and Ataka, between which ran the rail line that had brought us from Cairo.

As I sat there baking in the Ra sun of Egypt, I was suddenly aware of another presence other than the redoubtable Major Dunn. As he scanned the horizon with his field glasses I sat very still, taking short breaths and extending my senses.

It did not take long to locate it: a slight distortion coming no closer than fifteen or twenty yards from our position. It was a photic spirit—a smaller example of the larger one that lurked, malign, in the desert near Mehmet Nour's villa. And it was clearly hostile—openly so, enough so that when Major Dunn lowered his instrument and looked at me he could see the serious expression on my face.

You do not belong here, I heard in my mind. *You are exposed.*

"I make no attempt to conceal myself," I said aloud.

"Reverend—" Dunn began, but I held up my hand.

Of course you do, the silent voice answered me. *But soon, you go over water.*

"And?"

And you are largely beyond our reach.

"Such a shame."

But you are still exposed.

"I am not without resources," I responded. "Come closer and I will show you."

I am not so foolish.

"*You* are exposed as well."

As you say, the voice said. *But do not flatter yourself that you have passed unnoticed.*

I did not answer but instead caused my mount—which had suddenly become skittish, its nostrils flaring—to turn aside and face to the west, away from the canal works.

I made a mesmeric pass, drawing my hand upward with the palm remaining down, then suddenly clenching it into a fist just above my breastbone.

A sudden warm blast washed over us, like a wind that had whipped up out of nowhere. The sun became unbearably bright, causing both Dunn and me to shade our eyes for a moment. I kept my hand clenched in front of me, though it felt as if another hand was trying to pry the fingers loose one by one.

When the breeze died down and the sun returned to normal, the presence was gone.

When I remembered the incident later, I felt as if I had stood in a fulcrum moment—all of the events that had led me there seemed to be laid out like tracks across the barren desert, while the future was veiled in darkness.

At that time I had simply wanted to go home to London. I wanted to return to the time before the final encounter with James Esdaile, when things had been more clear. The Committee's objectives had been apparent; the sides were well-defined; and I flattered myself to think that I understood how the world worked.

A voyage to India, leaving my home domain, was nothing I would have contemplated. But what had brought me here made it impossible for things to return to their former state. The world had changed, and I needed to change with it.

With the arrival of the Peninsular & Oriental steamship, the tenor of life in Suez changed. Steamship passengers prepared to depart, gathering luggage and effects as soon as the ship was sighted; *Insh'Allah* became *Rahimakallah*—"may Allah bless you," particularly when one of those wealthy travelers produced a sufficiently large gratuity.

I had already obtained my passage ticket and I had little luggage; it made my journey across the low-lying water an easy one. Major Dunn accompanied me to the station: a tumult of people, packages, servants and steamship and railway employees. To an untrained eye it might have seemed complete chaos—but it was clear that the professionals followed specific paths and performed particular tasks. In less time than I would have suspected—a matter of a few hours—the ship was prepared for departure, bound for Aden—where it would recoal—and then across the Indian Ocean to points further east.

"We must part here, I'm afraid," Dunn told me. "Reverend Davey, it has been a pleasure to meet and assist you."

"The pleasure and honor are all mine," I replied. "I don't know if I would have survived the street Arabs without you."

"I suspect that you could have managed," he said, smiling. "You are a resourceful man."

"I'm to be on my own now."

"At least for a time. But you have contacts in Calcutta, I assume?"

"Only leads to follow. I know that it's not the same place it was before the unrest."

"Not hardly. But the elements that made it dangerous are no longer present. Still, these things are not settled in a day. I urge caution, sir. When I think of India, I am reminded of a lake with a shallow rim, deep in its center. You can wade in a few feet—and then suddenly find yourself over your head. It's particularly unnerving if you cannot swim."

"I can swim."

"I suspect that you understand my metaphor, sir. Some soldiers, some members of Parliament, some…clergymen think that India is a simple puzzle. The Mutiny taught us that it was not. I wish that I could help you further—that I could part the ocean for you, like Moses parted this sea." It was a singularly apt metaphor, given my earlier thought and our current location. He looked past the crowds on the gangways, at the water at low tide beyond.

I watched the passengers for a short time as they boarded the vessel. At one moment I thought I spied a familiar figure: an older woman, traveling alone, though I could not place where I had seen her. After a few seconds she was lost to sight and I turned back to Major Dunn.

"I don't think either of us have an east wind at our command."

"After what I have seen on this brief excursion, I would not be surprised to find that there was someone, somewhere, who does." He took my hand firmly, a soldier's handshake. "Godspeed, Reverend Davey. Do what you must and be safe."

"And you too, Major. God bless you."

Dunn smiled. "He does, I have no doubt of it."

We parted then; I had it in mind that I should make an effort to again cross the path of this remarkable young man. But it never came to pass.

I had expected that traversing the Red Sea would be a more uncomfortable experience than it turned out. Though flanked by dry desert to the east and broken dry land to the west, the open water was surprisingly calm and the air unusually temperate. I ascribed this to the possibility that, since it was now early December, this might be an unusually opportune time to travel in these latitudes—it might well be Hell's own furnace in high summer.

Malabar Princess was not the equal of *Empire Star*. It was, however, considerably more impressive than the French vessel that had taken me from Marseilles to Alexandria. The ship was fitted out for long sea voyages; the Peninsular and Oriental Steamship Company plied a route between Suez, India, Malaysia and Australia, carrying mail, passengers and the better sort of freight. Even then it was apparent that once the great engineering feat was complete, the Suez Canal would permit such ships to carry goods directly to Mediterranean ports and ultimately London itself without the need for a traversal of the Cape of Good Hope—which was about where *Empire Star* must have been as we steamed down the Gulf of Suez that first afternoon.

I wondered to myself if the Levantine were still aboard, or if he had realized that I was not to be found. I told myself that if he were, that I would have at least three or four weeks in Calcutta to prepare for his arrival—or to achieve my objective and be gone beforehand.

Time is a flexible thing, he had said to me in Manchester.

I was still unsure exactly what he had meant—but both he and Mehmet Nour had demonstrated the veracity of that statement: that time was something that could be manipulated. Science had changed our view of nearly everything—but I could not fathom how time could be experienced at any rate other than the normal one. It might be no more, and no less, than some sort of hallucination induced by a mesmeric power that far exceeded my own.

It took almost three days to steam from Suez to Aden, a trading port on the Indian Ocean near the mouth of the Red Sea. There was a decided difference in the tenor and atmosphere in Aden—where Suez was slow-paced, a place of gentle breezes and lazy shrugs, this port was a hive of trading activity—ships called frequently, coming and going with goods of all kinds. The wharves and markets seemed to be in constant motion from the time that the burning sun arose from the Indian Ocean on the east until after it had vanished behind the mountainous ridges of Yemen and the Hejaz to the north and west.

The only commodity no longer on offer in the markets in Aden was human chattel—and I was not entirely sure about *that*: I felt as if there were deals being made around every corner and behind every door. I remained close to the port, preferring to have no part of any transactions—either as buyer, seller or the goods being exchanged.

It took less than a day for the steamer to take on coal and water in Aden, along with passengers and goods bound for India and beyond. Well before it was due to depart I too was aboard. As I stood on the upper deck watching the last of those embarking for the East, my perceptions—dulled, I can readily admit, through the relative inactivity of the last several days—were suddenly attracted by the presence of a magnetic aura of a sort I had not felt since our borrowed moments with Mehmet Nour.

I could not determine at once whose aura it was: a number of people stood on the broad gangway, mostly of European origin, and almost all men: there were only two women—one older, traveling on her own—the one I thought I had seen at Suez—and the other younger, in the company of a young man. I immediately quit my observation post, intending to descend to the gangway, but collided with a crewmember. He was a young steward, and as we disentangled he apologized profusely; but by the time I was partway down the steps to the lower level I had lost track of the aura that had attracted my attention. It was not as if it had vanished entirely—it was more a matter of having the sensation lost in the crowd or blown away on the wind. When I reached the broad deck area where passengers were being received, I had entirely lost it.

As we steamed away from Aden and passed out into the Indian Ocean, I was left with the disturbing knowledge that there was another mesmerist somewhere aboard *Malabar Princess*.

CHAPTER 39

Unrequited hunger

WILLIAM DAVEY

Steamships are not sailing vessels: they obey the tides but not the winds, and tend to travel in straighter lines. They are also made of metal rather than wood—something that might have played a part in the events that unfolded on the ocean a few days later, and which helped fix the path of my journey through the subcontinent.

We left Aden under deep blue skies and burning sun, but within a week the sky had clouded and our vessel was beset with rain. It might have daunted a sailing ship, which might have changed course to avoid the storm—but a steamship is not a sailed one. We stayed the course.

The weather worsened: not gradually but in stages, as if the storm were descending and enveloping us. Rain and fog cloaked the ship and cut visibility so that it seemed that we were adrift and alone upon the ocean.

Belowdecks was decidedly claustrophobic. Those who had enough patience and temerity ventured on deck, staying under cover as much as possible, but making their constitutionals in oilcloth gear or under stout umbrellas. I stayed on deck but briefly, though I was less affected than some. It was colder and more raw than the passage aboard *Malabar Princess*, but no worse than the rain of a British autumn. Nonetheless, there was something unsettling about this storm. My senses were dulled belowdecks, but out in the rain I could acutely feel that *wrongness*. It was something I could not explain—and I had thus far failed to locate the other mesmerist.

Two nights into the storm, I was sitting at a first-class dining table enduring the pitch and roll of the ship (in better form than most of my fellow passengers, I should hasten to admit)—and I was suddenly aware of a presence: not the unusual power of a mesmerist's aura, such as I had felt as we departed Aden—but that of a *stoichios* of some sort, an elemental spirit with significant power.

It would not do to disturb the others at my table. Pleading an unsettled stomach, I retired from the dining room and made my way as quickly as I could to my cabin. I bundled myself in an oilcloth coat and hat and made my way up on deck.

"This is not a fit place, sir," one of the deck officers said to me as I came up through the hatch. "It's surely not safe."

"I need the air," I answered.

The man looked dubious, but gave me a salute. "Best stay away from the railings, Reverend. The deck will be slick and we don't want to lose you."

"I'd prefer that myself, sir."

He turned away to his duties, leaving me to the miserable scene. I waited for a moment, trying to orient myself; the sensation I had experienced belowdecks was redoubled above, and I found myself turning toward the bow. I tried to stay under cover as much as possible, but the rain battered me fiercely as made my way forward of the second great smokestack. I was presented there with a singular sight.

Out in the rain I could see a single figure—a young woman, neither dressed for the weather nor protected by an umbrella. The rain that crashed from the sky seemed to part around her, never touching her body or clothing.

Most unusually of all, she looked terribly, frighteningly familiar. Her profile conveyed her identity, and a crash of lightning showed her face.

It was Eliza Weatherhead Esdaile.

Except that it was *not*: it was a *chthonic* spirit, a fairly powerful one, in Eliza's shape. Only one *chthonios* could possibly be so expert at mimicking that image: the one that had possessed Eliza for nearly eight years.

And now she was aboard *Malabar Princess*.

"Reverend Davey," she said. "You are here at last."

"You know who I am." It seemed pointless to deny it or to attempt to conceal myself—if I could perceive her, she could perceive *me*.

"You are the reason my hunger is unrequited."

"I do not know what you mean."

"I shall enlighten you," she said, stepping forward. I braced myself and raised my hands in a warding gesture, unsure whether it would have any effect. To my surprise it did: she seemed to hesitate, either unwilling or unable to advance further.

"Please do."

"There was an arrangement," she said. "I was chosen to protect one of your servants—James Esdaile. He was to be *mine* when his life ended—but you induced him to commit suicide."

"I did nothing of the kind. I do not condone such an act, and was appalled when it happened."

"You did not look appalled at the time."

If I needed any further confirmation of the being's identity, this was it.

"I cannot account for my expression. I was…surprised."

"You *drove* him to this, William Davey. You threatened James Esdaile. You made him conceive of this evil plan to break his contract. As you have done this to *me*, I shall do this to *you*."

"Without negotiation."

"I am not interested in negotiation," she spat out. "I am not interested in discussion."

I wondered, much later, what my fate would have been if she had possessed the time-dilating abilities of Mehmet Nour or the Levantine. I concluded that it would have been quite unpleasant.

"You will forgive me for not immediately acceding to your request," I said, backing away. As I retreated, she advanced; I did my best to keep good footing, but found the deck slippery and treacherous, particularly moving backward.

I had to use one hand to brace myself while leaving the other in a warding gesture. The spirit—Fi—seemed to draw strength from this, and was also emboldened by a manifestation that I could see behind her, looming over the bow of the ship, illuminated by further flashes of lightning.

It was a nereic spirit—a power of the water. Unlike Fi, or even the Levantine, and disturbingly *like* the beings I had seen on Malta and beyond Mehmet Nour's villa, it seemed enormous and extremely powerful.

I wondered if she had offered to share the meal with this being.

The distance between us narrowed. What had been fifty or sixty feet was now no more than thirty as I retreated along the starboard side of the ship, attempting to keep my feet and stay away from the rails. Crew on deck had come to realize that something was happening—but I suspected that they could not see Fi, nor the malevolent nereic being that was crashing over the foredeck.

No one tried to stop me as I backed away, still holding my hand up in a warding gesture: it was if I were all alone on the storm-lashed deck—

Until I suddenly heard a voice speak my name.

"Reverend Davey," the voice said loudly and firmly—female, an older voice I thought I recognized but could not place. "Position yourself in the center of the ship."

I dared not look away, but tried to edge toward its sound. "Why?" I shouted.

"You foolish man," she shouted. "Do as I *say*. The two smokestacks—" A crash of water on the deck drowned out her words.

The two main smokestacks of *Malabar Princess* were located equidistant from fore and aft, thus dividing the ship into thirds. Unfortunately, the rough center of the ship—as the voice had described it—required me to climb a ladder to an upper platform, even more exposed to the weather. It also meant that I would have to completely abandon my warding gesture, allowing Fi to come as close as she was able.

I might be able to hold off a *chthonic* spirit such as Fi. I was certain that the nereic being was simply beyond my ability to withstand.

And the weather was on its side.

I let go of the handle with my left hand and made a swift mesmeric pass with both hands extended partway, thumbs pointing down, then sweeping them out to my right and left. Fi had been moving confidently forward and was caught unawares—or else she was less powerful than I even imagined: she was sent sprawling. As the ship undertook a significant roll to starboard, she slid sideways to her left, slamming up against an upright stanchion.

I could hear her cursing in a most unladylike fashion; but I had already turned and begun climbing the ladder directly behind me.

"There had best be a plan," I said over the din of the storm. A peal of thunder crashed through the air directly after I had said it, as if to punctuate my words.

When I reached the top rung, a gloved hand grasped under my forearm and helped me up on the slippery deck, pulling me into the lee of an overhang that at least took me out of the rain for a moment.

I found myself facing a woman, dressed for weather as I was. She was older, my age at least: she also seemed to be taking a moment to assess what she saw. I did not know her, but her face seemed slightly familiar—and then, despite the inclement conditions, I recognized it with a sudden rush.

I had seen her in Blackwell—and helped her remove her bags from the train. But she had been in disguise then as an older lady in a veiled hat.

And she had dismissed me with a casual mesmeric gesture.

I had seen her on the dock, and at Suez as well, and possibly on the gangway in Aden. She had clearly been on the scene since I had left Egypt—and was also clearly a practitioner of the Art.

"We have to reach the center of the ship," she said. "The two smokestacks function like magnetic nodes—similar to the water-towers at the Crystal Palace. In the exact center, the *chthonic* being will be severely diminished in power—long enough for us to deal with her."

"'Us'?"

"Yes, Mr. Davey. *Us*. We will need to get the cursed thing overboard into the ocean and let *that*"—she gestured toward the bow, where we could clearly see a distorted *something* at least thirty or forty feet in height athwart the steamship's prow—"*that* being deal with it."

Fi began to climb after us.

My unknown benefactor moved quickly along the side of the overhang, which ended in a dozen feet, after which we would be exposed again.

My mind raced as I scrambled after her out into the open, the wind blowing rain in my face, managing handholds on the deck as we moved, hands and knees, across the metal plates. Her plan was sound enough: position ourselves between the smokestacks where Fi's power would supposedly be diminished If this were true it would further explain the Crystal Palace phenomenon—the original site had not been a barrier to mesmeric power, but it had not had the two large round water-towers present at the current one. The smokestacks would function the same way.

Presently we stopped. She braced herself, peeled back one glove with her fingers and withdrew a coin which she placed on edge; it rolled a short distance and fell. She tried again, some inches away, with the same effect.

I turned and saw that Fi had reached the top of the ladder and was now making her way across to us. In the stuttering light of the storm her face wore a triumphal expression.

There was no point in asking for an explanation. My fellow mesmerist placed her coin once more; it seemed not to move quite as far, but its behavior did not please her, and she said something almost inaudible, and likely unladylike, under her breath.

"Madam," I said at last, "I do not think we have time for any further experiments."

"Just a *moment*," she said, placing the coin an inch or two to the left. Remarkably, it did not move. She snatched it up, slid to the place where it had been, and raised her free hand in a gesture. I managed a warding as well, but Fi continued to move toward us.

"What you did down below," the woman said very softly to me. "You must do it again."

"And?"

"And I will do the rest. But wait until she is almost upon us, because her own power will be the weakest."

"What *will* you do?"

"I must convince the nereic being that this creature would be more tasty than you. Clearly the *chthonios* is hungry: the *nereis* is no doubt hungry as well. Let us take your threat away, and sate it at the same time. Are you ready, sir?"

"Have I a choice?"

"Of course not."

"Then I am ready." I slid the toe of my boot into the nearest handle and propped myself on one knee. Then, with Fi less than six feet away, I took a deep breath and performed the same mesmeric pass as I had done below.

Perhaps the desperation of the circumstances strengthened me; perhaps my new companion's estimate of Fi's weakness was more accurate than I had expected.

And perhaps I was just more skilled than I had any right to expect, given the storm, the presence of a powerful elemental force and the pitching of the vessel. Fi's feet went out from under her and she slid once again, this time to port.

There was a flash of lightning that suddenly revealed the entire scene in stark detail—the rain-washed deck, the smokestack ahead, the tableau of my companion, Fi and the terrible nereic being—and for just a moment, another figure: a nearly naked man in a turban and brief kilt, crouching beneath the overhang from which we had emerged. A moment later, he was gone.

The mysterious woman beside me stood up fully, bracing her own foot as I had done, and began to *sing*.

It was no tune I could identify, and no language I understood, but it chilled me to hear it.

Her sinuous hand gestures, curving up and down, gestured toward Fi, who was holding on to a short metal loop embedded in the upper deck. The *chthonic* spirit's expression of grim satisfaction changed to one of surprise—and then horror, as she glanced at her hand and watched her grip loosen: first the thumb, then each finger in turn—four, three, two and then finally the last finger—and my companion's hands came together in a *clap*!

And Fi, in the shape of Eliza Weatherhead Esdaile, lost her grip and was flung off the upper deck and into the storm. I would have expected her to be hurled downward toward the main deck; for some reason, however, she was buoyed upward. The huge nereic being abandoned its post over the bow and moved at impressive speed to the port side of the ship. Fi's body was pulled into it, and then the being and its new captive were drawn down, down, down into the ocean.

The woman knelt—or, rather, dropped to her knees. I reached out to steady her, nearly losing my own purchase.

"That was well done," I managed. "Though it uses no discipline I recognize."

"I am not surprised, Reverend Davey. I learned it in Benares."

"I am significantly in your debt, madam. I regret to say that I do not know your name."

"I doubt whether it would be one you know, sir."

"Without knowing the name, I am in no position to judge."

"Very well," she said, wiping rain from her face as best she could, and straightening herself in her kneeling position. "My name, sir, is Georgiana Shackleford."

PART FIVE

Another country

If you do not change direction, you may
end up where you are heading.
—*Tao Te Ching*

CHAPTER 40

A blank slate

GEORGIANA SHACKLEFORD

Let me state at the outset that my sense of propriety is very firm, but I do not let it conflict with the desire to do what I feel is necessary—or what cannot be avoided.

Consequently, the idea that I should appear to be the... *improper* companion of an insane naturalist determined to experience a lightning-storm at sea firsthand does not trouble me a bit. People can believe what they want, and can speak as they please. What is important—indeed, what is critical—is that the deed was done. In a few days we shall be in Calcutta, and—

Yes, Reverend Davey. I said *we*, and I meant it. I did not track you down and follow you aboard *Malabar Princess* merely to save your life, though it is perfectly clear to me that it was an act of Christian charity to have done so—else *you*, not the *chthonic* spirit, might have been consumed by the nereic one. Once you reach India you will need my help. It is freely offered: better that you are accompanied by someone acquainted with the place than to have you simply stumble about. The stakes are far too high for that.

What is more, sir, I think we can readily dispense with the usual preliminaries in which you dismiss my contributions merely because I am a woman...ah. I am gratified to hear it. Knowing your views on that matter makes it easier to proceed.

I know a great deal about you, Reverend, but I assume that you are not acquainted with me in the least. It therefore is incumbent upon me to explain to you who I am, how I come into this adventure and why I know of you—and your objectives in India. *Le Maître* explained some of it, but as you are aware, he can be rather cryptic at times. He sent me to—

Well. Best to begin at the beginning.

Much of what I know about you, Reverend, is from conversations with Monsieur Dupotet, but my acquaintance with the Art dates back considerably further.

More than twenty years ago I met Dupotet for the first time, when he was exhibiting his skill in London. My Martin—we were married nearly fifteen years at the time—had taken a modest interest in the science—he refused to call it what the adepts did, "the Art"; we visited the Baron's salon in Regent Square and saw his experiments with the servant girl. Dupotet informed me without preamble that I had some innate talent with the Art, something which both Martin and I dismissed out of hand.

It was widely believed at the time that mesmerism was simply beyond the capacity of women to perform, as it might lead to the development of nervous conditions, hysteria and the like. Still, I welcomed the flattery; Martin regularly received the lion's share of attention in public, and I—the wife of a civil servant—was merely *decoration*. Dupotet told me that those who practiced the Art had the half-light to guide them: while not completely illuminating, it was a great advantage over the dark world of those who lacked talent.

I see that the expression is familiar. I suspect that he said something like that to every talented mesmerist he met.

In 1842, Martin obtained a posting to Calcutta as a customhouse inspector. Our daughter had already married, and our two sons were grown—we had purchased a commission for Arthur, and Theodore was in his second year at Cambridge. Some of my ladyfriends wondered that I would undertake such a perilous journey to such an inhospitable place, but I did not wish to remain in England and have my husband thousands of miles away. And it would be an *adventure*: a trip to a foreign, exotic place would be a tonic to my dreadfully boring existence. There is a large expatriate community in Calcutta, and I was sure I would be able to make myself at home there.

And so I did. There are two keys to getting along in society: the first is to know what people want to hear; the second is to *listen* to them. You must take care to notice not only what people tell you, but what they do *not*. I flatter myself that I was capable of moving in any society, and realized at once that to be in India meant to interact with *Indians*: I received excellent advice on the ways and means to set up a household in Calcutta. I listened to what was said…and not said…and learned what was expected. Martin and I made a life for ourselves in India. It was not London, of course, but it was comfortable.

Some ladies find refuge in polite distractions; I longed for something to *do*. I daresay that the Ladies' Society for Native Female Education provided me with an outlet for my energies. A Mrs. Huntingdon, whose husband had come out in the 1820s with the Company, was the most prominent member, and it was from her that we all took our lead. We were—

Men? Of *course* the governing officers of the Society were men, administering the spending of money and the relationship between our activities and the mandates of the Governor-General. Beyond that they took little interest in the Society's day-to-day affairs. Men in India found other distractions. Even my dear heart had his head turned by the occasional native odalisque, though I daresay he did not keep a harem of them as did some grandees.

You are shocked by that, Reverend Davey. You should not be—either for the act, or for my acceptance of it. Men follow their desires first, their hearts second, and their good sense third. While my husband was a sinner and not a saint, he was selective in his tastes and discreet in his indulgences. As far as I know, he left no legacies behind.

To be clear: I was not a *victim* of those tendencies—merely a bystander.

In any case, my distraction was in the nature of a great *project*. The young women we sought to reach had been kept distant from the light of Christian teaching, but that was the least of it; they could not read or write or do simple sums. In the most extreme cases when their husband departed this life, they were expected to lie down with the body when it was burned and die with him. It was a cruel, unjust fate for half of the population of that teeming country: Beatrice Huntingdon—a disciple of Mary Anne Cooke—and the rest of her followers, myself included, were determined to do *something* about it. The Englishwomen found meaning in their lives as well, I think. We could do something fulfilling with our time and our hands and our minds.

Yes. I think you are exactly right: we were still somewhat blind to the basic truth of the situation—that is, about what caused the Mutiny. But any subject of Her Majesty could be found equally guilty of that sort of hubris. India is a different, deeper place than most of our countrymen think—and it is not merely a blank slate on which we can draw our own vision of civilization. We did not even consider the possibility that the clay we sought to mold would resist the shape we wanted. It seems far simpler in hindsight.

I know that you are waiting for me to tell you how I came to be associated with Monsieur Dupotet. Before that, however, I must tell you that I know a great deal about *you*—some of which I have heard directly from *Le Maître.* I shall have your promise as a gentleman that you will eventually give me your part of the story. Since you know that I am an acquaintance of Eliza Weatherhead, then you know that she suffered a rather unpleasant fate at the hands of James Esdaile. I met Eliza at Hooghly, and even assisted in her brief wedding preparations before she left for Scotland with Doctor Esdaile.

I knew there was something wrong—I eventually learned what had been done to the poor girl, but to my regret I simply learned it far too late.

WILLIAM DAVEY

It took us most of two days to dry out and recover from our little jaunt on deck. No one saw anything of Fi or the nereic creature, of course: she had not been a passenger on *Malabar Princess*, and the creature had simply been a part of the storm. With it gone, the ship steamed into clear weather and open water. I was taken for a wild-eyed savant who had not had the sense to stay out of the storm, and Mrs. Shackleford played the part of my level-headed companion who had gone out there to drag me in. The ship's surgeon examined us, reproved us and released us on our own recognizance.

Word of our unusual diversion made the rounds of the passengers, and I was viewed either with newfound respect or with haughty bemusement. Mrs. Shackleford—Georgiana—determined that we should take our constitutionals and our meals together, and for the next two weeks we scarcely spent a waking hour apart. It was not a love interest: though neither of us strained ourselves to dissuade anyone aboard the ship on that account. On the other hand, neither of us had any interest in testing the other's prowess with the Art. She recognized my skill, and I hers. I was well out of my domain; if and when we were both back in Britain, there might have to be an adjustment to that relationship, but for the moment it could stand.

"It was the Mutiny that changed my life, of course," Georgiana told me as we sat out on the deck, spying the distant coast of Persia as we steamed eastward. "As it did so many in India."

"I can imagine."

"Many lives were lost in that terrible event, William." She had taken to addressing me by my first name, as I employed hers. Life-threatening combat against *stoicheia* granted access to that particular intimacy. "Including my husband's."

"You have not spoken of this before."

"There was no need. It is still painful, though the event itself freed me from a relationship that had long since grown cool. He was on a task for the Customs Service and was killed during a...fire." She looked stonily away from me, as if putting the incident aside in her mind—placing it in a compartment where it would be safe and could no longer hurt her.

Yet it still seemed to hurt.

"I am so sorry."

"He deserved better. But it was a terrible time, a dangerous time. Many of us felt unsafe: most nights, and many days, I would not even go abroad in the city. After Martin was killed, there was an intimation that I might be in danger.

"Then, someone rescued me. A *khansamah*—a sort of master butler."

"I know the term."

"From Eliza, I expect."

"Just so."

"Then you should be aware that the *khansamah* of whom I speak is someone who was known to her: a man named Gobinda Shah Ahmadi, who had served in the same house as Eliza when she was first in India."

"I see," I said. *Once again this man has come into the tale*, I thought. "How did this—Gobinda—help you, Georgiana?"

"He took me away from Calcutta. We journeyed to Varanasi—to Benares, as it has been Anglicized. Benares is one of many holy dedicated to one or another of their many deities; it is of particular significance to Lord Shiva, who is said to have founded it five thousand years ago. Gobinda had tried to secure a position for Eliza in Benares before I first met her: I advised her against it. Irony has an unhappy habit of catching up with us, don't you think?"

"Aptly put."

"Thank you," she said, with a gracious nod of her head. "Gobinda is an adept—a practitioner of the same Art you, Monsieur Dupotet and James Esdaile all employ…or employed. The disciplines of the school at Benares, however, are closely tied to the worship of Lord Shiva. A considerable body of knowledge was made available to me during my eight months in residence.

"Prior to the Mutiny there were very few Englishmen there, but a strong presence was stationed at Ramnagar Fort afterward, though the Kashi Naresh was not at all happy about it; because of the conflict Westerners were said to be disliked in the city. Most of them had no interaction with the natives, of course; I was even warned by the commander that I should consider withdrawing to Bombay or Calcutta—but due to my relationship with Gobinda, I was as safe there as in any city in India."

"This Gobinda fellow was your teacher in Benares. Did he convert you to become a Hindoo?"

"He most certainly did *not*," she answered. "And my progress in the Art as it is taught there was limited."

"Because of your unwillingness to embrace the Hindoo pantheon?"

"No, rather because I could not dance." She vouchsafed me a tiny smile, as if that explained everything.

"I see." I did not, but was unwilling to admit it.

"I must tell you, William, that Lord Shiva indeed exists. It is quite apparent to me that whatever He *is*, He is extremely powerful. The opponents we faced a few days ago are as children to Him. I… had a few momentary contacts with His avatar. I was terribly frightened by them, and by the realization that the Mutiny itself—though caused by deep resentments and strong feelings—was set off by something else, something completely different and dangerous."

"I suspect I know what that might be."

"I am sure you do. It is what is drawing you to India, William— and drawing me along with you. The Great Rebellion was set off in part by the effects of the artifact that James Esdaile left behind when he departed India nine years ago—a tiny bronze statue that only just contains a spirit more powerful than anything we have faced.

"We must find it, and find a safe place for it."

"'We'?"

"Of *course*, *we*," she said to me, as if it were the most natural conclusion in the world. "We have had this discussion already, William. You continue to assume that you can accomplish this task alone. *Le Maître* told me it was one of your great failings. You simply *must* be shut of this conceit.

"When we reach Bombay we should be able to gain some further insights and I can help you search for the object in Calcutta.

I was at James Esdaile's house the night Eliza was taken by the *chtho-nios*," she added, looking away from me. "If only for her sake I should like to make up for that."

I could recognize an irresistible force when I saw it, and saw no alternative than to say, "Madam, I shall be glad of your help."

CHAPTER 41

The changed land

WILLIAM DAVEY

Georgiana was amused as she looked at me, lowering the spyglass from my eye.

"I can see it."

"You look relieved, William," she said. "Or is that wonder I see in your eyes?"

"Wonder? No. I confess to relief. During the crossing I had the strangest feeling of isolation, as if the entire world was encompassed by this ship with nothing beyond."

"But you are much taken with the view."

"It is quite remarkable. I cannot see the harbor, but I thought I picked out a fort of some kind."

"Bawa Malang. It's in ruins now—and we are still some distance from the harbor; it is on an island set out from the coast. When we come closer you'll see that Her Majesty's Forces have seized extravagant and magnificent control—there are shore batteries and gun-ships, though I remain at a loss to know against whom they might be directed. The Rebellion is long past, and no other European power threatens Her Majesty's realm in India."

"It is called deterrence, Georgiana. Those armaments help *deter* mayhem."

"I cannot imagine that anyone would contemplate it."

"I do not think you understand how these things work, madam."

"I witnessed the Sepoy Rebellion in person, *Reverend*," she answered with some asperity. "I understand exactly how *these things* work."

I had no reply to that comment. Georgiana was always quite stubborn when she thought she knew what she was about.

"I have offended your male pride."

"Do not trouble yourself," I said.

She pursed her lips but did not immediately respond. We stood there looking out across the water, dappled by the sun.

At last she said, "You still don't trust me, William."

"I don't know what makes you say that. I owe my life to you, Georgiana."

"But you are still on your guard toward me."

"It is merely a habit of my profession."

She smiled. "I suppose I cannot blame you. I followed you all the way to India in secret; other than our little skirmish with the nereic and the *chthonic* beings, I have done little to gain your trust—"

"Surely," I said, "that is enough."

"I should have thought so. However, now that we are coming to another country, one that most Englishmen never see, you need to accept me as an ally."

"*Need?* I think you may overstate the case."

"I do not. I find your aloofness charming, William. But never fear: if you choose to trust me, I shall speak of it to no one. Your secret is safe with me."

GEORGIANA SHACKLEFORD

As was customary, our vessel docked at Apollo Bandar below Fort George to discharge the mail. The captain of *Malabar Princess* and the haughty customs official insisted on referring to it as Wellington Pier—but the old name, derived from the *palla* fish, and not the Greek god!—was still the vernacular. But as with the guns and ships, we have a tendency to attach the names of famous past heroes to anything in reach, though the indigenous people often stubbornly resist.

Within an hour we were again underway, proceeding along the east side of the island to Mazagaon, where the custom-house is located, so that we could disembark. That process could scarcely have been more disagreeable—not only for the rather undignified way in which the transaction was handled, but also for the odor from the nearby flats that permeated the air. But it was not the smell of fish that alarmed us as we waited for our luggage to be examined—it was the sense of something else all around us, waiting and watching.

By the time we emerged onto the crowded street opposite St. Peter's Church, it was clear to me that we had come to a changed land: not the India of the pleasant guidebooks, nor the India I had left a few years earlier, but a place with spirits that few people could see or feel. We two were among those few.

WILLIAM DAVEY

Our purser had made arrangements with a *dubash*, a sort of *valet de place* who had come aboard at Apollo Bandar to secure places for us at a small hotel in Bykullah, supposed to be nearby. I could only hope for the best, as I certainly had no idea. I was somewhat bewildered by Bombay, as we waited for the carriage.

When it at last arrived, I was made even more aware of the alienness of the place. The vehicle was harnessed to a pair of large bullocks. Porters obligingly piled cases and trunks onto the back of this conveyance—a *bullock-garee*, as it was called—and we took our places on broad benches. We were thus unceremoniously hauled over to Palanji's Hotel.

As we passed through the streets, I also had the sense of being watched: unlike the idlers on Regent Street or outside Fergusson's office, these seemed to be more inchoate and seemingly less malign—though Georgiana was on edge during our ride and even while we waited in the hotel lobby for our rooms. In the heat of the day we parted to take our rest; even in the winter, it was humid and warm, especially for a visiting Englishman. In the late afternoon, though, there was a sudden thunderstorm which unburdened us of much of the humidity in the air.

I met Georgiana in the hotel dining-room near dusk: we

resumed our roles as the natural philosopher and his amanuensis, sampling local cuisine. My companion did her best to steer me away from the most spicy dishes but the fare was still rather more than I was prepared to handle.

"You'd best get used to it, William," she said to me quietly as I wiped my brow and my eyes after a particularly savory forkful. "This is moderate for the native palate."

"I suppose one becomes accustomed."

"Or goes hungry." She set her napkin on the table and caught my attention with her glance. "Tomorrow we shall take a short voyage by steam launch to Elephanta."

"We shall?"

"We are going to visit Lord Shiva's temple. I hope that we shall gain some insight there."

"There are temples a-plenty here. Why must we make *this* voyage?"

She looked at me, frowning slightly. "This is not just any temple. It is a Shiva Linga—one might almost say that it is *the* Shiva Linga. Some Brahmins disdain the place, but I suspect you will feel its power."

"Tell me more," I answered, though I knew she would not hesitate to do so.

"Benares, the city where I learned the Art, is most holy to Lord Shiva," she said quietly. "But He is revered here as well. It is far too difficult to articulate all of the aspects of Hindu beliefs, so I will not burden you with them—but suffice it to say that the great cave on the island of Elephanta is a remarkable center of power. It depicts Shiva with three faces: the creator Brahma, the preserver Vishnu and the destroyer Rudra. It is called the *Trimurti*."

The description reminded me of something—though I could not place it at that moment.

"It is a remarkable likeness, I suppose."

"You do not have to resort to a mocking tone, sir. I can imagine that during your voyage here your eyes have been opened to things you have never seen—denigrating a place of power is not only impolite and impious, it might even be dangerous."

"You mistake my tone as a mocking one, madam. It is merely dismissive."

Georgiana looked as if she was prepared to retort angrily, but instead made a sort of *hmph* noise—then softened, realizing that I was only joking with her.

"I do not think Lord Shiva has a tremendous sense of humor, particularly with non-believers. Unfortunately, the great cave on Elephanta gets a great deal of them—Englishmen, mostly, though it is said that the Portuguese fired cannons into it to destroy the idols within. That Lord Shiva has not seen fit to retaliate may suggest that He simply doesn't think it's worth His while to do so."

"So I am safe in dismissing him."

"No," she said, sipping from her wine glass. "His inaction should not be used as an indication of his disinterest. *Post hoc* does not necessarily indicate *propter hoc*—or is it the other way around?" She smiled. "While I should like to impress you with the numinousness of the Shiva Linga, I shall have to leave you to sense it for yourself. In the meanwhile I am very troubled, William, by what I sense around us."

We are everywhere, the Levantine had told me. "I think the problem is more widespread than just India, Georgiana."

"I know that. But there is a certain…hunger here. If the Glass Door has been opened—"

"I rather think that we would know it by now."

"You have a tremendous confidence in your own abilities."

"It is a survival trait."

She sniffed, as if dismissing my survival traits. I might have considered it mildly insulting—except that I might well have owed my life to Georgiana, and could not help but respect her abilities.

"I suppose you are right. But this is not your domain—and it is not mine."

"Whose domain is it, then?"

"It is the domain…of Lord Shiva. But He has more than one

face. We must take care that the wrong one does not turn its attention to us."

We took to our separate rooms and slept as well as we were able.

In the morning, Georgiana and I boarded a steam launch at the P & O at Apollo Bandar dock and left the main island. Bombay harbor was still and shining in the sun; it would have been an idyllic, pastoral journey except for the feeling that weighed upon both of us as we stood out on the launch's main deck. The harbor was crowded with boats of every description—from the meanest rowboats to large steamships, berthed at the various docks behind us.

It took us less than an hour to travel to Elephanta Island, passing a smaller island on the way—the launch steered well clear of it, as it was apparently used for quarantine. The craft was thronged with pilgrims as well as inquisitive Europeans; the natives were respectful, while most of the Englishmen were garrulous and—I must confess—somewhat disrespectful. The lessons of the Sepoy Rebellion clearly did not include any regard for native culture: I wondered that I even took notice of it.

When we reached the pier we were all taken by the sight of an enormous mass of rock, cut in some bygone day in the shape of an enormous elephant, fifteen feet in length and nearly thirty feet around. Some of the head and neck had fallen off or been damaged—perhaps the Portuguese guns had done it. (I am given to understand that this great stone mass has long since been removed.)

The first inhabitants I noticed at the pier were not human at all—they were monkeys. Gray or dark brown, with long, curved tails, they seemed to have the run of the place; they capered around the visitors, hoping for food or attention, dodging canes and walking-sticks (at which they seemed quite adept), while we humans had to make an effort to keep our footing on the slippery pier, composed of large concrete blocks with gaps of several inches between them. We streamed steadily up the flights of steps; the more weary and infirm tended to stop at landing-places located at intervals, while others were carried upward—bump-bump-bump—by palky bearers. In comparison, Georgiana—who clearly had her destination in mind—moved at a resolute pace without pause, and I walked alongside. Monkeys kept us company, running along the stone railings and through the corinda bushes that covered the hillside.

We reached the summit of the hill at last, and were presented with the remarkable sight that Georgiana had brought me here to see: a cave temple cut into the rock of the hillside. It was composed of wide, squat pillars supporting a broad façade of stone resembling porphyry, dividing the cave-mouth into three broad openings. When it came into view, the native Indians immediately began to murmur to themselves; and even Georgiana hesitated.

"Shall we put our shoes from off our feet?" I asked quietly, in jest.

She stopped walking and grasped me by the forearm.

"I appreciate your dismissiveness—or is it disdain? But please understand, William: this is not the time, and this is *certainly* not the place."

She was deadly earnest—truly, even when we were opposed by Fi and the nereic being on the ship, I do not think I saw such a serious expression on her face.

"What is to happen here, madam?"

"I told you," she said, leading me gently out of the press to the left side of the great plaza. "We are here to learn more about the nature of our objective and what opposes us."

"And to see a three-headed god."

"This is one of Lord Shiva's most sacred places."

"I asked you some time ago if you had taken up the Hindoo worship, Georgiana, and you assured me that this was not the case. Would you care to reconsider your answer, and whether you intend something to which I might object?" I fingered the clerical collar at my throat.

"I did not choose this place by accident."

"That much is obvious."

"It is sacred to Lord Shiva, William," she repeated, and added in a whisper, "which means that certain beings fear it and will *stay away*. There might be no place more protected from a *chthonic* eavesdropper than this temple. Now I ask you to trust me, and bear with me."

"You are keeping things from me."

"Many, many things. And *you* are keeping things from *me*. I think that we can trust each other despite that."

"You ask a great deal."

"And so do you. Now let us enter the temple, sir."

I was acutely aware of the presence of the place, fifty yards from where Georgiana and I stood. Unlike the interior of the Crystal Palace, this place seemed to *magnify* my mesmeric senses: I felt drawn to it in a manner I had not experienced since I was aboard the Mediterranean steamer.

If Georgiana were leading me into a trap, I flattered myself that I should be able to anticipate that as well. But this far from my own domain and battered by recent experience and the continual revelation of worlds I had never seen, I found it difficult to be certain.

When I hesitated, Georgiana's expression softened.

"I realize that India is *terra incognita* for you, William, as it once was for me," she said. "But this is not the India I knew either: it is a changed land, torn by the Rebellion and now—inhabited—by things we must both consider inimical. If you wish to turn back, I cannot and do not desire to stop you."

"All right," I said. "Lead on."

CHAPTER 42

Three faces

WILLIAM DAVEY

"Come," Georgiana said as we passed between two of the great stone pillars that flanked the façade.

It was dark and cooler inside—but the first thing that struck me was the profound *silence*. It was not so much the reverent quiet of worshippers: truthfully, in some ways they were as animated as the disdainful Europeans had been in our journey across Bombay harbor. It was the silence associated with our separation from the world beyond those massive pillars—and I suddenly realized that outside I had been hearing the plaintive sounds of almost-voices... perhaps the *chthonoi* were asking me, in a voice I could scarcely hear and in a language I did not understand: *What do you want? How can we help you?*

And abruptly that chorus was struck silent. Within this ancient temple, a thousand or more years old, we were in the domain of Lord Shiva.

I could feel him—I refused to capitalize the pronoun then, and still hesitate to do so these many years later, for that would be to accord Shiva the status of deity. But his presence was apparent to anyone with the least sensitivity: and if not a god, he was clearly more than a mere mortal...and more than the nereic spirit out in the Indian Ocean, or the photic one in the Egyptian desert or the *chthonic* ones on Malta.

Shiva was, in truth, another sort of being entirely: powerful and without definite boundary, rather like a thunder-cloud in the sky. It was no wonder that Georgiana had been shaken by contact with him—especially if it had been deeper than the casual interaction I was presently experiencing.

My reverie was interrupted by Georgiana gently touching my arm.

"Come to the Linga Shrine," she said, and gestured to a large square structure on the west side of the cave. "A friend is here."

"A friend?"

She declined to answer, but indicated for me to follow.

We walked toward a doorway. Beyond I could see a square chapel, flanked by large stone statues that looked like Hindoo men leaning on smaller, dwarfish figures with curious, mocking expressions. As we passed beneath the square arch, I felt my aura tingle as if it had been assaulted by a mesmerist of considerable power.

Each compass direction held a similar square archway, so that the entire temple was open to the outer cave; in the center of the temple a smooth, conical stone about three feet across sat upon a round plinth.

Though the cave was crowded, this area was remarkably empty other than the two of us and a turbaned man with his back turned, who appeared to be contemplating the stone. At our footsteps he turned and offered a polite smile.

He was an elderly native gentleman with a carefully-trimmed beard and round spectacles. Animated eyes lay behind them.

"William," she said, "I have the honor to present—"

"No," I interrupted. "Let me guess. This must be the remarkable Gobinda Shah Ahmadi."

"Have we met, sir?" the Bengali *khansamah* asked, taking my forwardness in stride. Georgiana, by comparison, was speechless—I think that she had expected the man to be present in the cave and my reaction had thrown her completely off-stride.

Good, I thought. *Let's keep it that way.*

"You have me at something of a disadvantage," Gobinda said. "I suspect that you know more about me than I do about you. He glanced curiously at Georgiana. *What did you tell him?* he seemed to be asking.

"I take it that Georgiana did not brief you in advance when she set up this meeting."

"She…only just learned I was here. My friend and student…" he smiled toward Georgiana, giving the slightest mesmeric gesture, which I resisted, not letting my eyes travel from him to her—"has not been in India for a few years, and I have not left it. Despite our correspondence, Reverend Davey *Sahib*, I am unsure what you *know* and do not *know*. I do understand that you are a powerful practitioner…within your domain."

"And outside of it."

"I have no doubt of it," he answered.

"You and my new-found friend have arranged this meeting, sir. Perhaps you would be good enough to tell me what you want—or what you will do for me."

At this point I turned to Georgiana; she looked impatient and somewhat annoyed. I returned my attention to Gobinda.

"Your reputation does not do you justice," he said without explanation. "Nonetheless, I am here to assist you, and I shall do so. This is an important place to Lord Shiva, as I am sure Georgiana has told you."

I glanced around. "It keeps the *stoicheia* at bay."

"Just so. But there is more here than merely a barrier to elemental spirits. Consider, if you will, this stone."

He turned away from us to contemplate the object that dominated the center of the room.

"This is supposed to be a…part of Shiva, I presume," I said.

"Yes," he said quietly. "It represents…Lord Shiva in his character as a prolific power of nature."

"It is his—"

"*Nature*," Gobinda interrupted, before I offered a literal characterization of the thing, which I am sure would have led me directly to paroxysms of laughter, allowing the two of them to make short work of me.

"And it is, I assume, an object of veneration."

Gobinda did not turn to face me, but I saw him sketch a very subtle mesmeric gesture with his left hand. As he did, pilgrims and curious visitors began making their way into the hitherto empty temple area, as if he had just invited them.

"There are many places that mark mighty Shiva's worship. But outside of Varanasi itself, this might be the principal one. Do you not agree, Georgiana?"

"It is a place where He is revered."

"This is Lord Shiva's *home*. In any case, Shiva is powerful here. Younger spirits, therefore, are *not*. Particularly near the Linga. But look at this." He walked over to the north entrance, which was faced by an immense three-faced bust, perhaps twenty or more feet in height, depicting a huge figure topped with three faces, one looking directly at us, the others pointed left and right. Once again, the three-headed image reminded me of something that I was unable to bring to mind.

"The Trimurti," Georgiana said.

"Some traditions show Lord Shiva with five faces, but the more common representation is of three. The one facing us is Shiva as Brahma, the Creator—he is an ascetic, despite that jewel in his breast: he drinks from a gourd. On our right he is Shiva as Vishnu, the Preserver: see the lotus in his hand. These two faces are the benign aspects of Lord Shiva, who protects and cultivates. But there is a third face." He stepped a bit to the left and gestured. "That is Shiva as Rudra, the Destroyer. He holds a cobra wrapped around his arm, prepared to strike, and his third eye is visible but, thankfully, closed. When it opens, flame will erupt that will destroy the world."

"That is to be avoided, I trust."

He nodded. "For three thousand years, Lord Shiva has protected the land from perils—foreigners"—he smiled, inclining his head—"natural disasters, and of course *pishach*, or demons. There is a tale that the worst of these demons have been bottled up and tossed in the ocean or planted deep in the earth, for their essence is such that even Lord Shiva could not completely destroy them."

"The tale is true, as you know," I answered. "But the one I

pursue has not yet escaped. However, it has found a way to extend its influence beyond the bars of its prison."

"Where is it now? Where is its...prison?"

"I cannot say," I said. "It is what has brought me to India. I believe it was found, partially opened, and discarded before it could do further damage. But it clearly has done harm. It may have helped bring about the Mutiny itself," I added, as *sotto voce* as the echoes in the temple chamber would permit. "But there is something about it I do not understand."

"What is that?"

"The beings here in India do not seem to be particularly well-formed. They seem immaterial, partially inchoate. I have encountered their kind in a far better organized fashion. Enough," I said, looking at Georgiana, "that they could capably take a place in human society such that those without extended perceptions might not even notice their presence. I have seen none of that sort here in India."

"You might be surprised," Gobinda said quietly.

"How gratifying."

"If the *pishach* has not escaped by now," he said at last, "then perhaps it simply can not."

I looked up at the *Trimurti*, paying particular attention to the Destroyer aspect. The light was irregular inside the cave, casting some of the three-faced figure in shadow; but for just a moment I thought I saw the hint of flames behind the closed eye on the face's forehead: the fires of destruction, waiting to be unleashed.

"I should not like to take that risk," I said. "The object in which it is contained must be found and secured. Perhaps...Lord Shiva can help."

"If that is what He wishes. But if He desires that effort to fail instead. . ."

"Of the three faces," I answered, "that is the one I least wish to see."

CHAPTER 43

A prayer for sleep

WILLIAM DAVEY

We parted company from Gobinda before we left Bombay, with the assurance that we would see him again in Calcutta. I invited him to join us aboard the steamship but he declined, claiming pressing business.

For my part, I was relieved to have a respite to consider how I was to approach him—or make use of him—before circumstances forced me to do so. But I did not know how he might reach Calcutta otherwise in any reasonable amount of time—there was no direct train service. Perhaps he planned to call up a magic carpet. Georgiana seemed to entertain no doubts, so I let the matter lie.

After the voyage from Aden to Bombay, the passage to Calcutta was anticlimactic. We were not assaulted by *stoicheia* and met with no mysterious strangers. However, it was not without its eventful moments.

Our route took us entirely around the island of Ceylon, a large teardrop south and east of the tip of India. It seemed like an unnecessary detour for the ship, as opposed to passing through the Palk Strait into the Bay of Bengal, a shorter way as shown on a map. As we watched the approach to Ceylon's west coast from the main deck of *Malabar Princess*, I observed as much to Georgiana.

"It's not navigable," she said. "There's been talk of a ship channel, but it would cut through Rama's Bridge, which is clearly out of the question."

"Rama's Bridge?"

"There is a reef that extends from India to Ceylon. It's called Rama's Bridge because Lord Rama used it to reach the island, to recover his wife, Sita, from the evil Lord Ravena. It's all in the *Ramayana*. The story is that Lord Rama crossed on a bridge of floating stones—"

"Lord Rama."

"Yes."

"Another Hindoo god, I suppose?"

"He was likely a real king, in ancient time. A great hero—the perfect servant of *dharma*, which is—"

"Wait." I held up my hand. "I concede your knowledge of Indian culture. Let me assure you that, other than as it affects my purposes, I do not care very much about it."

"You *should*. I have already suggested to you—"

"Yes. That I might anger Lord Shiva, or Vishnu, or Rama, or whomever." I gave an exaggerated glance upward, as if there was a smiting on the way. "But I don't believe in all of it—not as religion. Do you?"

"I have told you that I do not."

"To be honest, I find that harder and harder to believe," I answered. "Whenever one of these pagan beings—I hesitate to refer to them as 'gods'—comes into the conversation, Georgiana, you accord him great reverence."

"I would not call it—"

"*Reverence*," I repeated. "I am trying…to maintain distance from what I see." I looked away from her, out at the verdant hills of Ceylon. The air was humid beyond belief—even in late morning mist covered the higher slopes, where rain was falling. "Somewhere ahead of us, I believe I will find an artifact that embodies a malign spirit, something dangerous enough that James Esdaile was willing to give his life and trap the soul of an innocent young woman—and, I must note, to defy *me* and the entire Committee to keep us from it. Gobinda called this thing a demon. I find the characterization not at all unbecoming.

"I *refuse* to be distracted by pagan nonsense that clouds the subject and confuses my aims. There is much that I do not understand, Georgiana, but—"

She put her hand over mine. I paused and looked at her.

"William," she said quietly, "there is much that *I* do not understand. You asked me whether I worshipped Lord Shiva and I told you I did not—but that does not mean I do not respect His power. I am not sure about the boundaries of divinity: what makes a being a deity, or god-like, or just something or someone we cannot comprehend.

"What is clear to me is that beings of such power have appeared in many cultures in the past."

"Yes, I accept that: the Vikings, the Egyptians and the Hindoos all seem to have devised ways to keep them at bay. But regardless of their power, it does not make them God."

"It makes them—" She removed her hand and adjusted her hat minutely, as if to better suit the fitful damp breeze that had sprung up. "It makes them *something* to be feared and respected. They may be different things, or they may be one thing viewed in different ways. Archaeologists call this *syncretism*: it's like the Greek Zeus and the Roman Jupiter."

"You are arguing the divine with a clergyman, Georgiana. I may be…I may be…many things, but I am still in a line of work that requires that I pay heed to certain standards. I also continue to adhere to those beliefs.

"Shiva—" I lowered my voice and caught her eye. I did not attempt a mesmeric pass: this was not a time for a test of wills, but I wanted to make sure I had her attention. "Shiva," I said very quietly, "is not God. Whatever the being whom you perceive happens to be, he or it is not God. If I were to travel that road, then soon I would attribute godhood to the terrible thing inside that statue. That way—that way lies madness.

"Do not try me, Georgiana. Do *not*."

I thought about using the Art again, decided against it, and began to turn to walk away; but she grabbed my sleeve. I shrugged it off but remained: she had something to say, and whether I was annoyed or angry with her or not, I needed to hear it.

"There was a time that such beings walked the earth," she said.

"They crossed bridges of floating stones; they raised great towers and changed the courses of mighty rivers. They blessed lands and scourged them. I believe *that*. I also am convinced that it happened a very, very long time ago. It is better to let such beings sleep, either by constraining them—or by offering them the proper respect and duty."

"Idolatry."

"I think of it more as...insurance. Whatever happens, William, whatever we do, we do *not* want them walking abroad again. Let them sleep."

We came upon Sangor Island in the first light of morning, the sun rising oily, orange-yellow from the Bay of Bengal. The island was an overgrown jungle that showed some signs of human habitation; some of the undergrowth had been hacked away to make room for docks, and there was a profusion of boats of various kinds. *Malabar Princess* was traveling under a fair bit of steam and none of these vessels approached—and our captain seemed to have no interest in heaving to long enough for them to do so.

Georgiana informed me that years ago not only did ships inbound for Calcutta regularly give over to this diversion, but that it was almost a necessity: the waters near the mouth of the Hooghly River were sufficiently hazardous that it was almost a requirement that a ship take on a foreign pilot to guide it into harbor. But those were still mostly sailing-ships; a packet steamer like *Malabar Princess* did not require such assistance.

Thus, though the ship slowed its pace as we approached and then entered the river itself—opening up a beautiful view, far superior to the initial impression—we approached the city without any intervention, coming at last to dock under the watch of Fort William, which dominated the fairly flat landscape. Soldiers were prominently stationed on the dock: as Jackson had pointed out to me a lifetime ago, this was a land that had only recently undergone a great upheaval. No natives with nasty knives were in evidence.

I could feel presences on shore—not only the sorts of inchoate spirits we had felt in Bombay, but also those who projected an aura indicating facility with the Art.

As we arranged our descent from the ship, I saw Gobinda on the dockside, standing serenely among the scarcely organized chaos of the import jetties which accompanies the arrival of passenger vessels anywhere in the world, patiently waiting for us to approach.

When we came close, he offered a perfect, courteous bow to Georgiana, and gave me a tight, careful smile.

"I am pleased to see you here," I said. "And to be honest, not the least surprised."

"I dislike dissembling," Gobinda answered. "I have been very busy since we parted, Davey *Sahib*."

"Of that I have no doubt."

"And *I* do not doubt that you did not expect me to arrive in advance of *Malabar Princess*," Gobinda said. "But as I told you, I have been quite busy since we last met."

"Indeed. And may I ask what *possessed* you, sir?"

"William," Georgiana said in a tone that seemed like a mild scold.

"You have an interesting choice of words, Davey *Sahib*."

"It was deliberate. I should like some answers, if you please."

"Answers?"

"It has become clear to me," I said, looking from Georgiana to Gobinda, "that there is a good deal of knowledge being kept from me. And while this is not my domain—" I lowered my voice a bit. "While this is not my domain, I still retain some power. I am not here to be a part of *your* plans but to execute one of my own. I shall do it with your help or without it, or in the face of your opposition."

"*William*," Georgiana repeated, with an expression of scarcely contained fury; but the *khansamah* held up his hand.

It was a subtle, but very powerful, mesmeric pass. I recognized it and felt it pass by me—and I cannot imagine that Georgiana did not do the same. In any case, she fell silent.

GEORGIANA SHACKLEFORD

Though I was aware of your purpose, it drew upon deep reserves of patience to refrain from an act of physical violence against you when you took such a tone with Gobinda. I have seen him angry—and I respect his power, William, even more than I respect yours; to his credit, he did not give in to that or any other emotion in his response.

You may have thought that you controlled the situation with your abrupt and brusque tone. But it did not seem that way to me. If it had been a cricket match, I would have declared your side's innings over.

Except, of course, this was no game, and all of us knew it.

"I fear," I said, "that as some say, you wish to put the imp back in the bottle. But I do not think that is possible."

"We must try."

"William," I said, "I believe that we must attend to mundane matters. When our luggage is arranged, we will have much to discuss."

"I have made an advance reservation at the Auckland Hotel," you told Gobinda—and me, for the first time. "If it would be convenient, we can meet in the lobby later today."

Without so much as a by-your-leave, you offered the merest of nods and turned away, walking down the jetty toward the queue of passengers awaiting entry to the custom-house.

Gobinda waited several moments and then allowed himself a smile.

"Georgiana Memsahib," Gobinda said with a slight bow, touching the ends of his fingers together.

"And I shall now call you *Guru*?" I glanced around; no one was paying any particular attention. "No. Merely names, my friend. And it is good to be back in Calcutta once more."

"You despise Calcutta."

"I do *not* despise Calcutta."

"Georgiana," Gobinda said, "when you departed Benares twenty-six months ago, you assured me that if your soul passed around the wheel of dharma five or six more times before you returned to Calcutta, it would be far too soon. I am sure your facility with the English language can characterize that as something short of *despising*, but it is a distinction without a difference."

"I spent many years in Calcutta," I answered, "but I concede that it is painful to be reminded what I left behind. It is the scene of my second-greatest loss," I said. "Losing Martin was painful…but I could have saved Eliza."

"This is old ground, Georgiana. The question of whether you, or I, could have saved Eliza is irrelevant and we can do nothing to remedy what happened. But she…survived," Gobinda said, looking thoughtful. "She survived."

"William has visited with her. She was—she is—a remarkable woman."

"Davey *Sahib* is going to be a problem, Georgiana. I am not sure what he precisely wants."

"What he cannot have. But he knows that, Gobinda. He has come to realize the limits of his, or anyone's power."

"You think so."

"I do."

"Such men sometimes realize the limit of their power, my friend. But it rarely prevents them from trying to exceed it."

WILLIAM DAVEY

Customs officials and native functionaries are the same the world over. They can be obeyed, flattered, bribed or compelled; the judicious application of humility, fair words, coins and the Art in the correct proportion and at the proper time will see a gentleman through the most onerous of inspections.

I did not wish to apply my abilities to any noticeable extent, but I did employ a few very simple passes when the dilatory nature of Her Majesty's servants became too much for me to abide. Based on what I had been told, the Company had been remarkable in its efficiency: the Government, by comparison, seemed to excel in just the opposite.

A palky took me from the Custom House to the Auckland Hotel, or (as it was locally known) Wilson's Hotel, across from Government House. This impressive establishment was as English as its surroundings were Bengali—an ornate white façade four stories high, rising above its neighbors on the crowded streets.

I entered the lobby of the hotel with my carpet-bag in my hand, and was at once on my guard: I sensed a presence, just as I had done on the docks in Bombay.

It was quiet away from Courthouse Street and cooler than I would have expected. I warily approached the concierge's desk.

"Good afternoon, sir," the English clerk said. He seemed nervous; I offered him a polite smile. He was not the presence I sensed: I wanted to turn and search the lobby, but refrained.

"My name is William Davey," I said. "I sent a letter from London—"

He glanced at me, and at a ledger-book opened in front of him. "Yes, sir. Reverend Davey. You are expected." He snapped his fingers and said a few words in Bengali to a junior clerk, who moved quickly to a side table. "I believe—we have some correspondence for you, sir. If you would be so good as to sign the guest-book?"

I would be so good. As I applied myself to the task I glanced around me, carefully extending my senses. Locating the being that had attracted my attention took only as long as was required to inscribe my name on the register.

"May I ask about your luggage, Mr. Davey?" the clerk said. "Your letter said that it would be aboard *Empire Star*, but that vessel has not yet arrived in port…"

"There was a change of plan. I arrived on *Malabar Princess*, which has only just docked. I may have a trunk aboard *Empire Star*, and would like to have it delivered here when that ship arrives."

The clerk looked a bit confused; I wasn't about to take the time to explain it to him. Still, he was well enough trained to nod and say, "Very good, sir." He took the guest-book in hand, and offered me a small bundle of letters.

I took them in hand along with my room key, thanked the clerk with a rupee coin, and set off across the lobby in search of my prey.

A figure sat in a wide armchair in the shadow of a square pillar. It was noticeably cooler in the vicinity; I tucked the key and the unread letters in my bag and stood a dozen feet away, my right hand held loosely by my side.

"Please, Reverend. Come and make yourself comfortable."

In the indifferent light of the lobby, I at last saw the figure of Dr. Richard Daniel, whose path I had not crossed since my visit to the sanitarium at Trafford.

"Dr. Daniel."

Empire Star had not yet arrived in Calcutta, but Daniel was already here. He clearly had not found the object of the search, or he would not trouble himself to seek me out.

"Welcome to Calcutta, Reverend Davey. I am surprised to see you here so soon. I have been waiting for you."

I could not readily determine if this was indeed Ann Daniel's husband, or some *stoicheia* playing the part. I concluded that I should assume that he was the genuine article unless proved otherwise.

"I didn't realize my itinerary was of any particular interest." I declined to sit in the offered chair, but remained instead at my ease standing behind it, leaving my free hand on the antimacassar.

"Oh, come now." Daniel leaned back in his own chair, pyramiding his fingers in front of him. "You must have realized that I—that we—would take notice of your intention to journey to India."

"There was a change of plans."

"Won't you sit?" He gestured to the chair opposite—with a mesmeric pass!—I gave the chair under my hand the slightest shove to interrupt the flow, making Daniel start in his seat. He glanced quickly to his left, then back at me.

"Have your friend join us," I said. It was a bluff, but it seemed to me that the chill I felt was not from Daniel after all—but it was close by.

"What friend?"

"Please do not trifle with me, Doctor. You have a companion—and, if I may say so, one who is presently giving you extremely poor advice."

"I don't know what you're talking about."

I lifted my hand very slightly, fingers together, the thumb extended rigidly at an almost right angle. Daniel began to say something else, but his breath caught in his throat.

"Introduce the *chthonios* or dismiss him. I don't give a damn which, but I'll not have someone lurking in the background."

Daniel's face began to redden. Again he attempted to speak and failed to make any sound. His face, which had been a mask of smugness and certainty, now betrayed a certain amount of alarm.

"Now, now. You don't want to make your Annie a widow, do you?"

Daniel glanced at me, then suddenly, definitely, at the space behind the pillar. There was a chill breeze—and then it was gone, replaced by the warm, humid air of Calcutta.

I waited ten seconds before letting my hand drop to my side. Daniel heaved a great breath, slumping forward, hands on knees. He did not look up at me for several moments; when he at last chose to favor me thus, he offered an expression of pure malice.

"That was unnecessary," he whispered.

I stepped around to the chair and took my seat, carpet-bag in my lap. "I will be the judge of that. And the jury and executioner, if you so choose. What are you doing here, Daniel? This is no place for amateurs."

"Is that...what you think of me?"

"I judge men by their deeds, or their inability to perform them. So yes, that is what I think of you. I think rather more highly of Miss Braid."

"Mrs. Daniel."

"Yes. Of course. She is a dangerous woman, or would be if she could walk."

"She *can* walk. With difficulty. That is a burden, but it will be overcome under my care. Her recovery is none of your business, I may add."

"And my business in India is none of your concern. *Malabar Princess* will clear out in a few days: I suggest that you be aboard."

Daniel seemed to have recovered his composure; he returned to his previous posture, pyramiding his fingers and smiling.

"I don't think that is in the offing, sir. I do not think that either of us expects me to simply depart because you say so."

"I should not like to have to insist."

"What does that mean?"

"You are not stupid, Doctor Daniel. Neither are you naïve. If you do not cease to be an irritant, I will have to resort to unpleasant means to rid myself of you."

"Even if I could be of assistance."

"Go home, Doctor, and tell your wife and her attendants that I have survived their little scheme, and that I am satisfactorily well educated regarding their nature that I shall be henceforth on my guard. I shall have no trouble—indeed, I shall take some pleasure in the act of eliminating you from the landscape if you interfere in any way with my undertakings. Do I make myself clear?"

"Are you threatening me?"

"You're not listening, are you? Of *course* I'm threatening you." I stood up, wondering if he was simply baiting me, or was truly oblivious to my imputations.

"You should take great care in issuing threats, sir. You have me at a disadvantage at present, but we are far from England, and—"

"And you still must breathe to live. Don't trifle with me, Doctor. I don't issue threats lightly—nor do I like being threatened. Good day." I deliberately turned my back on him and walked away, tensing for an attack of some sort, but none ever came.

CHAPTER 44

Going up the river

19 November, 1860

Davey:

I will not burden you with the tiresome details of my administration of this wretched band, but I must concede that your admonition has turned out to be perfectly true: this singular authority is as unrewarding as it is onerous. I therefore urge you Godspeed on your swift return to England so that you may resume it for yourself.

Regardless of my dislike for the task, I believe that I have acquitted myself appropriately and effectively in the duties laid upon me. I have managed this despite the annoying and sometimes obstructive efforts of your subordinate Mr. Jackson. While he is punctilious in his duty and possesses a remarkable memory, two qualities which would otherwise recommend him, I cannot but suspect that he is constantly working at cross purposes to my own—and therefore to your own interests. This may be for purely selfish reasons—unless, of course, you have given him secret instructions of which I am not aware. He retains his position at my sufferance, and also because it would do me no good to allow such a potentially disruptive force to be excluded from my consultations and thus work outside of them.

I hope to God that 1861 brings more good news than 1860 did: of that I have low expectations but high hopes.

Yours sincerely
T. Carlyle

28 November 1860

My dear Will:

It is not with any particular pleasure that I admit my errors, particularly when I must at the same time concede that you were right. Your choice of Carlyle as your deputy was, however, exactly correct: he has dismissed much which is foolish, responded to threats with firmness, maintained your mandate in preventing any of our committee from troubling Mrs. Esdaile—and, to my surprise, has exchanged friendly correspondence with Dickens. The Great Man has not appeared at any of our meetings, but he did send a modest pecuniary contribution despite his earlier avowed intention to cease doing so. This is no doubt due to the esteem in which he holds the great Carlyle.

As for the man who presently directs our affairs in your absence, his perception of his own worth is of a magnitude that even exceeds your own—an extraordinary thing, I assure you. It may break the bonds of credulity to conceive of it, but I assure you that it is true. Still, even despite the size of that self-image, he has backed up his assertions with his actions. I cover my chagrin with my well-known efficiency; Carlyle occasionally suggests—when he is at his most irascible—that he will dismiss me and replace me with Browning or some other literary victim, but has as yet not done so. I begin to think of this as no more than an acrimonious if somewhat playful threat on his part.

In short, matters are as well in hand as you might possibly have hoped, and I have little of consequence to report. Since you departed in November there has been scant news of our colleague, the new Mrs. Daniel; I presume that she continues to recover from her injuries. Daniel is almost certainly in India by now. If you cross his path, I trust that your low opinion of his abilities will be tempered by the power of that which he may be able to summon to aid him.

I hope that this short letter finds you well. I hope that you are able to find what we seek and that you come home safely. I wish you—well in advance—a very happy Christmas and remain

Your dear friend,
Jon'n W. Jackson

WILLIAM DAVEY

Georgiana and Gobinda joined me at the Auckland's *table d'hôte* that evening. The staff seemed particularly miffed at the idea of serving a native—whether due to his race or because of the recent unpleasantness between whites and natives—but not long after we were seated, a well-dressed manager approached us. He seemed to know Gobinda rather well and offered his polite greetings to Georgiana. But his most effusive apology was to *me*.

"I truly am sorry for any unpleasantness, Reverend," he said in a particularly unctuous manner. "The behavior of my staff toward the honorable Mr. Ahmadi is unacceptable, and I assure you that it will be dealt with."

"That is very kind of you, Mr.—"

"Wilson, sir. David Wilson." He took my hand and pumped it enthusiastically. "The proprietor of this hotel, your servant, sir."

"Wilson *Sahib* is too kind," Gobinda said, his head slightly inclined. I could see a hint of merriment in his eyes, perhaps with amusement at Wilson's discomfiture.

"I shall see that you are personally provided for," Wilson said, and offered another bow, then turned and hurried away. Out of earshot, he undertook a rather warm conversation with one of the head waiters, gesturing toward us.

"Your powers of persuasion are most impressive, Georgiana," I said, sipping a glass of wine.

"This is the most famous hotel in Calcutta, and David Wilson would like it to stay that way. He far prefers this position to his previous form of employment."

"Which was?"

"Confectioner," Gobinda said. He made a minute adjustment to his turban.

"That is a noble profession," I ventured.

Georgiana and Gobinda exchanged some sort of knowing glance. "Well—" Georgiana began, and Gobinda said, "Wilson *Sahib*—"

They both stopped, leaving me somewhat baffled. Gobinda extended his hand and gave a bow of his head.

"Mr. Wilson," Georgiana said, "is in the enviable position of being master of the most celebrated hotel in English Calcutta. He relies on the custom of patrons who come from all over the Empire—but he also benefits from having them in his lobby, at his dining-table, at his card-tables and in his salon. They speak of all manner of things, and he *listens*."

"And that information makes its way across the street," Gobinda added, gesturing toward the louvered windows that fronted on Courthouse Street.

"You mean he's a—"

"Loyal subject," Georgiana cut across my sentence, which I had intended to complete with the word 'spy'—but that was somewhat inaccurate, since he would more properly be termed an 'informant'. It made sense—but it also suggested a problem with our own privacy, even at a remote table in the dining-room.

"This is as secure a place as any," Gobinda said, as if perceiving the direction of my thoughts. "I have employed turn-aside gestures to keep intrusions away, and Lord Shiva casts confusion in their ears."

This time it was Georgiana who offered a secret smile. I did not quite know what technique Gobinda was using to 'cast confusion'…it was no doubt some skill taught in the Shivan mesmeric school.

"I still entertain some doubt regarding a conversation in this venue." When Gobinda began to protest, I added, "There is an… informant of another sort who is here. He was waiting for me when I arrived. He has nightfall creatures at his command—or at least on call. I do not know what Lord Shiva can do about that."

"You disbelieve in His power?"

"Mr. Ahmadi—"

"Gobinda is sufficient, Davey Sahib."

"Gobinda. I am on my guard against all manner of powers, and am skeptical of all types of claims. I have seen what—what a disciple

341

of your school can do." I looked over at Georgiana, who offered a smile in return. "But we are all in *terra incognita*, and with the stakes as high as they are, I prefer to take no chances."

"This caution belies the confidence I am told you possess in abundance. You seem to have had no lack of it on the docks this morning. I understood you to be bold and decisive."

"I am those things. But I tire of this banter, Gobinda. You know why I am here in Calcutta, I trust, and what I seek."

"Yes. Of course. Georgiana Memsahib—" he smiled. "Old habits die exceedingly hard. You seek the object. Georgiana and I have both had opportunity to be close to it, and would know it right away if we saw it."

"Or sensed it," Georgiana said.

"Indeed," Gobinda agreed. "If it is here in Calcutta, we would certainly know by now. I assume, therefore, that if it is anywhere nearby it is in Hooghly, where the Doctor Sahib practiced. Where he took his wife." The phrase had multiple meanings; we all knew that.

"Then we should go there. I am concerned, however, that this other informant may follow us."

"Then he must be dealt with."

Gobinda said the words dispassionately, as if *dealing with* Richard Daniel was something akin to swatting a fly.

"I hesitate to commit outright murder," I answered at last. "Regardless of the man's lack of innocence, I do not think that is appropriate."

"This is some species of gentlemanly courtesy. Or perhaps an example of Christian charity, I suppose. A few minutes ago you alluded to the stakes—does that not require any means to achieve the desired result?"

"No. Not anymore. Two years ago I would have agreed whole-heartedly—but not now. It has cost too many people too much. I will not stoop to *any* means: if I had employed that policy then…"

"This is where we are now, Davey Sahib, and your temporizing and regret do not change the situation. If it is your wish to absent yourself from this decision, I shall attend to it myself."

Gobinda's expression never changed: he retained his polite smile, his inclined head, his demeanor of indifference to the situation.

"You will do as you must," I said. "But it may not be that simple."

Gobinda did not answer, simply retaining his serene expression.

"Hooghly is a few hours up the river," Georgiana said at last into the silence. "And we can travel by train. Is there a reason to wait? We could leave tomorrow."

I spread my hands wide. I could offer no useful opinion on the subject.

"Some time would be required," Gobinda said. "A few days, at most, should be sufficient."

Georgiana seemed dubious about delay, but said nothing.

"And what are we looking for in Hooghly?" I asked.

"Answers."

The experience of being in a land as unusual—as *alien*—as India is difficult to describe. I was nearly fifty-three years old when I made this journey and had never previously been further from home than Paris or Edinburgh. Calcutta was almost halfway around the world, still raw from the wounds of the Mutiny, not yet transformed into the jewel in Her Majesty's crown. In Calcutta, I felt presences all around me: they were like little scraps of paper blowing in the air, ephemeral and invisible to anyone lacking the perception that skill in the Art provided.

Such beings come when called. I knew that when I was in Manchester and had my first direct encounter with the Levantine—I should have realized why he had been summoned, presumably to deal with Dr. Braid.

That was yet another casualty of my arrogance.

And even more than in Bombay, even more than in England, they were…*everywhere*.

It is very simple, Gobinda told me. *They are here at the behest of the being in the statue. They are here to help open the Glass Door.*

It would have been easy to despair in the face of the problem. Two years earlier, things had looked much different—my enemies would have accused me of dissembling, but I was extremely conflicted during that period in Calcutta; on the other side of the world my countrymen were preparing for the Christmas feast, while I was quixotically pursuing an item of unknown power in a mysterious land with allies who kept more secrets than I did.

Despair was not the answer. But kind-hearted trust was not the answer either. I refused to submit to the former or be gulled by the latter.

Eliza Weatherhead's Calcutta, which she had revealed to me during our interviews in early 1859, had no railroads in it. The roads there at the end of 1860 were the work of the Scotsman Turnbull, who had undertaken a number of large railway projects at the behest of Lord Dalhousie, the Governor-General, in the intervening decade. Still, compared to the evolved state of the railways in Great Britain, the 'fire-carriages' in the Bengal were archaic relics—uncomfortable and slow, using locomotives of a sort that had, on the home island, long since been replaced by more powerful ones. Steam hissed alarmingly and soot blew through the windows that, due to the heat, had to be left open.

Georgiana and I secured first-class seats through the judicious application of bribes and stout English determination—unwillingness to take 'no' for an answer. As for Gobinda, he remained in Calcutta, declaring his intention to locate and isolate Dr. Daniel. I am not sure that he simply disliked, or even feared, the railways—Georgiana did not say, and I did not ask.

The entire journey was thirty miles, though it took almost three hours to complete—in part due to some manner of mechanical failure near a place called Barrackpur. While the train was stopped, it grew uncomfortably hot within the carriage, but Georgiana expressed herself unwilling to disembark.

"Barrackpur is where the Mutiny began," she said quietly. "There is an aura here."

I wanted to ask more, but she seemed unwilling to offer further information. Instead, I looked through the window and extended my senses. It took only a few moments to feel that to which she had alluded: there were a number of presences here. They were not as strong as the ones in Calcutta but less inchoate, as if they were ready and able to take form.

Idlers. Idlers in search of someone to help—and to serve their own ends.

"What are they waiting for?" I asked Georgiana.

"The Raj government believes that the flames of dissent have all been stamped out," she said. "All that is necessary is to build academies and railroads and put all of the *coolies* to work, and soon India will be saved for civilization.

"But as long as *it* is here"—we both knew very well what she meant by *it*—"it will encourage more violence. Soldiers of the Prophet, servants of one or another petty king or *zamindar* or what have you…there are many natives, William, and altogether too few soldiers. What happened before can happen again. They are waiting…to be employed."

After the train at last got underway, we rode in silence. We finally came to Hooghly early in the afternoon. Georgiana observed that the prison was larger than she had remembered it, and the hospital meaner and not as well kept up; presumably those employed there after James Esdaile's departure were less devoted to its maintenance.

We made our way from the small train-station, Georgiana in the lead, walking toward the jail complex—she seemed to know where she was going. I assumed, correctly, that she was seeking something in particular; when we reached the outskirts of the prison she stopped, looking both annoyed and baffled.

"What is wrong?"

"They have erected walls," she said, gesturing toward the stout brick palisade that separated the building from the town.

"It *is* a prison. I am hardly surprised."

"The building itself was once sufficient. The person I seek—I expected to see her near there, serving food to those who work in the hospital."

"You look for Kajari Kaurá," a voice said behind us. We turned to face an older boy, perhaps no more than ten or eleven, but with deep eyes and a wary expression.

"Yes, that's right," Georgiana said. "I am looking for Kajari. Do you know where I can find her?"

"Of course, Memsahib," the boy said. "She is my great-aunt. She has a tea shop now."

"Can you take us there?"

"Of course, Memsahib."

The boy loped away, beckoning us to follow. He led us away from the prison complex, onto a narrow street with little shops of various kinds. His aunt's tea shop was a small one, with two steps leading up from the street. Even from outside, we could smell the pleasant aroma of spices and baking bread.

"*Tayi* Kajari," the boy said, running into the shop, "there is a *sahib* and a *memsahib* who are looking for you—"

A woman came out from the kitchen. She was not elderly, but clearly well into middle age; plain, but obviously strong—and her face was full of character, her eyes deep and piercing. She did not smile, but extended a hand with a gesture almost like a mesmeric one, silencing the boy in mid-sentence.

"Good, Janu," she said, without looking at him. "I believe you have an errand to do for me, yes?"

"Yes, *tayi*," he said. "But what—"

"None of your concern, little *bhanja*. Now run quickly and do as you were told."

Apparently there were not many *memsahib*s and *sahib*s who

came looking for the woman, causing the boy to hesitate for just a moment—but out of a sense of duty, or more likely fear of the consequences of delay or defiance, he dashed off, leaving us standing in the empty tea-shop.

"You have returned, Georgiana *Memsahib*," she said, hands on her hips. "I thought you said you would never come back."

CHAPTER 45

Reunions

WILLIAM DAVEY

Then, with no preamble, the two women embraced. Georgiana, as stalwart and firm as any woman I had ever met, even betrayed a tear or two as they reunited.

I remembered the Bengali woman from Eliza's account. She had been a gatherer of information: someone to whom everyone talked; she and Georgiana had been close. As I was not presumed to know all of this, I assumed the proper air of bafflement as the two women hugged each other in front of me.

At last Kajari pulled away, wiping her hands on the apron she wore over her long dress.

"I am so glad to see you, Georgiana Memsahib," she said. "I have missed you."

"And I have missed you, my dear friend," Georgiana said. "More than almost anything in Hooghly. There have been some difficult times between then and now. My husband—"

"Yes, I know. Now we are both widows," Kajari said, looking away. "The wheel of *dharma* has taken them away from us—but we do not choose *sati*."

"Certainly not. Not in any way. I am so sorry to hear about Mádhab—he was a good man."

"He left me two sons—and I have Janu as well, my sister's grandson. She, too, has no husband, and her son was in Delhi during the...events."

During this exchange I remained silent, without context as to the details of the events being described—except the realization that these two women's lives had been caught up and twisted by the Sepoy Rebellion, the event that had redrawn the map of India.

"You have done well," Georgiana said, looking around the shop. It was a small place, but neat and clean, its walls crowded with knick-knacks and little pictures from Indian legend.

"We were very careful with our savings," Kajari said. "When the government stopped permitting us on the hospital grounds, we made other arrangements. Hooghly is not what you remember, *Memsahib* Georgiana."

"No," Georgiana answered, glancing at me. "It is not. Tell me," she added as casually as you please, "is Doctor Noboo still working at the hospital?"

Kajari's brows furrowed, as if the question made her suspicious, but quickly covered it with a gentle smile. "No, he was dismissed— or resigned his position, I don't recall which—during the troubles. I believe he practices medicine in the country now."

"In the country?"

Kajari's face became stony. "The soldiers that fought the sepoys took pleasure in leaving destruction in their wake. They had heard stories of what was done to whites. Some of the stories were even true—but as a result, anyone with brown skin, and anything built or kept or raised by people with brown skin, was fair game for them.

"Doctor Noboo decided that his duty was to be a *doctor*, *Memsahib*. To find those who needed him and to care for them, whether they had an anna to their name or not. Most did not."

"Do you know where he lives?"

"Why do you want to know, *Memsahib* Georgiana?"

It seemed to me that Georgiana had not expected to be asked that precise question. It was clear that she had an old and established friendship with Kajari—the Bengali woman was clearly happy to see her, and they were clearly kindred spirits: but I suspect that my ally thought that her questions would be readily answered, either from courtesy or simple deference.

It was sufficiently surprising that Georgiana did not have any ready reply.

"I wish to speak with Doctor Noboo on an extremely important matter," I said, the first words I had offered to the conversation.

"Georgiana *Memsahib*," Kajari said quietly, "you have not presented me to your companion."

"Why, you are exactly correct," she said. "Kajari Kaurá, allow me to present Reverend William Davey."

"Davey," Kajari said, her eyes narrowing.

"A pleasure," I said, offering a small bow.

"You were a friend of the Doctor Sahib," she said. "A fellow doctor, perhaps. Someone from whom he received letters."

"That is true." *Fellow doctor* was as benign a category as I could have expected.

"He has come all the way from England to speak with Doctor Noboo," Georgiana offered.

Kajari did not answer at once, but seemed to examine me closely, as if considering what cut of meat I might be. Then she said, "I must look at the oven. Please excuse me for a moment," and turned away and walked into the kitchen.

Georgiana, usually the picture of decorum and composure, seemed a trifle discomfited by the exchange. She looked at me, a little surprised at how the interview had proceeded.

"She knows who I am," I said quietly. "She was a gatherer of information, wasn't she?"

"Yes, of course, but—" She looked at me sideways. "Have we discussed Kajari? I didn't realize that you knew about her."

I did not answer; my knowledge of Kajari had not come from her, but from Eliza, and I had just inadvertently revealed that fact.

"She knows who I am," I repeated.

"There is no way to be sure of that. And even if true, I am not certain whether that affects her disposition toward us. Toward me."

"You flatter yourself, Georgiana," I said. "We may have to find this Noboo ourselves. We—"

Kajari chose that moment to emerge from the kitchen, wiping her hands on her apron once again. I do not know for certain whether she had heard the entire exchange: to be honest, I would have been surprised if she had not.

"The country is not like the cities, Memsahib," she said to

Georgiana. She did not look at me at all. "There are no soldiers or government bureaucrats there—only natives. You might find that you would not be welcomed."

"The matter is urgent," Georgiana said. "Doctor Noboo has information that is very important."

"What sort of information?"

"Something important enough to bring me all the way to India," I said. "Mrs. Kaurá," I said, catching her eye and spreading my hands apart, "I was a friend of Doctor Esdaile—the Doctor Sahib, I believe you called him. He left some things with Doctor Noboo, things that were very important and that I am here to recover."

Kajari did not respond at once, but she was—to my surprise—remarkably receptive to the simplest of mesmeric passes. I saw the slightest tinge of anger color Georgiana's cheek: she had clearly not expected me to resort to the Art. I, on the other hand, was not disposed to let the situation spiral out of control merely to satisfy Georgiana's excessive inclination to propriety.

"Doctor Noboo was a good friend to the Doctor Sahib," Kajari said. "He did not want him to return to England."

"Doctor Esdaile spoke well of him. He even mentioned him in his book describing his time here in Hooghly."

"The Doctor Sahib respected the abilities of native doctors," Kajari said. "The Doctor Sahib was not a well man—he often complained of being tired. I told him he needed to eat more, but he did not listen to me. Perhaps his new wife takes better care of him."

"Doctor Esdaile died two years ago," I said. "I am sorry to bring you this sad news, Mrs. Kaurá."

"Died."

"Yes," I said. "He was not, as you say, a well man. His wife took care of him for eight years. I was…with him when he died." That statement was true, of course: but I did not intend to explain why I was with James Esdaile that particular morning.

"If you are here to tell Doctor Noboo of the Doctor Sahib's death, *Sahib*," she said to me, "you could have just sent a letter."

"Into the country?"

"Word would have reached him. But there is something you want from him."

"There is," I said agreeably. Kajari Kaurá was focusing directly on me now; I could tell, without looking away, that Georgiana was watching this exchange with annoyance, at the very least. "I would not trouble you—or trouble him—but it is a matter of great importance. I am certain that you can help me."

I offered her my best absent-minded-English-scholar smile, and added a subtle gesture that was sufficient to make her take a step forward. At any moment I expected Georgiana to interrupt my work, but she did not.

"Doctor Noboo is in Awadh somewhere," Kajari said. "I cannot say exactly where, but I have a cousin in Cawnpore who might help. But it is not a safe place for whites: General Havelock *Sahib* made many enemies as he searched for mutineers."

"I am no soldier," I said.

"You are a Christian priest," Kajari said. "The people in the country believed—some of them still believe—that the English were here to take away their gods and turn them all into Christians. What do you think they will believe when they see you?"

"I will conceal my profession," I said. "I am not here to change anyone's faith."

"Including mine, or Doctor Noboo's."

"No," I agreed. "No one, including you and Doctor Noboo. That is not why I am here."

We left Hooghly with a letter for Kajari's cousin and more warnings about the danger of traveling away from the cities.

As we stood on the railway platform, Georgiana—who had remained silent as we concluded our visit to Kajari Kaurá—rounded on me furiously.

"You subjected her to mesmeric persuasion, William. She will not even know what information she provided you."

"She was prepared to dismiss us entirely."

"She is under no obligation to *assist* us. And as for your 'friendship' with Doctor Esdaile—none of this would have happened if it had not been that he feared for his life, from *you* and your Committee."

"All of this would not have *happened*, Georgiana, if it had not been for the being in the statue we are going to find. This long ago stopped being about a particular disagreement between Esdaile and myself, or between Esdaile and the Committee. The *soi-disant* scholar James Fergusson handed Esdaile an object containing a being more powerful than the ones we met out on the Indian Ocean."

"You *mesmerized* Kajari—"

"Yes. And I will *mesmerize* Noboo as well, madam, if that is what is required to procure the statue."

"He is a practitioner of the Art."

"He will not be more skilled than I am—of that I am confident."

"I am surprised you have not attempted such with me," she said. "I presume that you do not consider me your equal—and it is clear to me that you have not taken me completely into your confidence."

"Nor have you done the same for me." I turned away from her and walked down the platform, then returned. "Georgiana, I will thank you to refrain from troubling me with your trifling scruples regarding assistance, however obtained. I know that it is customary to refrain from manipulating those unskilled in the Art without their consent: but the stakes are too high. My need is too great.

"Your friend was ready to turn us out. She knew that I was someone who knew Esdaile; she no doubt remembers that he left quickly, in the company of a wife he had *just met*. She may know about the statue, or what is within it. I do not know all she knows."

"But you clearly know about *her*."

"Eliza told me." I did not intend to elaborate. "If you have any information that I need, I may have to practice the Art upon you as well."

"You would not *dare*."

"Do not mistake what I might and might not dare, Georgiana. This is not a parlor game. Even if it played only a minor role, the being within the statue contributed to the great rebellion here in India. Esdaile believed it; Eliza believes it. So do I.

"Do not get in my way."

"Is that a threat, sir?"

"I do not trouble myself with idle threats."

We stared at each other for quite some time; the lady clearly was unsure what I might do next. I rather preferred that.

"You are a rather different man than I originally thought, William. I shall not be mistaken again."

To that I had no answer. At last, after some considerable silence, we heard the whistle and huff of a locomotive approaching, to take us away from Hooghly.

CHAPTER 46

Pro patria conamur

WILLIAM DAVEY

In order to prepare for travel into the country, we returned to Calcutta, where the English community was preparing for the Christmas holiday. The two cultures were decidedly distinct—more so since the Mutiny.

I must honestly confess that, while I had no doubt of our objective and was more than willing to undertake such a journey, I was not sanguine about our ability to do what was called for—to ride into the countryside, looking for a man I had never met, in a place that was said to be still hostile to Her Majesty's subjects. Even Georgiana's confidence was insufficient to overcome my fundamental concern—but I knew that I had not come all this way, and taken all this time, to stop short.

To our surprise, a solution appeared without any effort on our part to produce it.

A bellman knocked at my hotel-room door a few mornings after Christmas to tell me that a gentleman awaited me in the breakfast-room. There had been no word from Gobinda, and Richard Daniel had not made any further appearances at Auckland's Hotel or elsewhere in our path. I was not sure whether that was due to his improved skill at concealment, or that he had accepted my threat in earnest.

Upon inquiry, I was told that the person asking for my presence did not provide a visiting-card, which in England might be enough to refuse such an interview—but that was England, this was India and my curiosity overcame my caution.

As I entered the breakfast room a young military officer stood to greet me. He was not particularly tall or imposing, but like Major Dunn in Egypt he conveyed a sort of martial fervency that would have picked him out as a soldier even had he not been in a lancer's uniform. Still, he had an air of burdened exhaustion, as if he had spent too much time in the sun and wind.

Then, to my surprise, I discerned the very slightest mesmeric gesture as the young man offered me his hand.

I turned it easily aside, though not roughly—it appeared as if he might have even made it out of habit or custom rather than in any vain attempt to coerce me. I accepted the handshake and gestured toward an empty table.

"I shall order us tea, sir," I said. "To whom have I the honor of speaking?"

"My name is Wood, sir. Lieutenant Evelyn Wood, of the Seventeenth Lancers."

"I hope that I have committed no crimes that require the attention of Her Majesty's Forces."

We took our seats, and a servant placed a teapot between us. I poured a cup of fragrant Assam for Lieutenant Wood and then one for myself.

"I trust that is not the case, Reverend Davey. But I am not presently on duty. I shall leave such dispositions to other authorities. My purpose is not to interfere with your intentions, but rather to aid in them."

"I was unaware that my intentions were generally known. And," I added, lowering my voice, "I am not desirous of demonstrating my skill at your expense, so please refrain from such provocation."

The lieutenant appeared slightly abashed at my comment; he did not dissemble, but took a brief sip from his teacup and nodded.

"I was told that it would be a way to command your attention, Reverend."

"It has done so. I should like to know who told you so."

"A fellow soldier. Major Alexander Dunn—I understand you

recently made his acquaintance. He indicated that I might be of assistance to you."

"Are you acting at his direction?"

"Rather his *recommendation*. More proximately I am at your service due to the estimable Gobinda Shah Ahmadi, who conveyed information regarding your intended journey."

"If he trained you in the Art, he is remiss."

"He was not my primary teacher, but I will confess that it is not my strongest skill, sir." I raised my eyebrow at this; he continued. "I hope that I shall not need to employ it."

"I have great respect and admiration for Major Dunn," I said. "Did he have anything else to say?"

"He asked me to convey a message to you—that a mutual acquaintance, a Mr. Nour, has…lost one of his children."

"He said just that."

"Yes."

I realized at once what that might mean, and attempted to reconcile that piece of information with everything else. I found myself unable to do so effectively.

"Please continue, Lieutenant."

"It is my understanding that you intend to travel to the Awadh, and I would offer my services as guide and translator. My recent experience here in India makes me qualified in that capacity."

"Do you not have military duties that preclude such an expedition?"

"I have recently been called before a medical board here in Calcutta, sir. I am to be invalided home and am thus on leave from my brigade." He did not appear to be particularly happy to communicate this to me.

"I should not want to exacerbate your condition."

"The medical leave is not my choice, Reverend Davey. I would prefer to remain on duty, but the decision is not mine. A short ride in the country will make me no more ill."

"I cannot be the judge of that, Lieutenant. And I do not ask for your help."

"I am told that you are planning a trip into the country."

"Yes."

"And your command of the *Hindoostani* language is—"

"Nonexistent."

"Your marksmanship, Reverend?"

"I do not generally travel armed, Lieutenant."

"And your knowledge of the native culture, your contacts with persons in authority, your train of servants and guards—"

"Minimal, absent and of course lacking. Your point is made, Lieutenant Wood, but I am not planning a punitive expedition against a *nawab*: I am looking for one particular man, who has made no attempt to conceal himself or cover his tracks."

"You will now impute that this effort should not be that difficult."

"And?"

"And this is *India*, Reverend Davey. There is little in India that is simple or straightforward. Even dismissing the possibility of violence—a generous assumption, given the level of distrust of Englishmen in the Awadh—it presumes that you might find anyone there who would be disposed to assist you."

"And a cavalryman would be of inestimable assistance—"

"I arrived in India more than two years ago, and had the honor to serve under the late Sir William Peel, among others. I have been all through that country. I speak the language; I am an excellent shot. In short, you need my help if you wish to accomplish your task."

"Sir William Peel, you say." His father, Sir Robert, had been Prime Minister not too many years before.

"Yes."

"Your first teacher in the Art."

He paused for a moment before answering. "Yes," he said at last. "He was kind enough to share some of the techniques he learned from his father. It was from Captain Peel that I first heard of you, sir, in your...supernumerary capacity."

Sir Robert Peel, like his protégé William Gladstone and a

number of his other influential followers, had been a skilled mesmerist. They were all beyond the scope of my power, and beyond Edward Quillinan before me; Peel and I had never met and only distantly corresponded, but he was the sort of man who could have taken control of the Committee if he had so desired. Instead, he had always shown a circumspect deference to the Committee—and to Quillinan and, later, myself. In our circle he had his detractors, and I had always wondered if his death—thrown from a horse on Constitution Hill and crushed underfoot—might have been caused by one of our number.

"He was a great man," I said. "A credit to his nation and his Queen."

It was logical that he would teach the Art to his son, and that some of that knowledge would filter down. It appeared that Wood had respect for the discipline, though obviously not a great amount of innate talent.

"I shall have to consult with my colleagues."

"Colleagues?"

"I am not traveling alone. I do not know how my erstwhile ally will feel about the inclusion of a stranger. She—"

"'She'?" Wood picked up his teacup, then thought better of sipping from it and carefully set it down. "This is no work for a *woman*, Reverend. Particularly an Englishwoman."

"I wish you luck telling her so, Lieutenant. If you have served Her Majesty here in India, you clearly have some measure of bravery; it will require all of that and more to suggest to Mrs. Shackleford that she should not go."

Georgiana was not amused.

Indeed, she was quite annoyed at Gobinda, to whom she had formerly showed considerable deference. He had been her rescuer, her mentor and her teacher; he reminded me of the Trimurti, the three-headed Shiva we had seen in Bombay, looking in each direction and fulfilling each role in her practice of the Art. But she clearly did not wish to have him burden us with a young cavalry officer, confident in his own ability, leaping forward and doing his duty to protect us against any hostile natives who might come between us and Noboo. Hindustani speaker, crack shot and trusty guide he might be, but she had no particular reason to trust his motives.

Wood's regimental motto—*pro Rege, pro Lege, pro Patria conamur*—*we fight for Monarch, Law and Country*—was insufficient to convince me either. But neither of us could respond to the primary argument in favor of including him: we were far less likely to find Doctor Noboo, and therefore the statue that had drawn both of us to India, if we did not include Lieutenant Evelyn Wood.

Preparation, including the acquisition of suitable horses, took two more days. Georgiana realized that this was necessary, but chafed at Wood's tendency to take charge as if he were the commanding officer. Nonetheless, it was clear that he was more capable than any of us in accomplishing this task. When at last we departed Calcutta, we believed that we were ready for whatever we might encounter.

It goes without saying that we were completely incorrect.

It took almost a week to find Noboo. He had not taken up residence in a single place, but moved from place to place in the Ganges Valley attending to those who had no other doctor. We had just missed him in one village: he was expected two days hence in another.

The New Year was four days old when we rode into a small, dusty hamlet of two dozen houses on a high hill overlooking the Ganges. As we approached, we passed a crowded graveyard. From what we could see, there were more markers than the likely number of living residents. Lieutenant Wood was not in uniform, though as I had observed from the outset, his martial carriage could hardly be disguised; he drew the attention of villagers as we arrived.

A medium-sized covered cart drawn by two dray-horses was parked near the largest house, with a servant squatting on the ground nearby in their shade. The sun was an enemy, but apparently the flies were not; the horses' tails and a broad fan kept them at a distance. We dismounted nearby and walked up to the house.

As I went to knock on the shutter, someone from within opened the door and addressed me in a native language. Wood responded; the man—a servant, I supposed—immediately diverted his attention to Wood and spoke quickly and somewhat angrily.

"You will oblige me by translating," I said, without turning around or changing the tone of my voice or the polite smile on my face.

"He does not wish to speak with me," Wood answered. "Only with you."

"Very well, I—"

"And he knows your name," Wood added.

I did not respond. The servant opened the door and admitted me, reluctantly permitting Georgiana and Lieutenant Wood to follow. We were led through a dimly lit house smelling of spices and into a sitting-room, where an elderly Indian man reclined on a wicker armchair. He was draped in a light blanket, with the lower right corner turned back; where his right leg would have been there was a stump that had clearly taken on some sort of infection. Another man sat next to him on a low stool, applying some sort of unguent to the wound, who did not turn as we entered, but continued with his task. When he was done, he wiped his hands on a cloth and began to carefully wrap the member in a bandage.

During this procedure, the patient looked pointedly at the three of us, giving particular attention to Lieutenant Wood. I did not speak, and exchanged only a single glance with Georgiana; Wood affected an air of complete indifference, as if he were often invited into an Indian man's sickroom and caused to wait.

Finally, the doctor completed his task, wiped his hands again and stood, turning to us.

"I am Doctor Noboo," he said in excellent English. "I have been expecting you for some time, Reverend Davey *Sahib*."

CHAPTER 47
Do no harm

WILLIAM DAVEY

"We should not disturb the gentleman," I said, gesturing to the patient.

"Of course not," Noboo said. "But the *sahibs* really never paid attention to such things before." He looked pointedly at Wood, who met him with a level gaze. "But you have come far to find me, Davey *Sahib*. I must show you Bengali courtesy. You—and your companions, including Shackleford *Memsahib*," he said, nodding to her as if her presence were no surprise.

He beckoned us out of the sickroom and along the corridor to a verandah, where we sat in chairs.

"I have heard about your inquiries for me," he said. "I am no more than a doctor now: I seek to take care of the people in this valley, who have so few."

"That is very noble," I said.

"I was told at Hooghly that my services were no longer needed," he answered. "A foolish choice. Your people claim to have come to India to help us—you even set up universities to teach us! They graduate artists, poets...who can paint and draw and write like Europeans. One in fifteen, one in twenty is an engineer or a doctor.

"And then the bureaucrats of the Viceroy call us a stupid and backward people. As if they were not wearing bear-skins and fighting wars with clubs when Lord Shiva and Lord Rama walked the earth."

He sounded angry, despondent—but resigned to the categories into which British overlords had placed the native peoples.

"I am not here to debate the fine points of Imperial politics with you, Doctor," I answered. "Even if I could effect change—and I cannot—it is not my place to do so."

"Then what does bring you here?"

"I suspect you know that as well."

Noboo looked at me, then at Lieutenant Wood again.

"Lieutenant," I said, "I wonder if you might excuse us for a few minutes." I made a strong dismissing gesture and stood up, as if to show respect for his station, but in reality to strengthen the mesmeric command. Though Wood claimed to have been trained by the son of one of the most capable mesmerists of the previous generation, he complied at once, muttering something about a smoke, and walked off the verandah, offering a polite bow to Noboo.

"Does he—" Georgiana began.

"He might realize later," I interrupted, resuming my seat. "But in the meanwhile, we can speak privately."

"I suspect that I know what you desire," Noboo said. "You must be prepared for disappointment."

"Be as glib as you like, Doctor. I am adamant, and will brook neither obstruction nor delay."

"I think…an explanation is therefore in order."

MAHENDRA NOBOO

Twenty years ago, Reverend Davey *Sahib*, India was a very different place. There was no viceroy; there were really *two* Indias— one part was a land of petty states and princedoms, the other the islands of British settlement, bastions of your Western culture. In my India, the native land, where the *rajah*s and kings and other noblemen feared for their independence, if there was no heir to a prince's realm the Governor-General *Sahib* would declare the title lapsed and assume the government. Satara, the Punjab, Jhansi, Nagpur—all of them fell to the Company by the Doctrine of Lapse. Of all the things that enraged the sepoys when they rose in rebellion, that might have been the greatest.

The other part, the British part, was full of reformers—forgive me, Mrs. Shackleford *Memsahib*: you had beneficent and noble aims, but what you wanted, what all of you wanted, was for us to become *you*; except not quite as *good* as you. Calcutta is not London, Bombay is not Manchester, and never will be. India is India.

At university, I took a prize in Latin; I studied the history of Europe. I even learned to laugh at jokes about the *babu*s who try so hard to be English. When I took my medical degree, I realized that my best chance to do good—or at least to do no harm—was to find a place in *your* India. Thus I found myself at Hooghly, working with the excellent Doctor Sahib, James Esdaile.

He was already there when I arrived—he had come a few years earlier. His second wife had just died and he was therefore completely focused on his work with the patients at the jail hospital. There was a particular affliction called a hydrocele: a sort of large tumor—ah. You know of it, Reverend. Then I will not describe it further. Removing these hydroceles was exceptionally painful: we had no ether, nor indeed much in the way of medicines at all other than native remedies—and the chemists at the hospital dismissed most of those, since they had only been in use for a few thousand years…but in a *primitive* country, of course.

On a particular day in April of 1845—one I will likely never forget—the Doctor Sahib was facing a difficult problem. Mádhab Kaurá: you will remember him, *Memsahib* Shackleford, and his wife Kajari. Mádhab had been admitted with a double hydrocele in a most painful place. The Doctor Sahib told me that he was going to try a different procedure.

That is correct, Reverend Davey *Sahib*. He attempted to induce a mesmeric trance on the patient. It was difficult; he had only a few descriptions of the process, and did not think he had done it correctly. I stood by, with no role in the procedure, and after some time he looked up at me and said, "I am making no progress, Noboo. I am afraid it is a failure."

"But, Doctor Sahib," I answered, "look. The man is much more quiet and does not grimace quite so much."

And indeed it was true: Kaurá had become tranquil and still, his eyes fluttering.

"Are you still in pain, Mádhab?" the Doctor Sahib asked him, and when he said that he was, he was instructed to open his eyes and tell us what he could see. "Something like smoke," he said. He could see nothing, and he felt cold and sleepy. Then he fell into an even deeper sleep, one from which the Doctor Sahib could not awaken him—even by touching the afflicted area, or pricking him with a pin.

The doctor had never done this before, in my memory. He was surprised: more than that, he was shocked. Mádhab had not only become insensible, he had arched backward until the nape of his neck rested on the back of the chair and his breeches rested on the front edge, his arms crossed over his chest.

I asked, "What is happening?" and the Doctor Sahib said that he did not know—he called it a state of *opisthotonos*—extreme rigidity. He was not sure what it meant, or what he had done.

"You will remain here with the patient," he said. "I am going over to the Kutcherry to fetch Mr. Russell and Mr. Money to witness this singular event."

He left me alone there to watch Mádhab Kaurá. Except I was not quite alone—a powerful presence was nearby. I thought it might be Lord Shiva, or perhaps even Lord Ganesh. I was no mesmerist at the time, but it was clear that *something* was there. Only somewhat later I learned that the *something* was in the statue, which was always present when the Doctor Sahib performed his mesmeric work.

The Doctor Sahib tired easily: he was never well, always complaining about one or another affliction, though he was in far better spirits than he had been since before the death of his wife. Some of the mesmeric work became my responsibility, and he taught me what he had learned.

No, Davey *Sahib*, he did not fear the process—not at first. I did not know where he had learned the technique of mesmerizing: I assumed that it was from some medical journal. It seemed almost foreign to European medical practice; I learned later that it was much discussed in *alternative* circles, but that most doctors dismissed it as trickery or worse. But it was not trickery: it worked, reliably and repeatably. We had hundreds of cases in which we used the treatment.

I acknowledge your impatience, Davey *Sahib*. But you have asked me to tell you what I know, and I wish for you to understand the situation as completely as possible.

I served with the Doctor Sahib until the spring of 1851. Some time in the summer of 1849 he began to curtail his use of the treatment, claiming fatigue and difficulty concentrating. The statue was no longer in evidence in his surgery.

He favored me on one occasion with an invitation to his house, and I noted that he had placed the statue in his study, on the mantelpiece. I remarked upon it and he indicated that he felt that it no longer belonged at the hospital—just that, those words.

It was during a lull in the conversation that I thought I heard it speak to me. It was a woman's voice, very pleasant, I thought.

It did not know me by name—it asked me: *Mahendra*, I said in my mind, and it replied, "*Very good—'most courageous': a good name for you,*" for that is the meaning of my name in Bengali.

It then asked me how it could help me, how it might assist in the mesmeric treatments. It was with this sudden realization that I knew that the Doctor Sahib's success with mesmerism had been due to the statue's assistance. I told the voice that I would consider how it might be able to help. I pleaded indigestion and took my leave of the Doctor Sahib, but the experience left me much shaken. Whenever I visited his house, I would hear its voice again, but there was something about it that troubled me.

When the Doctor Sahib left India in 1851, after marrying Weatherhead Memsahib, he left the object in my custody. "Do not give this to anyone, Noboo," he told me. "Keep it safe for me."

I promised that I would. And I promised myself that whatever I heard it say, whatever it offered, I should not listen. After a time, I heard nothing. My suspicion is that the being within found the

Doctor Sahib unsuitable, and then found *me* unsuitable, and would have been happy to contact some other person whom it could assist.

The Rebellion caused me to lose my position at Hooghly, despite the protestations of a number of colleagues, English and Indian, as to my skill and my loyalty. In the summer of 1858 I went to live with my brother's family in Allahabad; I took my possessions with me, including the statue, concealed in the bottom of a box of medical books. Not long after, I received a letter from the Doctor Sahib, sent to Hooghly and forwarded to me by an English friend who still worked there.

I have retained the letter, Davey *Sahib*, for I knew that some day you—or someone from Britain, since the Doctor Sahib told me he had many enemies there—would come looking for me.

WILLIAM DAVEY

Noboo, with us following close behind, quit the house and went to his cart. He climbed up inside and returned presently with a wooden letter-box. He took a small key from his watch-chain and unlocked it, then reached within and withdrew a letter that bore familiar handwriting.

Sydenham
22 August 1858

My dear friend:

The news of the terrible events in India has greatly troubled me, for I am certain that the particular burden I left in your charge has contributed to them. I am certain that it is due to no fault in your conduct, but rather to the insidious nature of the item itself.

I should have realized from the outset that I was dealing with something far beyond normal ken, and that its goals were always malign. But I have obtained a solution to the problem that will remove the item from India, while not placing it in the hands of irresponsible men who would bring about even worse evil than we have heretofore witnessed.

Please pack the item carefully and arrange for it to be shipped to the address I have hereunder enclosed. Do not speak of this to anyone, and do not refer to it in any correspondence with me: I am unable to satisfy myself that any such intercourse would remain secret. It is of utmost importance that you strictly follow these instructions.

Your service to me during our time together, and your attendance to this important matter, confirm the high regard which I have, and always have had, for you.

With best personal and professional regards,
James Esdaile

I held the letter in my hands for several moments, rereading it and examining the address Esdaile had provided.

"Fergusson," I said at last. "You sent the statue to Fergusson."

"I did as the Doctor Sahib instructed," Noboo said. "It removed the item from India, which was a most satisfactory result. But it is unclear to me what that person would have done with it. Nonetheless, it arrived safely: I have a short note from Mr. Fergusson *Sahib* acknowledging its receipt."

My mind raced. I had visited Fergusson not long after Esdaile's death. He seemed impervious to mesmerism, but surely something as powerful as this statue could not be hidden—it was not in his office near the British Museum, but it might be in his house, or in a bank vault, or in some other safe location. It might be sitting on a shelf on display with pieces of statuary or shards of pottery.

It was obvious why Esdaile had not had it sent to Sydenham— Eliza, or rather Fi, would have known it was there. To Fergusson, it was no doubt one more artifact, even if it did not match anything in his collection.

"He lied to me," I said to no one in particular. "He was a part of all of this, and he lied to me. When he visited Sydenham late in 1858, he must have already had the statue—or known it was on its way."

"Where is it now?" Georgiana asked.

"It's not in India," I said. "Unless you, too, are lying to me," I added to Noboo, waving the letter at him. "I can satisfy myself on that account, and—"

Georgiana touched my sleeve.

"William."

"I am in *India*, Georgiana. I have traveled all the way to India for this object, if only to secure it somewhere so that the Glass Door is not opened. And now I learn—" I let my arm drop to my side. "I learn that it was sent back to England *two years ago*? I will make sure this time—"

"William," she repeated. "Why would Doctor Noboo lie to you?"

"Fergusson would lie to me because he perceived me as an enemy. Because he would think that I wanted to use the statue. The same could be applied to you," I said to Noboo.

"You will have to judge that for yourself, Davey *Sahib*," he said to me.

I turned to Georgiana. "Where is Lieutenant Wood?"

"Watching the proceedings," Wood said. He had been standing twenty or thirty feet away, leaning against a porch pillar. He walked slowly to the cart. "You need my help, Davey?"

"Your revolver."

Wood looked at me curiously, and unholstered his service revolver and handed it to me. It was a beautifully made Webley, in perfect condition. I hefted it, noted that it was loaded, and lifted it slowly, aiming it at Noboo.

"William, what are you—"

"Davey," Wood said.

"I confess that I am not as accurate a shot as Lieutenant Wood. He has established the truth of things more often than I have—I am accustomed to subtler and more pacific means.

"But I assume that this weapon, at this range, would cause a considerable amount of damage to your person."

Mahendra Noboo met my gaze levelly, showing the courage for which he was named. Georgiana did not speak, but wore a look of horror. Wood appeared unwilling to interfere in this procedure, or perhaps he was fascinated at the sight of a civilian being so bloody-minded.

"I think that your assessment of its firepower is correct, Davey *Sahib*. I would prefer that you not demonstrate it, but as you hold the pistol and I do not, the matter is entirely in your control."

"Did you send the statue to Fergusson?"

"I did as the Doctor Sahib asked," Noboo answered.

"So it is no longer in India."

"That is correct, Davey *Sahib*. You have traveled all the way here in vain. Now," he said, still looking directly at me, "if you are not planning to cause that considerable damage of which you speak, I have other patients to attend to."

"Give me the revolver, Davey," Wood said quietly. He did not reach for it, nor make any sudden move.

After a moment, I lowered the pistol and handed it to Wood, handle first, without looking at him.

"I believe I have done what I needed to do here," I said, and walked slowly away.

CHAPTER 48

A part of the epitaph

WILLIAM DAVEY

To my surprise, Georgiana hardly spoke to me on the return journey to Calcutta. She had demonstrated coolness in crisis situations, such as the confrontation on *Malabar Princess*, and she had, after all, survived the chaos of the Mutiny.

I had never actually considered shooting Noboo; she should have realized that. It had been a threat posed in order to satisfy myself that the Bengali doctor was in earnest, and no doubt satisfied him that I absolutely, certainly, unquestionably *expected the truth* from him at that moment. It seemed fair enough; Noboo offered no objection—he gave me the answers I wanted, and in turn I was not compelled to carry through on my threat.

I simply did not understand why Georgiana objected so strongly to the means by which I was able to achieve my completely necessary ends. After all of our separate and joint experience, she chose this passage to assume some position of elevated moral authority.

I was having none of it. It was my impression that Wood was also disinclined to humor her on this matter. He was not completely briefed on the situation: but he perceived my determination in the matter. He was a military man: he clearly saw the need for me to do whatever was necessary in pursuit of my objective.

At one stop at which we watered the horses, he stepped close to me and out of Georgiana's hearing said, "*Women, you know,*" with a knowing shrug.

"Yes," I said. "I know."

We should not have had her accompany us, he meant but did not quite say. *This sort of expedition is not for women.*

I assumed the veracity of Noboo's revelations. I had seen Esdaile's letter with my own eyes. It was now necessary for me to make my way back to England by the most expedient method. I also resolved to send information to Jackson—and not to Carlyle—on what I had learned; I was certain, in the way that hubris makes one certain, that Carlyle might try to take action on his own rather than to wait for me to return and deal with Fergusson.

It was a tragic miscalculation, but there was no way to know this at the time.

With no direct telegraph connection from Calcutta, the only means of communication was a letter that would travel by Royal Mail packet to Aden and then be transmitted from there. I provided the briefest summary for John Jackson, directed that he not act without me and left it to his discretion whether he should tell Carlyle what I had learned. I wanted him to observe, prepare and be ready to deal with Fergusson and locate the statue upon my return.

At Mr. Wilson's hotel, I was informed that my trunk had been delivered from the recently-arrived *Empire Star*. The steamer was being provisioned and refitted, and would depart in a week's time; both Lieutenant Wood and I intended to be aboard to return to England—he to an invalid post until he recovered from his India service, and I to whatever might await me. I did not want to delay in Calcutta that long, but I was at the mercy of the Peninsula & Oriental. An overland journey would have occasioned an even greater delay.

The afternoon after we returned from Awadh, I hired a palky to take me to the English Cemetery in Chowringhee. I suppose that I wanted to see the place where the Heath children and Eliza had come every Sunday. Wood and Gobinda had their own commitments, and Georgiana was scarcely speaking to me, so I was alone. Now I realize the folly of that choice, but I preferred it at that time.

I was let off at the Park Street gate, and let myself wander among the graves and monuments, which cast charcoal shadows over the grounds. It was a lovely, peaceful place, and truly very English, as if those burying loved ones far from their native soil needed reassurance that some aspect of their country surrounded that interment.

In addition to the gravestone for Mr. and Mrs. Heath, I found the marked graves of Mary Ann Esdaile and, in another section of the burial ground, Charlotte Esdaile: the one read *Beloved Wife*, the other *Faithful Companion*. Ten years after James Esdaile's departure from India, they were neglected and overshadowed, two graves among many, scarcely worth a passing glance. I did not know whether James Esdaile had ever visited either.

Just as I was making my way back toward the entrance, intending to take my leave, I stopped short as a brief bit of cool air blew toward me. I saw a familiar dark-skinned figure, impeccably dressed, loitering near the entrance. He was clearly waiting for me, and took note of my sudden halt in the open, thirty feet away.

I do not know why he did not directly approach me: he appeared hesitant to enter the cemetery, which—I determined—might provide me some advantage. I stopped close to an ostentatious marker placed in memory of some eighteenth-century military hero, and allowed myself to give it my closest attention.

"Reverend Davey," the Levantine said.

I ignored him. I was considering a number of possible courses of action, though none seemed particularly promising. I was alone: there were few other visitors, and my closest allies were not on hand. My choice to come alone now seemed like a top-notch tactical blunder.

"You intend to return to England," the Levantine said. "I am sorry to say that I cannot permit that."

"I am not interested in your threats," I answered without looking at him.

"They are not mere threats. You have become an obstacle, sir."

"And you had such high hopes for me. An obstacle to what?"

"My objectives. Our objectives."

"Pray enlighten me." I considered my alternatives. The

Levantine had bested me with ease in Manchester a year ago, but here he remained at the gate to the cemetery, talking. "What do you want?"

"Myself?" The Levantine laughed. It was harsh and disturbing, like the sound of a spade scraping on stony ground. "I would like to open the Glass Door. It is at long last within my reach, and I will brook no opposition."

"Thus I am to be prevented from returning. Forgive me, but I fail to understand why my travels have any effect upon your desires."

"It is the object, of course."

"The object?"

"Do not dissemble with me," the Levantine said. "The statue, of course. You know it is no longer in India. Now, so do I. You are clearly not the person capable of using the power of the statue; therefore, you shall not have it."

"You seem singularly well-informed."

"You have no idea."

"Enlighten me," I repeated, turning at last to face him. The Levantine remained at the gate. "Come over here and we can discuss it. Or perhaps we should find a crowded train platform. Though," I added, taking the opportunity to make a strong warding gesture, "I'm not sure that there are many places in India that *aren't* crowded."

The effort was sufficient to make the Levantine step backward. A rickshaw on Burial Ground Road was forced to suddenly veer, as if its driver was unwilling to make contact. However, the native did not hesitate to unleash a lengthy course of curses. I maintained my composure: derision has its uses, but it might have interfered with my concentration.

"I would prefer to remain here," the *chthonios* said. "I would not wish to offend your *delicate* sensibilities by entering a place you consider sanctified."

"Or you simply cannot enter."

"*Will* not."

"Tell yourself whatever you wish. I shall remain here—and you shall apparently remain there."

"Do not consider yourself completely protected," he answered. "Do you know what 'Chowringhee' means, Reverend Davey? It means *four-colored*. Long before this was Burial Ground Road, it was the road to Kalighat, the four-colored temple to the goddess Kali. Your friend Gobinda…"—he glanced around at the nearby burial markers and the road behind—"who is derelict in his duty to protect you…has characterized my race as servants of Kali, just as his school of adepts serve the Lord Shiva.

"It is an apt analogy; therefore, this is ultimately a place of power for *us* as well. Perhaps that is why he is not able to confront me here. After all, his school has fared poorly enough when our sides have met on *neutral* ground."

He laughed harshly again.

"Charming," I said. "But your Kalighat is dust now, isn't it? And this is sanctified ground." I briefly touched my clerical collar. "So we seem to be at a bit of an impasse."

"You will have to leave the Burial Ground some time, sir."

"How dreadfully melodramatic. You see, I am not alone."

"You lie poorly."

"I see no reason to pursue this conversation," I answered, and turned my back on him. I began walking slowly away, in the direction of the other gate. He could no doubt easily confront me there as well, but I had to conduct myself as if I were in control of the situation.

I was under no illusion that it was actually the case.

Accordingly I retreated as quickly as I could without actually breaking into a run. After some initial hesitation the Levantine began to follow.

The English Cemetery is a warren of headstones and great tombs, stands of trees and steps up and down. I had the advantage of having spent the last few hours there; I also possessed the energy of desperation. It was a humid day, and quite hot by English standards, but not as intemperate as it had been during our journey through Awadh.

It was also clear that the Levantine had spent little time chasing scoundrels. Slipping away and doubling back was almost too easy.

From a vantage behind a rather ornate monument that looked like a four-poster canopy bed, I watched the Levantine stop uncertainly. Chowringhee might be an ancient domain of the worshippers of Kali, but its more recent consecration seemed to confuse him. I imagine that I could have remained in my concealment for quite some time. I was prepared to wait until darkness if necessary.

After a short time, the Levantine drew out his pocket watch and made an unfamiliar mesmeric pass. A figure appeared in front of him—a man with dark skin, wearing a dirty turban and loincloth and little else. I recognized him at once: he had been one of the photic prisoners of Mehmet Nour—who had "lost one of his children", as Lieutenant Wood had told me.

"Effendi," the photic spirit said, looking at the Levantine.

"You have served well. Tell me: the mortal to whom you are attached. He is nearby—do you sense him?"

The photic spirit bowed, never taking his eyes off the Levantine and his pocket watch. "Effendi, I…"

The Levantine rubbed his thumb across the surface of the device. The spirit shuddered, and I felt a new chill and heard a far-off moan that set my teeth on edge.

"Answer."

"I should be able to sense him," the photic spirit said at last. "But I…but the connection is tenuous, effendi. He burned hot when he held the pistol and aimed it at the other mortal, but he does not burn hot now. The environment…"

"I do not care for your excuses. I need to know: can you feel him or not?"

There was a long pause.

The mortal to whom you are attached, I thought. *That's how the Levantine knows about the statue.*

I had been followed by a photic spirit—perhaps since Cairo.

"No, effendi," the spirit said. "But I—"

"Enough." The Levantine opened the pocket-watch wide. I heard a disturbing, unearthly sound that made me shiver. The photic spirit's face was twisted in horror and he appeared to be pulled forward, being drawn into the watch like smoke being pulled up a flue.

The Levantine snapped the device closed with a loud click.

The *chthonios* began once again to look slowly around, speaking words under his breath. I sensed, rather than heard what must have been their language.

He suddenly stopped. The Levantine's attention was drawn away by someone approaching from another direction.

It was Lieutenant Henry Evelyn Wood. I thought to cry out—based on my perception of his skill, he was no match for the Levantine. Even if he had been trained by Sir Robert Peel himself, he would not have been powerful enough.

Instead, I remained silent and listened.

"I do not think that you belong here," Wood said. "I will ask you politely to leave."

"I do not answer to you," the Levantine responded. "Whoever you are. If you think I can be controlled—"

"I am not looking to *control* you. I am looking to dismiss you. A *stoicheia* does not have any place among the honored dead. They cannot speak for themselves, so I will speak on their behalf."

"Surely you have other battles to fight, Lieutenant."

"None more important than this, nightfall creature. You may leave the cemetery, or I will remove your contact with the earth. During the Mutiny, I dealt with many of your colleagues in just that way, and the odylic force is not strong enough for them to reconstitute. You may not wish to take that chance."

"I have the man who accounts himself the most powerful adept in Britain cowering somewhere nearby, and I should find *you* threatening? Pray tell me why."

"Why, that is simplicity itself," Wood answered. "Your power, *chthonios*, such as it is, depends on one singular weakness—that you have something to offer anyone who might seek to control you. Power, advancement…something. You have *nothing* to offer me.

"And I do not seek to control you. I ask you once more to depart, or I shall show you exactly what I can do."

The Levantine did not answer. He took another glance all around him, his gaze lighting for just a moment upon where I stood. For a second time, I considered introducing myself into the scene, and once more I hesitated.

"Your bravery is commendable."

You have no idea, I thought. *After what Wood has seen on the battlefield, this must be like a stroll in the garden.*

"Shall we make that part of your epitaph?"

The Levantine waited for another moment—perhaps a bit longer than might have been comfortable.

"No," he said, with another glance toward me. "No, Lieutenant. Not today."

He turned on his heel and walked away, his figure shrinking and becoming insubstantial until it completely disappeared.

PART SIX

Full circle

Dum loquimur fugerit invida aetas.
(While we talk, hostile time flies away.)
—Horace, *Odes*, XI

CHAPTER 49

Traversal

WILLIAM DAVEY

The Levantine did not appear again, and Dr. Daniel was gone—perhaps as much as a week in advance of my intended departure aboard *Empire Star*. The entire trip to India had been fruitless, for the statue was at home somewhere after all. I had somehow brought along a photic spirit from Egypt, and the Levantine had somehow used it to spy on me. I was far out of my domain.

Lieutenant Wood had also arranged passage on *Empire Star*, which was a comfort—but that in itself was a further blow to my confidence. While Wood, brave soldier, had stared down the Levantine, I had done just as the *chthonios* had said—I had cowered and watched.

Wood dismissed the matter. "Some skirmishes are fought by cavalry and some by infantry," he told me. "Our skills are different, Reverend. But we fight on the same side."

I wondered to myself if that were true.

Georgiana and Gobinda saw us off from the *ghat* at Clive Street. The Bengali adept had the same serene expression I had seen at every turn; Georgiana seemed to have recovered her equanimity, and if she was still angry—or disgusted—with me, she concealed it beneath her customary courtesy.

None of us had any idea how I might thwart Richard Daniel or find the statue, wherever Fergusson had concealed it.

"You will remain in India," I said to Georgiana.

"I think there are some loose threads in my life waiting to be gathered," she said. "I will go to Benares for a time, and then perhaps the Society can find me useful occupation. Perhaps I shall learn to dance," she added, with a hint of a smile.

"A friend of mine in England told me that India was still a very dangerous place. A *chthonios* might be here, and might seek to hurt you—either of you—or Doctor Noboo. I trust you will endeavor to keep yourself safe."

"I appreciate your concern, Davey *Sahib*," Gobinda said, smiling. "But she is a formidable woman. Certainly you have seen that."

I glanced at Wood, who stood nearby, as if he were unwilling to intrude, and then looked at Gobinda. "It does not make either of you invulnerable."

"Our fate is what it is," he said. "And so is yours."

"I wish I could see it more clearly."

"It is not the fault of fate," Gobinda observed. "It is the fault of your own eyes."

I had no response to that comment, so I let it lie.

"If you procure the statue, William, what do you plan to do with it?" Georgiana asked me.

"I do not know if I can find it before Daniel does," I answered. "But if I do, I shall find a safe place to hide it."

"It has a mind of its own," Gobinda said. "And patience beyond human understanding."

"I will do my best."

"I know you shall," Georgiana said. She took my hand and gave it a polite squeeze. I looked in her eyes and saw some measure of affection—but I am not sure what she thought of me at that moment. I am certain, however, that I had come to want her respect; and I am not sure if I had it then, or afterward.

"A safe journey to you," she said.

Empire Star followed her course along the Malabar coast and around the tip of Ceylon, then struck westward across the Indian Ocean, bound for Aden and then East Africa. It was far more peaceful than my previous ocean voyage; no nereic spirits threatened us, no *chthonic* manifestations challenged us. Wood was invited to the captain's table every night, and I was so honored regularly—but often demurred, preferring solitude or the company of complete strangers, to whom I could spin a tale of scholarly pursuits—temples and ruins and forgotten cultures, and the ways in which the Raj was lifting up India to the standards of Her Majesty's Empire.

Wood and I took strolls on the promenade deck in fair weather. Neither of us suffered from seasickness. It did not trouble me, and Wood had been a sailor before he was a soldier and had considerable experience afloat. Indeed, that had been his first career.

I speak of him as if he was a man of great experience—which, as contemporary readers surely know, he was inevitably to become. But at the time I met him he had not yet turned twenty-three years of age. That happy occasion was to occur during our journey back to England.

Evelyn Wood had been favored with the privileges associated with birth into the gentry. He was the youngest son of a baronet, Reverend Sir John Page Wood, vicar of the parish of Cressing in Essex and later rector of St. Peter's Cornhill; his uncle was later Lord Chancellor of England. After a grammar-school education, he had entered the Royal Navy at fourteen as a cadet aboard H.M.S. *Queen*. Scarcely a week after his achieving a midshipman's rank, his ship had come under enemy bombardment at Odessa, and before he was sixteen he had been involved in a naval landing and had watched the Battle of the Alma from the tops of his vessel. As a part of the Naval Brigade, he showed sufficient gallantry that he was to be awarded the Victoria Cross, distinguishing himself to Captain Sir William Peel.

But that was apparently not to be, for he exchanged his station in the Navy for one in the Army as a cornet in the Thirteenth Light Dragoons—where he demonstrated his skill as a cavalryman, and was promoted to Lieutenant. His name was struck from the list of those recommended for the 'bit of blue ribbon and penn'orth of bronze'—as he had left the Navy—though, again, contemporary readers are aware that he was awarded the honor for service ashore not long after I met him.

Lieutenant Henry Evelyn Wood's life had truly been remarkable—I was twice his age and felt that I had scarcely done half as much. He was, however, a gentleman, and deferred politely to me at every turn.

Valor and determination may count for more than you think, Alexander Dunn had told me in Alexandria. I had at last begun to understand what he meant.

We arrived at Aden on a beautiful January day, with the sun already beginning to descend behind the distant hills. I was on deck for the occasion; Wood was not with me at that instant, but the hooting of the ship's horns brought him from belowdecks.

And as the port became more visible on the horizon, I became aware of a sensation: the presence of a practitioner of the Art—or, rather, the manifestation of a practitioner's power. For it to be noticeable this far out in the harbor, it was a prodigious manifestation indeed.

"Could your acquaintance have arrived here before us?" Wood said. He was speaking of the Levantine; the subject had not come into our conversations since we left India.

I thought about the matter for a moment and replied, "This is something different, I think."

Wood scratched his chin. "You are right, I am sure."

I was right.

When we disembarked—*Empire Star* would be laid over at Aden until the following morning—I saw a familiar figure approaching, someone whose power attracted me at once. Lieutenant Wood hovered nearby with the casual air of a military man who knew his business.

"Mr. Nour," I said when he was a dozen feet away. "I am surprised to see you here."

"Of that, I have no doubt," he answered. The Egyptian looked older and more weathered than I remembered. His glance went from me to Wood.

"Lieutenant Henry Evelyn Wood," I said by way of introduction. "Mehmet Nour. I believe you have not met."

"Sir," Wood said. "I count Major Dunn as a valued acquaintance."

"Indeed," Nour said. He had an aspect of weariness that stood in stark contrast to the energy in his blue eyes.

"While I am sure that your company is an honor, sir," I said, "I am curious why you are here."

"I am here because of *you*, sir. I received information that you would be aboard *Empire Star* and determined to be here to receive you."

"Thank you."

"It is an *obligation*, Reverend Davey. You owe your thanks elsewhere. Still, assisting you might help rectify the damage you have done."

"Excuse me—damage?"

"Yes." Nour swept his gaze along the great docks at Aden, then returned his attention to me. "You express surprise in seeing me. It is true that I have scarcely left my home in some years, due to my... charges. I am sure you remember them."

"Yes." I looked at Wood for a moment. "One of them escaped."

"The one with whom you spoke. I trust that you remember my injunction that you not speak with them—and your violation of that injunction. It was sufficient for the devil to attach himself to you. I see that is no longer the case."

He's trapped inside a watch now, I thought, but did not answer. Nour was going to explain something to me.

"It is not. I...did not know this had happened."

"Of course not," Nour said dismissively. "But—" He lowered his voice. "But the great devil—the one that the creatures called their 'father'—knew that one of his own was no longer in contact. I assume that it concluded that I had destroyed it. Its anger was… substantial."

"Your home—"

"If Major Dunn were here, I assume that he would offer the opinion that it was the logical outcome. Reaping the whirlwind, and so forth. My family is safe, but my home is no more. The greater devil, however, is contained." He touched his chest above his breastbone; I could not see it directly, but the bulge under his shirt was roughly the size and shape of the large pectoral cross. It might well be concealed out of sensitivity for the Mohammedan denizens of Aden.

I once more found myself held to account for circumstances beyond my control, due to power beyond my knowledge. I was once more the pawn of events, not their master.

It had been two years since I confronted James Esdaile and his *chthonios* in the Crystal Palace, and I still felt no closer to regaining the object of my attentions—or even completely understanding what it was and what I faced.

"What do you intend?"

He touched the cross through the folds of his clothes. "I have been informed that there is another man in pursuit of the object you seek, and he is likely to reach England before you do. I am to help to remedy that situation."

"By intercepting him?"

"Not exactly."

Nour gestured around us. I had not taken particular notice of what was happening nearby as Nour and I conversed. Suddenly, I became aware of profound quiet—there was no noise of any kind.

Around us on the broad dock, nothing at all moved: it was as if we stood before a great mural, an incredibly detailed daguerreotype of the scene. Cargoes hung still in midair as they were being unloaded from ships: people all around were frozen as they stood or walked—hands were raised, mouths open.

Mehmet Nour had stopped the world.

"With the help of the great devil," Nour said calmly, his steel-blue eyes holding my gaze so strongly that I could scarcely look away, "I will recoup that time for you. The Austrian Lloyd's Mail steamer departs Alexandria for Trieste tomorrow morning, as it does once a month; you may then proceed by rail from Trieste to Ostend and thence to London ahead of your rival."

"And then…"

"And then I *dismiss* the being, Reverend Davey. Against every instinct in my body, possibly at the cost of my own soul when I am called before the Throne of Divine Judgment. Rather than destroy this being utterly as my training commands me to do, I am *treating* with it—to assist *you*. Because those that ask have hold on my loyalties, and I cannot refuse."

CHAPTER 50

The edge of the storm

WILLIAM DAVEY

The effects of Nour's stolen time came to an end when we reached Alexandria—though the trip took almost four days by my perception, not even a single night passed. Nour had a boat at his disposal and mounts available at Suez, and the world remained in its unmoving state as we passed, unseen and unnoticed.

In the mind's-eye of my memory, however, the journey seemed like a dream in its entirety until I disembarked at Trieste. The waking world seemed to return only then with a rush, making me aware of its presence.

Despite the civil conflicts in the Italian states, the course of life in Trieste seemed unaffected, and it was a simple matter to embark at Trieste Centrale and travel on the *Südbahn* up into the Alps toward Graz and then Vienna. My German was less practiced than my French, but I was in no particular mood to be communicative. I sent a second telegram to Jackson before I left Trieste—again, instructing him to take no action until I arrived approximately five days hence—around the twentieth of February.

And during those days of travel I wondered to myself what I would do when I arrived in my domain once more—and how I would coerce James Fergusson to tell me what he had done with the statue. It had been two years since the confrontation in the Crystal Palace: two years that had taught me enough to leave me more ignorant than before.

I crossed the Channel on the morning of the twentieth of February, 1861. The wind blowing eastward from the Atlantic was fierce, enough so that the packet's captain was said to have considered turning back; I should have been very disappointed at the delay, and during a brief interview on the deck I imparted my urgency by a gentle use of the Art. Still, it was an uncomfortable passage, and I assumed the role of a proper clergyman in public, giving audible thanks when the vessel docked at Blackwall. The cold wind was fierce even there—the dockmen were trying to batten down everything they could, and there were two heavily laden barges at the pier that looked as if they might sink at any time.

I made my way by train into London, after directing my luggage to be sent on ahead to my lodgings, and made my way to Regent Street. Jackson lived in Southwark and I had rarely visited him there; I would be most likely to find him, or find word of him, at Vernon's rooms. With the windstorm outside there were no idlers—and no sign of the Levantine. I was under no illusions that he was gone forever—Wood had not caused him to "lose contact with the earth"—but he was not there to trouble me.

A servant took my coat and I was ushered into Vernon's drawing room, which was empty but for John Vernon himself. He looked troubled, and I immediately learned why: Carlyle entered from the library, his face past annoyance and falling just short of anger.

"The prodigal son returns," the famous author said. "You might have let me know."

"I like to be spontaneous. It's good to see you too, Carlyle."

"I suppose you let Jackson know that you were coming."

"Yes. Where is he?"

"I haven't any idea. I haven't seen him since sometime yesterday." Carlyle walked to the window and looked out at the lowering sky. The wind was gusting enough to half drive away the usual fog of London.

He turned to face me. "There is something wrong about this storm."

"What do you mean?"

"Your travels in foreign countries have dulled your senses, Davey. Tell me what you feel."

I paused and extended my senses. After a moment I nodded. "You're right. It feels like a *stoicheia*. I've...never sensed one like that."

"A pneumic *stoicheia*. Here. Timed with your arrival."

"I hardly think—"

Vernon cleared his throat at this point, and we both stopped and looked at him. Carlyle was clever and insightful enough to know that Vernon was not the fool he was often taken to be, but he demonstrated his usual disdain for anyone so forward as to interrupt him.

"I almost forgot," Vernon said. "This was left for you."

Carlyle stepped forward, but Vernon said with a mischievous smirk, "No, it was left for the Chairman."

He extended a small, sealed envelope to me. Carlyle's face reddened, but he said nothing.

I took the envelope and immediately recognized John Jackson's spidery handwriting. I took a letter-opener from an occasional table and slit it open.

Will:

Your messages indicated that Dr. Daniel might arrive at any time, and though he is not the most insightful, he might well have reached the conclusion that I have already done.

There is only one place that Fergusson could have concealed the statue—it is such an obvious location that I am amazed that we never considered it. He's put it somewhere in the Palace. I confirmed his continuing interest by careful queries at his home and his office—he goes to Sydenham regularly.

By the time you return from your dances with the brown-skinned men with nasty sharp knives, I should be able to present you with the prize we have been seeking. I cannot wait to see the expression on Carlyle's face when I do.

John

I folded the letter and tucked it inside my coat.

"The pneumic *stoicheia* isn't here for me," I said to Carlyle. "It's here for the statue."

By the time Carlyle and I were able to make our way to Sydenham—where the regular train had stopped running due to the storm—it was already dark. The wind had risen to a full-force gale, and it took little effort on our part to sense the elemental presence of the thing bearing down on the countryside.

Our progress toward the Crystal Palace was hindered by all manner of obstacles: fallen tree branches, debris and even garden walls were blown down by the fierceness of the wind. It was all we could manage to get up the hill, where the Palace was buffeted by gusts and driving rain.

The Palace was closed, of course, but we had little trouble entering "Joseph Paxton's Tunnel" beneath the structure—the long rail line that was used to transport items to and from the exhibition halls. We disembarked and made our way up through a service entrance into the main nave, where the dark night was continually interrupted by flashes of lightning and the terrible noise of the wind hammering at the glass panels dozens of feet above our heads.

"I suppose," Carlyle said, "you have some notion where to begin searching."

"The Nineveh Court," I answered. "It was Fergusson's particular interest."

Carlyle nodded and directed our steps toward the north transept. We made our way through the Alhambra Court; watch-lights were in place in sconces for the night watchman, though I suspected that anyone answering to that title was huddled in his own home this night. In the daytime, it would have been quite magnificent—the Court of Lions, named for the great fountain borne up by four carved animals, from which water continued to pour. It partially drowned out the howl outside.

We made our way through this structure without pause. I found it mildly unsettling in the half-darkness, with my mesmeric senses dulled by the geometry of the Palace itself; Carlyle might have been experiencing the same, but he moved with his usual grim Scottish determination toward the far end. We emerged into a vestibule; to the left we could dimly make out Roman columns in another great hall; to the right there was a chamber filled with coats of arms and examples of Moorish armor. We then passed under a wide arch and found ourselves standing before the entrance to the Nineveh Court: a huge stonework façade consisting of winged lions with the bearded heads of men, upon which the bases of huge fluted pillars rose to the ceiling of the Palace. Beyond—between the lion bas-reliefs—was a round arch leading to the court's interior.

As we stood there for a moment, stopped by the immensity of the architecture, we heard a sound that will remain with me until my final day: a screeching, groaning sound that drowned out even the howling of the wind.

"What in God's name—" Carlyle began. It was coming from

beyond the Nineveh Court—and it was growing louder by the moment.

A sudden flash of lightning illuminated the darkened arch beyond the lion figures and we saw as plain as day a young woman, dressed in colorful clothing but barefoot, a dagger held in her hand. She saw us—and turned and fled within the Court.

And just as suddenly, I sensed a distortion in the magnetic patterns around me, as if the Crystal Palace—in its mathematical exactitude—had just been *twisted*.

Carlyle did not hesitate further, but took off into the Nineveh Court at a run. I was a step behind.

It was completely dark within: no watch-lights here. I had the sense that we were in a huge hall, and could dimly make out four huge pillars holding up some sort of large ceiling; but I could discern no features of any kind.

Carlyle reached within his jacket and drew out a match, which he struck to life on the sole of his boot. The illumination was faint, but by the dim, flickering light I could see a figure sprawled on the floor twenty or thirty feet away—and then, by virtue of a flash of lightning, I saw one of the great water-towers that stood at the far end of the Crystal Palace through the glass roof beyond the north end of the Nineveh Court.

This great structure, several stories tall, *swayed* in the wind. It was the source of the hideous noise we had previously heard.

I hurried to the side of the sprawled figure and recognized it immediately from the extra-thick sole of the boot on his lame foot—it was John Jackson. He had been knocked to the floor and rendered unconscious by some falling pottery—he had a slight gash on his head. As I examined him, he awoke.

"Will?" he said softly.

"I'm here, Johnny."

"So is she."

"She?"

"She's here," he repeated. "She found her way out. It's—"

"Davey," Carlyle said. "Look." He gestured toward the ceiling beyond the Court.

"Where?" I asked Jackson.

"I…I don't know."

The screeching sound grew louder and louder.

"Can you walk?"

"I don't know. I—"

There was no more warning than the sight of that great tower, several stories tall, swaying and suddenly falling toward the roof of the Palace. I was trying to help Jackson to rise and follow: Carlyle was already backing away as fast as he could manage, the discarded match tossed aside…

Some time later I felt water on my face, and heard the wind howling even louder than it had been before—but not quite as strong.

I opened my eyes and found myself lying on a stone bench. Carlyle was nearby, jacket off and sleeves rolled up; he had procured a cloth of some kind and had attended to a rather nasty wound on my head.

The Alhambra fountain continued to gently spill water from the bowl supported by stone lions.

"We will need to find better shelter," he said. "Now that you're awake."

I tried to sit up and failed; then, with my teeth gritted, tried again and succeeded.

"Where's John Jackson?"

He gestured toward the arch leading out of the Alhambra Court. "Somewhere out there. Buried under masonry, Davey. When the water-tower fell, it destroyed most of the Nineveh Court. It's a wonder it didn't kill us too."

I could not speak. John Jackson, my friend and partner for twenty years and more, was dead—and Carlyle spoke of it as if it were a mere annoyance.

"The statue—"

"I don't know. But the Palace's mesmeric properties have been disturbed. I think your statue was found: either by Jackson or someone...or something...else. But we need to leave now."

"But what about—" I began. "No," I said. "It's got to be here. We were so close—"

"We need to *leave*," Carlyle said. He gathered his jacket and tossed the cloth onto the bench. He helped me to stand, and we made our way out into the main nave. Outside, the wind still howled, and it came in through the broken wall at the far end of the Palace.

Before we went outside, I stopped in what I perceived to be the center of the Palace. Carlyle looked at me curiously as I drew a coin from my wallet and set it down on the floor.

It rolled a short distance and landed, crown-side up.

"All right," I said. "Let's go."

CHAPTER 51

Torn asunder

During all Thursday the wind blew over the hills at Norwood with extraordinary fierceness… All stood well till about half-past 7 o'clock on Thursday night, when, during one of the fearful gusts which then swept over the hill…the huge tower fell over among some trees, and lay smashed into millions of fragments on the ground. In the course of two or three minutes more of the rest of the wing went, by 30 or 40 yards at a time, till a total length of about 110 yards strewed the earth, a mere mass of splinters of glass, wood, and iron. Anything more complete than the destruction it caused would be difficult to imagine. The appearance of the ruin rather suggests that every part of the building has been carefully broken into small pieces than that it has been merely blown down. A tremendous explosion could not possibly have shattered the place more effectually.

—The *Times of London*, Saturday, February 23, 1861.

WILLIAM DAVEY

For we know in part, and we prophesy in part—for now we see through a glass, darkly; but then face to face: now I know in part; but then shall I know even as also I am known.

Edward Quillinan had said that to me—or, rather, my mind had conjured a dream in which he had spoken those words.

Then he had said, *You'll have to peer through the dark glass and find this one out for yourself.*

And as I thought about that dream, I conjured the image of his commonplace-book in my mind. It was sitting on the stone bench at the ruined abbey next to Holyrood, and I could see that its cover bore an image—the Trimurti, the three-headed image of Shiva—

that I did not actually see until Georgiana Shackleford and I reached Bombay.

No, I thought. *I don't believe in coincidence.*

I wondered if I had already gazed through that dark glass. I had been in a cave on Malta, where ancient *chthonic* beings had warned me that they might be moved to take action; I had felt the presence of a large inchoate photic being, held at bay by Mehmet Nour outside of Cairo; and Georgiana Shackleford and I had done battle with a nereic being that had been summoned from the Indian Ocean to consume me, in place of James Esdaile. Finally, I had arrived in England at the same time as an enormous pneumic spirit, thus completing the elemental cycle—earth, fire, water, air.

In the morning the destruction was past. I returned without Carlyle, passing through a neighborhood that had seen an extraordinary amount of devastation. I had no idea what had happened to our carriage from the previous night; there was no sign of it.

There was still no train service, but I hired a coach; the driver was understandably grateful—the terrible storm had eliminated his usual customers, and with the Crystal Palace closed until further notice, it was difficult for business.

He drove me up the road through the beautiful gardens toward the structure, which brilliantly reflected the bright afternoon sun. It was clear that there had been considerable damage at the north end of the building; four great voluted columns poked up at the sky. The north water-tower was, indeed, missing from its former position.

As I alighted from the carriage, I was suddenly struck with an unusual sensation: the absence of any sort of mesmeric impression.

For those sensitive to the Art, it is scarcely possible to navigate a street without feeling some impression or another; strong emotions, ancient lines and patterns, and knowing or unknowing practitioners are found at every turn. But the absence of any such impression was quite singular.

It was as if the area had been wiped clean.

Avoiding the main entrance, I made my way through the lower gardens to the north end, where I was able to ascend a set of stairs and enter the remains of the wing, open to the air. Close up, I could see the trappings of the Nineveh Court, most of which was still under the great glass and steel roof. Shards of glass and metals, fragments of plaster and wood lay everywhere.

I picked out Fergusson at once: he was standing at a large stone block that had evidently been a pediment for an archway, now broken and lying about in shards nearby. A number of ceramic pieces were arranged in front of him; he had one in his hands, and regarded it with a serious expression.

He saw me approaching, and set the item down with great delicacy.

"Mr. Fergusson," I said. "Good day to you, sir."

"Reverend—Davey, was it? I am quite preoccupied, sir. Perhaps at another time—"

"I don't think this can wait," I said, as I reached him. "You have—or had—something I want."

"I beg your pardon?"

"I had a conversation with Dr. Mahendra Noboo," I said. "I saw Esdaile's letter."

Fergusson looked me directly in the eye. "I should infer something from that name."

"Fergusson," I said quietly, "I have traveled to India and back. It has taken me two years and more to reach the point of understanding I now enjoy. You have lied to me, sir, and I am willing to concede that your sense of duty, or your loyalty to the late Dr. Esdaile, or perhaps some knowledge you possess has motivated you in the past.

"But the time for all of that is over. You were sent the statue that you originally gave to James Esdaile nearly twenty years ago. I wish to have it. You will give it to me."

His expression conveyed the sense that he might try once more to dissemble with me, but then seemed to dismiss the idea as a bad one.

"Aye. So. If Jamie Esdaile did not wish you to have it," he said, "why do you think *I* would give it to you?"

"Because of what I can do to you," I said. "If not directly, then indirectly. But some things have changed."

"Such as?"

"I know what it does. It causes *wars*, Fergusson. It may have helped bring about the Sepoy Rebellion. In England, it could do immeasurable damage in the wrong hands."

"Aye, and *yours* are the wrong hands, Davey."

"I disagree."

"And," he said, holding up his hand in an almost mesmeric gesture, "it doesn't matter. I don't have it."

"Noboo sent it to you."

"Yes," Fergusson said. He looked weary of a sudden—like someone who had borne a great burden over a great distance. "Yes. He did. In October 1858, it arrived in my hands and I did as I was instructed: I placed it in the safest location I could imagine. *Here.* In the Crystal Palace." He lifted up one of the ceramic figures in front of him. "Inside a sculpture very much like this one.

"Within the Palace, Reverend Davey, mesmeric fields were neutralized due to the mathematics of its construction. Esdaile determined that for himself; it is why he chose this place to end his life. He told me that if the statue were concealed here, it would be undetectable. He was right.

"Until the night of the twentieth of February, it was in the safest place in the world: safe from you, from your Committee, and from everyone else. But now it is most certainly gone."

"Where?"

"God only knows. Perhaps someone took it as a souvenir. Perhaps it was smashed by the storm, allowing—its inhabitant—to escape. But it is not here, and I do not have it.

"And you cannot have it either, Davey."

"Do you have any idea what this means? Do you understand the serious nature of this circumstance?"

"No," Fergusson said. "To be honest, I do not. I only know that a man I regarded as a friend, a man whose life you threatened—directly or indirectly—asked me to perform an important task for him. I did so. He is now dead at his own hand. His wife is free, I understand; and my duty is discharged.

"And if you wish to do something to me—have at it. I am not without resources, and I have little regard or respect for your Art and its practices. Now, if you will excuse me, I have work to do."

I could think of nothing further to say. I extended my perceptions once more: if the statue had been concealed nearby, I am certain that I would have felt it.

I turned my back on Fergusson and walked away.

EPILOGUE

Home at last

WILLIAM DAVEY

I had visited Eliza Esdaile twice: immediately following her husband's death, and then a year later after the death of James Braid. Her house appeared completely unharmed by the storm, which had spent its wrath on the Palace.

With not a little trepidation, I presented myself for a third time at her door.

Her maid, Elizabeth, answered.

"May I help you?" she said.

"Is your mistress at home?" I asked. "I had the honor of being received by her in the past."

She considered and appeared to recognize me. She stepped back and admitted me to the front hallway.

"I am sorry, sir. Reverend. Mrs. Esdaile is not at home; she is traveling."

"Ah."

"I am not certain when she will return."

"If it is not impolite to ask, where has she gone?"

"Scotland, sir," Elizabeth said. "To visit family."

"I should like to leave my card." I reached into my vest and withdrew a calling-card and handed it to her. She took it and went to place it on a tray but stopped and turned to me.

"You are Reverend Davey, sir?"

"Yes. I visited Mrs. Esdaile some months ago—"

"There's a letter for you, Reverend. Mrs. Esdaile specifically instructed me that should you call, I was to give it to you." She walked over to the side table; next to the tray was an elegant japanned box. She opened it and withdrew an envelope and handed it to me.

Sydenham
24 February 1861

Reverend Davey:

If you have chosen to pay me another visit, you will not find me at home. I hardly regret this, for though your attentions have been unquestionably polite and solicitous, they also remind me of an exceptionally painful period in my life. But the recent damage at the Crystal Palace might draw you back.

I am traveling to Rescobie, where my brother-in-law has very kindly invited me to spend some time with his family. At last I am ready to make that journey, and I am looking forward to the chance to become acquainted with all of them. I shall also pay my respects at my father-in-law's grave.

David told me in his letters that you spent some time at Rescobie and did the same, and that he found you an interesting and courteous guest. But like me, he would prefer to remain apart from the world of the mesmeric Arts.

I hope that you find what you seek. I do not know if that includes the statue—it is difficult to imagine that Dr. Noboo would place it in your hands. All of us have been changed by encountering it. Each of us must find his or her own way home.

Sincerely yours,
Eliza Weatherhead Esdaile

It was a chimera.

I started from a different place than I ended, searching for the object for which I had been willing to end James Esdaile's life. All that I had heard, all that I had seen, suggested that Fergusson was right, just as Esdaile had been right: its power was not for me or anyone else to use. Perhaps it could have adorned a shelf in Henry Evelyn Wood's den, since he would no more succumb to its blandishments than he would accept an offer from the Levantine; but the best place for it would have been the Crystal Palace, where it was safe and undetectable, even by so powerful an adept as myself.

It made other appearances. It was present in Mexico a few years later, and was noticed at the court of the Ottoman Sultan not long after that. It was in the hands of General Gordon at Khartoum— and it made one further appearance, in a place and at a time I shall never forget. But it was never in my hands.

The Glass Door has not opened. I fear that it might someday; the inhabitant of the statue, a powerful spirit, might loose the mercurial, violent beings that our ancient ancestors banished to the poles to keep them away from civilization. We have enjoyed a long period of relative peace in this century, and I pray it shall long continue; though the statue's influence has brought violence from time to time, perhaps the field is fallow. Perhaps there will be no more wars like my father and grandfather knew.

That will depend on the vigilance of others, once my own revels are over.

Acknowledgments

Thank you to my wife for her patience and support; to the Hawthorne-Longfellow Library at Bowdoin College and Bellingham Public Library in Bellingham, Massachusetts for research assistance; and to my editor at Spence City, Vikki Ciaffone, who read this book and wanted to publish it.

About the Author

Walter H. Hunt has been writing all of his life, and has been a full-time writer since 2001. His writing draws on his knowledge and study of history in one form or another; truth is often far stranger—and more interesting—than fiction, and research is a touchstone for his work. He grew up in Andover, MA and received a B.A. in History and German from Bowdoin College in Maine. He now lives in Eastern Massachusetts with his wife and their teenage daughter. He is an active Freemason and baseball fan.